Mountain Boss

Mountain Men Book One

S.J. Tilly

Mountain Boss

Book One of the Mountain Men Series

Content Warning

This book contains mature themes, violence and... a touch of stalking.

BLACK MOUNTAIN LODGE

FOOD HALL

BUNK HOUSE

GUEST CABINS

THE LAKE

MR. BLACK'S HOUSE

STORAGE SHED

LAUNDRY CABIN

WALKING
PATH

GUEST
CABINS

v

This book is dedicated to the bears and to fictional men in flannel.
We love you.

CHAPTER 1

COURTNEY KERN

MY TITS MASH AGAINST THE STEERING WHEEL AS I LEAN forward, craning my neck to look up at the hawk flying just above me.

Or at least it feels like it's just above the roof of my Jeep.

Like if I could reach my hand through the glass, I could touch it.

"Pretty baby," I sigh.

I glance back at the road before looking up for one more glimpse of the amazing creature.

Oh, to be a bird.

To be able to float above the world.

To move, place to place, with ease.

The hawk tilts its wings, then disappears behind the tall pines and yellow-leafed aspens that line the road.

I sit back.

I have no reason to feel so jealous of the creature.

Not today.

Because today, I'm starting a new job.

Well, technically, I start tomorrow.

But it's still the beginning of a new adventure.

A new chapter of my life.

I let the smile form on my lips as I think about it. And how my fortune has finally changed.

I pat my dashboard, then grab my phone out of the cupholder to check the GPS.

My old Wrangler still runs well, but the screen has been out for a while.

Someday I'll get it fixed.

When my phone confirms that my turn is coming up, I lift my foot off the gas and start to slow.

There's no one on the road behind me.

Feels like there's no one out here at all.

The last town was probably thirty minutes ago, but I've seen driveways. Spotted the occasional *Private Property* sign along the road. So my destination is secluded but not isolated. Not really.

I follow the turn in the road... and my mouth opens.

Mountains.

Giant, beautiful, glorious mountains tower before me.

"Fuck," I whisper. "This was the right choice."

I've seen mountains on my drive today. Seen a few over the last couple days as I traveled from North Carolina to Colorado.

But this view...

The snowcapped peaks before me...

I am *in* the mountains.

I reach out and pat the dash of my Jeep again. "Just a little way left, old girl."

Consulting my phone again, I see that my turn is in half a mile.

Still no other vehicles in sight, I coast, squinting against the bright orange of the setting sun.

And then I see it.

The sign marking the next phase of my life.

I force myself to take a slow, deep breath.

Because I'm here.

Black Mountain Lodge

CHAPTER 2

STERLING BLACK

I PAUSE, TOWEL STILL DRAPED OVER MY HEAD.

It's faint, but after years of living out here, my hearing is attuned to catch the sound of tires on gravel through the open windows.

I yank the towel off and toss it over the edge of the tub.

My new employee isn't technically late, but they're pushing it by showing up at sundown since the roads out here can be treacherous with wildlife, sharp turns, and no streetlamps to speak of.

After pulling on a clean pair of boxers, I reach for the jeans I left on the floor and decide to be grateful the guy showed up now and not ten minutes ago. Otherwise, I wouldn't have heard him over the shower.

Buttoning my pants, I step into my bedroom and look out the window.

Sure enough, I spot the shine of headlights bumping their way through the trees.

I try not to think about Marty as I grab my flannel off the foot of the bed. Retiring so he can go live near his grandchildren isn't something I can actually be mad about. But having to train a new maintenance guy is going to be annoying as fuck.

My bare feet slap on the steps as I jog down to the main floor.

Black Mountain Lodge is a cluster of cabins spread through the woods rather than a single building, as the name might suggest.

My house is the only two-story building on the property. But it's still just a modest-sized three-bedroom A-frame structure with the main suite upstairs and everything else on the lower level, with an attached garage off to the side.

I shove my feet into my unlaced boots and step through the front door onto my covered patio.

It won't take long to settle Court into the Bunk House, and once he's moved in, I'm kicking my boots back off and spending the rest of the night on the couch in front of the TV.

Pulling on my flannel, I look around at what could be considered my front yard while I wait for my newest employee.

The gravel driveway ends in front of my house in a wide circle large enough for vehicles to turn around. And lining the driveway, then farther off into the trees, are the cabins. Several of them.

The paths between buildings, and leading to and from the driveway, are crude. Mostly just packed dirt from years of boots walking the same route.

At this elevation, over eight thousand feet, we don't have lawns, just sporadic ground vegetation, so I don't really bother with landscaping.

The approaching headlights crest the final hill in the driveway, and the outline of a Jeep Wrangler appears.

He's driving slowly, which is smart, probably taking in the buildings as he goes.

Back there, he's passing the communal bathrooms. One for men and one for women.

Now he's passing a pair of guest cabins.

Off to my right is another cluster of cabins. And a little past that is the second largest structure, the Bunk House, where my five—soon to be six—employees sleep.

Not far from the Bunk House is the Food Hall—a single-room cabin with an industrial kitchen. There are picnic tables inside and more under an overhang outside.

A path runs from here to there, but it's thin since I'm pretty much the only one who travels it.

To my left are a few more structures. A Laundry Cabin, which will be used by the new maintenance guy, and the Storage Shed.

The setup is simple but effective.

And all mine.

I fill my lungs with the clean fall air as the Jeep finally comes to a stop several yards from the bottom of my porch stairs.

The sun reflects off the windshield, making it hard to see the form inside.

For a long moment, nothing happens. Then the engine shuts off, and the driver's door opens.

I take one step forward.

Then I stop.

Because the person who climbs out of the vehicle before me isn't my new employee.

It's a woman.

She's standing so I can see her head between the open door and the side of her Jeep. And the dwindling sunlight glows off her light brown hair.

Hair that's been twisted into two braids.

Braids that instantly give me inappropriate ideas.

I clear my throat.

I was expecting Court, so I hadn't bothered to button up my flannel, but now my fingers twitch at my sides as I debate the merits of leaving my shirt open or trying to button it before she can round her door.

But then she does just that. Stepping fully into view. And I don't care about my buttons anymore. Because all I can focus on is her.

Her tits straining against her white T-shirt.

Her thick, clutch-able waist.

Her full hips covered in tight denim, and, pretty please, let there be a rounded ass to match.

This time when my fingers twitch, it's for a whole different reason.

I don't even care that my new employee is late. Don't care if he shows up at all. I can certainly pass the time with this lost lady.

Maybe offer up a cup of coffee.

A blanket.

A bed to sleep in.

I take another step forward, descending the stairs to meet her.

CHAPTER 3

COURTNEY

HOLY. FUCKING. FLANNEL.

I bite down on the urge to gulp because the man striding toward me is the most handsome, most sexy, most built man I've ever seen in real life.

I can't quite tell if his hair is black or if it just looks that way because it's wet.

Wet and tousled, and, *good god*, he's hot.

The beard covering his jaw is trimmed and just as dark as his hair.

And I'm sure he has an eye color, but my gaze keeps dropping. To his bare chest.

Bare, because he left his shirt open.

Because I'm pretty sure he was just in the shower.

Naked.

I smooth my hands down my sides, then reach out and push my door shut.

The man's heavy boots crunch noisily over the driveway as he crosses the distance between us, stopping just feet away.

The edge of his mouth is pulled up, and I don't miss the way his eyes drop to take me in. "Evening. Can I help you find your way somewhere?"

His voice rumbles over my skin, and I silently beg my nipples to behave.

"I, um." I pause to take a calming breath. "I'm looking for a Mr. Black."

His lips part, drawing my attention to their dusky pink color, but then they close.

My normal nerves at meeting someone new twist into something more.

When his smile disappears, I slowly lift my eyes to meet his and find them full of suspicion.

That *something more* in my belly morphs into something bad.

He's silent for another second before he answers. "That's me."

This extremely attractive, open-shirted man is my new boss?

Okay. That's fine.

I'm cool with it.

Totally chill.

"Oh, well, it's nice to meet you." I clear my throat and hold my hand out. He slowly puts his palm against mine. "I'm Courtney."

"Courtney." He repeats slowly.

I try to smile, but I feel it fall sideways. "That's me, uh, Courtney Kern. Reporting for duty."

I swear his jaw clenches, then his head starts to shake.

CHAPTER 4

STERLING

"Courtney?" I say it again.

"Yes..." She nods, her brows knitting in confusion.

I shake my head again. "The application said Court."

"Oh, um, that's weird. Sorry about that." She tacks on the second sentence when my expression doesn't soften.

There is no fucking way Marty hired a woman.

No. Fucking. Way.

My eyes drop again.

And not just any woman. A woman cut from the exact type of cloth I crave.

A woman who looks like she could take anything I wanted to give her.

A woman I'd much rather have in my sheets than in my employ.

Long dark lashes blink up at me, flashing those bright hazel eyes.

"No." I say the word out loud, but I still don't release her hand.

Her half smile drops. "No, what?"

"No." I keep shaking my head. "You can't work here."

Chapter 5

Courtney

Panic replaces every other emotion fighting for dominance inside my body.

I must have heard him wrong.

He can't fire me before I even start.

Can he?

"Sorry, but there's been a miscommunication." His fingers flex around mine.

"But..." All the reasons why I need to stay spiral through my mind.

I have my entire life packed into my Jeep.

I don't have another place to go.

I have two hundred dollars in my bank account and twenty dollars in my purse, and no way to pay for a hotel for more than a single night before I'd be forced to live out of my car. With no way to even fill the gas tank.

"But I was told I got the job." I struggle to keep the anxiety out of my voice.

"Sorry."

Sorry?

All he has to say is sorry?

His warm grip still encompasses my hand as he attempts to literally ruin my life.

"Did you hire someone else? Because if the maintenance role is filled, I can take a different position. Anything." I know I sound desperate. But that's because *I am* desperate.

He shakes his head again, his damp hair shifting with the movement. "No, I just—I can't have you working here."

My mouth pulls into a frown. "Why?"

"This is a working lodge. And there's only one cabin for all the employees to sleep in." He says it seriously. Like it's some sort of big deal.

I nod. "Yeah, that's fine. I can sleep anywhere."

"It's not fine." He grits the words out.

"Why?" I ask because I really don't understand.

Hearing voices, I glance over and see a pair of men walking through the woods toward us.

A quick tug on my hand pulls me forward and off-balance.

My head jerks back to face Mr. Black as I stumble.

He loosens his grip, and my hands dart out automatically. Catching myself against the closest surface.

The heat is instant.

But not just where my palms are pressed against his bare stomach.

No, the warmth of his skin is just the beginning.

My panic is still real, but the lust from before is fighting its way back to attention.

"Can you fix a well pump?" His muscles flex with each word, and the feel of it has me snatching my hands back.

"A well pump?"

He's even closer now, and I'm forced to tip my head back to make eye contact.

"Yeah, do you know how to fix a busted well pump?" He moves like he's going to cross his arms, then realizes there isn't enough space between us for his biceps and lowers them.

"Do you have internet?" I ask my own question.

Mr. Black dips his chin. "This is a lodge, not a cave."

Such an attitude.

"Okay, well, if I have the internet, then I can fix it." I sort of lie.

Of fucking course I don't know how to fix a well pump.

I've spent the majority of my life living in an RV where the water comes from a hose. Then in dorms and apartments, where my water comes from the city. But it doesn't mean I won't look it up and try. I'll master scuba gear if it means I can stay.

He's back to shaking his head. "It doesn't matter. You can't stay."

My stomach sinks. "But why?"

He glances in the direction of the men, then leans down until our faces are only inches apart. "Look, I'm sorry for the mix-up, but on the application, your name was filled out as Court, not Courtney. I thought I was hiring a man. I can't have a woman working for me."

My eyes slowly widen as my mind races. "Like... legally? You're not allowed around women?"

Is he a sex offender? Is that the rule?

I start to take a step back, but Mr. Black darts his hand out, gripping my upper arm.

"I don't know where the hell your mind is going, but this has nothing to do with legalities." He looks like he's trying not to growl at me. "I just can't have a woman on staff. I can't have you sleeping in the Bunk House with my five *male* employees."

"But I don't care." I try to sound convincing. I do care, but I don't have a choice. "I'll sign a... *paper* stating it's fine."

"No. It wouldn't be right."

Right?

Who cares about right?

I need a place to sleep until I can get a handful of paychecks.

His grip on my arm gentles as he stands back to his full height.

"Sorry you drove all the way here." He says it without inflection. "I'll reimburse you for your time and gas."

It's my turn to shake my head.

I need to stay.

I need to change his mind.

Like, right now.

"It's illegal to fire someone for their gender." The words are out of my mouth before I have time to think them through.

They also came out much louder than intended.

"Are you threatening me?" Mr. Black's voice is low.

CHAPTER 6

STERLING

HER TEETH PRESS INTO HER LOWER LIP BEFORE SHE straightens her shoulders. "I'm not threatening you. Just pointing out you can't fire me just because I'm a woman."

Irritation layers on top of my frustration. Because she's not wrong. "You can't—"

"I can take care of myself." She talks over me. "I can sleep in the, uh, Bunk House, or whatever you called it. But if you're that worried about them, you know, *doing something*, then maybe you should fire them instead of me."

I grind my teeth. "I'm not worried about them *doing something*. I'm worried about the distraction you would cause by being around." I'm trying to keep my voice down. I saw Cook and Fisher earlier. Saw them veer off to go around behind my house. And since the workday is over and they have no reason to head that way, I'm sure they're hiding behind some corner, trying to overhear this conversation.

We don't get many pretty ladies randomly showing up by themselves.

Even if they don't know who she is, she's still the most interesting thing to happen all day.

"I won't be a distraction," the woman promises.

That's the most untrue statement I've ever heard.

She's being a literal distraction to my workers as we speak.

She'll be disruptive.

Enticing.

Alluring.

And I'd sooner smash my hand into a tailgate than put her in that cabin with five messy, stinky men.

"I'm qualified," she continues. "I'm a hard worker. And I've signed my paperwork to start tomorrow."

If it wouldn't look absurd, I'd figure out a way to kick myself right now.

This is what I get for delegating a hire for the first time ever.

Yes, I posted the job. Sifted through the handful of applicants. And sent my top three to Marty.

From there, I told him to interview and hire his replacement.

But for whatever fucking reason, Courtney appeared on the application as Court.

Maybe it got cut off. Maybe it was a typo. Maybe she did it on purpose. Either way, that was the name I sent to Marty.

But he interviewed her.

Or at least he said he did.

I draw in a sharp breath through my nose, nostrils flaring. Because ultimately, if I hadn't been such a sulky bitch about getting a new maintenance person, I might've taken the time to look at the final contract and seen her full name.

And it's my company. My responsibility.

Still, Marty is getting an earful from me.

But since I don't want to get fucking sued this week, I guess I'm hiring my first female employee.

I release the hold I have on her arm and step back.

"Fine," I grit out.

Her shirt strains as she takes a deep breath. "Fine, I can stay?"

I nod as I try to shove the memory of her hands against my bare skin out of my mind.

The moment I saw her, this creature named Courtney, I wanted her.

I secretly hoped she was lost and that this was going to turn into some X-rated Hallmark *in the woods* scene.

But *no*. Now I need to be professional.

I need to keep my hands off her.

I need to keep my dick in my pants.

And I need to make her quit.

CHAPTER 7

COURTNEY

RELIEF CRASHES INTO ME SO HARD I NEARLY COLLAPSE.

I'm staying.

I suck in a breath.

I get to stay.

Pressing the tip of my thumb into the tip of my pointer finger at my side, I school my features.

I'm a professional.

"Thank you." I heave out the words. "You won't regret this."

Mr. Black grunts, indicating that he already does.

"Can you show me to the Bunk House?" I prompt when he continues to stare at me.

His intense glare makes me want to look away, but if I do that, I know my eyes will drop to his exposed chest, so I hold his gaze.

"I already told you. You're not staying in the Bunk House." He turns away from me. "You'll be staying over here. Alone."

With that ominous statement, Mr. Black starts walking.

I press my lips together to keep from saying something under my breath and hurry to follow.

Our footsteps are out of sync, sounding loud in the quiet, and it reminds me of those two men I saw earlier.

I have no idea where they went, but I suspect they didn't go far.

Jogging a few steps, I catch up to my boss's long stride, then keep pace behind him.

He's heading for the big cabin, the one I watched him exit when I first pulled up.

He wouldn't...

No. There's no way he'll try to make me stay in there. With him.

Right?

I mean, maybe there are extra rooms in that house, but he came out half dressed. He has to live there.

Maybe there's a Mrs. Black in there too?

And he said he had a Bunk House for his employees.

There's no way he would have me sleep in his home rather than the employee building.

Before I can spiral further, he turns away from where those other men were walking, off the other side of the driveway.

I'm gonna need a damn map of this place.

I watch my step as we go, avoiding the occasional tree root that sticks up through the packed dirt.

"This is you." Mr. Black gestures as he comes to a stop.

I lift my eyes from the ground and find that we're stopped in front of a cute little cabin.

It's the same mahogany brown as the other buildings I've seen. Same rectangular windows with the trim painted a forest green.

The front door is the same shade of green, making the yellow word stenciled across the top stand out.

Laundry

Mr. Black climbs the three steps in one large stride and closes his hand around the doorknob.

I make a mental note that there are no railings along the steps.

I do not want to face-plant off the edge when I come out tomorrow morning.

The door creaks when my boss opens it, and he reaches inside the cabin a second before the interior lights flicker on.

"There's no lock." He turns back to face me. "But the bears have a hard time opening the round doorknobs, so you should be fine."

I stare at him.

Bears.

Like Yogi, Smokey, Care?

He takes the stairs one at a time as he descends them, his attention focused on my face.

Is he fucking with me?

I mean, I know bears are real. But they wouldn't try to open doors... Would they?

I decide that saying nothing is the best option.

He stops in front of me. "Work starts at seven."

Then, without so much as a welcome or a goodbye, he leaves.

So nice to meet you, I mouth to myself as I valiantly resist the urge to watch his ass as he walks away. Because he might have a good-looking ass, but he *is* a good-looking *ass.* And we don't ogle assholes.

Human assholes.

People who are assholes.

I press my fingertips together.

Get your shit together, Courtney.

Chastising myself only half works because now I'm thinking about assholes and how I've never really seen one in person. Because it's not like I can look at my own. And even though I'm not a virgin, I've never seen the buttholes of the guys I've been with...

The sound of a door slamming snaps my attention over to the main house.

There are some trees and bushes between here and there, but the view is mostly unobstructed.

And even though the man is unpleasant, I'd be lying if I said I didn't want him close.

Not because of his looks. Because I need someone within hearing distance if I end up screaming for my life.

"No bears, please," I mumble.

Then I look up through the still-open door of the Laundry Cabin, a.k.a. my new home, and focus on the positives.

I have a job.

I have a place to stay.

I have some eye candy for the next three months, even if his flavor is sour.

And—I inhale deeply—I'm surrounded by the most beautiful scenery I've ever seen.

Not all bad, indeed.

The listing for this job was only for three months, a temp position, starting tomorrow—October first to December thirty-first.

I was hoping to dazzle my new boss with my work ethic and abilities in an effort to get those three months extended. But now I'm thinking I need to utilize my downtime to find a new position for the new year. Which sounds all fine and good on paper, but if this year has taught me anything, it's that it's not easy—or quick —to find a job that also includes room and board.

Sighing, I turn around and head for my Jeep.

Maybe if I keep my spending to the absolute minimum and save every freaking dollar I make working here at Black Bossy Lodge, I could have enough for a deposit on an apartment by January first. Then I'd just need to find a *regular job* and not one that includes a living space. And for once in my life, I'd have some separation between work and sleep.

I open the passenger door and pull my backpack off the floor, slipping my arms through the straps. Then I move to the rear of the Jeep, where I sling another bag over my shoulder before I lug my large suitcase out, setting it wheel-side down on the gravel drive.

Last, I tuck a small box into the crook of my arm and accept that's enough for the first trip.

For a moment I debate whether I should park closer to the Laundry Cabin rather than in the driveway. But Mr. Black didn't tell me to move my Jeep, and parking on the *lawn* might piss him off more.

Opting to leave it where it is, I slam the rear door shut and grab the suitcase handle with my free hand.

My luggage bumps over the gravel until I turn off the drive and onto the dirt walking path.

It's only been five, maybe ten minutes since I did this walk with Mr. Hot and Cold, but I can already tell it's darker out, the day slipping past sunset and into dusk.

And I can't help but think about bears.

Chapter 8

Sterling

I run my hand through my hair.

You can't go out there.

Helping her move in would completely defeat the point of putting her in the Laundry Cabin.

Below me, Courtney stops at the bottom of the steps leading to her cabin and releases the handle of her suitcase. And I watch as it does a slow tip forward into the dirt.

"Super." She doesn't say it loud, but out here, in the silence, voices travel.

Not as far as you might think, not in the woods. Which is how people get lost so easily. But with line of sight and the windows open—because at eighty-five hundred feet above sea level, open windows are nature's air conditioning—I can just make out her words.

Muttered curses float into my bedroom, and I take a step back, making sure I'm out of view should she turn around and glance up.

I didn't put her in the Laundry Cabin because it's the closest to my house.

And I certainly didn't put her there because I can see her front door from my bedroom window.

I put her there because it has a bunk in the back.

Because even if I trust my guys with my life, I'm not putting a woman in a cabin with five men. People need privacy. And I know my men don't give a fuck about changing in front of each other, but that would change with a lady in their midst.

And I can't just put her in one of the guest cabins; it could be seen as preferential treatment. Not to mention the fact that she'd have to move into the Laundry Cabin when all the guest cabins end up in use anyway.

This saves a step.

And as my new maintenance person, she's also responsible for cleaning, which includes laundry. So, really, it makes sense.

And if the cramped surroundings make her want to leave...

I turn my back on the window.

So be it.

CHAPTER 9

COURTNEY

I LOWER MY SHOULDER, CAUSING THE STRAP TO SLIDE down my arm, before dropping my bag the rest of the way onto the floor.

"Cozy." My eyes bounce around the space, which is as surprisingly clean as it is sparse.

The cabin is a rectangle, with the front door on the short end, closest to the main house.

To my right, lining the wall, are two washers and two dryers of the industrial type and revolution.

They're all front loading, and a few inches above them is a plain white shelf boasting a jug of detergent and a half-empty box of dryer sheets.

Beyond the farthest appliance is a deep utility sink with a cabinet above it.

A sink and counter space... basically a full kitchen.

Or it will be when I get my toaster and electric kettle set up.

To my left... is a tiny round table with a single chair.

It looks antique.

And looks like the chair legs might jump ship if I sit on it.

Setting my light cardboard box on the table, I decide to consider the table and chair as decorative only.

I can sit on the bed when I want to relax. And I've become a pro at eating off my lap. So, not a big deal.

Before I venture farther into my cabin, I put my backpack on the floor and go back outside to fetch my suitcase.

Pretending my heart is beating wildly because of exertion and elevation and not because I'm worried about bears in the dark woods behind me, I shove my suitcase into the cabin and kick the door closed the second I'm inside.

I spent my formative years living in an RV with my mom, parked in various campgrounds in various states. So you'd think I wouldn't be such a chickenshit. But apparently, it's been too long since I've been around nature, because the idea of having to walk down one of these paths after dark is making me sweat.

Please, mountain gods, let that door beyond the sink lead to a bathroom.

I saw the two restroom buildings on my way up the driveway —one door stenciled with *Men*, the other with *Women*. Another reminder of my campground days. Drafty showers and wet flip-flops.

The restrooms weren't far from here, per se, but if I'm forced to find them in the dark, I'll probably pee my pants before I get there.

I leave the suitcase and all my things where they are and move farther into the cabin.

Passing the sink, I step into the narrow hallway—though, *hallway* is a stretch—that separates the front of the cabin from the back.

The mini hallway is just long enough for a door.

I hold my breath as I pull it open, then exhale in relief when I see the beautiful porcelain throne.

It's just a powder room. With a toilet and the tiniest sink known to man. No shower. But I can shower in the public restroom when it's daylight. That's easy-peasy. Peeing in my own cabin? Straight luxury.

I lift my hand and press my pointer and middle finger to my lips, then press my fingers against the door.

"You'll be well taken care of, Bestie," I tell the bathroom.

I have a set of bright green hand towels that will spruce the place right up.

Backing out of the bathroom, I have to shut the door so I can continue past it to the back part of the cabin.

Instead of a door, there's a curtain rod secured high across the end of the hallway, with a navy blue curtain hanging from it.

I push it aside and step through.

It takes a moment. A few breaths. But not long.

Not long to see *it*.

I press my lips together.

I pinch my fingertips together.

I try *so hard* to hold it together.

I even lift a foot and stomp it to the floor.

Because... fuck him.

Fuck that man—my new boss—so fucking much.

Hot anger builds in that spot between my eyes.

"Fuck you," I whisper.

Along the wall that separates this space from the bathroom is a dresser.

This space.

I press my fingertips together even harder, my thumbnails digging into my flesh painfully.

This is not a bedroom.

A bedroom has a bed.

This room...

I swallow.

This room has a homemade structure straight in front of me, lining the back wall of the cabin. Sturdy legs support a platform made of plywood. Something I would call a bunk.

The bunk is under a window that has a curtain to match the one across the hallway, and it's tall, above hip height for me. So there's plenty of space for me to shove my things underneath.

But it's not what's under the bunk that has a traitorous tear rolling down my cheek.

It's what's on top.

Nothing.

No mattress.

Nada.

Nothing.

Just a bare slab of plywood to sleep on.

I turn to the dresser and pull open the drawers, thinking maybe there's a vacuum-sealed mattress pad magically wedged inside.

But just like the bunk, the drawers are empty.

I close my eyes.

I have a pillow in my suitcase.

I have a blanket in my bag.

It's thin, but I can sleep in a sweatshirt if I'm cold.

I open my eyes and stare at the bare bunk.

What I don't have packed in my things is a mattress.

I clench my jaw as another tear escapes.

"Stupid jerk."

If that man thinks he can scare me off, make me quit, with a little rough sleeping, he's wrong.

I brush at my cheeks and almost laugh.

How quickly my excitement for this new start has diminished.

But no matter what he does, no matter how miserable he tries to make me, I'm not quitting.

I stare at the bare board, willing my eyes to dry.

I'm not tough. But I am desperate. And sometimes, that's the same thing.

CHAPTER 10

STERLING

To: Marty2003@email.com

    Subject: WTF Marty?

    From:BlackMountainLodgeAdmin@email.com

    Seriously, Marty, what were you thinking hiring a woman? She's already threatened to sue me. I had to put her in the damn Laundry Cabin. I'm sure she'll be complaining in no time.

    Tell me those other candidates are still available.

    Sterling

Chapter 11

Courtney

My alarm beeps, and I have to fight the desire to scream.

It feels like I just fell asleep.

Like literally. It feels like unconsciousness just took me under and that I hardly slept at all.

I reach my arm up over my head to where I left my phone on the edge of the platform, and groan in pain.

I'm thirty, and my body is way too old for this shit.

After silencing my alarm, I slowly lower my arm back to my side.

Six a.m.

I blink at the ceiling.

I took my time unpacking last night—feeling like a chicken for not wanting to go back outside for the rest of my stuff in the dark. And then, even though I was exhausted, I still couldn't force myself to climb into *bed* until midnight.

When I finally did, it was impossible to get comfortable. Because, as it turns out, laying all your clothes out into a flat pile on top of a board does not a mattress make.

I shift and let out a pitiful whine.

Everything aches.

I've had some less-than-ideal sleeping situations in my life, but this... this takes the fucking cake.

I'm almost tempted to sleep in my Jeep rather than spend another night on this literal board. Even if the cold and fear of the forest would keep me up all night.

I blink, waking myself up more.

I wiggle my toes.

I rock my head side to side.

And I groan again.

Because I won't sleep in my car.

I can't give Mr. Black a single reason to fire me.

Filling my lungs, I mentally brace myself, then roll onto my side.

Soreness has me grunting, but I don't stop.

And as I roll the rest of the way off the bunk, the rough edge of the plywood digs into my hip. I'm glad I slept in sweatpants and a hoodie last night, so at least I don't have bare skin exposed, because getting a scrape or a splinter right now would truly be the final straw.

My feet hit the floor, and the impact radiates up my shins.

"Owie," I whine.

I shift my weight around, trying to ease the pins and needles dancing up my legs. Through the socks I wore to bed, I can feel the coolness of the wood floor beneath my feet.

I've been living in hot climates for too long. This new chilled world is going to take some getting used to. But I did spot a base-board heater behind that dinky table in the main room, so at least I won't freeze to death.

Rolling out my shoulders, I notice the same thing I noticed last night... the quiet.

It's so damn quiet out here I—

My phone starts to beep again, and I nearly jump out of my socks.

I slap a hand over my heart before I turn it—and my backup alarm—off.

The sun isn't exactly up, but there's enough early morning light coming in through the windows. Especially from the front room since the curtains up there are a thin white linen.

I shuffle to the bathroom, and while I brush my teeth, I curse my cowardice from the night before, remembering that my food box is still in the Jeep.

It's nothing exciting. A rather pitiful collection of ramen, peanut butter, crackers, and off-brand beef jerky. The basics, and all nonperishables, which is good because there's no fridge in the Laundry Cabin.

I look at my phone to check the time.

I have fifty minutes before my first shift at Black Mountain Lodge starts.

Just enough time to shower, change into work clothes, get my food box, and eat a few spoonfuls of peanut butter.

I eye the front door as I shove my feet into my tennis shoes.

Knowing it was unlocked did not help me fall asleep last night.

Even if Mr. Black believes bears won't be able to turn the handle, men can. And he was adamant about me not sharing the Bunk House with his male employees. So it seems a little counterintuitive that he wouldn't care about an unlocked door.

But I suppose out here in the middle of the woods, there isn't really a need to lock the Laundry Cabin. Because while there might be a platform in the back room, clearly this building wasn't meant to be used as housing.

Still, I tried to wedge the little dining chair under the door handle, like how I've seen it done in movies. But the dinky chair wasn't tall enough. So I just added a nice little layer of fear to my discomfort last night.

How cozy.

Going on my tiptoes, I reach over the dryers and pull the curtain aside.

I don't see anything out of place.

No movement.

No bears or men or other creatures.

I let the curtain drop back into place.

"Looks clear," I tell Spike.

My small cactus doesn't reply. But that's to be expected. She's been a little testy after spending the last few days in a box.

I purse my lips and glance at the window above the table, then back at the one above the dryers.

Which way is west?

Do cacti do better in sunrise or sunset?

Does it make a difference?

Spike and I have been rooming together for two years, but it's been in an apartment, and not a corner unit, so I've never gotten to choose what type of sunlight she gets.

"I'll google the answer once I get on the Wi-Fi, okay?" I tell her, then I pick her up and set her on the windowsill above the table.

It's not like Mr. Black couldn't easily walk around the back of the Laundry Cabin and see Spike, but I figure facing her out back is better than in the window that faces the driveway. I don't need my boss to accuse me of being *too girly* by *decorating*.

I glance at my phone again.

"Shit."

Five minutes have passed, and I need to get a move on.

I snag the plastic grocery bag filled with my shower supplies off the counter and yank open the front door.

Cool air gusts through the doorway, and I hurry to step out, pulling the door closed behind me.

No railing, I remind myself and focus on my steps until I'm safely on the ground. Then I turn down the little path that leads to the driveway.

I'm mid-yawn when I lift my gaze from the ground and let out a sound that's half scream, half choke.

Fifteen feet away from me, walking up the driveway, is Mr. Black. Carrying an honest to fucking god log on his shoulder.

He looks like a lumberjack.

An *angry* lumberjack.

And, unfortunately, he looks even sexier than I remember.

CHAPTER 12

STERLING

MY NEWEST EMPLOYEE SPINS ON HER HEEL AND RUSHES back to her cabin.

Torn between amusement and annoyance at her flight, I tell myself her jumpiness is a good thing. Means she'll be gone soon, and I can go back to my usual routine.

A routine that doesn't include a pretty girl dressed in sweatpants screaming at me before daybreak.

A routine where I wake up with the normal amount of morning wood. Not the raging hard-on I woke up to today, which I was required to *take care of.*

But even that release didn't relax me because I felt more on edge after it than I did before.

Because my mind stayed stuck on thoughts of *her.*

Wondering what it would feel like if *her* fingers were wrapped around my dick.

Wondering what she would do if she could hear me through my open window.

My heavy breaths. My grunts as I neared the edge.

Wondering how bad it would really be to sleep with someone in my employ...

Which is how I ended up here—hauling logs to stock the pile I have behind my house for splitting.

It was too early to use the axe, which would have been a better exertion, but the cardio of carrying heavy things was doing the trick to blank out my mind.

Until *she* appeared.

Courtney doesn't pause as she rushes up the steps to the Laundry Cabin, disappearing from sight with a snap of the door.

Good.

I turn my focus back to what I'm doing and continue walking, not at all thinking about how she looked.

How her eyes were still sleepy. Not quite open all the way. Those damn lashes lowered, blocking my view of her pretty irises before she realized I was there.

How she looked warm and adorable in that hoodie.

How her hair was a mess. Strands hanging loose around her face, her braids coming undone.

She looked the way she would look waking up after a long night of fucking.

I grip the front of my jeans and adjust the material.

She looked like *I need to keep my fucking distance.*

CHAPTER 13

COURTNEY

AT FIVE TO SEVEN, I OPEN THE FRONT DOOR. AGAIN.

After running into, then away from, Mr. Black, I spent the rest of the hour hiding in my tiny bathroom, getting dressed for the day.

I can shower and eat food later.

Stepping out onto the top step, I pull the door shut behind me.

Mr. Black didn't give me any real direction for today. Just that we start at seven.

So I'm ready. Or as ready as I'll ever be.

I stuck with my routine of SPF moisturizer and mascara. And since I couldn't tame my hair with a shower, I stuck with my usual and twisted it into two French braids, one over each shoulder. With that done, I put on my work clothes. Dark green cargo pants that are snug on my ass but fit wide past my thighs. They aren't attractive, but they don't need to be. And the pockets are practical. Then I layered a gray long-sleeved shirt tucked into my pants under a cropped olive-green crew neck sweatshirt.

Back home... or rather, out east, I didn't need the extra layer.

And maybe the cropped shirt isn't professional, but I'm

completely covered, so who cares if it happens to highlight my tummy. It will keep me warm, and I can take it off if I need to.

Plus, if I have to crawl around to fix or clean something, I don't want a big baggy sweater in the way.

Then again, Mr. Black already made his distaste for me being here known.

I give the bottom of my sweater a little tug.

What if he sees my clothing as a distraction?

Maybe I should change.

A throat clears.

And my pulse jumps.

CHAPTER 14

STERLING

THOSE FUCKING BRAIDS.

I want to crowd her right back into her cabin and guide her to her knees with a grip on those goddamn braids.

I clear my throat.

I don't even mean to.

I just suddenly find it hard to swallow.

Courtney's eyes snap to meet mine, and even though we're separated by a dozen yards—me standing on my front deck, her standing on her top step—it feels like I could reach out and touch her.

Grab her.

Drag her against me.

I see the hint of her tongue as she wets her lips...

Pure distraction.

This woman is a pure fucking distraction.

Courtney raises a hand in the most hesitant wave I've ever seen.

She is clearly going to pretend that we haven't already seen each other this morning, and that's fine with me.

I dip my chin, then tilt my head toward the driveway.

She starts down her stairs, and I start down mine.

CHAPTER 15

COURTNEY

I SHOVE MY HANDS INTO MY POCKETS AS I WALK TO meet Mr. Black in the driveway.

It shouldn't matter that he's good looking.

It's not like I've never been around hot men before.

Not hot like him.

Okay, maybe he's the hottest man I've met in real life, but I'm an adult. I can handle this.

My work boots crunch on the gravel as I slow to a stop.

His dark hair is mostly tamed. His beard...

I can't look at his beard. Something about it does something to me, and I can't deal with that right now.

He's wearing jeans, possibly the same ones from yesterday. His flannel is red—and buttoned. And he's carrying a steaming mug of coffee.

Motherfucker looks like he belongs in a damn Folgers Christmas ad. Just toss some snow on the pine trees, and he'd sell coffee by the truckload.

Then I notice the clipboard in his hand, and he no longer feels very Christmassy.

CHAPTER 16

STERLING

"MORN... ING." COURTNEY'S GREETING FALTERS AS I hold out the clipboard.

She takes it, flipping it over so the top sheet of the well-used legal pad is facing her.

Across the top of the paper, partially hidden by the clip, is the word *Maintenance.*

I watch her flip through the pages, the top three filled with a dozen tasks each.

I didn't create the list last night. This isn't some prank. This is the collection of ongoing projects that need to get done around the Lodge.

Marty started the list months, maybe years ago. He was thorough in his observations... He just also happened to be very slow.

But I don't share those details with Courtney. She can make whatever assumptions she wants regarding the timeliness of these items.

"Before you start on the list, your first job every morning is making coffee," I tell her.

Courtney hugs the clipboard to her chest, then makes a point of looking at the mug in my hand.

I take a sip. "This is coffee from my house. You need to make a pot in the Food Hall for everyone."

"Oh." Her brows furrow, confusion coloring her tone. "Where's the Food Hall?"

A seed of guilt begins to sprout in my chest.

I'm being an asshole.

I wouldn't be this short with the male version of Court I thought I was hiring.

The sun reflecting off her hair.

The tip of her tongue peeking out between her lips.

I turn my back on Courtney and stride toward the Food Hall.

It's *be an asshole* or *seduce her.*

So I guess I'm gonna keep being an asshole.

CHAPTER 17

COURTNEY

I FOLLOW MR. BLACK ACROSS THE DRIVEWAY AND down a path that leads away from my cabin.

The trees are thicker over here but not oppressive.

As we walk, we pass larger cabins with numbers painted on the doors. I'm assuming they're the guest cabins, but I'm not willing to break the heavy silence by asking.

Ahead of me, my grumpy boss lifts his hand and points to an even larger cabin farther down the path and to the left. "That's the Bunk House. The guys clean it themselves, so you have no reason to go there."

I'm not a cartoon lion, so I don't feel the immediate urge to go where I was told I can't. But still, being told I *have no reason to* irks me.

"Did you hear me, Court?" He stops as he asks the question, looking back over his shoulder.

Court?

I stop a step later, bringing us closer than we've been since last night, when I touched him.

"I said, did you hear me?"

Why does it seem like he's looking at my mouth?

"Yeah." I hold the clipboard tighter against my body. "Stay out of the Bunk House."

He nods once, then continues walking.

Did you hear me? I mouth behind his back.

His attitude is making him uglier by the moment, and I'd take solace in that, except when I first met him yesterday—before he knew who I was—he was nice. Smiling. Pleasant. So I know he's capable of kindness. He's just also capable of turning it off.

When we hit a Y in the path, Mr. Black veers to the right, away from the forbidden Bunk House.

Following his footsteps, I spot our destination.

Same paint colors as the rest of the cabins, but this one is different because the roof extends over the front, creating an over-hang that shelters four picnic tables.

Bossy walks around the tables to the door with yellow letters.

But instead of opening it, he turns to face me. "The code is on the top of the second page."

I stare at him.

He stares back.

I look at the door.

The code?

And then I see the little keypad above the handle.

It's locked.

The Food Hall locks, but the cabin I sleep in doesn't.

I bet if I looked at the doors on all the other cabins, I'd find locks.

Cool.

I dig my thumbnail into my index finger.

He made that damn comment about the bears and round handles and...

I grit my teeth.

And everyone else gets a damn lock.

Lock it down, Courtney.

I refuse to show him my frustration.

Not today.

Keeping my eyes away from Mr. Black, I loosen my hold on the clipboard and lift the top page.

In the corner, I see a four-digit number.

No label. No explanation.

3324

I lower the top page.

Moving to the door, I'm grateful that I've used these exact locks before, so I know how to work them.

I type in the code, the lock whirs, and I open the door.

Dawn is coming through the uncovered windows—windows that are much larger than the ones in the Laundry Cabin—but I still look for the light switch.

Finding it, I flip it on, illuminating the one-room building.

More picnic tables are inside, and a wood-topped island separates the tables from the back wall where the oversized appliances are. A fridge, freezer, giant oven-stove combo, and another stretch of countertop hosting a coffee maker from the same era as the washer and dryer in my cabin.

"Is this the—"

When I turn around and find myself alone, I stop talking.

The door is standing open, and I step back outside in time to see Mr. Black's form disappear between the trees.

"Wow," I whisper. "What a great onboarding session."

My eyes dart around the woods, checking for bears. And coworkers.

I don't spot any, but not wanting to be observed by either while I figure this machine out, I pull the door closed.

Just make some coffee, then you can work on the list.

Remembering that I'm still holding the clipboard, I quickly scan the pages. But—and this should not come as a surprise—there are no instructions on how to work the coffee maker.

Moving over to the machine in question, I set the clipboard down.

The stainless-steel monstrosity stares back at me.

"So, are you one of the old kind of appliances that performs like a workhorse? Or are you a finicky bitch?"

It doesn't reply.

Propping my hands on my hips, I take a deep breath.

"You can do this, Courtney."

Saying my name reminds me of Mr. Black calling me Court earlier.

I don't mind the nickname. I've always wanted someone to give me one. But why he would call me the name that offended him so much yesterday, I don't understand.

Unless this is him pretending I'm a guy?

Joke's on him, though, because I've been working in the male-dominated field of maintenance for years, and I've heard it all. So a shortened version of my real name is hardly insulting.

I step closer to the coffee maker and start inspecting it. "Alright, Big Joe, you treat me good, I'll treat you good."

It takes some work. Some digging through cupboards. Some guesswork on quantities. But twenty minutes later, the scent of coffee fills the room.

While the oversized pot fills, I poke around in the large cabinets.

All the dishware is metal, which makes sense, durability and all that.

Then there's bulk groceries filling the other shelves. Canned goods, dry goods, baking supplies...

Big Joe lets out a loud click.

I shut the cupboard and move back to the coffee machine to check out my work.

The pot is made of metal, like everything in this place, so I can't see the color of the coffee, but it smells right.

The drips from the basket above slow to a stop, and I assume the click sound was meant to announce the shutoff.

I did it.

Feeling absurdly proud of myself, I try to release a little piece of tension by relaxing my shoulders. But the forced movement sends a twinge down my spine. Reminding me that Mr. Black-heart made me sleep on a goddamn board last night.

Pretty sure I'm gonna have to sleep on that board again tonight. And tomorrow.

On and on until I can afford to buy one of those inflatable camping mattress things.

Afford.

I spread my fingers at my side, stopping myself from pressing my fingertips together.

The application for this position stated the flat per-week pay I'd get, but it didn't say *when* I'd get paid.

Since the amount was listed as weekly, I'm hoping the pay is weekly. But I'll have to find someone to ask.

Someone other than my surly boss.

My stomach gives a twist, reminding me I'm hungry.

Along with leaving my food in the Jeep overnight, I also left my kettle and instant coffee, so I am both hungry and un-caffeinated. Which is practically a crime.

I won't take food out of the pantry behind me because that feels far too much like stealing, but Mr. Black did say I was making coffee for everyone.

I purse my lips.

Everyone does include me, right?

I only stand in indecision for approximately four minutes before I cave and snag one of the metal coffee cups out of the cupboard.

The pot is heavy, and I embarrass myself with how much I struggle to pour it, but I manage to do it without spilling.

Winning.

Careful to hold the cup by the handle, I tiptoe to the window that faces Mr. Black's house.

I don't know what I expect to see, but I don't see him. Or the house. Just trees.

Feeling safe from prying eyes, I step back and finally take a sip of coffee.

My eyes start to close but open wide as I swallow.

"Damn, that's good."

I stare down into the brown liquid.

Clearly, I made it correctly, but this is more than the machinery at work. This is good coffee.

My eyes move back to the window.

So, Mr. Black is a dick. But he still buys quality coffee beans for his employees.

Interesting.

CHAPTER 18

STERLING

I WATCH COURTNEY AS SHE HUGS A LARGE BOX TO HER chest and uses her hip to shove her Jeep door closed.

It's 12:10. And ever since she stepped out of the Food Hall this morning, after mastering the coffee maker, she's been working.

I wasn't being weird. I just happened to be close enough to see her head to her Jeep, and curiosity kept me watching.

I expected her to maybe finish unpacking her stuff, but she surprised me when she took a toolbox out of her vehicle.

A real one that looked heavy and banged-up and wasn't just for show or painted some wild color.

She carried it into her cabin, then reappeared with a screwdriver sticking out of her pocket.

I had to bite my lip.

Because *fuck me*, a girl with tools is hot.

Then I started to picture her in a tool belt.

In only a tool belt.

And I had to turn away.

Now, I'm back at my kitchen window, about to head to the Food Hall for lunch, but I can't bring myself to exit the house and interrupt whatever Courtney is doing.

48

She slowly moves up the stairs to her door, like she's being extra careful with her steps, then she props the box between her hip and the doorframe as she reaches for the handle.

After she goes inside, I wait.

I wait five minutes, but she doesn't come back out.

We didn't discuss any sort of schedule, other than when to start. But it's safe for her to assume that the lunch break starts at noon.

I would've thought she'd like to partake in the included lunch, but maybe she's feeling shy.

I could keep her company.

I roll my eyes at my horny inner voice.

I'm not asking the girl to sit with me.

CHAPTER 19

COURTNEY

STEAM WHISTLES OUT OF MY KETTLE AS THE LIGHT ON the base turns off.

I lift the pot carefully and add the hot water to a bowl already containing a square of hard ramen noodles covered in the powdered flavoring.

Once it's full, I place my plate over the bowl, sealing in the steam. Then I pour the rest of the hot water into my coffee mug, the instant coffee already scooped into the bottom.

The one cup I had from Big Joe this morning is not going to be enough to get me through the day.

I blow on the surface of the hot coffee as I wait for my lunch and take in my new *kitchen*.

It didn't take long to set up.

I put my food away in the small cabinet above the sink. And on the end of the counter next to the sink, over the first washer, I lined up my kettle, my toaster, and my stack of dishes for one, with my set of silverware sticking out of my old cracked mug that isn't good for liquid but is good for storage.

It looks a tad meager, but it's not like I need a second plate for my pretend friends.

My first sip reminds me that I still haven't eaten today, and the next four minutes are going to feel like forever. So, I take the peanut butter out of the cupboard and use my spoon to scoop some out.

There's no fridge in here, but maybe we're allowed to use the fridges in the Food Hall? If we are, then after payday, I'll get some sandwich stuff. It'll be a splurge, but it will be nice to not eat the same thing for every meal.

When four minutes pass, I lift the plate off my bowl and daydream about sandwiches and sturdy chairs as I sit on my hard bunk, eating noodles and mumbling curses about my dark-haired, dark-eyed boss.

CHAPTER 20

STERLING

"So..." Fisher starts two seconds after I sit on the bench across the picnic table from him.

I hold his gaze as I lift the burger to my mouth.

He's worked for me too long—for years, like all my guys—so my stare rarely works as a deterrent anymore.

"Is it true?"

I take my time chewing. "Is what true?"

Simpson drops onto the bench next to me. "You really hire a girl to take over Marty's position?"

My head snaps over, his incredulous tone annoying me. "You have two daughters. You really want to tell me I can't hire a woman?"

I'm being a total fucking hypocrite, but clearly, I'm unwell. So what's one more offense?

He holds his hands up. "Course not. Just... wasn't expecting it."

Yeah. Me either.

I take another bite.

"Where'd she come from?" Fisher is still not put off by my attitude.

Fisher is by far the youngest guy on my crew at twenty-eight.

And the closest in age to Courtney. The rest of the guys are near, or over, my forty-five.

I eye him. Trying to decide whether a woman would find him attractive.

Baby face. Shaggy hair in his eyes. Lanky.

I shove more of the burger into my mouth.

"Her plates are from North Carolina," Cook chimes in from the other side of the counter, his graying mustache twitching with a smile.

The door to the Food Hall opens, and we all turn toward it.

Every shoulder slumps when Leon enters.

He pauses. "What?"

Cook snickers. "We were hoping you were the girl."

As the oldest of the employees, Leon rolls his eyes, his bushy brows lifting with the motion. "You're a bunch of fools."

I fill my mouth with the final bite of my burger.

He's not wrong.

It's not until I've put my plate in the dishwasher and brushed my hands off on my jeans that I realize the obvious.

None of the guys have talked to Courtney.

No one has met her.

And if no one met her, then no one told her about lunch.

She wasn't being shy by staying in her cabin; she didn't know.

The burger rolls in my stomach.

I really am an asshole.

CHAPTER 21

COURTNEY

I DRAG MY SWEATER OFF AND USE THE BUNCHED-UP material to wipe at my forehead.

I've been fighting with this cabin door all afternoon.

The list said *Fix the front door on cabin two.* So I went to cabin two, which turns out to be the closest one to my Laundry Cabin, and found the front door wasn't exactly straight, causing it to stick when you try to open it.

Not a huge deal. I've fixed doors before. My last gig had me replacing more than one after a break-in or a fight.

However, stripped screws, rust, and a bent hinge quickly dampened my confidence.

Even under the best circumstances, two people are best for hanging doors.

But I don't have a second person.

And I'm hardly working under the best circumstances.

So I struggled.

I found branches on the ground to use as props.

I used screws out of my toolbox because no one showed me where to find tools here.

And there have to be tools here.

Throughout the process, I bit my lip more than once to keep the tears at bay.

But I didn't cry.

I didn't dare.

Not when Mr. Blackasshole could appear around any corner.

I am giving zero reasons for him to fire me.

Mentally unstable? Never heard of her.

Wiping my forehead again, I marvel at the weather here.

This morning it was chilly, but with the sun shining down between the trees, the day has gotten warm.

I eye the interior of the guest cabin.

The kitchenette and full-size fridge.

The pair of bunk beds mocking me with their mattresses...

I'm tempted to sit on one of the adult-sized chairs at the table for four.

I'm even more tempted to collapse onto one of the *four* glorious mattresses. But instead, I gather my tools and pull the door shut as I move onto the steps outside.

The door clicks shut smoothly.

"Not too shabby," I sigh to myself.

It might have taken me longer than I would've liked, but I did my job.

My muscles protest as I lower myself onto the steps.

I was hoping my aches and pains would loosen up as the day went on, as I moved around, but that has not been the case. If anything, I feel worse.

My butt hits the step, and the grunt I let out could be mistaken for one of the bears I've been stressing about all day. And as I blink at the clipboard on my lap, I almost welcome the idea of a bear approaching.

Maybe I could befriend it. And it could carry things around for me. And by things, I mean me. I want it to carry me around.

Or maybe it would just swallow me whole.

Either option would make the rest of my day easier.

With a huff, I pull the pen out of my cargo pocket and drag the tip across the paper, crossing out the *Fix the front door* task.

Voices carry across the property, but I don't look up.

I've heard evidence of other people throughout the day, but no one has approached me.

Possibly because I've done everything I can to stay hidden.

I'm sure they're nice. Sure they won't be like Mr. Black. But I'm just not up for small talk today.

The lack of sleep. The moodiness of my boss. The measly amount in my bank account. The lingering hunger from not eating breakfast and rushing through lunch since I didn't know how long of a break I was allowed...

It's all caught up to me.

I hang my head forward as I flip through the pages on the clipboard.

I started from the top of page one, but I need to find an easy task to end the day with.

I still don't know how late I'm supposed to work each day.

Since it started early, it should end early. Right?

It's not like I have some pressing engagement, but I do want to shower before nightfall.

My eyes snag on a line of text.

Fix leaky faucet in women's toilet.

I make a face at the term *women's toilet*, but that's the building with the showers—please, Ourea, let there be showers in the *women's toilet*.

Reaching up, I grip the railing—since the guest cabins have railings—and haul myself up.

With all my things gathered, I take the short path from the front of the cabin to the slightly wider path that runs parallel to the driveway. Then I follow that path to the bathrooms.

Cleaning is a part of my job description, so as I open the door labeled *Women*, I pray once again to the god of the mountains that the bathrooms aren't gross.

The high square windows don't let in much light, but when I

find the switch for the overhead fluorescents, I'm pleasantly surprised.

Hooray for one thing going right.

Ahead of me is a long counter with four sinks.

I look down the length of the building and see four stalls with metal locking doors, and then four stalls that stick out farther and have shower curtains instead of doors.

I'd prefer doors over curtains for showering, but... I look over my shoulder at the main door and see it can be locked from the inside.

"Basically a spa."

Before I start on the leaky sink, I walk down to the shower stalls and pull one of the curtains aside.

My second pleasant surprise comes when I see the second shower curtain splitting the front part of the stall from the actual shower part. This means I can put my clothes and towel on the small bench without them getting wet.

All in all, not a bad setup.

As I work on the sink, I daydream about the shower I'm going to take as soon as the clock strikes five.

CHAPTER 22

STERLING

THE LIGHTS SHUT OFF IN THE FRONT HALF OF THE Laundry Cabin, telling me Courtney is going to bed.

I wonder what she wears to sleep.

A T-shirt and underwear?

Those baggy sweatpants I saw her in this morning?

A lacy little dress?

Nothing at all...?

I press my palm against the front of my boxers.

If my little worker is heading to sleep, then I will too.

My lights are already off, so I pull back my quilt and drop into bed.

Lying on my back, I keep my hand on my dick as I think about *her*.

I think about those wet braids I saw when I spotted her coming out of the showers.

I had another moment of guilt, realizing I hadn't even thought about showers since the Bunk House has two full bathrooms. But the majority of our guests are men, so she'll pretty much have that whole women's bathroom to herself.

I was standing there, working on convincing myself that was actually a perk, when she shifted the bundle in her arms.

The wet towel, presumably wrapped around clothes, soaked the shirt she'd just put on.

Her thin T-shirt.

I was no longer thinking about showers because I was looking at her nipples.

At her hard fucking nipples, straining against the cotton, showing the perfect outline.

I slide my hand inside my boxers and grip my length.

And I start to stroke.

Thinking about her soft tits and hard nipples.

About how her skin would've been damp and warm.

I think about her right now, climbing into bed, settling onto her pillows.

I think about her getting comfortable, letting out a moan.

I think about her slipping her hand into her panties, thinking about me.

CHAPTER 23

COURTNEY

I USE THE LAST OF MY STRENGTH TO CLIMB ONTO MY bunk, the height feeling taller than it was last night.

Kneeling, I straighten the layers of clothing on the plywood before lying on top of them.

I took some Tylenol with my multivitamin after dinner.

My body still aches, but at least I won't get scurvy.

I pull my blanket up as I settle on my side.

It takes some shifting and some rearranging of shirts, but I find a position that doesn't actively hurt.

Staring into the darkness, I think about my boss.

About how I might actually hate him.

I slide my palms together, entwining my fingers, and close my eyes.

I've been on my own since I was nineteen.

I'm used to it.

I should be used to it.

My fingers tighten around each other, pretending I have someone's hand to hold other than my own.

Maybe it's the darkness outside.

Maybe it's the quiet.

Maybe it's the fact that I'm literally stranded here.

But here, tonight, I feel a whole lot lonelier than I have in a long time.

Chapter 24

Sterling

I pause at the open cabin door, the feminine voice inside claiming my attention.

I've been looking all over for Courtney, so walking into the guest cabin she's occupying isn't spying. It's work.

I cross the threshold.

"Well, I'm sorry. If someone had done this sooner, it wouldn't hurt so much."

Wouldn't hurt?

What the fuck?

I stride through the cabin, following the sound of her voice to the bathroom at the back.

Who's with Courtney in here?

"Just a little more," she coos.

I turn into the small room. "Who are you—"

Courtney lets out a shriek of surprise as something falls from her hand into the toilet's open tank.

There's no one with her.

She's all alone.

So when the toilet water splashes up, it only hits her.

Courtney looks down at her shirt, but I think the expression of horror on her face is for the toilet water dripping off her cheek.

Her gaze slowly lifts to meet mine, her hands held out to the side.

I clear my throat. "I, um." I clear my throat again, torn between wanting to help and wanting to laugh. "I wanted to let you know that Cook serves lunch for the employees from noon to one in the Food Hall."

She brings her forearm to her face, using her long sleeve to soak up the droplets. "Is it included in the room and board, or is it extra?"

An uncomfortable emotion slithers across my sternum.

Most of the guys who work for me don't have much. Some have houses elsewhere that they rent out, but most of them don't. Either way, they're all happy to take a free lunch.

So why does it feel different when Courtney asks me if it's included or extra?

My hand rubs the flannel over my chest before I realize what I'm doing and drop it. "It's included."

She uses her other sleeve to wipe her cheek again. "Okay. Thank you for telling me."

I nod.

I don't have anything more to tell her, but I'm reluctant to leave.

"Was there something else?" Her voice doesn't have a bite exactly, but it's clear she doesn't want me here.

I start to shake my head, then remember why I barged in here the way I did. "Were you talking to the toilet?"

Courtney eyes me for a moment before she lifts a shoulder.

When I continue to hold her gaze, she answers. "I'm used to being—working alone. It passes the time."

I make a humming sound, not sure how to take what she just said.

I step back out of the small bathroom.

"Don't forget about lunch," I remind her.

Then I leave.

CHAPTER 25

COURTNEY

I STAND STILL, NOT SHIFTING MY FEET UNTIL I HEAR the front door shut.

Then I let out the high-pitched whine that's been caught in my chest since I got splashed in the face with *toilet water*.

"What the fuck, World?" I snap at the room.

I tug at my shirt, pulling the wet fabric out and away from my face as I drag it over my head.

Not that it matters, because I already got *toilet water* on my *fucking face*.

I grit my teeth and let out another sound of frustration.

"Why?" I ask the toilet as I throw the shirt down on the floor, leaving me in a tank top.

I glare down at the gray material clinging to my tits because that's wet too.

"Not cool. Not fucking cool."

I spin around in the small bathroom and turn the faucet on to hot, leaning my face over the sink.

Thankfully there's a hand soap dispenser on the counter.

After filling my palm with the *mountain rain* scented liquid, I slap my hands together and lather roughly.

"Why?" I can hear my fragile mental state when I ask it this time. "Why did that have to happen in front of *him*?"

I fill my lungs, then hold my breath and scrub my soapy palms all over my face.

When my chest starts to burn, I cup my hands under the running water and scoop it up over my mouth.

Suds clear, my lips part, and I suck in a big breath.

Once all the soap is washed off, I pump more into my hand and start the process all over again.

Toilet water.

On my face.

Fuck. Me.

CHAPTER 26

STERLING

THE WAIL ALMOST HAS ME TRIPPING OFF THE LAST STEP. Catching my balance, I stand still, listening.

"What the fuck, World?" Courtney's voice is clearer than it should be as she cusses out the planet.

That girl can flip from meek to crass in a second.

"Why?"

I narrow my eyes at hearing her again.

Stepping carefully, I turn the corner on the side of the cabin and see the culprit.

The open bathroom window.

I also see Fisher and Cook standing a few yards off with grins on their faces.

"Not cool. Not fucking cool." Courtney's tone is still angry, but there's a hint of distress coming through that keeps my mouth in a flat line.

When the guys look like they might say something, I shake my head and point down the path, silently telling them to keep their mouths shut and to move on.

"Why?" Her voice is quieter, and I'm sure I'm the only one who can still hear her. "Why in front of *him*?"

Him.

Me.

The now familiar guilt pushes me back a step away from the window.

I'm her boss, I tell myself.

She doesn't want to look incompetent at her new job, I try to reason.

She hates me and doesn't want to show weakness to the enemy, I accept.

CHAPTER 27

COURTNEY

FACE WASHED AND TOILET FLUSHER FIXED, I BUNDLE MY shirt in the hand towel I dried my face with and hold it at my side.

Looking around the bathroom, I try to see if anything else is out of place.

The powder room is larger than the one I have in the Laundry Cabin, but it's still just a toilet and a sink. So, apparently, I will be sharing the public showers with our guests.

As I'm wondering how many women come to Black Mountain Lodge, my eyes stop on the window.

The *open* window.

I tip my head back and clamp my teeth down on the urge to scream.

But I can't scream now because the flipping window is open, and if someone was outside, they'd hear me.

I set down my bundle and reach up to close the window.

The other reason I can't scream now is because if I did, there's a strong possibility it would turn into a sob.

Pulling the window down, I go up onto my toes to look out the glass.

No one is out there. Just trees. And an empty path.

I stare at the path. Was it empty the whole time? Or did someone witness my meltdown?

I drop my weight back onto my heels.

What's done is done.

Plus, if Mr. Black heard me, he'd probably have come back into the cabin and scolded me.

Gathering the shirt and towel again, I wonder if that's actually true.

He felt different today. Not exactly *different nice* like he was in those first few moments we met. But nicer. And he lingered like he wanted to say more.

But what he did say...

Lunch.

He didn't sound hesitant exactly about telling me, but there was something there.

Maybe he felt bad about not telling me yesterday?

I think about how hungry I was most of the day and kind of hope he does feel bad.

Yesterday sucked.

At least this morning, after I peeled myself off that damn board, I made two packets of cinnamon raisin oatmeal and added a big spoonful of peanut butter. It was good. And it meant I didn't start my day hungry.

I bite down on my lip.

I hated asking if the lunch was included, but I needed to know.

If, at the end of the week, my paycheck was going to be less, I'd need to know by how much before I agreed.

I could live off what I have in my cupboard for a while.

But not today.

The idea of eating with all my coworkers—whom I haven't met—does stress me out. But I'll stay focused on the fact that I'm about to have some free food.

And free food is always delicious.

VOICES FILTER OUT THROUGH THE PROPPED-OPEN front door of the Food Hall.

I'm a little later than I meant to be. But when I got back to the Laundry Cabin, I still felt the toilet water on me, so I stripped everything off and threw it—and the hand towel I used—into one of the washers. Testing out my cabin's namesake for the first time.

Then I used a washcloth to scrub my face and body.

Then I put on different clothes.

But since the day is half over, I put on my outfit from yesterday—since no one but Mr. Black saw me in it anyway.

So by the time I did all that and re-braided my hair, it was quarter after noon.

And now here I am.

Late.

I force myself to keep walking to the open door.

"Suck it up, Buttercup," I whisper to myself.

Were you talking to the toilet?

The question would've been funny if my answer wasn't so depressing.

I thought I caught myself well though.

And it wasn't a lie. I have worked alone for a long time.

But I've also been alone for a long time. Thankfully I didn't finish that sentence.

A loud laugh makes me jolt.

I'm not working alone anymore.

Hoping for the best, bracing for the worst, I step into the Food Hall.

CHAPTER 28

STERLING

I SEE HER BEFORE ANYONE ELSE DOES. BECAUSE I'M watching.

Waiting.

Three of my guys are sitting at a table. Cook is behind the counter. And another is filling his plate.

But my hip is against the counter, and my eyes are aimed at the door.

She's changed. Back to the outfit she wore yesterday. The one that had me staring at her from around corners like a fucking stalker.

Her face is flushed.

Her braids are smooth.

And I know the moment the guys spot her, too, because the room falls silent.

I straighten. "Guys, this is Court."

Courtney's eyes dart to mine.

I called her Court earlier as a way to keep distance between us. But also the idea of anyone other than me calling her by her full name... I don't like it.

So they'll call her Court too.

But when I'm alone. When I'm thinking about her. She'll be my Courtney.

The pretty woman raises her hand in a shy wave. "Hello."

"She's the new Marty. She's staying in the Laundry Cabin. And you'll keep a civil tongue in your mouth when she's around." She scrunches her face at my last sentence.

"Oh, that's not necessary," she tries to argue.

"It's necessary," I say before pointing to the table. "That's Glen, Simpson, and Leon." I use my thumb to indicate the men near me. "Cook is behind the counter. And this kid is Fisher."

I purposefully point out his young age.

He's not mature enough for her.

She needs someone older.

"Nice to meet you," the kid says, leaving his plate on the counter and walking over to shake her hand.

I'm tempted to trip him. But I don't.

Because I'm mature. Unlike him.

Then Courtney smiles at Fisher, and I regret the not-tripping.

CHAPTER 29

COURTNEY

I SLUMP IN MY SPOT ON THE BENCH.

The grilled chicken melt with potato salad was as delicious as it smelled, and I'm in definite danger of slipping into a food coma.

"Anyone want more before I put it away?" Cook asks as he gets up from the bench across from me.

Fisher gets up for more potatoes, but the rest of us pass.

Lunch wasn't nearly as awkward as I expected it to be.

After everyone stood and shook my hand, reminding me of their names, the group spread out over two of the picnic tables, and I ended up in the middle of it all.

They included me but didn't grill me with questions, and it wasn't long before I relaxed into my meal.

The only person who didn't talk was Mr. Black.

"Court." Leon, one of the older guys, gets my attention. "You any good at baking?"

"Leon," our boss snaps.

"What?" Leon holds up his hands. "I ain't asking cuz she's a lady. I'm asking cuz no one here can make a pie to save their soul."

I smile at his argument.

Leon looks back to me. "Can ya, Court? You good at pies?"

I press my lips together, keeping my eyes off Mr. Black, and nod.

A chorus of whoops fills the Food Hall.

"What'd'ya say, Sterling?" Cook asks from across the room. "Can our Court here use her time to bake the occasional pie?"

Sterling?

Who's Sterling?

Mr. Black, my boss, stands from his spot at the other picnic table. "I don't care." He picks up his plate. "If Court agrees, you two can make fucking pies."

"Civil tongue." Fisher fake coughs.

A few guys snicker, but *Sterling* ignores him. Just like he ignores the rest of us as he puts his plate in the dishwasher and strides out of the building.

My coworkers resume talking among themselves, but my brain is still stuck on the revelation that my Black-souled boss has a first name.

And, of course, it can't be boring or bland. No. It has to be *Sterling*.

It has to sound strong. Masculine.

It has to remind me of the way his stomach felt under my hands.

Remind me of the way his muscles flexed under my touch.

"Earth to Court?"

I blink out of my stupor and find Fisher grinning at me.

Mr. Black, a.k.a. Sterling, called Fisher a kid when he was doing introductions.

With his sandy-colored hair curling over his eyes and his long limbs that remind me of a growing teen, he is definitely *the kid* compared to the rest of the crew. Though he can't be much younger than I am.

"Sorry, did you ask me something?" I smile back at him.

His grin widens. "Cook's food puts me to sleep too."

"That's a compliment," Cook hollers from across the room.

"Didn't say it wasn't," Fisher calls back. "Anyway..." He

shakes his head and turns his attention back to me. "I gotta hit up the Storage Shed after this. Has anyone shown it to you yet?"

"Uh, no," I tell him truthfully.

There's another building out past my Laundry Cabin, and I assume that's what he's talking about. But Mr. Black certainly hasn't mentioned it.

His hands-off approach has been... trying. But it's better than him hovering. I don't think I could handle him looking over my shoulder all day.

Though I would think he'd want to at least check my work. Or ask what I did at the end of the day...

But maybe he has been checking and just hasn't said anything about it.

"I'll take you over there now." Fisher stands.

"Okay, thanks." I twist to the side to lift my leg over the bench, and a groan of pain escapes my throat before I can stop it.

Simpson, who is still seated, snickers. "You're working too hard. It took Marty three days just to get started on one of those clipboard items. By my count, you've already crossed out a few."

I pause, straddling the bench. "Oh."

It's good to know that the bar is set low if Marty's speed was acceptable.

And it's just for me to know that most of my pain comes from sleeping on a wooden bunk, not from the work I've done.

Keeping the rest of my groans internal, I get to my feet and put my plate in the dishwasher before following Fisher out.

"So." He slows his long stride to match mine. "How's the first couple days going?"

I open my mouth, then close it and purse my lips.

This guy seems chill, but they were all acting casual at lunch, so I don't know how much I should share.

Fisher laughs. "Aww, it can't be that bad."

Not wanting to get in trouble for talking poorly about the job, I shake my head. "No, no, it's going well."

He chuckles again. "You don't gotta lie on my behalf, Court."

I eye Fisher as we keep walking, then sigh. "It really is fine. I just don't know how I'm doing."

Fisher tilts his head. "What do you mean?"

"I didn't really get any... direction. Beyond telling me to make the morning coffee, Mr. Black hasn't told me what he expects." I give him the truth, if not all of it.

"Mr. Black?" Fisher chokes on those words. "Did Sterling really tell you to call him that?"

We're approaching the driveway, about to cross right in front of the home of the man in question, so I lower my voice. "I didn't even know his name *was* Sterling until someone said it at lunch."

Fisher reaches a hand up and rubs the back of his neck.

Great. I made it uncomfortable.

"How long have you worked here?" I change the topic.

"Five years," Fisher says with pride.

As we approach the building behind my cabin, he tells me about graduating from college but not knowing what to do with his degree. How he knew a guy who came to Black Mountain Lodge for a fishing retreat. How he himself loves fishing. And how he came here, knocked on Sterling's front door, and asked to be considered for a guide position.

Fisher opens the door to the shed after typing in the same lock combo as the Food Hall.

"And he just hired you?" I ask, stepping into the space that's more of a garage than a shed.

"Not exactly." He snorts. "But I wore him down."

I hum, wondering if he was also forced to sleep on the board in the laundry room.

As I wander around the Storage Shed—circling the large cluster of shelving in the middle of the space—Fisher explains about the guests. How sometimes there's just one cabin's worth of people at a time, and sometimes every bunk is full.

"What do you guys do when there aren't guests?" I ask, wondering what they do on days like today.

"Mostly prep for the next round. Plan the routes we'll take.

Make packing and grocery lists. Prep gear... Each group fills out an intake form, and we adjust accordingly. So not every outing is the same."

"Makes sense," I muse.

We stay a few more minutes, and I make a mental note of where the items of interest are.

"You sure it's okay I take this?" I hold up the short step stool as I meet Fisher back at the door.

He nods. "Totally. This stuff is for any of us to use."

I stop myself from grinning like a fool as I imagine using the steps to get into bed tonight and how much easier that's going to be than climbing onto the bunk like a clumsy koala.

I shift my grip on the step stool as I step outside. My sore shoulders remind me that climbing into the bunk might be easier now, but it won't make sleeping any more comfortable.

Which reminds me...

"When is payday?" I ask Fisher as he locks the door.

His back is still to me when he answers. "Last day of the month."

Last...

My back rounds, like I caught the answer with my chest.

Last day of the month.

But it's only October second.

I won't get paid for another twenty-nine days.

"We always go to the bar..." Fisher keeps talking, but I don't hear him.

My brain is too busy calculating what I have in my cupboard, plus how expensive groceries are and...

That fucking board.

I can't sleep on that fucking board for another twenty-nine days.

Tears burn in the corners of my eyes, and I try desperately to blink them away.

It's okay.

I'm going to be okay.

I've been in shittier conditions.

I have a roof over my head.
A private bathroom.
Limited food.
Half a tank of gas.
Two hundred dollars.
And a board to sleep on.

"I'm headed this way." Fisher's words break through my spiral.

I glance up, making sure to smile. "Thanks again."

"Anytime. See ya." He spins away from me.

My smile drops.

End. Of. The fucking month.

Defeat feels heavy around my ankles, making it hard to lift my feet.

Maybe I could ask Mr. Black for an advance?

I take a step toward my cabin.

Maybe I could convince him to pay me weekly. Just for my first month.

Maybe...

My eyes lift at the sound of footsteps.

A pair of dark brown eyes stare back at me.

Sterling narrows his gaze.

And I feel it.

I feel the cool track of a tear sliding down my cheek.

My stomach sinks with that roller-coaster feeling.

I force my mouth into another smile.

But I think I get it wrong.

I think I make it too big.

And I know... I know I can't ask this man for money.

Even if I've earned it.

Even if I'm going to keep working for it.

Even if I'm worth it...

I can't ask him.

Because he'll say no.

I feel a second tear ready to fall. But I can't let it.

Can't let him see it.

Dropping my gaze, I rush forward and off the trail, moving around Mr. Black without a word.

I see movement out of the corner of my eye as I pass him. As though he may have been reaching for me.

But I keep moving, silently cursing myself for being so weak.

It's just one month.

It's just twenty-nine days.

CHAPTER 30

STERLING

I TURN AND WATCH COURTNEY RETREAT DOWN THE path, folded up step stool bumping against the side of her leg as she goes.

I don't know what the hell Fisher could have said to put that look in her eyes.

That fucking tear on her cheek.

I start to follow her. Ready to...

What?

The whole reason I came over here was to break up whatever chat-fest she was having with Fisher. And now, well, now they aren't chatting anymore.

But...

I turn back around and head in the direction Fisher went.

Anger and jealousy and other emotions I'm not used to dealing with twist up my insides.

The idea of those two flirting was making me fucking lose it.

But that fake-ass smile. And that fucking tear...

I open and close my fists as I follow the small trail that goes up behind my house.

I can't deal with people crying.

I don't know how.

Blame it on being raised by an overworked single mom. Or the fact that my brothers handle their emotions about as well as I do. But I never learned the skill.

All I know is I'm going to peel Fisher's skin off if he was mean to her.

Passing my back deck, I glance over at my hot tub.

I bet Courtney would like the hot tub.

My steps slow.

Maybe I can offer it up for her use.

It wouldn't be pervy; the guys know they can use it whenever they want. They just don't take me up on it much.

And I don't feel a bone-deep urge to join them in the bubbling water.

Turning away from my deck with images of Courtney in a swimsuit, dripping wet, I face the view.

It's hard to tell from the front of the house, but the land dips back here. And the forest splits around a small lake. Sparkling water below, mountain tops above... it's the reason I built where I did. When this was just my home, not Black Mountain Lodge.

I bet Courtney would like this view too.

I roll out my shoulders and continue down the path.

Focus.

I catch up to Fisher a moment after he reaches the shoreline.

A long bench sits near the water, and it opens to reveal a dozen or so fishing rods. As our resident fishing guide, this is Fisher's territory, and he keeps them maintained and organized.

I've never had the patience for the sport, but this kid could—and does—do it every day.

But if he deliberately made my Courtney cry, he'll have a hard fucking time threading lures with broken fingers.

He spots me, straightening from his position, rod in hand.

"Hey." He fiddles with the reel for a second before looking back up at me. "What's up?"

That's the question, isn't it?

But... what if he doesn't know about Courtney being upset?

If I ask him why she was crying, I could out her over something she was trying to hide.

But I need to know what was said between them.

I need to understand why she was crying.

Isn't that what you wanted?

I ignore my inner voice.

Yes, I want Courtney out of my employ. But I don't want her fucking crying.

I can't take her crying.

"What were you and Court talking about?" My tone is angrier than I intended.

And I didn't mean to blurt my question out like that. But I'm obviously a fucking mess.

Fisher's face scrunches. "Huh?"

"I just bumped into her." I strive to sound casual. "She looked... in a hurry."

Fisher's confused expression clears, and he chuckles. "She was probably sick of listening to my life story."

That's not it.

There's more.

"Hmm." I slide my hands into my pockets. "She didn't say anything about where she was going?"

Fisher shakes his head. "She'd just asked if it was okay to take that step stool. I told her it was fine. And she asked about payday, but I told her it was at the end of the month, so it's not like she was hurrying off to get her check." He snorts at what he must assume was a joke, but I don't see the humor.

And I don't say more as I turn away from Fisher.

Was she crying about payday?

That shouldn't have been a surprise. It's in the contract.

It should be in the contract.

And even if it wasn't, monthly pay is perfectly within my rights as a business owner.

If she doesn't like it, she can leave.

I lift a hand and rub it over my chest.

It's been two days. Two damn days, and already I can feel my resolve wavering.

Which is all the more reason to get Courtney out of here.

If she's here for the full three months...

I won't make it.

There's no way I'll keep my hands off my curvy little worker that long. So, tears or no tears, I need to continue keeping my distance.

CHAPTER 31

COURTNEY

ON MY HANDS AND KNEES, I HUNCH MY SHOULDERS, then stretch them out like a cat.

It doesn't help.

I still feel like I was rolled down a hill.

The plywood beneath my hands groans with the movement.

"Quit your bitching. I'm getting up."

I crawl to the edge, then reach down with one foot until I find the top step of the mini ladder.

The steps did make it easier to get into bed last night, but this —I shift and reach my other foot down—is less easy.

When I fell asleep with pitiful tears on my pillow, I told myself I'd wake up feeling better.

I know the situation.

I can create a plan.

I can figure out a budget.

But when I get my feet on the floor. And I feel the throbbing in my shoulder from sleeping on it.

I accept that I don't feel better today.

I slowly move my head side to side, willing the knot at the base of my neck to go away.

Maybe a hot shower will help.

I could take one now *and* one tonight. Really indulge.

Knowing I have time, since I never changed my alarm from the first day, I brush my teeth and gather an outfit for today—jeans and a worn-in crew neck sweatshirt.

I'll have coffee in the Food Hall, but I quickly scoop a spoonful of peanut butter out of the jar and shove it in my mouth before opening the door.

My foot halts over the top step.

The clipboard.

With my mouth glued shut, I glance around, eyes lingering on the view I have of Mr. Black's front patio. But I don't see anyone.

Picking up the clipboard I left in the Food Hall at the end of the day, I see a new sheet has been added, and *Costco* is written across the top.

There's a shopping list of groceries, a business membership credit card tucked under the clip, and a scrawled note across the bottom of the page that says

Use the card to fill up your gas tank.

I blink at that last line, reading it over and over.

Gratefulness he doesn't deserve lifts some of the weight off my shoulders.

He might not realize it, and this might just be standard policy, but my boss just handed me a lifeline.

It's not enough for me to suddenly afford a mattress. But it's a free scouting mission.

And it's a trip to the Costco food court.

My stomach grumbles simply at the thought of a slice of pizza.

With a genuine smile on my face, I look over at Spike.

"We're gonna eat good today."

CHAPTER 32

STERLING

I watch the brake lights disappear as Courtney maneuvers down the driveway.

I saw her look my way when she first found the clipboard.

She didn't see me, didn't notice the face in the kitchen window.

But I saw the way she smiled. And I saw her say something out loud over her shoulder, like she was talking to someone inside.

I also saw her walking back from the showers.

Her hair in damp braids.

The jeans she was wearing the first time I saw her back on and clinging to her ass.

I made sure to turn away before she got close.

Not needing to know how she smelled right out of the shower.

Not needing a scent memory to torment me alongside the regular memories of Courtney when I go to bed tonight.

Except...

I glance around, confirming no one else is nearby.

Except I need to know more about her.

I step off the driveway and onto the path leading toward the Laundry Cabin.

She's my employee.

I'm responsible for her, whether I want to be or not.

And there's something about her that says she needs help.

But I can't help her until I understand her.

Which is what I keep telling myself as I approach the steps to her front door.

I stare at the knob for a long moment.

The fact that it's not locked—because it doesn't lock—makes me feel like an asshole, because even though no one here would do her harm, it's the only building that doesn't lock.

But that's because we never needed it locked. No one is going to steal laundry. And the only time anyone sleeps in it is when they're sick and the rest of the Bunk House doesn't want to hear coughing all night.

It's been months since anyone slept here, so it's not like it's contaminated. It's just a convenient place to stash the female.

Also, the *not locked* detail serves to make this feel a little less like breaking and entering.

Plus, the cabin is mine.

I own it.

I own everything here.

So is it really trespassing...?

Before my conscience can remind me why this is wrong, and before any of the guys can catch me, I climb the steps in one stride and open the door.

CHAPTER 33

COURTNEY

WHEN I TURN ONTO THE MAIN ROAD, I HIT PLAY ON MY phone and set it in the cupholder.

My car stereo might not work, but the cupholder acts as an amplifier, making the music loud inside my Jeep.

I don't own headphones, and since I don't want to be a *distraction*, I don't listen to music while I work. But now, on my way to Costco, with a full tank of gas on the horizon, I play it as loud as it will go.

CHAPTER 34

STERLING

ORANGES AND FLOWERS.

I take a deep inhale as I close my eyes.

I didn't want to know. Didn't need to know what she smelled like fresh out of the shower.

But now I do.

Fucking oranges and flowers.

Some combination of shampoo and lotion. And I want to fill my palm with the scent before I wrap my fingers around my dick.

I open my eyes.

I will not jerk off in Courtney's cabin.

Thinking about how she spoke back through the open cabin door earlier, I clear my throat.

I feel stupid talking to the empty space, but I do it anyway. "Hello?"

No one answers. Obviously.

I shake my head. This girl is always talking to herself, so I shouldn't be surprised she talks to her damn cabin too.

It's been a while since I've been in here, but it looks pretty much the same.

Courtney has a little kitchen area set up on the counter above the washers. It's not much, but it's neat and organized.

There isn't a refrigerator in here, but she can use the ones in the Food Hall. Probably already has.

Doesn't look like she uses the little table, and I'm hard pressed to remember where it even came from.

I grip the back of one of the chairs and wiggle it.

My mouth pulls down at how flimsy it feels.

I'm tempted to sit on it, just to see if it collapses, but I don't want to leave any sign that I was here.

The thin curtain covering the window flutters.

It's a nice day out, and Courtney must've opened the window above the table to let in some fresh air.

The fabric catches, and that's when I notice the small cactus sitting on the windowsill.

I pull the curtain out of the way.

It's in a little ceramic pot and there's an orange string bow stuck in the spikes.

Cute.

I let the curtain fall back over the plant.

I'm tempted to open the cupboard, but that feels a little too intrusive. Though I have no trouble opening the bathroom door.

It's perfectly clean, and there are a few bottles of lotion and other items lining the small sink.

I take one second to wonder if there's a way to get a shower in here, but the thought is quickly dashed. There's no room.

And she won't be here long.

Which is what I want.

I say it to myself twice, trying to make it more true.

My mind is on Courtney as I step into the bedroom.

I let my eyes drift over the dresser.

Is she here because she really wants to work here?

Is she drawn to the mountains?

Did she find the Lodge randomly, or did someone suggest it?

Did she just want to get away from the East Coast?

Is she running from something?

I step closer to the bed, seeing how she has the step stool positioned near the end, like it's a top bunk bed rather than just a slightly tall frame.

But I suppose she is pretty short, so it's probably hard for her to climb in and out of bed without the steps.

A single pillow with a gray pillowcase is on the other end of the bed, and a gray blanket to match covers the bunk.

The color surprises me. I would have pictured her with something else. Maybe green, because she wore that color on the first day. Maybe pink, because I'm a dumb man and don't know what colors women actually like.

I reach out and place my hand on the bedspread, wanting to feel the material.

With the material between my fingers, I can't help but picture her in bed with someone. Breathing heavy. Arms over her head.

Is she running from a relationship?

Is she married?

Getting a divorce?

That would explain a lot.

The move across country.

The vehicle filled with her possessions.

Does it explain the tears from yesterday?

I run my hand down the blanket and frown.

Why does this feel so lumpy?

I reach up and grip the top corner of the blanket.

I shouldn't be touching her bed.

I flip the blanket back anyway.

And I stare.

At clothes.

"What the hell?"

I look back at the dresser.

Did she fill the drawers already and... what? Decided to hide her clothes rather than leave them in a stack?

I slide my fingers under one of the sweatshirts to lift it.

And I pause.

Because my fingers touch wood.

I shove the sweatshirt to the side.

Plywood stares up at me.

My exhale gets knotted in my chest.

I push more of the clothes aside, exposing more of the rough board below.

I...

I can't make sense of what I'm seeing.

I shove all the clothes away.

There's no mattress.

I turn away from the bed and look at the walls, like a mattress might be propped up somewhere.

There isn't.

There's no fucking mattress.

I look under the bunk.

But it's just boxes and Courtney's suitcase.

And the bunk is just a bare piece of fucking plywood.

I look back at the pile of laundry now bunched at the foot of the bed.

And I feel like the biggest piece of shit on the planet.

My Courtney has been sleeping on her clothes because I gave her a cabin without a mattress.

I plant my hands on the bunk.

The weight inside my chest threatens to drag me to the ground.

Why wouldn't she say something?

Why the fuck wouldn't she ask for a fucking mattress?

But the answer is obvious.

She thinks I did it on purpose.

Guilt glides over my skin, seeping into my being and filling me with a level of self-hatred I haven't experienced before.

Courtney thinks I gave her this cabin knowing there was no mattress.

I didn't know.

I swear, I didn't know.

But why would she think otherwise?

I've been dismissive and rude to her since the moment I found out who she was.

Flashes of her filter through my mind.

Courtney seeing me that first morning and going right back into her cabin. After sleeping on a fucking board.

Courtney not eating lunch with us because I didn't tell her.

Courtney with toilet water on her face and shirt after her second night sleeping on a fucking board.

Courtney last night, with tears in her eyes and a fake smile on her lips, on her way to spend another night on a fucking board.

Courtney asking when we get paid. Probably because she wanted to buy a fucking mattress to sleep on.

Courtney this morning, smiling over a trip to Costco, after sleeping on a fucking board.

I have to clench my jaw.

Have to press my lips together.

Have to force myself to breathe.

I wanted to make her leave.

But not like this.

Not like this.

Swallowing down the emotion that threatens to choke me, I bend over the bunk and claw her clothes back into place.

I need to know what it was like.

When I have her clothes back in a thin layer—the way I found it—I climb onto the bunk and lie down.

The clothes do nothing.

This feels exactly like lying on a sheet of plywood.

She must fucking hate me.

I fucking hate me.

I stay where I am, looking at the ceiling, forcing myself to experience this.

Courtney spent three nights sleeping like this, and my body is starting to protest after five minutes.

How she managed to work... and work hard, without a single complaint...

I don't know how she did it.

Because she had no choice.

I may not know her circumstance, but I know no one would put up with this, and me, unless they had to. Unless they were desperate.

I think about the projects she's already completed. Specifically the ones in the guest cabins. Each one fully stocked, each bunk covered in a mattress. And she still didn't say anything.

She didn't sneak one into her cabin.

Didn't ask if she could use one.

Courtney didn't say a fucking word.

I roll to my side, groaning because I'm lying *on a fucking board,* and swing my legs down.

The edge of the plywood catches my shirt.

If that was on my bare skin, it would have left a mark.

I glare at the bunk.

Then I turn and stomp out of the cabin.

I'm storming across the driveway when I spot Cook between the trees, walking from the Bunk House to the Food Hall.

I freeze.

Cook keeps walking.

I listen to the faint sound of him whistling until he disappears from view.

I should've been more careful exiting Courtney's cabin.

If anyone had seen me...

How would I have explained being in there?

I can't.

So I also can't let anyone see me hauling a mattress around. And I can't explain her not having a mattress without exposing the fact that I was snooping.

I can't even pretend she asked me for one because why would she have waited three nights?

No. No one can see me.

I step off the driveway into the woods.

Moving quickly, I stay behind the trees and make my way to

the cabin closest to the Bunk House. It's the one we use the least, only when the rest of the cabins are in use. There's nothing wrong with it. It's stocked the same as the rest. But why put guests so close to my guys if I don't have to?

A creak alerts me to the front door of the Bunk House opening, and I take a quick stride forward so I'm covered by the corner of the guest cabin.

Totally not sketchy behavior.

I lower my feet carefully, keeping the sound of my steps quiet as I circle the back of the cabin.

There's enough forest between the cabin and the Bunk House that I can move around the other side undetected until I make it back to the front door.

We changed the locks last year—one of the projects Marty actually finished—so now all the buildings have code locks rather than key locks.

It's handy. Especially now.

I type in my personal code that gets me into every lock on the property.

0690

Because I'm a child.

The door opens with a faint sound, but I step through quickly and close it behind me.

That shitty feeling hasn't left my chest. And as I look at the four unused mattresses, that feeling just gets worse.

Unused.

I think about how many mattresses have been sitting unused over the last three nights.

How Courtney saw them.

Knew they were there.

"Fuck."

I rub my hand over my stomach.

"Fuck." I say it a little louder.

Then I stride to the closest bed, grip the bare mattress, and start to pull it off the bed frame.

It has a mattress protector on it. One of the kinds that zips all the way around the full-size mattress like a giant pillowcase. The bedding is in the closet, put away to keep it from getting dusty.

I pause my efforts, the thin material not feeling luxurious in my grip.

Growling in the back of my throat, I shove it back into place and climb onto the cramped bunk.

I lie down.

I roll on my side.

I lie flat on my back.

And I grit my teeth.

It sucks.

This mattress fucking sucks.

"God dammit." I shake my head as I shove my hand into my pocket and pull out my phone.

As the call goes through, I roll out of the bunk.

It takes two rings before Marty answers.

"Hey, Sterling." Marty greets me as I grip the mattress one handed. "Before you start, I saw the email already—"

"Fuck the email, Marty. I need to know where to order new mattresses." I grunt as I drag the mattress all the way off this time.

"Uh, a mattress? Like for your bed?" Marty's confusion annoys me, even if it's understandable.

"Not for my bed, for the cabins," I bite out.

Marty makes a sound. "Have a round of food poisoning or something?"

I pause, propping the mattress up against the wall. "What... no." I grimace as I visualize the implication of his question. "Hell no."

"Oh." He sounds even more confused.

"We just need new ones, alright?"

"Alright. No questions. Got it." I can picture the old man rolling his eyes. He worked for me too long to not recognize my bad moods.

"Do you know where I can order... thirty-something mattress-es?" I ask in a calmer tone.

I can hear him scratching his beard as he thinks. "I bet Rocky would have a connection. Want me to call him?"

"No, I'll do it. Good thinking."

"I live to serve." Marty snorts.

I hang up. Then text Rocky.

He owns a bar and motel in the next town over, along with several other hotels.

I don't know if we're friends exactly, but I know him well enough that I should've thought of him.

Text sent, I go to the closet and pull out a set of sheets and a quilt, then I peek out the window next to the door, checking if the coast is clear.

CHAPTER 35

COURTNEY

HOPPING DOWN FROM MY JEEP, I LOOK AROUND THE mostly full parking lot.

It took almost an hour to get here, but it's hard to complain about a sunny drive through the mountains.

I push the sleeves of my sweatshirt up.

It's also much warmer down here, at this lower elevation.

I take a deep breath, imagining I can tell the difference and wondering how long it will take before the high elevation of the Lodge stops killing me.

The Lodge...

I know I can't linger and spend all day here, even if I want to, but I will enjoy myself.

With the list folded in one pocket and the company card in the other, I head toward the massive building, ready to spend Sterling's money.

CHAPTER 36

STERLING

CAREFUL NOT TO LET GO OF THE MATTRESS, I PULL THE cabin door shut behind me.

It takes some maneuvering, but I get the mattress behind me, grip the sides, and then bend forward so I'm carrying it like a disproportionate turtle shell.

Retracing my steps, I stay as hidden as possible as I dodge low branches. And when I reach the edge of the woods, I stand still for a moment, listening. But since I don't hear anyone, I break from my cover and stride across the driveway.

I don't run into anyone, but by the time I'm at the front door of the Laundry Cabin, my lower back is about two steps away from spasming.

Lucky for me, there are three steps before I'm inside.

"This is your penance, you old fuck," I grumble to myself with my forehead pressed against the door.

I should've put the mattress down and then opened the door. But... I'm a stubborn dumbass.

Shifting to the side, I tighten my grip with my left hand and let go of the mattress with my right.

The mattress immediately starts to slip, so I twist the doorknob as fast as possible and use my head to shove the door open as I reach back to stop the mattress from completely falling.

The weight tries to pull me back, so I bend forward even more.

But the width of the mattress is wider than the doorframe.

I stumble one step to the side and catch my balance before I fall off the edge of the damn stairs.

Focus.

Taking a breath, I stand up straighter, then angle myself so I'm shuffling sideways through the door.

As soon as I clear the threshold, I drop the mattress, letting the bottom edge fall to the floor, then flop against the dryers.

My phone chimes in my pocket with a text, and I take it as a sign to take a break.

Not that I need a break.

I could easily carry this mattress into the bedroom right now.

My muscles are barely even warm.

I kick the door shut as I read the text from Rocky, giving me the email address for *his mattress guy.*

And since I'm a man of action, I keep standing here as I type out an email with my purchase request.

I know it's going to be a large expense, ordering more than thirty mattresses all at once. But Rocky mentioned that his guy would haul away the old ones for donation—*if they're not disgusting*—so I might as well bite the bullet and do them all.

Plus, it's an investment in my property.

Something I can advertise.

I'm not dropping a few thousand dollars just for Courtney.

My eyes raise toward her bedroom as I slide the phone back in my pocket.

I'm not going to leave the mattress here in the front room for her to struggle with.

I'm going to put it on the bunk for her.

But for that, I'll need to move her clothes.

And if I move her clothes, do I fold them? Or spread them back on top of the mattress?

Reaching up, I pull the sheets and blanket off my shoulders, where I draped them like the world's biggest scarf.

As I start to haul the bedding through the cabin, I wonder what her reaction will be to finding the mattress.

My first thought is wondering if she'll be all sweet and smiley when she thanks me.

Because it's not like she won't notice it.

Even if she doesn't see it until she's climbing into bed, she's going to know that *I* put a mattress onto her bare bunk.

I pause on the threshold, looking at the wooden bunk and the stepstool she uses to get onto it.

Of course she isn't going to thank me.

She probably won't bring it up at all.

I'm positive Courtney didn't tell me in the first place because she thinks I did it on purpose. So me replacing the mattress now will probably make her think it was some fucked-up test. Some sort of trial to see if I could bully her out through inhumane sleeping conditions.

And why wouldn't she believe that?

What sort of owner doesn't know his own property?

I even opened the front door for her.

I opened the door but didn't step inside.

Didn't look at the conditions I was leaving her in.

But I'm looking now.

And anger wraps warm fingers around my neck as I stare at the rough edge of plywood running the length of the bunk.

"Fuck."

I turn and storm back out of the cabin.

CHAPTER 37

COURTNEY

Turning off the main road and onto the Black Mountain Lodge driveway, I quiet my music.

My stomach is full.

I still have half a cookie in a paper sleeve on my passenger seat.

But the closer I get to my cabin, the duller my happiness becomes.

My Jeep bumps over a divot, and it's enough to remind me that I need to pee, badly, after spending the drive home sucking down a frozen mocha.

I didn't notice it the first night I arrived, but a part of the driveway cuts off to the left, leading to a clearing where all the guys park not far from the Bunkhouse.

But no one has told me if I should park somewhere special, so I continue on and don't stop until I'm even with my Laundry Cabin. I put it in park with two wheels off the side of the driveway, leaving plenty of room for other vehicles to pass.

I'm not looking forward to lugging all these groceries over to the Food Hall, but at least I took long enough on my outing that lunch is long over. So there's no need for anyone to see me struggle.

Turning off the engine, I shove open my door and slide out until my feet hit gravel.

My body aches in protest, and I press my palms against my lower back.

Today wasn't as strenuous as the last couple of days, but the shitty sleep is catching up to me big time.

Leaning across the driver's seat, I grab my cookie and the mostly empty to-go cup.

It was hard to walk past the home goods inside the store—the fluffy blankets and discounted pillows calling my name. But the splurge on lunch was all I could justify.

"Find everything?"

Sterling's deep voice startles me so badly that I nearly pee myself.

Chapter 38

Sterling

The girl has no awareness.

She doesn't hear me approach.

Doesn't notice me a few yards away as she stretches her back.

Doesn't seem aware of the way she's pushing her tits out.

And clearly doesn't know I'm behind her when she reaches into her Jeep, going up on her tiptoes as she sticks her ass out to reach across the seat.

The movement makes her shirt rise, and I can see the top sliver of red panties above the band of her jeans.

I tip my head back and exhale.

When I drop my gaze back down, she has one foot in the air, leaning even farther into the vehicle.

I want to hook my arm under her raised knee and bring it up and out, opening her for me as I press my cock into her heated slit.

I want to fuck her against this fucking Jeep.

And I want to do it with my other hand twisted in her braids, holding her head up, craning her neck back so she can look at me with those pretty eyes while her pussy swallows my dick.

She starts to straighten.

"Find everything?" I blurt the question, my voice coming out rough because I'm fighting not to get a hard-on. But I just end up sounding angry.

Something thuds against my chest as Courtney spins around.

Reflex has me catching the item. And even if I couldn't smell the dessert, I've had enough of these to know what it is.

"Sorry," Courtney gasps, then averts her gaze as she reaches out and plucks the cookie from my hand. "Sorry."

"It's fine." I try to reassure her, but I still sound just as angry. Which *makes* me angry because I'm not trying to be an asshole right now.

"Um, here." Courtney holds the drink to her chest with her forearm so she can hold the cookie with that same hand. Then she reaches into her pocket.

I hold out my palm, expecting the card back, but instead she puts a folded receipt and a few bills into my hand.

I start to unfold the paper.

"I-I didn't realize it was going to charge the card when I ordered, but it's all there." Her voice is strained, but when I look up, she's not meeting my eyes.

With the receipt unfurled, I read the items.

Hot dog, slice of pepperoni pizza, frozen mocha, chocolate chip cookie.

The ten-dollar bill and three single dollars are wrinkled and warm.

I know money is filthy, but I want to press the bills against my cheek since her body warmed them.

But I don't.

Courtney's cheeks are red when she starts speaking again.

CHAPTER 39

COURTNEY

As soon as my lunch got charged to the company card, I was mortified.

It was my private meal. My little joy for the day. And as much as I've reminded myself that I'm not ashamed of it, that it's okay to eat a big lunch, I knew I'd be embarrassed handing over the evidence to *him*.

I was hoping I could just leave it on his porch, attached to the clipboard.

But instead, I get to do it standing face-to-face. After throwing what's left of my cookie against his solid chest.

I clear my throat.

"I have the receipt for the gas too." I reach into my back pocket and pull out two pieces of paper. One for gas, the other for the groceries.

Sterling takes them without a word, flattening the receipts on top of the first.

"They didn't have the chocolate muffins." I don't meet his eyes. "But they had a lemon version that looked good, so I got that. And the red apples looked a little weird, so I got the green ones instead." I press my fingertips together on my free hand. His continued silence is making my stress worse. "They were two dollars more. But they should last longer. And they're good for baking. But I can pay for the difference."

"I don't care."

I force my gaze up to meet his. "I just—"

"Cookie, I don't care."

My mouth snaps shut.

Cookie.

I lower my eyes.

He called me Cookie.

I try to look down to see if I have crumbs on my shirt. If that's why he called me that. But insecurity flares bright behind my eyes, making it hard to see.

Maybe he meant it in a cute way. I try to convince myself.

But Sterling Black doesn't say cute things.

He's never been hurtful.

Not...

I press my free hand against my not-flat stomach.

Not until now.

Now, when he saw the receipt for what I ate.

Now, when he commented on it.

I bite my lip. Hard.

I don't want to be here anymore.

I want to leave.

I dig my nail into my thumb pad, knowing that my situation hasn't changed.

I'm still stuck here.

And even half starving, I'm still as *not thin* as I've always been.

The urge to throw the rest of my cookie away hits me right in the sternum.

And that makes anger swell within my sadness.

Cookies shouldn't go in the trash.

Only men.

"You guys need help unloading?" one of my coworkers calls out.

I think the voice might belong to Cook, but it sounds like more than one set of footsteps approaching.

Sterling turns away from me, and I use the opportunity to flee.

"I'll be right back," I practically whisper as I dart past him. "Bathroom."

I don't look back as I hurry down the path to my cabin.

CHAPTER 40

STERLING

"DIDN'T MEAN TO SCARE HER AWAY," COOK SAYS AS HE and Simpson cross the driveway.

I glance over my shoulder.

Courtney is speed walking away. "Not you. She said something about the bathroom."

At least, I think that's what she said. I could hardly hear her.

Cook grunts and opens the back door of the Jeep, reaching for one of the overflowing boxes.

I look at the Laundry Cabin just as Courtney climbs her stairs, and wonder if she'll venture into the bedroom before coming back out.

Certain she won't say anything to me, especially in front of the guys, but not wanting to chance it anyway, I turn to Simpson. "Text the guys and tell them to come over now and help."

Then I stack two cases of beer and lift them both.

Chapter 41

Courtney

I press my back against the door after closing it behind me.

Maybe you heard him wrong.

Maybe it wasn't meant to be... mean.

Maybe Mr. My Heart is a Black Hole wasn't hugged enough as a child.

I close my eyes.

The words of men will not define me.

The opinion of others will not destroy me.

I open my eyes.

I have a job to do.

And I will not let this man defeat me.

I wipe my fingers below my eyes.

It's exhaustion.

That's why I'm letting him hurt my feelings.

Just exhaustion.

Pushing off the door, I feel the breeze from the open window and halt.

After setting my drink and cookie down, I reach over the little table, pull the curtain aside, and shut the window.

"We got this, right, girl?" I say to Spike as I straighten her bow.

Somewhere in one of the boxes under my bunk is her wardrobe. And since it's October, I suppose it's time for her little witch's hat.

"We'll switch clothes this weekend, alright? Give us something to do," I tell her, even though we both know it will take all of five minutes.

She silently agrees with the plan, and I wonder if cacti years are the opposite of dog years since—in theory—they live so long.

I hurry into the bathroom and let my head hang while I'm on the toilet.

Then I face the music while washing my hands and look at the mirror.

Through pure willpower, I was able to keep most of my tears at bay, but my eyes still look glassy and red.

I hold my fingers under the cold running water before pressing them to my eyelids.

Then I straighten my shoulders and head back outside.

I STARE AT THE EMPTY JEEP.

Everything is gone.

"How...?"

Movement catches my eye, and I turn as Sterling emerges from the woods and cuts across the driveway to his front steps.

He couldn't have done this all by himself in the few minutes I was gone.

Blowing out a breath, I close the doors on my Jeep and turn toward the Food Hall.

Clearly Cook and whoever else walked up must have helped, meaning I owe them a thank-you.

Chapter 42

Courtney

Sighing, I climb the steps to my cabin and let myself in.

I helped Cook sort the groceries while he explained how it works when guests are here. He makes three meals a day while they're on the property, and all staff members are allowed to partake in each meal.

I tried to keep my eyes from widening because every time my boss does something dickish—like calling me freaking *Cookie*—I find out something surprisingly generous.

After just a few minutes, Cook caught on to the fact that no one has explained anything to me, so he took the time to tell me the basic timeline. Like how the guests will arrive, spend a night or two here, then go off to another location—staying in either cabins or tents. They do their outings for a few days with their designated guides, leaving the Lodge very quiet. Then they all come back for a final meal, then leave after lunch. Occasionally leaving the next day.

Simple enough.

And all of this is important for my role as the resident custodian.

The day before guests arrive, I need to spruce up the cabins—

dusting and making the beds. And after they leave, I have to deep clean and use my Laundry Cabin for actual laundry.

I also found out that there is a washer and dryer set in the Bunk House, and I'm eternally grateful for that fact.

The guys have all been great, but standing here in my cabin, I know I need this space to just be mine. No matter how uncomfortable, or unlocked, this cabin is my home for the rest of the year, and I don't need to know who wears boxers and who wears briefs.

Heading to my little bathroom, I wash my hands, then go back out to my *dining table* and pick up my leftover cookie and the sandwich Cook saved me from lunch.

I nearly cried all over again when he handed me the turkey club wrapped up in wax paper.

But I kept it together.

Like a professional.

Snagging my water bottle, I take my dinner to my bedroom.

There's still enough of a sunset outside that I leave the lights off.

I'll have my food with some mood lighting and a little YouTube scrolling. Because honestly, logging onto the Lodge internet has been the only thing keeping my sanity around here.

I dump my armful of food onto the bunk, then move over to my step stool.

Gripping the top rail, I put my foot on the bottom rung, step up, then shift my palms to the bed as I lift my other foot to the second step.

And then I freeze.

My heart beats once. Twice. Three times.

"What?" I whisper.

I flex my fingers into my blanket.

Soft.

Squishy.

"What?" I say it louder.

I shift my weight around.

The surface under my hands shifts with me.

"What?" My voice cracks this time.

I scramble off the step stool and flip my blanket back.

There's another blanket.

Another blanket.

That too-familiar feeling of tightness behind my eyes starts to build.

My hands start to tremble as I grip the edge of the new blanket and pull it back.

A huff that sounds too close to a sob leaves my mouth.

Because I'm looking at a mattress.

A mattress covered with a fitted sheet.

A mattress with several inches of padding.

I lay my hand on it.

It's still there.

I put my other hand on it.

The mattress squishes beneath the pressure.

A laugh spills out of me as I bend and press my face into it.

I have a mattress.

I straighten back up.

I have a mattress.

After three nights of sleeping on that fucking board, Sterling gave me a mattress.

The smile I hadn't realized was stretched across my face falters.

Why now?

I run my hands over the sheet.

Was this all some sort of test?

Was this his plan all along?

Or did seeing me cry last night convince him to cave early?

Is that why he sent me shopping today? So he could replace the mattress when I wouldn't see it?

I purse my lips, thinking about him in here, all alone, with my things.

My eyes move to the edge of the bunk.

He would've seen my bed of clothes when he came in here.

My cheeks start to heat.

But I quickly tell my body to knock it off.

I won't be embarrassed about trying to make myself comfortable. Even if it didn't work.

Speaking of my clothes...

Glancing around the room, I don't see a pile of laundry.

I grip the mattress and lift it.

No clothes.

But... there's another bedspread. Under the mattress.

I tilt my head and look at where the edge of the plywood board should be visible. The rough edge that's caught my clothing more than once.

There's a thud as my water bottle rolls down the angled mattress, landing in the space against the wall.

But I stay focused on the bedspread.

"Are those...?" I try to reach out, but the mattress is awkward to hold one handed, so I let it drop.

Then I crouch down and look at the underside of the board, where the blanket has been wrapped around the raw edge and stapled into place. Confirming the little bits of silver I saw above were also staples.

I stand back up.

He covered the board with a blanket, securing it in place so it won't scrape me anymore.

I lightly trail my fingers over the edge.

Was this part of the test too?

I frown.

That doesn't feel quite right.

The mattress, though cruel, has the feel of a test.

A *tough it out* situation.

But the edge of the board, the bit that can inflict actual injury... even though I've endured it for days, it feels... wrong.

Like maybe he forgot.

Or maybe when he took the mattress out, it hadn't occurred to him that it would expose the edge.

I shake my head.

He didn't know it was *me*—a woman—arriving.

Sterling had planned for *male me* to sleep in the Bunk House. And after I blackmailed him into letting me stay, he brought me right here. No time to remove a mattress as a punishment or test.

He just knew there wasn't one.

I run my hand over the newly protected edge again.

Hope he felt like a jerk while he was stapling the blanket in place.

Then I remember my clothes.

They aren't under the mattress.

I don't see them on the floor.

I turn in a slow circle.

No piles in the corner or on the dresser.

No...

I drag my eyes back to the dresser.

"He wouldn't..."

I dig my teeth into my lip as I take the few steps over to the dresser.

He seriously wouldn't...

I open the top drawer.

My socks, bras, and underwear look the same as I left them.

"Okay."

I push the drawer shut, then pull open the next one, which should only be half full with tank tops.

I bite my lip harder.

It's all the way full.

The tank tops are there... and so are the T-shirts I'd been sleeping on.

All folded.

My heart rate picks up a step.

I shut the drawer and open the next.

It's filled with perfectly folded long sleeves and cardigans.

More items I'd been sleeping on.

The next drawer is the same, filled with folded sweatshirts and sweaters.

The next has my sweatpants and pajamas.

The final bottom drawer has all my jeans and cargo pants.

He... He folded my clothes.

I shove the bottom drawer shut, then reopen the one with my pajamas.

"No fucking way."

I leave it open and rush out of the bedroom.

Stopping in front of the dryer, I yank the door open.

Empty.

"No. Fucking. Way."

I stare at the empty dryer.

This motherfucker didn't just fold the clothes that I'd been sleeping on. He emptied the dryer and folded those too.

I turn to Spike. "Why would he do that?"

She doesn't answer.

I turn back to the dryer. "Why would he do that?"

Spike silently tells me to stop repeating myself. And I silently tell her to quit judging me. I'm having *a moment*.

Back to biting my lip, I look at the door.

If this is also part of the test, I have no idea how to handle it.

Am I supposed to go thank him?

I mean, I *am* grateful for the mattress. And the blanket over the board.

But the clothes...

Am I supposed to thank him for folding my laundry?

It seems... weird.

It *is* weird.

But would I rather he have tossed them on the floor in a pile?

I lift my hands and rub them over my face.

I can't think straight. I'm too exhausted.

I lower my hands.

I won't be exhausted tomorrow.

Because I get to sleep on a real live mattress tonight.

I shake my head.

I will never take a mattress for granted again.

Thinking of my new cushy setup, I head back into my bedroom and go straight for my step stool.

The moment my knees land on the mattress, I let out a squeal.

Then I plop onto my butt and drop onto my back, letting out another sound of excitement.

This boss of mine might confuse the hell out of me, but right now, I don't care. He can Jekyll and Hyde me all he wants, so long as he doesn't take this mattress away from me.

Thinking of the moment he called me Cookie reminds me that I still have half my cookie left.

I sit up and find it, along with my wrapped sandwich and water, in the six-inch crevice between the mattress and the wall.

Crossing my legs, I peel the paper away from the sandwich.

Usually I take my time eating. A habit from mostly eating alone with no place to be. But tonight, I eat fast.

I'll probably suffer a stomachache from it. But, again, I don't care. I want to enjoy this mattress as soon as possible. And I can ride out my stomachache on my new mattress.

After finishing my food in record time, I brush my teeth and go through the motions, not thinking about Sterling folding my pajamas.

It's still early, but with the lights off, the curtains closed, and *both* my blankets pulled up to my chin, I know I'll be asleep in moments.

Clasping my hands together, I close my eyes and pretend.

I pretend that I could make friends here.

That I could make a life here.

That I could be wanted here.

CHAPTER 43

STERLING

I SET THE CLIPBOARD DOWN ON THE TOP STEP OF THE Laundry Cabin and turn away.

It's early.

Really early.

But I couldn't sleep.

I watched out my window last night as Courtney turned off her lights. And I thought about her climbing into her bed. Onto the mattress.

The arguably shitty mattress, but still a mattress.

And I couldn't turn my mind off.

Couldn't stop thinking about what she must be thinking.

Couldn't stop wondering how much she hates me.

I shove my hands into my pockets as I cut between bushes, my boots tamping down a path between her front door and mine.

And I still can't stop thinking about her clothes.

How they felt in my hands.

How small they seemed.

How tempting it was to slip a pair of her panties into my pocket.

How I did.

And how I put them back.

But I didn't put them back because I'm a good man.

I did it because they were clean.

And what use do I have for panties that smell like dryer sheets?

I take my front steps two at a time, my dick thickening at the thought of having a pair of Courtney's panties that smell like her.

That smell like her hot little pussy.

I'd hold them against my face as I—

I shove my front door open with one hand and shove the other down the front of my jeans.

I got too close to her yesterday.

I can't do that again.

I'm going to set some new boundaries for myself.

Just as soon as I jerk off.

Again.

CHAPTER 44

COURTNEY

I PAUSE AT THE SIGHT OF THE CLIPBOARD ON MY FRONT step, once again moved from where I left it in the Food Hall.

I don't know if there's a clipboard protocol around here—if there is, no one told me. But since I start each day making coffee, I figured I'd leave my lists by Big Joe so it's ready for me each morning.

But this is Sterling. And he makes no sense to me.

Grabbing the clipboard, I step back into the cabin.

There are still the usual pages of tasks. Except there's also money attached.

I tug the cash free.

It's thirteen dollars.

The same thirteen dollars I gave Sterling yesterday.

Below, on top of the usual pages, is a single sheet of paper with a single line scrawled out.

Lunch is included.

Yawning and climbing into bed freshly showered and hair braided, I wonder if it's a coincidence I didn't see Sterling all day.

Or if he's avoiding me.

CHAPTER 45

STERLING

"FUCKING HELL." I CLENCH MY JAW AND CHANGE direction.

I managed to avoid Courtney all of yesterday and was hoping to do the same again today. But this girl...

I stalk up behind her.

She has a ladder propped up against the front of one of the guest cabins, and she's reaching up with a rag to clear the spider-webs and dust off the light bulb above the door.

It's a task off the list I gave her. *Clean outdoor light fixtures.* But the bottom of the ladder is on the top landing of the stairs and only a foot away from the top step.

If she falls...

My insides twist at the thought.

If she fell...

If I witnessed her fall...

I lengthen my steps.

She removes one foot from the rung so she can stretch up even farther.

I see a wobble.

In one stride, I'm up the three steps.

She lets out a sound of worry as she puts her foot back in

place. Then she lets out a cry of surprise when I wrap my arms around her waist.

She's partway up the ladder, and with our height difference, that puts her ass at my chest.

I haul her against me, pulling her feet off the rung.

"What...?" She turns her head to see who's touching her. "Sterling?"

I squeeze her tighter.

It's the first time I've heard my name on her lips.

And fuck me, it's affecting my pulse just as much as her ass is.

"What are you doing?" Her voice is breathy, and I can picture her saying those exact words as I peel her clothes off.

"Saving you from yourself." I try and fail to not sound angry.

Her legs move, and without looking, I know she's trying to get her feet back on the rungs.

I take a step back.

She lets out a squeak of fear, pulling the top of the ladder close to her body and away from the wall.

"Let go," I snap.

Her braids swing as she looks to the ladder in her hands, then back over her shoulder. "I'll fall."

"No, you won't." I slide one of my arms farther up her body until my forearm is just touching the underside of her tits. "Let. Go."

"But—"

"Courtney," I growl. "Do as you're told."

I slipped up and used her full name, but it gets the needed results.

She lets go, and the ladder thuds back against the wall.

Her hands fly down to my arm—one of her hands gripping my elbow, the other hand wrapping around my fingers against her side.

"Put me down," she pants.

I'm going to.

I have to.

But I hold her against me for a moment longer than necessary before I slide her down my body.

Her ass drags down my stomach.

Over the waistband of my jeans.

Lower.

She's still gripping me with her little hands.

And when her ass slides down against my cock, I feel her breath hitch.

I feel her body tense.

And I feel her fingers tighten on my arm.

I don't press my hips forward.

I don't have to.

She feels it.

Feels me.

And as twisted as it is... I revel in it.

That's right, Cookie. Feel what you do to me.

Feel what I have hidden for you.

Think about it tonight when you're in bed alone.

Before I lower her the rest of the way, I lean my head forward, placing my lips near her ear and my nose against her hair. "Be more careful, Miss Kern. Those things are dangerous."

Her puffed exhale makes my dick twitch.

Before I can make any more ill-advised decisions, I lower her the rest of the way.

Chapter 46

Courtney

My shoes touch the ground, but my brain is too focused on the hardness pressing against the top of my ass to worry about balance.

Sterling loosens his grip, and I sway.

His fingers flex against my sides, then he drags his hands across my stomach until he's no longer hugging me to him.

Heat pools between my thighs as zings of awareness skitter across my skin.

"You good?" His voice is rough. And hard to understand since my attention is still on the fact that I can feel how hard his cock is.

I take a shaky step forward, and his hands drop away from me.

Grabbing the railing, I turn to face my boss.

And I can't help it.

My gaze drops.

To the large bulge pressing against the front of his jeans.

"Eyes up here, Cookie."

I can feel the color in my cheeks deepen as lust turns to embarrassment.

Slowly, I do as he says and lift my gaze.

Sterling searches my face, not repeating his question despite my lack of an answer.

But he must see something in my expression because he dips his chin. "Go to lunch."

Then he threads his arm through the ladder, lifts it onto his shoulder, and carries it down the steps.

I look up at the light above the cabin door.

Then I look at Sterling as he walks away.

My hands go to my stomach, sliding across the softness, feeling what he felt.

Eyes up here.

I squeeze my thighs together.

I can't believe how hot that was.

Can't believe I got caught looking at my boss's junk.

Can't believe I felt his junk.

Can't believe he got hard from holding me.

I watch his back as he retreats, the ladder still on his shoulder like it weighs nothing.

He held me like I weighed nothing.

I press my fingertips together.

He called me Cookie again.

While he had a boner.

I relax my hands, spreading my fingers apart.

Does he hate me?

Is he attracted to me?

Or is it both?

CHAPTER 47

STERLING

STANDING IN THE STORAGE SHED, I CLOSE MY EYES AND will my dick to settle down.

That was a mistake.

I think about the way she felt against me.

Think about the warmth of her tits against my arm.

Think about the way her breath hitched when she felt my dick against her ass.

Huge fucking mistake.

Because now I know.

Know what I'm missing.

Know what I want.

And know that I'm going to have her.

One way or another, I'm going to cave and take a bite of my Cookie.

The only question is when.

CHAPTER 48

COURTNEY

"HEY, COURT." COOK GREETS ME AS I ENTER THE FOOD Hall.

"Hey, how's your day going?" I ask, hoping my voice sounds normal.

"Oh, ya know, the usual," he starts, then jumps right into a story about how someone moved his can opener.

I nod along, trying my hardest to engage since I'm the first one in here, but my mind keeps circling back to my boss.

I was so caught up in the intensity of the moment, distracted by the way his body felt against mine, that I didn't take the time to think about how wildly inappropriate the situation was.

And I don't just mean his massive hard-on.

Because it was massive.

I mean him lifting me off the ladder in the first place.

Sure, I was feeling off-balance right before he grabbed me, but he could have just held the ladder. Or said my name.

He did say my name. Courtney.

Cook laughs, and I blink.

A few more minutes pass before the rest of the guys start to filter in. And then a few more before we're all sitting at the tables with our plates of ham salad sandwiches. Something I haven't had since I was a kid and thought I hated. Turns out I just needed Cook to make it.

I try to stay present—as present as possible when my panties are damp—but I can't settle as I sit here waiting for Sterling to show up.

Not Sterling. Mr. Black.

I need to keep it professional.

Professional, like his dick against your ass.

I shove another bite of sandwich into my mouth.

"Howdy, Boss," Glen calls out.

My eyes snap to the doorway.

Sterling is walking through, eyes straight ahead, but he grunts in reply.

The chatter keeps up, and I nod along with something Simpson is saying, but Sterling is still in my line of sight, and I can't stop my gaze from gravitating to him.

He picks up the plate Cook left out for him, but he doesn't bring it to the tables. He just leans his sexy hip against the counter and takes a bite of his sandwich.

Not sexy.

How are man hips even sexy?

I trail my eyes up his torso.

He's in another flannel, which seems to be the only type of shirt he owns. And I wonder if he's wearing a T-shirt underneath or if his chest is naked under the soft fabric, like it was that first night I arrived, when he came out with his shirt unbuttoned and his toned, hairy chest on display.

Stop thinking about his chest hair.

And since when do I like chest hair?

Oh my god, stop thinking about him!

He's a dick!

My eyes drop to his dick.

As I stare, Sterling reaches down, cups the front of his jeans, and adjusts himself.

My gaze snaps up.
And meets his.

CHAPTER 49

STERLING

MY COCK TWITCHES IN MY GRIP.

My little worker is showing her hand.

And the temptation to take her in hand is nearly too much.

I let go of my pants and pick up my sandwich, shoving the rest of it into my mouth.

As soon as I'm done, I set my plate down and clear my throat.

It's not loud, but everyone quiets and turns to look at me.

I keep my eyes away from Cookie.

"We have a delivery coming tomorrow morning at ten," I tell them. "I need all hands on deck to get it sorted."

"What's the delivery?" Fisher asks.

"It shouldn't take long if everyone pulls their weight. Then, as you know, the next round of guests will be here the day after. So let's stay on top of everything. Yeah?"

There's a chorus of mumbles in agreement.

I don't hear Courtney's voice in the mix, so I shift my gaze to hers.

"Yes, sir." Her voice is quiet, but she says it just as everyone else goes quiet again.

Sir. Christ.

I slide my hands into my pockets, hoping the movement will distract from the movement in my fucking pants.

Someone snickers, and I hear a snorted *sir*.

Courtney's cheeks flame red.

I push away from the counter, needing to leave.

"Uh, Mr. Black?" Courtney's voice stops me.

Her tone is full of uncertainty, like she's trying to think of something to call me other than sir.

But it causes more snickers, because no one calls me Mr. Black.

Call me Sterling, Cookie. Come over here and call me fucking Sterling.

"What is it, Court?" I enunciate her shortened name. It's still what I want everyone else to call her. And I want to put that perceived professional distance between us.

I plan on obliterating that distance. But the guys need to believe it's there.

Her cheeks are still pink, possibly pinker. "Can I, um, have a moment?"

A moment?

A year?

A lifetime?

Yes.

"No" is all I give her before walking out the door.

CHAPTER 50

COURTNEY

"Sir?" Cook laughs after the door swings shut behind Sterling.

I bring my shoulders up to my ears. "I wouldn't even know his first name if it weren't for you guys," I defend myself. "He never gave me permission to use it."

Simpson shakes his head. "You don't need permission, Court. We don't stand on ceremony out here."

"Yeah, yeah." I sigh.

I think they can tell I'm still embarrassed, so Glen changes the topic. "What's the delivery tomorrow?"

I look around, wanting to know too, but notice everyone is looking at me.

My eyebrows lift. "You're asking me? How should I know? *Sterling* won't even talk to me."

"He has been in a bit of a mood." Simpson pats me on the back. "But he'll snap out of it."

I make a sound that could possibly be taken as agreement, even though I'm not convinced.

When I finally step out of the Food Hall, I find two things.

Next to my clipboard, which I left on the outdoor picnic

table, is something that looks like a mix between an over-long broom and a toilet brush.

The handle has to be six feet long, and the large dome-shaped brush on top would be perfect for getting rid of hard-to-reach spiderwebs.

I bite my lip.

This will make cleaning those outdoor lights much easier.

The second thing I notice is the fresh paper attached to the clipboard.

I pick it up and read the list.

It's the same as before, except...

I flip the page.

And bite my lip harder.

He rewrote the list.

All the tasks that require ladders have been removed.

Chapter 51

Courtney

The rumble of a large truck has me stopping at the edge of the driveway.

I check my watch. Nine thirty.

The sound gets louder, and I see the top of the large box truck cresting the drive.

I look around, wondering if anyone else has heard that the mystery delivery is early.

I literally have no idea what this is going to be, but since everyone else seemed to think I should know, I stand my ground.

If it's expected of me as the maintenance person, I guess I'll take the lead.

I glance over at Sterling's house as the truck nears.

He disappeared after lunch yesterday, and as much as I wanted to talk to him about the mattress—unsure if I would thank him or question him—I chickened out.

Instead, I spent the rest of yesterday using my big brush thing to clean off every outdoor light I could find.

I step off the side of the driveway as the truck approaches and wait for it to roll to a stop.

The engine cuts a moment before the driver's door opens.

I lift my hand to shield my eyes from the morning sun as a person climbs out. Cowboy boots hit the gravel in a poof of dust.

And then I have to work to keep my mouth closed because he's cute.

Like *really* cute.

His mouth pulls into a wide grin. "Howdy, ma'am."

I blush.

Even if my recent tastes seem to run to brooding older dark-haired men, this guy—who is probably around my age—is just too damn good looking not to notice.

"You in charge here?" His grin goes nowhere as he asks.

I shake my head and chuckle. "Hardly. But I was warned about a delivery." I tip my head toward his truck. "Should I assume you have some stuff for us back there?"

He props his hands on his hips and nods. "You're as smart as you are pretty."

I notice the small bite of pain in my thumbs before I realize I'm pressing my fingers together.

I relax my hands.

I am normal.

Normal and flustered.

"So..." The driver is still watching me. "You want them all in one place?"

I blink. "Huh?" I can't think straight with his flirty tone.

"The mattresses."

"The mattresses?" I repeat, like I've suddenly forgotten the English language.

His grin grows. "You sure you work here?"

I huff out a laugh. "I'm beginning to wonder."

His chuckle is loud, and I find myself smiling along with him.

The man opens his mouth, but before he can say more, his gaze moves to over my shoulder.

His grin stays in place, but he stands up a little straighter. And I know. I just *know* that Sterling is behind me.

"Morning," the driver says.

A large, warm palm lands on my shoulder, and I nearly jump out of my pants.

"Court, go tell the men the delivery is here." Sterling's tone is sharp, and it makes me feel like I'm in trouble. Even though I've done nothing wrong.

I drop my gaze, not wanting to see the driver's reaction to my boss's attitude.

But as I turn to go, Sterling turns with me so both of our backs are to the driver.

His hand is still on my shoulder, and I can feel the heat of his body as he leans into me.

"I don't want to catch you flirting with other men again, Cookie." His breath is hot against my ear, and it takes everything in me to stay upright. "Say *yes, sir.*"

A small sound crawls out of my throat, and I can only hope he doesn't hear it.

But the way his body curls over mine tells me he did.

"Say the words, Courtney." I can feel each syllable as it rumbles out of him and through me.

"Yes, sir," I breathe.

His fingers flex against my shoulder again before he lets go.

I stumble forward, thankfully catching myself before I face-plant into the dirt. But my heart is beating wildly as I hurry toward the Bunk House.

I don't know if the guys will be in here or scattered around the property, but I don't care. I just need distance between myself and the sexual frustration that is *Sterling.*

As I reach the cabin, my brain replays everything that just happened, and I slow.

Did that delivery driver seriously say his truck was full of mattresses?

That can't be true.

Where would they be going?

I've been in all the cabins. Mine was the only one missing a mattress.

Maybe they're for Sterling's house?

No, that's dumb.

He might have a couple of beds in that place, but not a truckload.

I climb the steps to the Bunk House—the place Sterling once told me I had no business going.

Before I can knock on the door, it swings open.

And it says something about my frazzled state when I scream.

Fisher lets out a yell in reply before slapping his hand over his heart. "Jesus, Court. You trying to kill me?"

I mirror him with my hand on my chest. "You're the one who scared me."

Glen steps up behind Fisher. "What's going on out here?"

I was already nearing cardiac arrest before this jump scare. If I make it through the day, it will be a damn miracle.

I take a calming breath. "The delivery is here. Sterling told me to come get everyone."

Both guys lift their brows, but Glen is the one to ask the question. "Do we know what it is?"

"Mattresses?" I don't sound confident.

They wrinkle their noses in confusion, and the continued synchronicity makes me smile.

"I think you might be spending too much time together," I tell them.

"Huh?" they say at the same time.

I snort. "Like I said." Then I heave out a breath. "Come on." I start to step back. "Er, is everyone else in there?"

Fisher shakes his head but pulls out his phone. "I'll send a message in the group chat."

My smile falters a little.

A group chat for all the employees.

Except me.

"Okay, thanks," I say instead of asking to be included in the text.

I don't even have their phone numbers.

Three minutes later, I approach the open back of the truck with Fisher and Glen. Cook, Simpson and Leon converge from other directions.

Everyone accounted for.

A large tarp is spread out on the ground off to the side, and as we stand there, Sterling appears from the other side of the truck with a mattress on his back.

As we all watch, Sterling tilts his shoulders and drops the mattress onto the tarp with a thud.

"Start with your own beds." Sterling stands straight and addresses our group. "Grab a new mattress and bring it to your bunk." He points at the open truck, and I notice the driver standing inside. He's leaning against a stack of mattresses, his mouth pulled up into a smirk and his eyes on me. I blush, again, and quickly look back to my boss. "Then bring your old mattress here." He points at the tarp. "Team up so you're not throwing your backs out. When the Bunk House is done, move on to the guest cabins. This shouldn't take too long."

"What's the occasion?" Cook asks as we all just stand there, dumbfounded.

Sterling lifts a brow. "You don't want a new mattress?"

Cook holds up his hands. "No questions. Got it."

As everyone shuffles toward the truck, I turn to Fisher. "Will you help me carry one to my cabin?"

"Yeah—" Fisher starts to nod.

"Yours is done," Sterling snaps out as he walks in front of us.

I turn my head to follow his direction. "Mine is done?"

But, of course, he doesn't answer. He just reaches into the truck, drags a whole-ass mattress out, swings it onto his back, and stomps off.

"Boss seems to be in a mood." Fisher shakes his head.

I bite my lip instead of replying as we step up to the back of the truck.

Why would Sterling do mine?

I tip my head back and look up at the truck full of mattresses.

Maybe he wanted to see if I put all my clothes back on my bed?

Jokes on him, though, because if I'd known he was going into my cabin today, I would've put all my dirty clothes through the wash so he could fold them.

It's arguably *incredibly* inappropriate that he did that once already, but he did a really nice job.

Shame about the pile of dirty laundry on my floor.

CHAPTER 52

STERLING

I USE THE WEIGHT ON MY BACK TO FORCE MY BODY TO focus.

I don't know why Courtney looked so surprised that I did her cabin for her.

She wouldn't be able to carry a mattress by herself.

And no way in fuck am I letting someone else help her. No one but me is setting foot in her cabin so long as she lives here.

She should save that surprise for when she finds a pair of her dirty panties missing.

CHAPTER 53

COURTNEY

I'M SO TIRED WHEN I PULL THE SHOWER CURTAIN BACK that I half regret taking the time to shower rather than just falling into bed. But I spent all day prepping the cabins for the guests who arrive tomorrow, and I felt too grimy to *not* shower.

And no way was I going to dirty my brand-new, incredibly comfortable memory-foam mattress.

As I brush out my wet hair in front of the mirror, I think about those damn mattresses for the hundredth time.

I crossed paths with Sterling multiple times as Fisher and I carried mattresses back and forth across the property, but I never got the nerve to ask Sterling about them.

Especially after the way he shut me down in the Food Hall the other day.

But it doesn't make sense—Sterling buying all those new mattresses.

It seemed too coincidental that he bought brand-new ones just days after giving me that other one. But him buying them *because of me* seems even more unlikely.

I set down my brush and twist my hair into two braids.

I don't have much experience with men. But I swear Sterling

has to be the most complicated one I've ever met. He's been hot, cold, and scorching since I started.

He's avoided me. Ignored me. Insulted me.

He's forced me to sleep on a board.

He's gone through my things.

He's folded my damn clothes.

He's hauled me off a ladder.

He's whispered in my ear.

He's pressed his big, hard body against mine.

Heat builds in my stomach as I think about him, and I know I'm going to end tonight the same way I ended last night, with my hand in my pajama pants, thinking of *him*.

I put face lotion on my fingertips and rub it into my cheeks. Then I repeat the process with my jasmine-scented body lotion. I found it on a sales rack months ago and have been using it sparingly since. I'm already dreading the day I run out and have to go back to the cheap stuff still tucked away in a box under my bunk.

When all my items are squared away in the corner of the long counter, I bundle up my dirty clothes and hold them against my chest.

I don't know if any of the guests coming in are women, but even if the entire group is women, I don't think they'd mind my things here.

The shower stall I've commandeered might be another thing, but I can move my stuff out of there if it's necessary.

Since I still won't get paid for weeks, I haven't been able to buy a carrier to haul my things around. But one day...

Daydreaming about a big paycheck, I turn off the lights and push the bathroom door open.

I hesitate.

It's dark out. Like *dark out*.

There's just a sliver of a moon, and even though I feel like I can see a billion stars, they do little to light my way.

I left my phone charging in my cabin, and as I start down the path back home, I vow to never do that again.

The flashlight on my phone might not be that powerful, but it's better than nothing.

The evening chill seeps through my cotton pants, and even though I pulled a sweatshirt on over my sleep top, I have to fight a shiver.

Winter comes early this high up in the mountains.

As my foot lowers on my next step, I hear a branch break.

I stop, looking down.

There is no stick beneath my foot.

I hold my breath.

The silence is deafening as I listen for movement, making my heartbeat feel like a drumline.

I lift my foot.

Another crunch.

My chest starts to burn.

I suck in air.

A large form lumbers into view a dozen feet in front of me.

My feet pedal backward.

I exhale my breath in a scream.

And my heel catches on something.

I drop my clothes.

My body tips backward.

And the big-as-hell bear turns her head to look at me.

My butt hits the hard earth, knocking the rest of the oxygen out of my lungs.

She takes a step toward me.

Looking at me.

Fear twists around me like a wire.

"H-hi," I whisper, the word cracking.

She tilts her head.

"You're a pretty girl, aren't you?"

I don't know how I know she's a she. But I can feel it. The mama bear energy.

She takes another step toward me. Her eyes glinting in the dark.

Please think of me as your cub.

I'm no threat to you.

Her nearness has fear clogging my throat, trapping the words, so I hope she feels them.

She stops, tilting her head the other way, then she turns back toward the woods and takes off.

I slump in relief.

Then I stiffen.

What scared the bear?

"Courtney!" Sterling shouts my name just as I see the beam of a flashlight fanning across the driveway.

My adrenaline crashes, and I drop onto my back.

"Courtney!" He sounds more frantic than I've ever heard him.

I lift a hand. "Here."

Instead of settling him down, I listen to his footsteps quicken until I'm sure he's running.

"Courtney, what the fuck happened?" He drops to his knees next to me with a thud. "Are you okay? Where are you hurt? What happened?" He places his hands on the ground next to my shoulders, leaning over me.

I blink up at him.

He shifts his weight and brings one of his hands to my cheek. "Tell me." His calloused fingers are so warm against my chilled skin.

"She was *right there.*"

"Who was?"

I inhale Sterling's masculine scent and relax just a bit more. "The bear."

Sterling sits back on his haunches and looks left, then right.

"She's gone," I tell him.

He heaves out a breath. "I heard you scream."

I grimace. "Sorry."

He shakes his head as he looks back down at me. "You're not supposed to play dead for black bears. You're supposed to fight."

I widen my eyes at him. "I'm not fighting a fucking bear. Duh. Plus." I start to push myself back up to sitting, but then he distracts me by helping me with a hand on my back.

"Plus?"

"Plus, I think she liked me."

Sterling shakes his head but grabs my hands and pulls me up to standing. "Of course the bear would fucking like you."

Before I can ask him what he means, he grips my shoulders and turns me around.

I think I hear him grumble something about *rolling around in the dirt*, then his big hands brush down my back.

Standing still, I look down and see the clothes I dropped.

Oh right.

Without thinking, I bend over and grab my clothes.

Those big hands leave my back and grip my hips. "Christ, woman. Do you have no survival instincts?"

CHAPTER 54

STERLING

I GIVE HER HIPS A SQUEEZE, AND COURTNEY straightens up, her clothes in her arms.

"Sorry." Her apology is a huff as she turns in my hold to face me. "Not all of us are survivalists or whatever."

"I don't need you to be a *survivalist or whatever*, but I do need you to survive."

Her stance changes. From defiant to defeated.

And I fucking hate it.

"What just happened?" I shift closer.

She shakes her head, her braids bumping against her shoulders.

I reach out and loosely grip one of those braids, slowly dragging my hand down the length like I've wanted to since I first saw them.

I open my mouth to demand she tell me what she's thinking.

"Hey! Everything okay?" Fisher shouts from somewhere in the dark.

I let the braid slip from my grip. "Go to bed, Courtney."

Without responding, she rushes past me, disappearing into the night just as Fisher appears.

"Coulda sworn I heard someone scream," Fisher says, looking around.

I bend to grab my flashlight and shotgun off the ground, confirming Courtney's lack of awareness since I'm certain she didn't even notice the firearm. "Court had a run-in with a bear."

"Oh shit," Fisher breathes out. "She okay?"

I want to grip him by the front of the shirt and tell him that *she* is none of his fucking business. But instead, I let out a chuckle that I hope sounds convincing. "She scared herself as much as she scared the damn bear."

Fisher shakes his head. "Sounds about right."

I dip my chin. "Turn your flashlight on."

I know he has one on him. All the guys do.

Then I look in the direction of the Laundry Cabin.

Not a survivalist, indeed.

Chapter 55

Courtney

My nerves are lit up as we wait for the guests to arrive.

Talking to Cook this morning while I made the communal coffee, I found out that just two of the cabins will be in use tonight, but then there's another group coming tomorrow. They'll overlap some, and then they'll all be gone by the end of the weekend.

I also found out that the past week without guests is a bit of an abnormality this time of year. But it was planned to accommodate the *switchover* from Marty to me.

It makes sense, but also, if Sterling was concerned enough about the new maintenance person, then it seems like he would've spent more time—*any time*—walking me through the position and what was expected.

Sighing, I plop down on the top step of my cabin.

I've been pacing around for the last twenty minutes, waiting for these people to arrive, but it's not helping me to calm down.

I don't even know why I'm nervous. My job, according to the new sheet I found sitting next to Big Joe, is to *stay away from the guests* and to *make the beds* and *clean the bathrooms and kitch-*

enettes while the guests are out of the cabins—doing whatever they do between one and four.

I reach into the thigh pocket of my cargo pants and let my fingers trace the button on my new flashlight. Which was the other thing sitting next to the coffee machine this morning. And another reminder of my run-in with Sterling, and a real live fucking bear last night.

The metal is cool on my palm when I grip the flashlight.

When he told me he needed me to survive...

I pull the flashlight out of my pocket so I can look at it again.

I wanted to tell him that surviving is all I've been doing.

And I'm sick of it.

I want to do more than that.

I depress the button with my thumb and shine the light onto my opposite palm. It's so bright I can see the beam even in the daylight.

I turn the flashlight off.

One of these days, I'll get there.

One of these days, I'll thrive.

I HUM AS I PULL THE BLANKETS UP TO MY CHIN.

Today was... anticlimactic.

The six men arrived over a period of two hours in four vehicles. Leon and Simpson are the guides for their outing, so they were the ones to greet and settle the guests in.

Everyone else just went about their day, and I went back to work on my list of things to fix—spending my afternoon tightening a couple of railings and replacing burned-out bulbs.

But after the bear and what felt like a near kiss from last night, I'm okay with boring.

Closing my eyes, I shimmy my shoulders against the new, ridiculously comfortable mattress.

And in what has become my nightly norm, my mind goes to Sterling.

I still don't understand what's going on there—between me and him. But there's been a change.

From moment one, he was hot and cold. But it's like the thermostat has been set to high, and then someone broke the switch. Causing the heat to build with every interaction.

And I can't ignore it.

Can't ignore him.

Can't ignore the way my body reacts to his nearness.

But I can't let myself forget he's my boss.

That he's my employer.

The reason I have a roof over my head.

The reason I'll eventually have more food in my cupboard.

And even though I'm nearly positive that sex with Sterling Black would be... *chef's kiss*, it's not worth losing my job over.

I open my eyes and look at the dark ceiling.

Would it really be jeopardizing my job?

It's not like Sterling is going to fire me for some fraternization rule over sleeping with the boss when *he* is the boss.

I shake my head.

I can't sleep with my boss.

I'm living here for the next two months and three weeks. That would be a long fling. And if we're doing *that*, but then something happens and we're not doing *that* anymore, I'd still have to see him.

Or worse, I'd have to watch him bring women home.

I make a face.

We've barely interacted, but the idea of seeing him walk into his house with another woman already fills me with slimy green jealousy.

If we slept together...

I heave out a sigh and roll onto my side, adjusting into my usual sleep position.

It's not a good idea.

Now, if it gets to the end of the year and I'm about to leave... then all bets are off.

CHAPTER 56

STERLING

THE BARK IS ROUGH, EVEN THROUGH MY SHIRT, AS I lean against the tree.

This is my favorite part of the morning, watching Courtney enjoy her cup of coffee on the Food Hall patio.

Sure, out of context, it might seem creepy. But I'm an employer making sure my employee is doing her job. And her drinking a cup of coffee after making a pot for the crew is quality control.

I'm just supervising.

From a distance.

Today, she's standing, her hip leaned against a picnic table.

Other days, she'll sit on one of the benches facing the woods.

She doesn't look as tired as she did those first few mornings. And now that I know what she was sleeping on, it makes sense.

And it makes me feel like shit all over again.

I tap my fingers against the side of my coffee mug.

I should go talk to her. Explain that the missing mattress was an accident.

It doesn't have to get heated.

We can just talk.

I can behave myself.

As I'm debating the pros and cons of walking over there, Courtney straightens.

Her head is tipped up, looking at something in the rafters.

She sets her coffee down on the table, then turns in my direction.

Courtney takes a few quick steps, and I push off the tree. Getting caught lurking will not help my case.

But she's not looking into the woods.

She's looking at the ceiling duster she left propped against the wall of the Food Hall.

She grips the pole and holds it high as she moves between the picnic tables, looking up.

I watch her reach her arms up over her head, pointing the bristles at the peak of the rafters.

It's not reaching.

She eyes the bench, and I take a silent step forward.

If she climbs on that, I'm gonna pluck her off it and lay her over my knee.

Courtney shifts her grip to the very end of the long pole.

Good girl.

She reaches up again.

The bristles brush against the ceiling, then Courtney swipes it violently against the wood.

I tilt my head.

Courtney flings the pole away from herself with a strangled cry.

She jumps back, eyes down, after dislodging what has to be a spider. Or some other bug.

She wipes her hands down her chest, moving backward, when she bumps into a bench.

Which shakes the table.

And sloshes coffee out of her mug.

"Shit sticks!" Her curse cuts through the woods.

I'm fighting a smile when she stomps inside the Food Hall,

mug in hand. And my smile wins when she comes out a minute later, her mug replaced with a soup pot.

It looks awkward to carry, one hand on the long handle. One under the pot.

She's holding it higher than seems necessary, and I can't help but hope she spills that water all over her tight long-sleeved shirt.

I swear I saw her in a sweater on her walk over, but it's off now, and I bet that fabric would cling if it got wet.

Courtney tries to slowly pour the water onto the coffee spill, but the handle twists in her grip, dumping out all the water at once.

It splashes everywhere.

Including across her shirt.

"Morning," Cook says from beside me.

I jolt, and the coffee in my mug sloshes over the side and down my hand. "Shit."

Cook chuckles. "Too much caffeine is bad for the heart, Sterling."

I shift my mug to my other hand and shake the liquid off my fingers. "Fuck off." I don't say it with heat. And Cook just clicks his tongue before walking past me toward the Food Hall.

CHAPTER 57

COURTNEY

WAKE UP.

Make instant oatmeal in my cabin, in my one bowl, with hot water from my teakettle.

Get dressed and ready for work.

Make coffee in the Food Hall.

Drink a cup.

Work on my list.

Eat lunch.

Clean the cabins.

Work on the list more.

Shower.

Eat ramen in my cabin, in my one bowl, with hot water from my teakettle.

Climb into bed.

Pass out.

Repeat.

CHAPTER 58

COURTNEY

I HEAR THE CRUNCH OF TIRES ON THE DRIVEWAY, AND my pulse skips a beat.

They're back.

I want to turn around and watch the vehicles pull up, but I keep walking toward the Food Hall with my armful of clean hand towels.

The guys have been gone for three nights. Which was expected.

But for some reason, I wasn't expecting Sterling to go with them.

So I haven't seen him for three long days.

No glances.

No hearing his voice.

No getting too close.

But now he's back.

I open the door and step into the scent of caramelizing onions.

"The guys are back," I tell Cook as I set the folded towels on the counter.

"Good." He nods as he stirs the onions. "Go tell Sterling that everything will be ready in thirty."

I roll my lips together before turning back to the door.
If you say so.

CHAPTER 59

STERLING

THE THREE GUESTS IN MY TRUCK ARE STILL TALKING when I pull to a stop in front of my house.

If I were considerate, I would have dropped them off at the path leading to their cabin. But considering how much energy they've had to fucking gab the entire two-hour drive back, they can carry their packs the extra hundred yards.

Plus, I need to shower before I hunt down Courtney.

As soon as I turn off the engine, I unbuckle and throw my door open.

I was a last-minute add to this outing, and normally I'm happy to go off property, but normally I don't have a curvy little sexpot living on my land.

The guys follow me out, clustering around once they've gotten all their shit out of the truck.

"Go grab showers if you want," I tell the guys. Our site had an outhouse and a well spigot. No plumbing otherwise, and the smell on the drive home was the proof of it. "There will be time to pack up anything else after lunch." I look at my watch. "Food should be ready in forty-five."

"Thirty, actually," a quiet feminine voice says from behind me.

"Aw, hey, Court," one of the guys facing her says. "Did you miss us?"

I narrow my eyes at him, annoyed he remembers her name from their brief meeting, before I slowly turn around to face my little worker.

Yeah, Court, did you miss us?

Her cheeks are pink, and she nods. "How could I not?"

She hasn't met my gaze yet.

"Showers," I snap. "You all smell like fish guts."

They chuckle, as though I'm joking, but disperse.

Leaving me dangerously alone with Courtney.

I keep my eyes on her, and she keeps her eyes on my chest.

But I can't have that.

I need to see those pretty hazel irises.

Need to see them look at me from under her long lashes.

"Eyes up here." My voice is a rumble.

Courtney slowly lifts her gaze.

And when her eyes meet mine, I take a step forward.

Her lips part, and I hear her little exhale, and *fuck me*, I want to put my mouth on hers.

I *need* to put my mouth on hers.

A car door slams, and Courtney glances past me.

Fisher and his guys have climbed out of his vehicle, and I can spot another vehicle coming up the drive behind them.

"Lunch in thirty." Courtney repeats herself, then turns and hurries away.

CHAPTER 60

COURTNEY

THE FOOD HALL IS NOISY AS ALL THE GUESTS GET IN line to grab lunch.

Cook made caramelized-onion grilled cheese sandwiches and a thick tomato soup. I got to taste some earlier, and it's damn near magical. And perfect since the weather is decidedly starting to turn cold.

I'm trying to hold out a little longer, but I'm going to have to turn the heat on in my cabin soon.

"Come on, darlin', get in line." One of the guests stops beside me, holding his arm out.

"Oh, I'll wait for you all—"

"No can do. Ladies first," the older man insists, and since my stomach is growling, I cave and move into the line.

The first evening, when the guests arrived and everyone was still at the Lodge, we employees sat at our own picnic table. But now that everyone is back and the guests have bonded with their guides, it looks like seating is a free-for-all.

As I shuffle closer to the food, I hear the door open, and I can't stop myself from glancing over my shoulder.

Sterling.

His hair is damp. His flannel is only half buttoned. And he looks so good, and so much like he did the first time I saw him.

He moves into line behind us, and before I do something stupid, like drool, I look away.

The man next to me starts talking about the fish he caught, and the man in front of us chimes in, claiming he's exaggerating. So the first man pulls out his phone, insisting I look at the photos.

"It's a big fish." I nod.

"See?" he calls back to his friend.

I don't know fuck all about fish. Mine come breaded and frozen. But sure, it looks big.

The line moves forward, and I take a plate from Cook, sandwich already cut in two and spread around the base of a bowl of soup. A pack of crackers is on the corner of the plate, and I smile at Cook when he winks and drops two more packets on my plate.

No one else is paying attention, so I don't have to feel embarrassed.

I don't know how Cook put together that I need a little help in the food department, but whenever there's something nonperishable, like crackers, on the menu, he always gives me extra.

Maybe he's noticed that I don't put anything in the fridges, and maybe he knows I don't have a fridge of my own, but no matter his reasoning, I appreciate it.

With my water bottle hooked around my finger, I pick up my plate and search for an open seat.

One table is full, two more are mostly full, and since I don't feel like wedging between people, I move to one of the empty tables and sit at the end of the bench, with my back facing the wall.

The man who caught *the big fish* sets his plate across from mine, dropping onto the bench with a groan.

"I'm gonna sleep like the fucking dead tonight." He shakes his head as he opens his crackers. "No idea how you guys do that rough sleeping all year round."

I purse my lips, wondering if he's forgotten my role and thinks I'm a guide too, when a plate gets set down next to mine.

Flannel flashes in my periphery, and that's all I need to see to know who it is.

CHAPTER 61

STERLING

THE MAN WHO HAD BEEN BEHIND ME IN LINE SNORTS AS
I set down my plate.

The fucker was making a beeline to sit next to my Courtney.

I shoot him a narrow-eyed look.

He dips his chin, fighting off a smile as he moves around to sit
across from me.

That's right, buddy, move fucking along.

CHAPTER 62

COURTNEY

I TRY MY BEST TO ACT UNAFFECTED AS A LONG LEG steps over the bench inches from my hip.

Act normal.

Sterling shifts, bringing his other leg over, then sits beside me.

He's so big. His shoulders are so wide. I feel like I should scoot over to give him more room.

But he's the one who sat so close. And I'm already on the edge of the bench.

Plus—I discreetly inhale through my nose—he smells too damn good to move away.

Like soap and sandalwood.

And he's probably extra warm from his shower.

Does he take his time?

Does he rush through?

Naked... Slippery with suds.

I start to lean toward him before I catch myself.

What the fuck, Courtney? Get your shit together.

You cannot be sniffing your boss.

Pressing my lips together, I look up, hoping no one noticed my sway toward Sterling.

The table has filled up in the minute I've been daydreaming. And everyone seems to be in conversation.

But then my eyes lock with the guy sitting across from my boss, and he's grinning at me.

Shit.

I pick up my sandwich and dunk it into the bowl of soup.

Eating quietly, I get through three bites before Sterling shifts. Adjusting himself on the bench. Widening his stance. Until his thigh is touching mine.

I chew slower.

It's not just *sort of* touching me. Sterling's large thigh is pressed against the length of mine.

I can feel the heat of it. Of him. Through our layers of clothes.

And it's too much.

I swallow.

It should be innocent.

Just two people sitting a little too close on a crowded bench.

Except it wasn't crowded when he sat down.

And him pressing his leg against mine has nothing to do with lack of space.

And I'm not moving away.

CHAPTER 63

STERLING

I DON'T EVEN TASTE THE FOOD AS I SWALLOW IT.

All I can focus on is the woman next to me.

Her warmth.

Her scent.

Her nearness.

The way her thigh feels against mine.

She's the soft to my hard.

The gentle to my rough.

And without even trying, she's consuming my thoughts more than any other human ever has.

It doesn't matter that we've hardly touched.

That we haven't kissed.

That we've barely talked.

And even though I want to know everything about her, the lack of information isn't important. Because there's nothing in her past that would keep me from wanting her.

Needing her.

I shift my arm, pressing my shoulder against hers.

Courtney doesn't move away.

A second passes, and the pressure between us increases as she leans into me.

Something hot slithers down my rib cage.

It's lust. But it's something else too.

Being leaned on.

Being depended on.

Being trusted.

I reach out with my opposite arm, the one not touching Courtney, and pick up my water.

My throat feels uncomfortably tight.

I take a large gulp.

Then another.

It's been so long since I've felt...

I set down my glass.

I don't even know what this is.

Purpose feels like too big of a word.

Lifting my sandwich, I pretend to naturally adjust my leg, pulling it away from Courtney just the smallest bit.

The clothing between us feels instantly cold without her touching me anymore.

But then she does it.

She follows me.

Spreading her thighs to keep the contact.

And that feeling inside me expands.

Whoever this girl is, she was sent to me.

Through the universe.

Through a twist of fate.

Through a fuckup of Marty.

I don't care if the Devil herself sent Courtney to my Lodge.

I'll take whatever punishment comes to me over what happens next.

I grab my napkin with the hand closest to Courtney and wipe it across my mouth.

Then, like a man with class, I lower the napkin to my lap rather than putting it back on the table.

The move should look natural.

And it feels natural.

Feels so fucking natural to drop my napkin and set my palm on Courtney's thigh.

CHAPTER 64

COURTNEY

THE MOMENT STERLING'S LARGE HAND RESTS ON MY thigh, my stomach explodes with fireworks.

The kind that makes every minuscule muscle in my core clench.

The kind that feels like magic.

The kind that you know is dangerous, but the risk of injury is worth the excitement of the explosion.

I try hard to remain still.

To appear unaffected.

But my heart is racing.

And I can feel the heat pooling between my legs, preparing for detonation.

CHAPTER 65

STERLING

I TURN MY WRIST UNTIL MY FINGERS ARE CUPPING THE inside of her thigh.

Then I pull her leg tighter against mine.

It's not enough.

I slide my hand farther down until my fingertips are against the wood of the bench.

I want to move my hand the other way.

Toward her core.

I swear I can feel the heat radiating off her pussy, from inches away, and I want to touch it.

I want to cup her there, between her legs.

But if I do that, I won't stop until she's coming on my fingers.

So I keep my hand where it is, tugging her closer, even though closer isn't possible.

With my free hand, I pick up my grilled cheese again.

And while I take a bite, I rub my thumb in a slow circle on the top of her thigh, feeling her thigh muscles flex and relax beneath my touch.

Courtney leans forward, resting her elbows on the table.

She's affected.

To cover my urge to grin, I shove more food into my mouth.

And I nearly choke when Courtney's other leg presses in, trapping my hand between her thighs.

CHAPTER 66

COURTNEY

I'M GOING TO COME.

I squeeze my thighs together, the feel of Sterling's large hand between my legs making it hard to think.

Hard to fucking breathe.

And I swear to Aphrodite, if he shifts his hand up. If he so much as grazes his fingers over my zipper, I'm going to literally come in my pants.

CHAPTER 67

STERLING

A POT CRASHES TO THE GROUND, AND ALL EYES IN THE room turn to look at Cook.

"Whoops." He holds his hands up, one clutching the towel he'd been using to dry said pot. "Nothing to see here."

As everyone chuckles and goes back to their conversations, Cook moves his gaze pointedly to mine.

Not being as sneaky as I thought I was.

Courtney jumped when the pot dropped, and the feeling of all her muscles tensing went straight to my dick.

With my free hand, I pick up my bowl and drink down the rest of the contents in two swallows, finishing what's left of my lunch.

I don't want to move from this spot.

I want to stay like this forever.

But for both our sakes, I need to stop now before I do more.

I flex my fingers against Courtney's thigh, signaling to her and memorizing how she feels.

Her thighs spread ever so slightly as I do, and as I stand, I move my hand toward her true north.

My pinkie grazes the seam of her pants.

And I clear my throat, covering up the sound of her inhaled breath.

Chapter 68

Courtney

My feet slap against the floor as I pace my cabin.

"What was that?" I direct my question to Spike.

If she could, she'd lift her spiny eyebrow at me.

"It's not like *I* instigated it," I huff, crossing back into the bedroom.

And it's not like I put a stop to it.

I groan and drape myself over the edge of the bunk.

"What am I doing?" My voice is muffled by my sweet, squishy mattress.

A knock at the door cuts off my inner chastisement.

I jerk upright and turn to face the front of the cabin.

Is Sterling at my door?

Should I answer?

I start walking across the floor before I can lie to myself.

Of course I'm going to answer.

"Court, you in there?" Cook's voice filters through the door.

The tension drops out of my shoulders as I heave out a breath.

No need to stress over will I or won't I fuck my boss, *I guess.*

I open the door. "Hey. What's up?"

"You wanna come make some pies or something before the

fire?" Cook takes a step back, like I'm going to immediately follow him.

"What fire?"

"The one we have after the first guests of the season leave." He waves an arm for me to get moving.

I put my hands on my hips. "Those were hardly the first of the season."

"Okay, fine. We do it pretty much every time a group of guests leave."

I drop my arms. "If it's tradition..."

CHAPTER 69

STERLING

FLAMES CRACKLE BETWEEN US.

The bright orange causes shadows to dance across Courtney's features.

I couldn't sit beside her. Not when we're all just sitting on logs with no tables to cover our laps.

So I chose the second-best spot, directly across from her, with the fire between us.

I'm on my third mini apple pie, unable to stop myself even after the dinner Cook and Courtney put together.

I'm not usually a sweets guy, but knowing her hands were all over every one of these... they taste better than they should.

And tonight, I'm here to indulge.

Except for alcohol. I'm still on my first beer, nursing it, same as Courtney.

These post-guest campfires are for unwinding, which is usually done by drinking. But I'm unwinding a different way tonight.

And neither of us can be drunk for that.

"Who needs another?" Fisher asks as he gets up and walks toward the cooler.

Most of the guys call out an affirmative.

But I stay silent, keeping my eyes on Courtney.

Like the good girl she is, she flicks her eyes to mine.

I shake my head.

No, Courtney, you may not have another beer.

"Court?" Fisher directs his question at her.

I watch her roll her lips together. Like she's deciding whether she's going to listen.

I slide my tongue along my teeth, keeping myself from scolding her aloud.

But she finally shakes her head. "No, thank you."

Simpson snorts. "You're always so formal."

The look that comes over Courtney's face is so fucking cute that I have to lift my mostly empty beer to cover my smile.

"I am not formal." She sounds so affronted. "I literally clean toilets every day."

Simpson shakes his head. "Doesn't matter what you're doing. You're out here saying *no, thank you* and *sir* and *Mr. Black.*"

I feel gazes turn toward me, but I keep mine on Courtney.

"We already talked about that." She lifts her brows, like she's reminding him of something.

"Ah yes, our boss never told you his name." Simpson smirks.

Courtney finally looks at me. "He did not."

Cook clicks his tongue. "Bad form, Boss."

I lift a shoulder, holding Courtney's gaze. "She never asked."

She lifts a matching shoulder. "Just a part of the new employee hazing, I suppose."

Some of the guys laugh.

But I don't.

And neither does she.

Because Courtney still thinks I made her sleep on a bare bunk on purpose.

Simpson laughs. "Nah, there's no hazing at the Lodge."

I can see the thoughts turning in her brain, wondering if she should bring up the mattress.

Which makes me wonder why she never said anything to anyone else about it. Because even if she thinks I knew, she couldn't possibly believe everyone was in on it.

Because they weren't.

Because there was nothing to be in on.

"Guess those new mattresses made up for it, then." Courtney chuckles, but I'm the only one in on the joke.

Glen slaps his hands down on his thighs. "Speaking of, I'm gonna go haul my ass to bed."

While the guys are giving him shit, Courtney silently stands up.

"Aw, not you too," Simpson whines at her.

"Sorry. It's been a long day." She pulls something out of her pocket. "But I'll see you all in the morning. Hopefully Big Joe keeps acting sweet to me."

I stand. "Who the fuck is Big Joe?"

I said that louder than intended, drawing everyone's attention.

Courtney presses her lips together as she widens her eyes at me.

"Maybe you missed the rule about no sleepovers," I tell her.

It's the truth. But that's more because the guys all share a cabin, and having a *bedroom guest* would cause all sorts of awkward problems. That's what the Inn down the mountain is for.

But since Courtney has a cabin to herself, there really isn't a good reason for her to follow the rule.

Nevertheless, the rule stands.

"Yeah, Court, who is Big Joe?" Cook's tone is antagonistic.

Courtney turns to him. "Why, Cook, you don't need to ask. You already know him."

Everyone's attention is ping-ponging between the three of us. So at least I'm not alone in not knowing Joe.

"You got a boyfriend?" Leon asks.

My jaw aches with how hard that question makes me clench my teeth.

She better fucking not have a boyfriend.

Courtney huffs, "I do not. And it's certainly not Big Joe. Because *he* is the oversized coffee maker in the Food Hall."

CHAPTER 70

COURTNEY

"Good night." I wave at the group of laughing men as I back away from the fire.

Sterling is still standing beside the fire, watching me, when I turn around.

I can't believe he was acting that jealous over a coffee maker.

I try to think of it as silly, but as soon as he's out of sight, my heart starts beating faster.

Turning my back on him feels like that time between turning off the lights and jumping into bed. Like an invisible monster is chasing you.

But I won't run.

Not from this particularly dangerous creature.

Lifting my hand, I press the button under my thumb, and the flashlight flares to life.

CHAPTER 71

STERLING

THE FLASHLIGHT BEAM BOBS THROUGH THE WOODS, showing me exactly where my girl is.

My pulse thrums as I cut between the trees, closing the distance.

Chapter 72

Courtney

I slow.

Did I hear something?

I stop.

The darkness is quiet around me.

I'm losing it.

I take a step.

"You need to pay better attention." Sterling's voice sounds from behind me.

I spin around on instinct, flashlight outstretched.

Sterling catches my wrist before my swing can connect with his body.

The contact makes my hand open, and I drop the flashlight.

He lets go of my wrist and catches the light. Then he closes his fingers over the end, muting the glow.

"Jesus, Sterling," I gasp.

"Just Sterling will do."

I huff, "Oh, *now* you tell me what I can call you?"

He steps toward me, and I take a matching step back.

"I like everything you call me. Sterling." Step. "Mr. Black." Step. "Sir." Step.

I keep backing up.

I don't *want* to move away from him. I just have to.

The monster from the dark has found me. And even though I want him to catch me, my body won't surrender.

Not yet.

He lifts his fingers from the light, aiming it at our feet. "And what do you like to be called?"

I swallow. "Courtney."

"That's all?"

"What else is there?"

"Cookie." He drops his eyes to my chest, then lower, taking me in.

"I don't like that one," I whisper.

He lifts his gaze. "No?"

I shake my head.

"Why?"

I cross my arms over my body. "Because... because of why you call me that."

He raises the flashlight, shining the light on where my arms are crossed over my chest, the edges of the beam lighting my features. "And why do I call you that?"

My stomach twists.

His tone is heated.

The looks he gave me across the fire were loaded.

And the memory of his hand on my thigh is still freshly burned into my mind.

But so is the hurt from the first time he called me that.

"Because of how much I ate. Or *what* I ate that day at Costco," I admit.

He tilts his head as he drops his hand to his side, the light swinging down. "What?"

"You saw my receipt, and you called me Cookie," I remind him. Reminding myself as well. "I know I'm... bigger. But I don't like the name."

I take another step back.

Sterling stays where he is.

It's too dark to see exactly where his eyes are looking, but I know he's staring at me.

I take another step.

"Courtney." His seriousness stops me. "I need you to listen to me real fucking carefully."

I press my lips together.

"I called you Cookie for two reasons. And neither of them had anything to do with the shape of your perfect fucking body." He takes a step closer, finally following me. "Reason one." He steps forward again, raising his hand and holding up one finger. "You *literally* threw a cookie at me. And two." He holds up a second finger. "I call you Cookie because you're sweet and delicate and"—he reaches out and grips one of my braids—"I want to *eat* you."

The air gets tangled in my lungs.

He... what?

"I know I shouldn't." He drags his hand down my plaited hair. "But I can't resist anymore."

"Resist?"

"Yeah, *Cookie*, I can't, won't, resist the urge to touch you any longer." He lets my braid fall from his fingers. "And you have until the count of three to get out of reach if you don't want this."

Awareness scratches over my skin.

Sterling wants me.

My boss.

And he's going to act on it.

Now.

I pull in a deep breath.

I should run.

"One."

I don't move.

Sterling's fingers cover the light again, leaving the smallest glow visible.

"Two."

This is really happening.

Excitement pounds through my veins.

So does *flight.*

I spin.

He doesn't say three.

And I don't have time to shout my surprise before his big palm is over my mouth and his hard body is pressed against mine.

Chapter 73

Sterling

With one arm wrapped around her middle, I walk us forward. The flashlight still in my grip bounces with every step, causing shadows to dart through the woods around us.

The hand I have pressed over her mouth muffles her sound of surprise.

I tip my head down, putting my lips against her ear. "Not fast enough, girl."

I tighten my arm across her stomach, nearly lifting her feet off the ground.

Her hands clutch at my arm, and it's just like when I pulled her off that ladder. Because she's not trying to push me away.

She's clinging to me.

And it's divine.

Each step has her body bumping into mine. My hard-as-steel cock grinding into her rounded ass with each movement.

Only this time, I'm not letting her go until my hand is covered in her scent.

CHAPTER 74

COURTNEY

I CAN FEEL EVERYTHING.

Everything.

And each stumbling step I take sends my heart rate higher.

"I need you to be quiet." His breath against my skin is hot. "So I'm keeping my hand here." He strokes his thumb across my cheek, letting me know he's referring to the palm over my mouth.

Honestly, I'm glad he's doing it. Because I'm not quiet.

Not when I'm working alone.

Not when I'm touching myself.

And certainly not during whatever he's about to do to me.

"But if you need me to remove it, just tap the back of my hand. Okay?" Sterling asks as he keeps walking us forward.

I'm beyond thinking about all the reasons why this is a bad idea.

So I nod.

Sterling presses his nose against my temple and inhales.

The move sends goose bumps dancing across my skin, and I moan.

He tsks. "My noisy girl."

All I hear is *my girl*. And I melt further into his hold.

Sterling chuckles, and it's not fair how sexy it sounds.

He turns us, and I finally look up.

He's taken us around the back of my cabin, putting the structure between us and everyone else.

"Brace yourself."

I don't understand his command until he loosens his hold on me, the flashlight dropping to the ground, the beam facing the cabin.

I reach my hands out, bracing them against the building.

I expect his arm to slip away completely, but he just moves it. Shifting it up until his hand is on my chest, just below my throat.

The neckline of my shirt is high enough that he's not touching skin, but my body doesn't seem to know the difference. It's lighting up over every millimeter of contact.

"I'm not taking you inside to your bed." He slides his hand down a few inches until the base of his palm is over my cleavage. "Because if I do." He shifts his hand and palms my breast. "I'll fuck you." I moan, and his fingers flex against my cheek at the same time that his other fingers flex, squeezing my tit. "And I'm not fucking you tonight." I whimper. He slides his hand down, away from my chest, over my stomach. "But I am going to make you come."

Sweet baby Zeus.

My body shudders.

I need him to do what he says.

I need him to—

His hand moves lower. His fingers work on my pants button.

"Are you already wet for me, Courtney?" He flips the button open. "When I stick my hand in your panties, am I going to find them soaked?" He pulls down the zipper.

I tell him *yes*, unsure if it was a rhetorical question, but under his palm, my answer is unintelligible.

"What was that?" Sterling nuzzles his face into my neck.

I nod my reply.

He flattens his hand on my lower stomach and pulls my hips back.

It's his turn to groan.

The sound is... primal.

And I arch into him. Pressing my ass against the hardness I feel behind me.

He rocks his hips into me. "Keep doing that." He grinds into me harder. "Keep your ass right here, Cookie." He rolls his hips. "Let me pretend I'm inside you."

I tip my head back, resting it on his shoulder, as I shift, pushing back into him like he asked.

Teeth drag across my bared neck. "Such a good listener."

The fingers against my stomach twitch, working their way between the top band of my underwear and my skin.

I tense.

I knew it was coming. Knew what he was going to do when he undid my pants. But now that it's happening, my insecurities flare to life.

The way I'm soft all over.

The way I haven't shaved in... forever.

The way—

Fingers slide over my curls, not stopping until they reach my drenched slit.

Sterling presses his open mouth to the side of my neck as he groans. Loudly. And just like that, my insecurities disappear.

Dissolving into the sound of Sterling's groan against my skin.

There's no room for negative thoughts when he presses his middle finger into my wetness.

"Christ, woman." He lifts his mouth just long enough to speak. "You feel like hot fucking heaven."

I shove my hips back, grinding against my boss's hard cock.

He rocks his hips forward.

I brace against his strength.

He pushes his finger farther inside me.

I moan against his palm.
He slides his hand up, fingers dragging over my clit.
My body clenches.
And he starts to rock his hips against me.

CHAPTER 75

STERLING

THE TIGHT, WET HEAT OF HER PUSSY IS TOO MUCH.

I circle her clit as I rub myself against her ass.

I can't stop myself.

I won't stop myself.

I push my finger back into her slit.

She moans.

I push a second finger inside.

She writhes.

I drag them out, then push them in.

She opens her mouth beneath my palm.

I change the position of my hand and shove two fingers into her mouth, filling her in two ways.

I lift my head to watch.

Courtney looks up and back, locking eyes with me.

I push my fingers farther into her mouth. "Suck."

CHAPTER 76

COURTNEY

MY EYES ROLL BACK AS I WRAP MY LIPS AROUND Sterling's thick fingers.

My tongue licks along the intrusion, then I do as he says and suck.

His reaction is instant.

The other pair of fingers inside me, the ones shoved deep inside my slit, drag out, then push back in.

In and out.

He mimics the motion in my mouth.

In and out.

My fingernails dig into the wooden siding beneath my palms.

He said he wasn't going to fuck me, and technically he's not, but this might be the best sex I've ever had.

My whole body is lit up with awareness.

In and out.

Fingers drag over my tongue, rub against my G-spot.

I moan and arch my back.

Sterling pushes his fingers deep, then holds them there and groans.

As he holds me in place by my pussy, I feel him bend his knees, lowering himself a few inches.

Then he rocks his hips up.

My eyes roll back.

I can feel the friction of his cock against my ass.

Can feel how if there was no clothing between us, his dick would be snug between my ass cheeks. How he'd be practically fucking me. How easy it would be for him to slip inside me.

He grinds his palm on my clit.

I moan around a mouthful of Sterling and feel more wetness gather between my legs.

Sterling grunts and presses into me harder.

I straighten my arms, locking my elbows so I don't collapse against the cabin.

Then I let my eyes close as I take it.

CHAPTER 77

STERLING

"Fuck." I drop my forehead against her shoulder as I hump her ass.

Courtney swirls her tongue around my fingers, and tightness forms in my balls.

"Fuck," I repeat between my teeth.

I rub my fingers deep inside her channel, reveling in the way she clamps down around me.

She feels like silk against my calloused fingers.

And she's starting to tremble.

I increase my pressure.

And I thrust up harder.

"That's it, Cookie." I rub my palm in a circle over her perfect little bundle of nerves. "Come on my fingers. Give me something to taste."

Her mouth opens as she lets out a whine of need.

I lift my head to watch her profile.

Her arms are shaking as she arches her neck.

Precum leaks out of my tip.

I slide my fingers out of her mouth and down her neck until her perfect tit is filling my palm.

Her bra is thin. Unpadded.

"Sterling," she gasps.

I pinch her nipple. "Call me Mr. Black."

My hips jerk forward.

My fingers rub.

"Mr." She sucks in a breath. "Black."

With my name on her lips, my girl starts to come.

She moans. And arches. And goes up onto her toes.

She tenses. And vibrates. And leans into me as she pulses around my fingers.

My little worker takes me to the edge.

I release her tit to hug her tightly, my hand in her pants still moving, dragging out her orgasm.

I thrust again and again.

Bouncing her body.

My cock grinding into her.

The friction is nearly painful, my thin boxers all that's between me and the back of my zipper.

Then she turns her head and looks at me.

Her eyes are hazy with lust but locked on mine.

"Deeper." Her request is a pant.

I curl my hand, shoving my fingers deeper.

And with her eyes on mine.

With her heat squeezing around me.

I hold her in place, fingers deep inside her pussy, and tip over the cliff.

She gasps, and I lock my mouth over hers.

My cock pulses painfully as she kisses me back.

I come against her ass.

Groaning as I jerk my hips against her.

My abs contract as my balls unload.

Courtney starts to collapse against the cabin, but I keep her in place with my arm around her waist.

She makes another sound as I pull my fingers free from her heat and drag my hand out of her panties.

Lifting my head, I raise my arm and bend it so the inside of my elbow is against the front of her throat.

Then I tip my head forward, sucking my fingers into my mouth.

My cock pulses again, coating the inside of my boxers as Courtney's taste explodes across my tongue.

CHAPTER 78

COURTNEY

"Holy hell." I sag back against Sterling as I watch him suck his fingers clean.

I have never been so ready to go again so soon after, but watching *that*... Pretty sure watching that would make a straight man come.

Sterling groans once more before opening his eyes and sliding his fingers out of his mouth.

"Delicious." His tongue peeks out to slide across his lower lip.

My pussy clenches around nothing.

My heart hops over a beat.

He slowly moves his hands to my shoulders, then turns me to face him. "Time for bed, Miss Kern."

Still breathing heavily, I manage to nod.

Bed is good.

Collapse is moments away.

Sterling dips to pick up the flashlight, then, with a hand on my lower back, he lights the way as we walk around to the front steps.

I try to discreetly button my pants but settle on holding them up with one hand.

I want to say something...

Thank you for the phenomenal orgasm.

You can stuff that big dick in me if you want.

Did you just come in your pants?

But I'm too busy trying to stay upright to ask questions.

When we reach the stairs, I finally lift my head to look up at Sterling.

His eyes are dark, the flashlight in his hand casting shadows over his features.

So I settle on the only thing I can think of to say. "Good night, Sterling."

He watches me for a beat. "Good night, Courtney."

His voice is more gravelly than normal, scraping across my nerves.

I press my lips together, then turn and climb the few steps to my door.

My hand is on the doorknob when he speaks again.

"Oh, and Cookie? I didn't know the bunk was bare."

I turn back to face him, my brow furrowed. "What was that?"

He holds my gaze. "I didn't know the mattress was missing. It was supposed to be in there."

His words crawl through my brain.

He... didn't know?

"It was an oversight and never should have happened."

I blink at him. "You... You didn't do it on purpose?"

He shakes his head. "I'm an asshole, Courtney. But I never would've made you sleep like that. Not ever. I wish you'd told me, but I understand why you didn't. And that's what I'm really sorry about."

My throat tightens as memories and emotions crash into each other.

He didn't know.

He didn't know, and if I'd said something, he would've gotten me one.

Something that feels a lot like relief fills my chest.

I melted under his touch, not knowing if he'd been testing me.

And now I know.

He takes a step back. "Go to bed," he commands for the second time.

Then he turns the flashlight off and disappears into the darkness.

CHAPTER 79

STERLING

Standing in the trees, I wait until Courtney is inside the cabin with the door shut behind her before I walk away.

On the way to my house, I accept two things.

One, for the first time in thirty years, I came in my pants tonight.

And two, a single taste of Courtney is not going to be enough.

Not even close.

I picture her disappearing into the cabin and accept a third truth.

She needs a lock on her door.

One that will accept my master code.

Chapter 80

Courtney

I slump against the door.

How am I still out of breath?

I'd like to blame the elevation. But it's not that.

It's Sterling's hand in my pants.

Sterling's fingers inside my pussy.

His fingers thrusting in and out of my mouth.

It's his grunted words against my ear.

Sterling's hold on my body.

His cock grinding against my ass.

I push away from the door.

I need to get ready for bed immediately.

If I stand here thinking about what just happened—what I just did with *my boss*—I'll either have a mental breakdown, or I'll walk out my door and straight to his, begging for more.

"Go to bed," I tell myself.

I go through the motions.

Stripping out of my clothes, cleaning myself up, pulling on pajamas.

I brush my teeth and undo my braids, my usual style feeling too tight against my scalp on my overstimulated body.

While I wash my face, I inspect my cheeks.

They feel a tiny bit sore from the hold Sterling kept over my mouth, but I don't see any marks. Not yet.

I squeeze my thighs together as I remember the feel of his strong hand holding my sounds in.

I'm not inexperienced. Not a virgin. But I'm not *experienced* either.

My history has been fairly... vanilla.

What happened tonight was *not* vanilla.

It was... rainbow sherbert. Or whatever the opposite of plain is.

And if my inkling is correct, it was only the tip of the iceberg of what Sterling has to offer.

Thinking of all these cold things while standing in a loose T-shirt makes me notice the nip in the air inside my cabin. But I still feel flushed from my *encounter*, so I decide to wait another day before turning the heat on.

Turning the light off in the bathroom, I step into my bedroom.

I stop in front of the bunk.

I didn't know the mattress was missing. It was supposed to be in there.

I never would've made you sleep like that. Not ever.

I reach out and touch the mattress. The new one that was delivered days after Sterling apparently found out I was sleeping on a board.

There are still so many questions.

Like how he found out I didn't have a mattress in the first place.

Clearly, he was in here. There's no other way for him to have found out.

Unless someone else was in here and told him...

I shake away that thought immediately.

We might not have been on speaking terms back then. *Not that we've really spent any time speaking since then either.* But hindsight lets me recognize Sterling's possessive behavior even back then. He may have still wanted me gone, but I don't think he'd let one of the other guys in my place.

So he comes in here to... snoop. Sees the missing mattress. Replaces it with one from some other cabin. And then... decides to buy new mattresses for the whole damn Lodge?

Heaving out a breath, I climb up the step stool and crawl across my new mystery mattress.

If I ever have a full conversation with the man who just worked my body over like a pro, I'll ask him.

But for now—I tug the blankets up to my chin and curl onto my side—I'll let the answers be as much of a mystery as the man himself.

CHAPTER 81

STERLING

I WALK THROUGH MY DARK HOUSE, IGNORING THE staircase that leads up to my bedroom and continuing out through the sliding glass door onto the back deck.

Using Courtney's flashlight, I illuminate the access panel on the side of the hot tub.

After opening it, I loosen some of the connections.

CHAPTER 82

COURTNEY

I SLAP MY PHONE UNTIL THE ALARM STOPS.

My body aches in weird places as I roll onto my back and force my eyes open.

I'm pretty sure I didn't move an inch once I fell asleep last night. Or rather, when I *passed out* the second I closed my eyes.

Last night...

I stretch my arms up over my head, and my forearms protest. Holding myself up against the cabin apparently strained some muscles.

I flex my toes, and my thighs reply with a similar ache.

Lowering my arms, I put my hands over my face.

In the cold light of day, I need to accept that we fucked up.

No matter how good it felt, nothing good can come from messing around with my boss.

The man whose property I live on. Who will be providing me with an income.

I groan.

What was I thinking?

I wasn't.

I wasn't thinking at all. At least not with my brain.

I drop my hands with a shiver and roll out of bed.

Today I'm making better decisions.

And I'm turning on my heat.

Fisher sets his plate down next to mine on the picnic table.

"How goes it?" He drops down onto the bench.

I finish chewing my bite of Italian sub. "It goes."

We have today and tomorrow, and then guests arrive again, so I've been putting my Laundry Cabin to use washing bedding all day.

And I know this schedule because when I made coffee this morning, I found a note on my clipboard. Which was right next to Big Joe, along with my flashlight.

I'd completely forgotten that Sterling had taken the light last night, so of course, when I saw it again, I had to stand there, fanning my face, for three solid minutes while picturing him backing away into the dark.

Once I was done with *the fanning*, I noticed the Post-it stuck to the front page of my clipboard.

> Two days to reset cabins.
> Fix hot tub.

I hadn't even known there was a hot tub. But thankfully, Simpson came in for coffee while I was still staring at the note and told me there was one on the back deck of Sterling's house. And that *the boss* doesn't mind if we use it so long as we put the cover back on it when we're done and don't leave any trash behind.

After that, I went into the cabin I was cleaning and sat on a bunk for another three minutes as I pictured Sterling in a freaking hot tub.

Beads of water trailing down his—

Fisher grunts as he takes a bite of his lunch.

I clear my throat. "You one of the guides again for the next round?"

"Yeah." He chews and swallows. "Think almost every time we have guests for the rest of the year, I'm going out with one of the groups."

I lift my brows. "Guess people like to fish."

He barks out a laugh just as the door opens.

My eyes flit to the entrance just as Sterling steps into the Food Hall.

He's looking right at me. Our eyes are locked. And it reminds me of another moment from last night.

It reminds me of our kiss.

My pulse jumps as I think about the way his lips felt against mine.

Firm and demanding.

But so warm. And so coaxing.

It was short.

I was so turned on I could hardly concentrate.

But it was the best kiss of my life.

My hand starts to lift, to touch my lips, to feel the skin around my mouth—where his beard felt wonderfully scratchy.

My arm jolts as Fisher bumps me with his elbow. "Maybe you can come out with us sometime. Eating fish fry in the woods is about as legit as life can get," my young colleague tells me.

I send a smile to Fisher before glancing back up at Sterling.

His eyes are narrowed, glaring at where Fisher's arm is still touching mine.

I reach for my sandwich, breaking the contact. "Fish fry sounds good." I strive for a casual tone. "But I don't know about sleeping outdoors."

I keep my focus on my food but watch Sterling out of the corner of my eye as he passes by our table.

Fisher uses his sub to wave off my concern, pieces of shredded lettuce falling onto his plate. "Nah, it ain't that bad. Really depends on where you go."

"Like what river you go to?" I ask, not understanding.

He hums around his food. "That too, but I meant like what campsite. Some of them have cabins. Not like ours here. There's no mattresses or nothing." I can feel Sterling approaching, so I keep my gaze down. I don't want to see what expression he's wearing while Fisher talks about sleeping on bare bunks. "But they got four walls, sleep a whole crew, and some even have little wood stoves to keep 'em warm." He shoves another bite into his mouth, muffling his next words. "But there's other sites that are just clearings of bare earth, and we gotta sleep in tents. That's arguably less comfy, even if you're sleeping on those little inflatable pads. Which we use in the cabins too."

"Oh." It's the best reply I can think of.

Fisher chuckles. "You ever been camping, Court?"

I open my mouth to reply, but a plate drops down across from me, startling a squeak out of me.

Fisher snorts. "Easy, Boss. Our girl here is jumpy."

CHAPTER 83

STERLING

FIRST, HE TOUCHED HER.

Now he calls her *our girl*.

I've never been more tempted to kick a kid.

I lower myself onto the bench across from *my girl*.

As irritating as Fisher might be, his idea of bringing Courtney out on a trip has merit.

If I'm on that trip.

And she needs help staying warm at night.

CHAPTER 84

COURTNEY

I HALF EXPECTED STERLING TO BLOW UP WHEN FISHER called me *our girl*. But instead of snarling or glaring or any of the other things I've watched Sterling do, he did nothing.

And it makes a weird sort of unease unfurl in my stomach.

Is he done with me now?

Did he get his taste, and that's all he wanted?

I pick up a potato chip and stare at my plate as I break it in half before eating it.

But really, so what if he's done?

He's my boss. It was fun, but we never should've started... whatever it is that we started.

I eat the second half of the chip.

Good news, he pretty much ignores me around the Lodge anyway, so no one will notice a difference in behavior.

But... The other half of my subconscious pipes up. *He wasn't acting like a man who only wanted to finger you once and call it quits.*

"I'm not taking you inside. Because if I do. I'll fuck you. And I'm not fucking you tonight."

He made it sound like he wanted to. And that he had intentions to *do it* another time. But I still don't understand why he didn't want to fuck me last night.

And *ohmygod why am I being such a crybaby about this?*

It's not just up to Sterling.

I can call it quits too.

This is in my control as much as it's in his.

But then I look up. And I know I'm doomed.

CHAPTER 85

STERLING

Holding Courtney's gaze, I lift my water to my lips.

This is fucking torture.

I knew getting physical with my Cookie would complicate things. That much was obvious. But I hadn't planned for the way my body would ache to touch her.

Hadn't considered how much my blood would boil at not being able to announce her as mine.

And we can't do that.

Not yet.

Possibly not ever.

For both our sakes.

Because I know how guys can be. Even the decent ones. I'll get a pat on the back for *getting some*, while she'll be viewed as the woman sleeping with her boss.

The only way this can come out is if we're officially together.

And I can't do that until I'm certain this is going to last.

The best things never do.

I take another drink of water, those pretty eyes watching me.

She's young. Talented. Smart.

And I don't know what she wants with her future, but I won't be accused of stifling her.

I'll never force her to stay here.

I lower my water bottle.

And if Courtney is still working for me when she decides she's done with *us*, I don't want everyone else to feel like they need to take sides.

I look away from the beauty across from me.

I won't stop pursuing her, but I won't fool myself into thinking this is more than it is.

No matter how much that hurts to admit.

CHAPTER 86

COURTNEY

I INCH MY FOOT FORWARD UNDER THE TABLE.

Something just happened.

Something... *sad* just crossed Sterling's eyes.

"You in?" Fisher asks from beside me.

I turn my head to face him. "Sorry, what?"

"Bunch of us are going to the Inn for drinks tonight. You wanna come?" His brows are lifted. Hopeful.

I've heard them mention this *Inn* before, and a night on the town sounds fun. But... *two hundred dollars in my bank account.* "Thanks, but I'm feeling tired, so I'll stay home—er, here, tonight." My cheeks heat.

This is my home. As much as anywhere has ever been, but I've never called it that in front of someone.

"You sure? Simpson usually heads home early. You could always ride with him." Fisher offers up our coworker.

"I'm sure. But thank you for inviting me."

Fisher sighs, then turns to look at Sterling. "How about you, Boss? Wanna hit the town?"

I do the same as Fisher and look at our boss.

"I have some errands to run." He starts to stand. "But I'll meet you guys there."

Oh.

Sterling picks up his empty plate and turns away from the table.

He's going to the bar.

With the guys.

To hit the town.

I pull in a long inhale through my nose.

None of it means anything.

Not last night. Not the bar. None of it.

What we did was no strings attached.

No promises.

No future.

Just fun.

I pick up another chip.

I can do casual.

I don't watch Sterling put his dishes away.

I don't watch him walk back past our table.

I don't notice the way he looks at me.

I don't do any of that.

Because I'm casual.

Super chill.

No hurt feelings.

Not at all.

CHAPTER 87

STERLING

A FILLED-TO-THE-BRIM DRAFT BEER IS SET DOWN IN front of me.

"Thanks," I tell Jessie, the bartender and sister of the owner.

She lifts a brow as she rests an elbow on the bar. "You can thank me by telling me who pissed in your Cheerios."

I scrunch up my nose as I drag the beer closer. "Thankfully, no one. That's disgusting."

She rolls her eyes. "Sorry, I forgot you were a prude. Let me rephrase. What has your panties in a twist?"

"Dammit, Jessie, I don't want to hear you talking about fucking *panties*." Rocky, owner of Rocky Ridge Inn, settles onto the stool next to me. "If she's being inappropriate, I'll write her up." He turns to me, hand out.

I shake his hand in greeting while Jessie cackles out a laugh.

"Who you gonna write me up to, human resources?" She uses a thumb to gesture to the giant tiger muskie mounted on the wall with HR scrawled beneath it.

The Inn, as everyone calls it, is low key. Gets a little loud on the weekends, but it has the classic dive bar feel, with a limited menu and cheap rooms in the attached motel.

I don't really know how long Rocky has owned this place, but it's been a while.

The man himself is about my size. Tall and broad but probably a decade older.

You wouldn't know it from his build, but his white beard and messy gray hair give him away.

Jessie gets her looks from the other side of their family, slender and dark haired, and she's somewhere around my age.

Rocky sighs. "Never work with family."

The side of my mouth pulls up. "That's a rule I can adhere to."

Jessie, for all her faked attitude, sets a beer down in front of Rocky. "Maybe you can get our boy here in a better mood."

Rocky lifts a brow. "She talkin' about you?"

I shrug and pick up my beer.

Jessie nods in my direction. "Sterling's never been a talker, but his aura of gloom is a bit much tonight."

"I don't have an aura of gloom," I argue. But I'm not convincing. Because I know I do.

Jessie makes a sarcastic sound of agreement before moving down the bar to refill a raised glass.

I take a gulp of my drink, trying to dispel said gloom.

It doesn't work.

I spent all afternoon thinking about Courtney. Wondering if I should've said no to the Inn and spent the evening with her.

Talking.

Fucking.

Both.

But I ended up here anyway because I couldn't decide what was right.

I know I'm not done with her.

I know I'll let this play out until she's ready to move on.

But I don't know if I'm supposed to wait a few days before approaching her again.

She looked a little crestfallen at lunch when I agreed to come out tonight. But she also hadn't acted any differently toward me.

Not that I expected her to save me a seat and bat her lashes at me over the picnic table. But I also didn't expect to walk in and see her acting all buddy-buddy with Fisher.

It only took one minute of hindsight to accept that wasn't on her. That's on my youngest employee. I just can't tell if he's being normal friendly or flirty friendly, and it's testing the boundaries of my sanity.

A part of me can admit it's jealous over how easily Fisher can talk to her. And how easily she seems to respond. Whereas I, a grown-ass man—who comes in his pants while fingering the girl he likes—can't seem to ever find the right words for Courtney.

In one of my weaker moments today, I googled *How long should you wait after sleeping with someone to do it again*?

The answers were inconclusive.

I also didn't know how to deal with the emotions that swept over me when she referred to the Lodge as *home*. But there isn't a good Google search for that.

A hand pulls out the stool on my other side, and Cook sets his beer on the bar before boosting himself up onto the high seat.

Cook picks his beer back up and tips it toward the bar owner. "Evening, Rocky."

Rocky does the same. "Cook. You don't know anything about this gloomy aura Sterling is giving off, do ya?"

Cook hums. "Not exactly a phrase I'd use, but I bet I know the source."

Rocky swivels his stool to face Cook. "Work or woman related?"

I take another drink of beer.

"Why, what an interesting question." Cook swivels to face Rocky.

Stuck in the middle, pretending I'm not here, I down half my glass.

"Oh? Why's that?" Rocky exaggerates his words.

"Because... the answer is both." I can hear the smile in Cook's voice.

"No one likes a snitch," I grumble at Cook, but he ignores me.

"Damn, Sterling." Rocky shakes his head. "You finally sleep with a guest?"

I almost say *I wish*. Because Devil knows it would be easier if it was a here-then-gone guest. But I don't say that. Because from the first moment I saw her, Courtney has ensnared me. And if she was a guest I only had a few days with before she disappeared, she would've haunted my thoughts. Possibly forever.

So complicated or not, this is better.

"Not a guest." Cook answers for me. Then looks around, making sure none of the guys are close, before he leans into my space and lowers his voice. "An employee."

"This that female employee I got wind of?" Rocky glances at me as he asks.

I roll my eyes.

"That's the one." Cook snickers, like I have any other employees I'd be sexually interested in. "Came over from North Carolina, I think."

I lean back since he's practically pressed up against me. "Can you quit acting like you know everything?"

Cook straightens. "You're right. I've just caught you spying on her from the woods and feeling her up under the lunch tables. But what do I know?"

"You're a prick." I mean it, but there's no heat to my tone.

Rocky leans an elbow on the bar. "Now, when you say spying..."

"It's not as bad as it sounds," I answer.

"Nah, it's exactly like it sounds." Cook snorts. "But considering the way she looks at him, I don't think she'd mind. And from the way he's always fucking watching her, I don't think she'd be surprised."

"Huh." Rocky narrows his eyes on me. "You spy on her before or after you started sleeping with her?"

I point at Cook. "I don't *spy* on her. And we aren't sleeping together. It was just..." *Fingering. Grinding. Dry humping.*

I down the rest of my beer.

"If you want my advice." Rocky shrugs the arm not braced against the bar. "I say sleep with her."

I set my empty glass down and give him a *Really?* look. "Good advice."

It's not. But I am going to sleep with her, so technically, I'll be taking it.

"She's a sweet girl." Cook mirrors Rocky's position. "But she's had it rough."

I narrow my eyes on him. "What do you know?"

He shakes his head. "Nothing specific. But even if she didn't show up with all her belongings like some of the guys do, you can just see it. It's in her eyes."

I swallow.

I've seen it too.

Along with the tears I've witnessed and caused.

My stomach churns.

"So you think he shouldn't sleep with her?" Rocky asks.

Cook shakes his head again, slower this time. "No, I think he should. I think he could be good for her. But." He gives me a pointed look. "Sterling needs to get out of his own way and let her in. Because she could be good for him too."

Rocky makes a sound of understanding. "So it's like that?"

Cook nods. "It's like that."

I look back and forth between them. "When did this happen? Why are you two so chummy?"

They ignore me.

"So does this mystery girl have anything to do with the truckload of new mattresses your boss called me about?" Rocky asks Cook.

"That's another good question." Cook turns his attention

back to me. "Care to explain why you ordered the whole Lodge new mattresses a handful of days after Court arrived?"

Because I felt like shit for making her sleep on a motherfucking board for three nights.

"No," I answer instead because there's no way I'm admitting that mistake to anyone. Ever.

"Interesting..." Rocky reaches up and strokes his beard.

"There's a lot of opinions over here for two old single guys." I gripe.

"Old?" Rocky straightens, pulling back his shoulders.

"Yeah, old," I deadpan. "You could be her father."

He smirks. "Don't discount it. Some ladies dig the daddy kink."

Cook cracks up.

I pull a face. "Please don't ever say *daddy* around me again."

He lifts a big shoulder. "Whatever you say."

"I say that's all I can take for the night." I push my stool back. "See you back at the Lodge." I nod to Cook, then point to my glass. "And thanks for the beer."

"What..." He looks at the glass. "Hey!"

I smile as I back away. "Make sure to tip the bartender. Bye, Rocky." Then I turn into the crowd and head toward the door.

There's somewhere else I'd rather be.

CHAPTER 88

COURTNEY

I BLINK AS THE STEAM INTERRUPTS MY VIEW OF THE stars.

It's so quiet out here. So... peaceful.

I close my eyes.

It's obviously been a bit of a rough start, learning to enjoy the outdoors again. But...

I pull in a deep breath of the fresh mountain air.

I could get used to this.

The quiet. The beauty. The change of seasons.

I lift my hand out of the hot tub's heated water and hold it up, letting the night air cool my damp skin.

If Sterling wasn't a consideration, I think I could be happy to work here forever.

I lower my hand back beneath the surface.

What is it about that man that just gets to me?

It's not just his looks. It's his... strength.

His control.

Never in a million years would I have thought I was the type of person who would sleep with my boss.

But it's like my body takes over when he's near.

When he's touching me.

I press my hands to my stomach.

When he pulled me off that ladder and held me against him...I swear my brain chemistry changed.

I've never been handled like that.

And then last night.

We hadn't even kissed, and he had his fingers buried in my pussy and my mouth.

"Suck."

My hands slide lower.

I've been on my own for so long.

I've been independent since before I was ready.

I've been teetering on the edge of desperate for years.

Letting go, giving in to Sterling—Mr. Black, my boss, Sir—was too easy.

Dangerously easy.

My fingers slip beneath the band of my underwear.

I don't have a swimsuit, so I grabbed a matching set of underwear, light green brief-style panties and a non-padded bralette. In case I run into anyone, hopefully I can play it off as a bikini. If they don't look close enough.

Though I have a feeling that anyone looking at all would set Sterling off.

I might not be able to get a solid read on him, but his jealousy always seems to be simmering just beneath the surface.

I stare up at the sky, dragging my hands off my waist and letting my arms float at my sides.

It's been dark for hours, and I have no idea what time the guys will be heading back. So rather than touching myself in Sterling's hot tub, I should get back to my cabin.

I can touch myself there.

Sliding off the seat, I lower myself until my chin is partially submerged, my braids soaking up more water.

I left my clothes and bath towel in a pile on the chair next to the house, a dozen strides away.

The temperature outside keeps dropping, so I need to prepare for the cold by getting myself as hot as possible now.

And I need the guys to go out more often because my muscles feel looser already, and I want to soak in this tub every damn night.

Bracing myself, I exhale and stand.

My thin bra does nothing to block the cold, and my nipples harden. The sensation isn't entirely unpleasant since my body was already primed from thoughts of Sterling.

Careful not to slip, I climb over the edge of the hot tub, reaching my foot down to the steps.

The wood is cold but dry, and I let go of the hot tub as I plant both feet on the deck.

I heave out a breath, watching how it condenses in the night air.

Then the cloud dissipates, revealing the back of Sterling's house.

And the open back door.

And the man standing on the threshold.

CHAPTER 89

STERLING

COURTNEY STANDS FROZEN ON MY DECK.

Her nearly nude form silhouetted against the starry night sky.

And I am a man who is not above temptation.

I step forward.

CHAPTER 90

COURTNEY

HE'S PROWLING TOWARD ME.

I step back.

He doesn't stop.

I can't catch my breath.

He's nearly on me.

I bump into the hot tub.

Sterling doesn't say a word.

He doesn't have to.

The consequences don't matter.

Not at night.

Not like this.

With my heart pounding behind my ribs, I tip my head back.

And he slams his mouth down against mine.

CHAPTER 91

STERLING

COURTNEY PARTS HER LIPS, AND I PUSH MY TONGUE into her mouth.

Our kiss last night was too short.

We were both too distracted.

But right now, in this moment, I'm fucking focused.

Feeling her tongue against mine.

Feeling the scrape of her teeth.

Feeling the vibrations of her moan.

Tasting her.

I reach down and grip her ass. Her practically bare ass. And I lift her.

Her hands claw at my shoulders until I set her down on the edge of the hot tub, then she wraps them around my neck.

Heat rolls off her skin. Off her tongue.

I pull back enough to look down.

The light from the moon sparkles across her form.

Her soft, pale form.

I groan and slide my hands up her sides, slipping my fingers in the front of her thin bra and pulling down.

When her glorious tits spill out, I groan again.

My fingers grip. Feel. Pinch.

Courtney gasps, and I seal my mouth to hers again.

She clings to me tighter as I roll her nipples between my fingers.

She's so... tender. So ripe.

And then her knees spread.

And I step closer.

CHAPTER 92

COURTNEY

STERLING WEDGES HIS HIPS BETWEEN MY THIGHS, AND I moan into his mouth.

He returns the sound, his hands dropping from my breasts.

I arch my back, wanting his touch back.

But then something presses against my core, my panties all that's between my pussy and his hand.

His thumb strokes up my entrance.

I break the kiss to gasp in a breath.

Staring into his eyes, I expect him to reach for the front of his jeans.

Expect him to undress.

Need him to take his cock out.

But he slides his hands to my thighs and lowers to his knees.

CHAPTER 93

STERLING

COURTNEY CLUTCHES AT THE FLANNEL COVERING MY shoulders, holding onto me to keep her balance on the edge of the hot tub.

When my knees connect with the hard deck, I shuffle forward and push her thighs wider apart.

Then, with my eyes locked on hers, I lean forward and place my open mouth over her pussy. Licking the length of her seam.

Her fingers twist in my shirt as her mouth drops open in a silent cry.

I smile against her.

I can taste the chlorine from the hot tub, but I can taste *her* too. Her slickness has soaked through her wet panties.

I lick again.

Her breaths are loud in the night.

Pressing my nose against her mound, I close my eyes and inhale.

I recognize the scent from the panties I stole.

I inhale again.

Heaven.

I sit back and pull the fabric covering her pussy to the side, exposing her to me.

233

"Sterling." She gasps my name.

My cock throbs in my jeans, and I know if I'm not careful, I'm going to come in my pants again.

I lean in. "Hold on to me."

She starts to say something, but I push a finger inside her channel, and her words turn to groans.

Her thighs try to close, but I keep them open with my shoulders as I close my mouth over her clit and suck.

CHAPTER 94

COURTNEY

STARS EXPLODE IN MY VISION, AND I TOSS MY HEAD back.

The motion causes me to tip, but before I can fall into the water, a big hand presses against my back, angling me forward again.

Sterling's mouth never leaves my core.

He keeps lapping. Sucking. Circling.

I grip the fabric of his shirt tighter and curl forward.

The hand on my back returns to my thigh, keeping me spread.

I can't stop my sounds.

Can't stop the way I keep tugging him closer.

Can't stop the buildup inside me as he devours me.

As Sterling *eats me*.

My thighs start to quiver.

My core starts to clench.

"Sterling." My pussy squeezes around the finger he has buried inside me. "I'm... I'm so close."

He moans, pressing his face harder against my body.

Then he flattens his tongue against my clit. Pressing. Rubbing.

And I can't hold back anymore.

Sterling licks the orgasm out of me. Holding me tight as my body convulses. As I soak his tongue.

CHAPTER 95

STERLING

My cock is painfully hard as I slide my finger out of Courtney's pussy and lick my lips clean.

Her head is hanging down, her back rising and falling as she tries to catch her breath.

Standing, I grip Courtney's sides and lift her off the edge of the hot tub, setting her feet on the deck.

Her hands move to my sides, balancing herself.

With my hold on her, I can feel the shiver that runs through her body.

Sure she won't collapse, I let go of her and make quick work of the buttons on my shirt.

She lifts her head and watches me shrug my flannel off, lifting her hands from my sides to allow me to remove my shirt.

I drape the flannel, warm from my body, over her shoulders.

Courtney looks up at me as she threads her arms through the sleeves.

Then her hands move... to the front of my jeans.

I grip her wrists, but she doesn't stop, her fingers working on the button.

"Courtney." I say her name sternly.

I didn't do what I just did so she'd return the favor.

But then she looks up into my eyes as she drags my zipper down. "I need to see it."

Fuck.

I clench my jaw.

She blinks those long lashes. "Please."

I loosen my hold on her wrists.

And she goes to her knees.

CHAPTER 96

COURTNEY

I drag the front of Sterling's jeans down, my fingers catching in his boxers, bringing them with.

The base of his dick is the first thing I see.

I lean forward and press a kiss to it.

Strong fingers wrap around my braids, and the tug on my scalp is divine.

He holds me in place, and I open my mouth, licking the inch of flesh I can reach.

Sterling groans and tilts his hips.

With my face pressed against his body, I pull his clothing down more.

And more.

Until his cock is free and pressing against my neck.

I grip it with both hands.

It feels hot to the touch. And so hard. So thick. Longer than my stacked hands.

I let out a sound of urgency.

And he uses my braids to pull my head back.

I look up at him, holding his cock an inch from my mouth.

His gaze is full of fire.

Promising everything I need.
I part my lips and stick my tongue out.
He thrusts forward.

Chapter 97

Sterling

Her lips close around my cock, and my balls squeeze, giving Courtney her first taste.

She moans. And the pressure of her swallowing nearly does me in.

I use her braids to pull her back off my cock.

"Eyes up here." My voice is gravel.

Courtney opens her eyes, mouth still open, one hand on the base of my cock, the other braced against my thigh.

I memorize the view.

"I'm going to work my cock into your throat." I warn her, and she pants out a breath. "If you need air, tap my hip." Her eyes are so bright as she stares up at me. "Tell me you understand."

"I understand, Sir." Her breath is hot against my tip.

"That's my good girl." I tighten my hold on her braids. "Now, breathe through your nose."

I drag her mouth onto my dick as I push my hips forward.

Courtney's eyes water as her throat convulses around me.

She's untutored.

Unable to deep throat.

And her innocence spurs me on.

Her eyes roll back as I retreat, then push back in.

She lets go of my cock and holds onto my thighs with both hands.

She pulls in air through her nose.

She chases my dick with her tongue when I pull out.

She fucking undoes me.

Then she moans. And when she blinks up at me, I watch a tear roll down her cheek.

And I come.

I hold her in place, watching her eyes widen as my cock pulses, filling her mouth with my release.

I let go of one braid and grip my dick as I pull out past her lips.

The next pulse splashes against her throat.

I tug her head back with my other hand.

The next and the next coat her exposed tits.

The last of my release drips down her stomach.

It's lude.

Vulgar.

And the hottest fucking thing I've ever seen.

Kneeling before me is the curvy goddess of my dreams, covered in my lust, gaze full of satisfied wonder.

I bend down and kiss her.

My taste is on her lips.

And it feels like ownership.

CHAPTER 98

COURTNEY

My eyes close as Sterling kisses me softly, his tongue lightly caressing mine.

My mouth still tastes like his release. And it makes this kiss... more.

More real.

More intense.

More devastating.

He brushes his thumb across my cheek, then he moves his hands to grip me under my arms.

Sterling rests his forehead against mine, breaking the kiss, before he lifts me.

My feet tingle as they once again press against the deck. And my knees ache from kneeling on the wood. But I've never felt sexier, standing here in my underwear and Sterling's flannel, with streaks of *him* all over my body.

Stepping away, he crosses the deck and grabs my towel.

I hold my hand out, but instead of giving it to me, he reaches past me to dip the edge in the water, then uses the warm, wet corner of the towel to clean me off.

Dragging it over my breasts. Across my stomach.

He wets it again, then even more gently wipes it up my neck. Across my chin.

It's sweet.

Familiar.

Caring.

But then the sound of tires on gravel reaches us. And I know the moment is over.

CHAPTER 99

STERLING

I DROP THE TOWEL AND REACH FOR THE FLANNEL, buttoning the sides together. "It's cold. I shouldn't have kept you out here so long."

Her tits are still hanging out of her bra, but pulling the damp material back into place feels too intimate right now, so I cover them with my shirt.

Courtney opens her mouth, probably to deny being cold, but then she trembles.

"Shit," I curse and do the buttons faster.

But then she lets out a light laugh that hits me square in the throat.

My fingers pause, and I look up from the buttons to take in her features.

She's smiling.

At me.

I let go of the shirt and palm her cheeks.

Then I kiss her.

Because I can't do anything else.

Her lips melt against mine.

Courtney was smiling at me.

Giving me one of her laughs.

She gave me that moments after being the sexiest thing I've ever seen.

I shift forward, pressing our bodies together and forcing her to tip her head back.

Her lips pull up even as I still have mine pressed against hers.

She's smiling again.

She's too good for me.

Loud laughter filters through the forest.

Either the guys are taking a detour, or they're just being extra loud, but either way, I need to get Courtney to her cabin before anyone sees her like this.

Heaving out a breath, I break the kiss and step back. "Sorry. I couldn't help it."

Courtney presses her lips together, like she's trapping in another laugh. "No apology needed." She wraps her arms around herself. "But if you could hand me my pants, my legs are getting a little cold."

"Right." I turn and find them, then hand them to Courtney. "I'd like to walk you back, but I should go through the house to head off anyone who might be drunk wandering."

Courtney nods and bites down on the start of another smile.

"What?" I ask.

Her smile wins. "You, um, might want to put your dick away."

I look down.

My torso is bare. My jeans are undone. And my dick is hanging out the front of my pants, half hard from the kiss we just shared.

I look back up to her. "You don't think this is a good look?"

Courtney snorts, then slaps a hand over her mouth.

I shake my head, my own lips pulling into a smile. "Put your pants on."

CHAPTER 100

COURTNEY

MY LEGS ARE DRY, HAVING BEEN OUT OF THE HOT TUB long enough, so it's easy to pull my thin sleep pants on. My underwear still feels damp, but I'll take those off as soon as I get back to my cabin.

Sterling struggles a bit to get himself tucked away, making me smile all over again.

Palms on my cheeks.

Lips against mine.

My smile fades, just a bit.

His reaction to my laugh was so... heartbreaking.

He looked so... surprised.

And not just surprised. Completely caught off guard.

Like he'd witnessed a rainbow in the middle of a blizzard.

I swallow, fighting down the urge to go to him. To smile at him again.

Sterling has been a gruff man since day one.

A hard man to get along with.

A closed-off man.

And I always just attributed it to his nature.

That he was just like that.

But...

I swallow again.

Maybe he wasn't always that way.

Sterling looks up at me, his mouth half turned up. And it's like he's a whole different person than the one I know.

His half smile starts to slip.

And it's my turn to close the distance between us.

His eyes heat.

He reaches for me as I place my hands on his bare chest.

His muscles tense under my touch, and I witness a full-mouth smile on Sterling's handsome face as he jolts.

"Your hands are fucking freezing."

I automatically start to pull them away, but his palm against the back of my neck holds me in place.

"Warm me up with another kiss," he demands, his lips an inch from mine. "Then go to bed before I take more."

I'm tempted to tell him he can take as much as he wants. But something stops me.

Something in my chest that tells me not to rush this.

That there's no need to rush this.

That, *please, gods, don't let me ruin everything by rushing this.*

The hand on my neck flexes as I close my eyes and push up onto my tiptoes.

Sterling moans against my lips.

And I feel his other hand drag down the length of my braid.

I open.

He takes.

We're making up for the lack of kissing last time. And his taste is familiar to me now.

Familiar and addicting.

We pull back at the same time.

My fingertips drag down his bare skin, feeling the rough chest hair that I fantasized about touching after seeing him that very first time. When his flannel was undone and his body was on display.

I slide my hands down to his sides.

I want to move them around to his back.

I want to hug him.

But I take a step back.

Not tonight.

Not when I need to hurry away.

My hands drop away from his body. "Good night, Sterling."

His fingers release my braid. "Sweet dreams, Courtney."

Scooping up the rest of my clothes, I slip my feet into my shower sandals.

I take the few steps off Sterling's back deck to the ground, and when I'm about to enter the woods, I look back.

Sterling is still there.

Shirtless in the moonlight.

Watching me.

And with a sense of safety I'm not used to, I step into the dark.

CHAPTER 101

STERLING

COURTNEY DISAPPEARS INTO THE WOODS, AND I CAN'T separate the feelings inside me.

The soft feelings are twisted together with feelings of hesitation. With the feeling that this is temporary.

But I don't want to be that person.

I don't want to be the surly man who grows old and dies alone in the woods because he won't give anyone a chance.

I won't be that man.

Grabbing Courtney's towel off the deck, I head back inside.

When I got home earlier, my plan was to go up to my bedroom and stare down at Courtney's cabin to see if I could tell if she was awake or not.

But then I paused by the back door, the steam from the uncovered hot tub catching my attention.

And like a mirage in the desert, the steam parted and there she was.

My Courtney, sitting in my hot tub.

It was exactly what I'd hoped for when I fucked with the wiring behind the panel.

Even though I'd stopped counting on hope a long time ago.

But I should've known better.

Courtney tips everything on its head.

Stepping back into my house, I shut the sliding door behind me, the heated air of my home prickling against my cold skin.

I watched her for too long. Unsure if I should join her or let her be. Until she stood up.

God damn.

When she stood up, I nearly groaned out loud.

My pretty little worker, using my hot tub in nothing but her underwear.

I head toward my stairs before I remember I'm supposed to be making sure the guys stay away from the Laundry Cabin.

Changing direction, I snag an extra flannel I left hanging off a dining room chair and shrug it on.

I'll do my job now, but before I go to bed, I'm ordering Courtney the smallest, skimpiest, easiest-to-remove bikini I can find.

CHAPTER 102

COURTNEY

A BRANCH CREAKS OFF TO MY SIDE, DEEPER INTO THE woods.

I hug my clothes tighter to my chest. "Lady Bear, if that's you, I'll be out of your forest in ten more steps."

My heart leaps, but I force myself not to run.

"Five more steps."

I swear I hear a huff.

Two steps.

Okay, I might run up the stairs.

And I might trip on my flip-flops.

But I wrench the door open and get inside before I hear any more signs of Lady Bear or Sasquatch or anything else that hopefully can't open a round door handle.

The light I left on illuminates the room, and I give Spike a sheepish look as I drop my laundry in front of the washer. "Don't judge me."

As I move through the cabin, stripping down to nothing, I realize that it's just as cold in here as it is outside.

"What the hell?" I stick a washcloth under the running sink water. "Sorry, Spike. I thought you were side-eyeing me for giving my boss a blow job." I quickly scrub my skin, getting the rest of what Sterling missed earlier, as I stick my head out of the bathroom and talk to my cactus. "But you were just cold."

Ideally, I'd shower off the chlorine clinging to my skin, but with *mystery creature* outside, I don't plan on hiking to the bathrooms tonight. So I wet down the cloth again and do a quick once-over under my boobs and where my waterlogged bra was clinging to me.

Shivering, I hang the washcloth over the faucet, then grab Sterling's flannel and pull it back on.

It's a little damp where my bra was across my back, but the comfort it brings me is worth it.

I button it as I move into my bedroom.

Looking like an idiot, I button it all the way up to my neck, then flip the collar up. For warmth.

And if that means I can turn my head and sniff the collar, smelling Sterling's scent... so be it.

I tug on a pair of sweatpants, then shuffle back out of the room to the thermostat next to the front door.

I frown.

It's on.

The heat is set.

The little screen is working. Showing that it's... fifty-nine degrees in the cabin.

"Well, fuck."

I fiddle with the settings, then get on the floor and crawl under the table to put my ear next to the baseboard heater.

Not a sound.

"That's probably not good."

Crawling backward until I clear the table, I shift onto my butt and use my phone to google possible issues.

Ten minutes later, with the small metal panel removed from the end of the heater, I accept that I'm fucked.

Sometime since the previous winter, when the heater was last used, some small creature got in here and chewed the wires. Which are hardwired into the unit and way above my pay grade.

And from what I can tell, it costs just as much to have an electrician repair this as it does to just install a new unit.

I bite down on my lip.

The cost is... It's too much.

Anywhere from four hundred to twelve hundred dollars.

And I have two hundred to my name.

Fighting the urge to cry, I stand and pull Spike off the windowsill.

"Promise I'll figure this out," I tell her. Then I place her on top of the counter over the dryer. "This will help in the meantime." I twist my discarded sleep pants around her, gently resting the material on top of her spines.

I go back to the thermostat and turn it off.

I don't know if there's a risk of fire or if turning it off even mitigates that risk completely, but it makes me feel like I'm doing something.

Back in my bedroom, I pull on my thickest socks and I drag my sweatshirt on over Sterling's flannel before climbing into bed.

Lying in the dark, I run through the list of *should I or shouldn't I.*

I should tell Sterling because it's his building on his property.

I shouldn't tell Sterling because he wouldn't have to fix the heat if I wasn't staying here.

I should tell him because I think he would want to know.

I shouldn't tell him because he'll feel obligated to fix it. And then he'll spend lots of money on something that's just for me, and that makes me feel weird. Especially since I'm already dependent on him for a place to live. And for the money I'm earning. And because even at the end of the month, when I get my first paycheck, I still won't be able to afford to live anywhere else.

I shouldn't tell him.

Another shiver runs through me, and I pull the blankets up to my nose.

I can ask one of the guys if there's a space heater available. Keep it on the down-low.

I just need it warm enough so the water pipes don't freeze.

Once I get paid, I can get my own heater. Maybe a heated blanket too.

Closing my eyes, I snuggle deeper under my bedding.

If Sterling extends my work past December, I'll probably have enough money to fix the heat.

And if he doesn't...

I roll onto my side.

It's still October.

That's future Courtney's problem.

I have enough to worry about. There's no use getting ahead of myself.

A GASP BURSTS OUT OF ME WHEN MY ALARM STARTS beeping.

Still on my side, my hands are under my chin, but instead of being gently clasped, they're clenched together painfully.

I reach out for my phone and groan because everything aches —giving me flashbacks to my first morning here when my body hurt from sleeping on the board.

But today, the groan hurts my throat too. And it only takes another moment for the throbbing in my head to make itself known. Only this time, my maladies have nothing to do with my mattress.

I pull my arm back under the blanket.

It's so fucking cold in here.

I knew the heat wasn't working last night, but I underestimated how fast the temperature would drop inside the cabin.

And going to bed with wet hair probably didn't help.

"Fuck," I croak. I instantly regret it because talking hurts worse than groaning.

I press my lips together, breathing through my nose.

I can't get sick right now.

My multivitamin has betrayed me.

I want nothing more than to go back to sleep, but I need to get up.

And drink water.

And take the hottest shower I can stand.

If I had any sort of medicine, I'd be taking that too. But a bag of tea is about as close as I can get.

Maybe there's some honey in the Food Hall I can steal.

With careful movements, I climb out of my bunk.

And that's when I realize the blankets were trapping a lot more heat than I was giving them credit for.

Keeping all my layers on, I grab my backup towel—since my other one is either still on Sterling's deck or in his house.

Before I step out the door, I pause and grab Spike, pants and all, off my counter.

No need for both of us to suffer.

"I'll be back, I promise." I adjust Spike's position on the counter in the women's restroom.

Guests are coming tomorrow, but on the off chance anyone comes in here, I can't imagine they'd disturb Spike.

"This is better than the cabin," I reassure her while pressing my fingers against my throat.

It's an assumption because I'm too lazy to look it up. But I think it has to be better for a desert plant to be in a warm, humid room than a dry, freezing one.

With a final wave, I leave Spike and hurry back down the path to my cabin.

It's supposed to be sunny today, and hopefully that will warm things up, but I need to dig through my boxes for my hair dryer. Because if I walk around all morning with wet hair in this frigid weather, I just might perish.

CHAPTER 103

STERLING

I PACE THE LENGTH OF MY KITCHEN FOR THE FIFTH time, two mugs of coffee in hand.

Mine and hers.

I stop and stare down at the drinks.

What am I doing?

I don't know how she takes her coffee.

And I can't just randomly start bringing one of my six employees coffee in the morning. Not to mention this particular employee is the one who makes coffee for everyone every day.

Big Joe.

I almost smile thinking about the jealousy that stormed through me when I thought she was talking about a man.

It was obviously misplaced, but the jealousy was real.

The way I feel about her is real.

A growl builds in my chest.

This is my property. My business. *My Courtney.*

I should be able to do whatever I want.

Considering the two coffees, I decide I can be subtle.

Lifting the mug filled with my black coffee, I chug it down, the hot liquid scorching its way down my throat. Then I pull open the cupboard next to the sink, take down one of my insulated Black Mountain Lodge travel tumblers, and pour the lighter, sweeter brew inside.

With the lid secured, no one will be able to tell it's not my usual drink.

Satisfied with my sneakiness, I stride out of my house, ready to see what my little worker is up to.

AFTER GETTING SIDETRACKED BY FUCKING EVERYONE, I finally spot Courtney walking between two of the cabins.

She's weighted down with a huge pile of bedding, tilting to the side, and wearing a maroon winter hat pulled low on her head.

I stand still, watching her, lifting the cup of coffee to my mouth. Before I remember it's her coffee and... I don't have to watch from a distance anymore.

I can touch her now.

Grinning, I stride toward her.

Then I pick up my pace to a jog when she stumbles.

She's at the steps of the next cabin when I reach her.

"Courtney," I say quietly as I scoop the pile of sheets out of her grasp with one arm. "Make more trips."

"Huh? Oh, sure." She sounds confused.

I lower the bundle so I can see her pretty face. And I frown. "What's wrong?"

"Hm?" Her brows lift. "Nothing. I'm fine."

She's not fine.

She's pale.

And a sheen of sweat coats her cheeks, even though she's wearing that hat like she's freezing.

The temp has definitely dropped in the last twenty-four hours, but it's not as bad as all that right now.

Courtney starts up the stairs to the next cabin before I can stop her.

And that's when I see the flannel.

My ribs flex around my heart.

Below her sweater is *my* flannel.

She's still wearing it.

She's... disappearing into the cabin.

"Shit."

I climb the steps in two strides and find her already pulling bedding off one of the mattresses.

I drop the bundle I took from her onto the ground. "Cookie, stop for a second."

I hate that she thought I called her Cookie for bad reasons. Fucking despise it. But I've thought of her as my Cookie for too long already and can't stop.

Plus, it usually gets a reaction. And I need her attention.

She sucks in a breath, like I startled her. As if she didn't expect me to follow her in.

Moving to her side, I place a hand on Courtney's shoulder and turn her to face me.

She wavers.

I set the coffee down on the top beam of the bunk, then grip her other shoulder.

"You're not feeling well." I make it a statement.

She tries to shrug, but it's more of a tremble. "I'm fine."

I shake my head. "You're not fine. And I mean this in the nicest way..." I let go with one hand and tug the front edge of her hat up, giving me a better view of her bloodshot eyes. "You look like you feel terrible."

She huffs, then covers her mouth with her hand as it turns into a cough.

My shoulders droop.

She looks miserable.

"Why didn't you tell me?" I murmur as I pull her hat up higher and place the back of my hand on her forehead.

"I'm fine." Her voice sounds painful.

She feels warm, but I don't know if it's a fever or if it's from her hat.

"You need to go back to bed," I tell her.

Courtney shakes her head. "We have guests tomorrow."

I drop my hand from her forehead and cup her cheek. "I'll get the guys to help. We'll take care of it."

She shakes her head again. "I can do it."

I match her movement. "No. You can't. You're sick."

"But..." Her chest rises with deep breaths, like she's exhausted from talking. "I..." Her eyes lower. "I can't skip a day."

"Skip a day?" I don't understand.

I feel the movement in her cheek as she swallows. "I can't afford to skip a day."

My brows furrow.

I can't afford to skip a day.

My brows furrow more.

Does she think...

"Courtney." Her eyes stay lowered. "Courtney, eyes up here."

I don't want to talk about pay with her. I don't want the stark reminder of our boss-employee situation. But I need her to understand how things work around here.

A long moment passes before she meets my gaze.

But when she does, I wish she hadn't.

It's my turn to swallow.

The fucking emotion in her eyes.

I swallow again.

It's the look of someone who doesn't want to do something but knows they have to.

The look of someone pushing through because they have no other choice.

It's that look of fucking defeat that I've seen her try to hide before.

And it's killing me.

"I'm not going to dock your pay for resting when you're sick." My voice is quieter than I meant it to be.

"I just... Maybe if I just take a nap. I'll—"

"No." I can't stand to hear her say anything else. "You will stay in bed. Take some cold medicine. Drink your water. And stay in bed until tomorrow. And if you're still not feeling well, you'll stay in bed tomorrow too."

She's watching me like she's trying to find the trick. "But the guests..."

"The guests will be fine," I reassure her.

Her gaze drops to my chest. "And it won't affect my pay?"

Courtney blackmailing me to keep this position.

Her double-checking that the Food Hall lunch was included.

Courtney crying after Fisher told her we get paid at the end of the month.

Her crinkled cash for the Costco meal she ate.

"It won't affect your pay." My words come out as a whisper. "I promise."

"Okay." Her voice is small. "And you'd do that for anyone?"

I nod.

I nod because my throat feels too tight.

Because I feel like a fucking asshole.

My girl, my employee, is standing here, working through illness, because she doesn't want to lose a single day of pay.

And even as I'm telling her to rest, she's asking me if I'd do this for everyone. Because she doesn't want special treatment.

I just fucking can't.

I slide my hand from her cheek to the back of her hat-covered head and pull her into my body.

Courtney tenses.

I hold her tighter.

Then I feel her back hitch through a breath before she wraps her arms around my middle.

Her body shakes again as she inhales.

"Fuck." I hold her firmly against me with one hand and run the other up and down her spine.

We stand there, holding each other for several quiet moments as she slowly relaxes into me, her fingers loosening their grip on the back of my shirt.

"Courtney…" It feels awkward to say this, but I think she's crying, and I can't take her fucking crying. "If you need money…"

Courtney pulls back, already shaking her head. "Please don't finish that sentence." She wipes at her cheeks even as she forces herself to look up at me. "I'm fine. I mean, I feel crappy enough that it's making me cry a little. But I'm fine. I just…" She brushes away another tear, like they're no big deal. "I earn my way. I don't want any favors."

I nod my head once. Because I get it.

I don't like it. But I get it.

"Is there anything else I can do? Anything you need?"

Courtney, of course, shakes her head. Asking for nothing.

"Alright." I let my hands slip from her body. "Go to bed. I'll finish up here."

She glances around. "If you're sure."

I don't miss the way she reaches out to touch the bed frame to steady herself.

"Want me to walk you back?"

"No." She turns down my offer.

I want to argue.

Demand she let me carry her.

But I can't do that with the rest of my employees milling around the property.

"Fine. But go right to bed."

She makes a sound of agreement, and then I uneasily watch as she exits the cabin.

I'll check on her soon.

Chapter 104

Courtney

Embarrassment and unwellness swirl inside me as I shuffle down the path.

I can't believe I cried in front of Sterling.

Again.

I reach up with the cuff of my sweater and wipe away another traitorous tear.

It's just because I don't feel good.

I glance down at the damp fabric and wince.

Sterling's flannel is peeking out beneath my sweater. Everywhere.

He must think...

I brush at my other cheek.

I have no idea what he must think of me.

The negative part of me wants to focus on the bad.

Like the fact that he, my boss, has seen me cry more than once.

Or the fact that he knows I'm broke.

I start to choke on a laugh and press my palm to my throat.

I thought I'd been mortified before, but him offering me money. That was a new low.

He meant well.

Said it because he wanted to help.

But I'm not a charity case.

Pretty fucking close, my inner self points out, but I ignore her.

So yeah, Sterling probably thinks I'm a helpless girl on the edge of despair.

Not exactly wrong.

But he also looks at me like he wants me.

And that might hold more weight than the rest of it.

Maybe.

Hopefully.

I stumble up my steps and into my cabin.

The temperature inside is basically the same as outside, but maybe it's not so bad.

As I shuffle to my bed, I pull all the curtains open.

At this point, the sunlight isn't going to be enough to keep me awake, and maybe it will heat the place by a few degrees.

Leaning against the bunk, I paw at my laces until I can kick my boots off.

I put my hand on the step stool to climb into bed but pause long enough to strip off my work pants and replace them with my sweats.

Leaving the rest of the layers on, I finally flop onto my mattress.

It's firmer than I remember, but it's not enough to keep me awake.

Eyes closing, my last thought is of Sterling.

And the way he hugged me.

CHAPTER 105

STERLING

I SLAM THE DRYER CLOSED AND HIT START.

All the beds are made in the guest cabins.

The guys helped me get everything sorted, and I washed the dirty bedding in my laundry room so I wouldn't disturb Courtney. But now it's well past dark, and I haven't seen her since this morning.

She didn't come out for lunch, and I never got to give her the coffee I made.

With the final load of sheets going, I grab a can of beef stew out of my pantry.

I know chicken noodle is the typical sick nourishment, but this is the only flavor I have.

I'm a simple man.

A man not prepared for caretaking.

The can weighs heavy in my hand as I walk the trail to the Laundry Cabin.

With Courtney's darkened windows in sight, I start to second-guess myself.

There are no lights on in the cabin, and I don't want to wake her, but I need to get my eyes on her. Just to make sure she hasn't gotten worse.

As I open her front door, I remember the new lock I have sitting on my kitchen table.

I'll install that tomorrow.

The door opens with a quiet creak, but silence greets me.

I step inside and kick my boots off.

I told myself I would just check on her. But I know I'll stay for a while.

There's no way for me to stop myself.

The curtains are all open, letting in enough dim moonlight to light my way.

I'm halfway to the bedroom when I realize how fucking cold it is in here.

The air feels as chilled as it did outside, and the floorboards are freezing beneath my sock-covered feet.

Stopping, I go back to the thermostat by the front door and use my phone to illuminate the unit.

It's off.

What the fuck?

I push the tab from *off* to *heat*.

Nothing happens.

I seem to recall some rattling last time I turned this unit on. But maybe I'm misremembering.

Sighing, I turn back toward the bedroom. This is probably why she got sick.

Was it not bad enough that she slept on a damn board already? Now she's self-sacrificing by sleeping in a damn frozen room.

The form in the bed doesn't appear to stir as I enter the bedroom, but when I get closer, I can see she's shivering.

"Courtney?" I whisper.

She doesn't react.

I stand in indecision for a minute, unsure if it's the right call to wake her—to see how she's feeling—or let her sleep to get better.

Her body trembles again.

"Dammit," I huff.

I'm annoyed with myself for not bringing more than a can of fucking stew. But I didn't know what else to do. And I didn't count on the heat being off.

Stepping up to the edge of the bunk, I place a hand on the mattress and lean over Courtney's sleeping body.

She's curled up on her side, facing away from me, blankets up to her damn nose.

"Court—" I trail off as I place my other hand on the mattress beside the first.

Why does this mattress feel so fucking hard?

I lift and lower my palms, checking the firmness.

Christ.

I grit my teeth.

It's so cold in here the memory foam has gone hard.

Does she think I wouldn't allow her to turn the fucking heat on?

She's the damn maintenance person. I know she knows how to work a thermostat.

I grip her shoulder with one of my hands and give her a gentle shake. "Courtney."

She groans and tries to shrug me off.

"Cookie." I raise my voice louder.

"What?" she grumbles, not moving otherwise.

"You gotta turn the heat on, Honey. You'll freeze to death." *Honey? I've never called someone Honey in my fucking life.*

"Doesn't..."

I can't catch the second word.

"What was that?" I lean closer.

"It doesn't work." She's hard to understand, still half asleep.

"The heat doesn't work?" I clarify.

She grunts a reply.

I glance back toward the main room. "The thermostat was off."

This time her groan sounds annoyed. "I know," she tries to snap but is still too groggy. "I didn't want a fire."

"A fire?" She tries to pull the blankets up over her head, but I move my hand from her shoulder and grip the fabric so she can't. "What are you talking about, Cookie?"

"The cords are chewed up," she murmurs like she's falling back asleep. "Too expensive. Can't afford one."

Can't afford one?

The fuck?

"That's not for you to worry about." Barbed wire twists around my rib cage. What the hell is she talking about saying it's *too expensive*? "I'll fix it, Courtney. It's my responsibility."

She makes a sound in the back of her throat. "...a burden."

I close my eyes.

I couldn't make out the first part of what she said.

But I didn't need to hear it.

I could feel it.

"You're not a burden," I whisper as those barbs scrape across bone. "You're never that, Little Worker."

But her breathing has changed, her body relaxing again into sleep, so she can't hear me.

I lower my head to her shoulder and rest it there.

If this woman doesn't strangle me through sexual tension, she's going to drown me in guilt.

She's here freezing herself and literally sick because she thinks it's too expensive to fix the fucking heater.

Because she thought she'd have to pay for it?

Because she felt like a burden.

Because she's felt like a burden before.

I rock my head back and forth.

If she was in the Bunk House, she wouldn't feel this way. Because the heat would be for everyone. But she's here. Alone.

The only one in the cabin. The only one using the heat.

Anger with myself floods my system.

She's suffering, again, because I singled her out.

But she's sure as shit not moving into the fucking Bunk House, so she's just going to have to deal with it.

Or she could move into the main house with me.

I stay there, bent over, head on her shoulder, for far too long with that idea crawling around in my brain.

I want that.

I want her with me. Badly.

But that would single her out even more. And it would out the fact that I'm not only treating her differently. I'm sleeping with her.

And I will be sleeping with her.

That wire tightens even further, my chest constricting.

Last night, after we left my back deck, I went to my nice, warm bed, and she slept like this.

On a hard mattress in a cold room.

I couldn't've known.

I tell myself that, try to convince myself of that. But these cabins are my responsibility.

I should have known.

When I assigned her the Laundry Cabin, as a way to purposefully isolate her, as a way to try to make her quit, I should have checked.

If I had checked, she never would've slept on that fucking board.

She never would've slept in the cold.

She never would've gotten sick.

It's my fault.

All of it.

And I need to fix it.

A shiver runs through Courtney, and I straighten.

I can't change the past, but I can help her now.

Striding back to the main room, I close the curtain over the bedroom doorway, then flip on the light.

I'll give her some medicine now so she can sleep through the night.

The more restful sleep she can get, the quicker she'll recover.

Moving around the room, I pull the curtains closed. They

aren't blackout, but I don't want the sun waking her up tomorrow.

As I'm tugging on the curtain above the crappy table, I pause.

Where's that little cactus?

I glance around the room, not seeing it anywhere.

A question for another day.

Curtains closed, I look at her little setup on the counter. She has the electric teakettle, but I don't see any tea. Or cold medication.

I open the cabinet over the sink.

And I stare.

That fucking barbed wire sinks all the way into my skeleton.

This is everything she has.

A handful of ramen packets.

A—I lift it—nearly empty container of oatmeal.

A jar of peanut butter, over half gone.

A bottle of off-brand vitamins.

Instant coffee and six unlabeled bags of tea.

I push the items around.

Nothing else.

I push them to the other side of the cabinet.

Still nothing.

No real food.

No medicine at all.

My heart clenches painfully.

I go into the bathroom, hoping she has a little pharmacy set up here.

On the edge of the sink is a small bottle of Tylenol.

This is it.

I grab it and go back to the other room.

This is all she has.

I turn in a slow circle.

No fridge. No microwave. No place for groceries. No stockpile of drugs.

What has she been eating?

My stomach twists.

Are her cheeks thinner than they were before?

The urge to be sick floods my mouth with saliva.

Has she been hungry?

I look at the stupid fucking can of stew I left on her counter.

I brought her a spare item from my pantry.

A throwaway meal.

Literally nothing.

And it's the most nutritious thing in this whole fucking cabin.

The bottle of painkillers creaks in my hand as I clench my fist with incompetent rage.

How she can even fucking look at me, let alone touch me.

Or let me touch her...

I close my eyes and breathe.

Just make myself breathe.

Another inhale as I try to picture what I have in my medicine cabinet, wondering if there's anything that will help her.

I don't know.

I can't remember.

I should look, but I don't want to leave her.

Shaking a pair of pills into my palm, I spot Courtney's water bottle near the sink and pick it up.

Back in the bedroom, I shake her shoulder again. "Courtney."

She groans.

"I need you to wake up and drink some water."

"Later," she mumbles while trying to pull the blankets over her head again, but I stop her.

"Now. Then you can go back to sleep."

I don't know how much these will do, but they can't hurt. And if I don't do something to feel like I'm helping, I'm going to lose my shit.

Her eyes finally flutter open, and I hold the water bottle out in front of her.

She sneaks her hands out from under the blankets and takes it from me.

Courtney lifts her head, and I wait for her to take a sip from the short straw.

"Open up," I urge her.

Not arguing for once, she parts her lips and, reaching around, I press the pills into her mouth.

She drinks more water, swallowing them.

"That's my girl," I praise her. "Just a little more."

She takes another mouthful before dropping her head back to the pillow.

I take the water from her hands and set it down on the bunk above the top of the hard mattress.

I have a space heater in one of my closets, but I'll get it later.

For now, I'll be her heater.

I strip down until I'm in nothing but my boxers and socks, then I climb into bed behind her.

Courtney makes a disgruntled sound when I bump into her. But when I get under the blankets and wrap my arm around her middle, pulling her back against me, she lets out a contented sigh.

She's still tense. Still curled on her side.

I wiggle one arm under her pillow, pressing as much of her back to my front as I can manage.

It'd be better if she was wearing fewer layers, but it took enough of her energy to drink some water. I won't try to make her strip.

Searching for any skin-on-skin contact, I use my top hand to feel for hers.

They're clasped together under the blankets, palm to palm, but her fingers still feel cold.

I wedge my fingers between her palm, then use my hand to push hers apart until her hand is clasping mine. Her other hand resting on top of mine.

She surprises me when she squeezes our entwined fingers.

"This okay?" I ask, with no intention of moving.

She nods. Her breath hitches once. And then she exhales, relaxing against me.

I close my eyes and focus on keeping my tone calm. "Honey, what have you been eating?"

The endearment feels right. And I'm done fighting my feelings for the person in my arms.

"It's not my stomach," she replies sleepily.

"No, I mean, what have you been eating for your meals?" I keep my voice quiet to match hers.

"I eat lunch in the Food Hall. Like you said."

"That's only lunch." It's getting harder to keep my tone even.

"But I can have the guest's food still, right?" Exhausted confusion laces her question.

"Yeah, you can always eat the guest meals." I flex my arm to hold her tighter. "But what do you have for breakfast? Or dinner when guests aren't here?"

And why am I only asking this now?

Why didn't I wonder?

Why didn't I fucking think?

"I have food." She says it like she means it. And that makes it worse. I open my mouth, but she keeps going. "Sometimes I make toast in the Food Hall." She sounds almost drunk, clearly on the verge of falling back asleep. But it's making her honest. And I don't care if it's unethical to talk to her like this. I have a feeling it's the only way I'll get a real answer. "But I've kept track."

"Kept track?" The question sounds broken. "Of the toast?"

She hums. "So I can pay you back."

"Courtney..."

You don't have to pay me back for toast.

It's what I want to say. But that barbed wire has reached my throat. And I can't say anything.

"But not until the end of the month." She sighs, relaxing farther into me. "I'll get the good ramen then too."

I close my eyes.

The fucking good ramen.

Pay me back at the end of the month.

I suck in a breath.

If she's waiting to buy *good ramen*, I doubt she has any plans to buy cold medicine.

How have I been so fucking blind?

She squeezes my fingers again. "This is nice."

Courtney is relaxing, falling back asleep, while I feel like I'm on the verge of a complete mental breakdown.

I expect my pounding heart to keep her awake, but as I hold her, she slips into unconsciousness once more.

I bury my nose in the back of the hat she's still wearing.

How she can sleep next to me... How she can trust me...

I bend my knees so my thighs are flush against hers.

Thoughts spiraling, I lie wrapped around my girl, willing my body to heat hers.

Needing to help her when so far all I've done is disappoint her.

Chapter 106

Courtney

My bladder wakes me up.

I climb out of bed, wondering if Sterling has been here.

But I'm too sleepy to think.

Another pill is pressed between my lips.

I take another sip of water.

Then a glass is held to my mouth, and I down something fruity and medicinal.

There's a mechanical humming from somewhere in the cabin.

But Sterling tells me to go back to sleep.

So I do.

Something wakes me.

It sounds like a drill.

But the warmth filling the room feels so nice.

Sleep finds me again.

MY EYES FLUTTER OPEN.

I stay still for a moment, taking stock of my body.

My head doesn't hurt as much.

I swallow, and that feels better too.

I flex my fingers and toes.

My muscles ache, but that's probably from staying in bed for so long.

I finally notice the bright daylight lining the curtains.

"Shit." I groan, annoyed that I forgot to set an alarm for myself.

Guests are coming today, and I haven't finished the cabins.

Rolling off the edge of the bunk, I marvel at the softness of the mattress while forgetting my legs are unsteady and nearly collapse to the floor.

I grip the edge of the bunk, keeping myself upright.

"Okay. A little slower."

I take my time getting my balance before letting go.

The curtain over the doorway is pulled shut. Something Sterling must have done while he was here.

My cheeks heat thinking of him as I pull the curtain open.

It's all a bit fuzzy, but I remember him checking on me. Giving me water and...

I sag against the wall.

How...?

When...?

Tears fill my eyes.

There's a space heater in the middle of the floor. The source of the hum I heard earlier, filling the whole cabin with wonderfully warm air.

And...

A half laugh, half sob catches in my throat.

There's a mini fridge.

A plain black one, on top of the new square table, tucked into the far corner.

It's a folding table.

Nothing fancy.

But it's strong enough to hold a mini fridge... and a microwave.

And the two exposed sides of the table have matching folding chairs.

Nothing fancy.

But sturdy enough to sit on.

I cross the room and open the fridge with trembling hands.

It's stocked.

Deli meat and sliced cheese. Cans of soda. A jar of jelly. Some type of milk and short bottles of orange juice.

I close the fridge and slowly turn around.

On the counter, next to my kettle, is a pile of cold medication. Way too much. The evidence of a panicked shopping trip, buying every sort of decongestant, fever reducer, cough suppressant, and immunity booster in sight.

It's unnecessary. Over the top. And the nicest thing anyone has ever done for me.

I almost wish I still felt bad, that it was a real cold and not some twenty-four-hour thing, so I could use all this.

"Oh, Sterling," I whisper.

Gratitude and guilt and wonder all crowd in around me.

My eyes tick over to the cupboard over the sink.

He must've looked in there.

Must've seen how little I had.

It's hard to swallow, but not from illness.

I slowly step over to the sink and pull open the cabinet door.

My food shelf... is full.

Three stacks of microwavable soup.

A row of *just microwave* Asian noodle dishes.

Crackers and bread. Packets of flavored oatmeal and those little cups of fruit suspended in Jell-O.

It's too much.

It's way too much.

I'm stumbling to the door before I even realize where I'm going.

I have to find Sterling.

Have to tell him to take it all back.

A tear rolls down my cheek, and I tell myself it's because I'm still not feeling one hundred percent, and not because this man is starting to mean more to me than he should.

It's not because this man has somehow managed to flip my fortune around in a matter of one night.

I tug on the door handle, but the door doesn't open.

I blink down at the matte black handle in my hand. And at the deadbolt above it.

He gave me a lock for my door.

Tears I can't explain away drip down my cheeks, and I unlock the deadbolt.

The thud is solid.

The lock sturdy.

When I open the door, something falls onto my feet.

My clipboard.

Keeping a hand on the door, I bend down and pick it up.

There's a new page clipped over the rest.

The cabins are ready.
Guests arriving at three.
Dinner at five.
Rest until then.
That's an order, Cookie.
PS the deadbolt code is 5683

I clutch the clipboard to my chest.
And my heart thumps an extra beat for Mr. Black.

CHAPTER 107

COURTNEY

THE PINCH ON MY FINGERTIP JERKS MY ATTENTION away from the Food Hall ahead of me.

Forcing my hands to relax, I take a breath and keep my steps steady.

I got through a shower and back to my cabin before the guests started to arrive. Then I took a nap after eating some soup, resting like Sterling ordered me to do.

But now it's dinnertime.

If it's the same as last time, the employees will mostly eat together tonight. But I'm not worried about seeing my coworkers.

Just my boss.

And not *worried* exactly. I'm excited to see Sterling. Just not excited to talk to him.

Voices sound behind me, more people heading this way for dinner, but none of them sound like Sterling, so I keep my gaze forward as I open the door and enter the Food Hall.

The room is crowded and loud with chatter.

I think it's two groups at the same time again, based on the way the tables are filling. And like I'd hoped, the farthest table is just Black Mountain employees.

It only takes a second to spot Sterling.

His back is to me as he stands at the counter, talking to Cook.

His shoulders are stretching the limit of his green and gray flannel.

My eyes lower.

His butt looks amazing in those jeans.

I want to—

Someone bumps my shoulder. "Sorry, Court." Simpson shakes his head with a laugh as he steps up beside me. "I'm too hungry to see straight."

I smile at the man. "I'll forgive it."

He nods. "Good of you." A pair of strangers moves past us into the short line to get food. "You feeling better? Heard you were under the weather." The genuine concern in his voice reminds me he has daughters and that he's said I remind him of them.

I give him a real smile. "I do feel better, thank you."

For a second, I wonder if he knows about all the new stuff in my cabin, but I don't think so.

"Glad to hear it." He claps his hands together. "Let's eat."

"Go ahead." I wave him forward. "I have to show Mr., uh, Sterling something first."

There's a laugh behind me, and we both turn to see Glen. "I'm gonna call you Miss Courtney until you remember to just call him by his name."

"Call who by his name?" The deep voice comes from my side.

I don't need to look up to see who it is.

But I look up anyway.

Dark eyes connect with mine.

"Talking about you, Boss," Glen replies for me.

Sterling lifts a brow.

I shoot a fake glare at Glen for tattling. But he did give me the perfect opening.

I shift to face Sterling. "I was just saying that I needed a moment to show you something before dinner."

Sterling lifts his plate. "Eat first while it's hot. Then you can show me."

I roll my lips together, wanting to argue, but I know there's no good argument for me here.

Also, the sight of his BBQ meatloaf and garlic potatoes has my stomach grumbling with hunger.

"Get your dinner, Court." His tone is gentle. And I can tell, just from how he says it, that he wants to call me something else.

But he can't.

Because no one here can know what's going on between us.

Nodding rather than replying, I get in line with Glen and Simpson.

Before long, we have plates piled with steaming food, and as a trio, we walk over to the *employee table*.

Leon and Fisher were already seated across from each other. Simpson climbs into the free spot between Leon and Sterling. And Glen moves to sit directly across from Sterling, leaving the only open spot between Glen and Fisher, over one and across from Sterling.

Cook rarely leaves his spot at the counter when guests are here, so the six of us fit perfectly, albeit a bit snugly, at one table.

"You feelin' better, Court?" Leon asks, mouth full of meatloaf.

I have my fork raised, the first bite of potato inches from my lips.

"Already asked her that." Simpson leans forward so he can see Leon around Sterling.

Sterling, who is also slightly leaned forward, focused on his food, doesn't lean out of the way.

I shove the potato into my mouth to stop from smiling.

I don't know why him being a bit of a dick seems funny to me now. But I guess sucking on someone's private parts can change your perspective.

Then I remember all the things Sterling bought for me today, and my partial smile is suddenly too heavy to hold up.

Even if he didn't purchase all those things. Even if he had the table and chairs and mini fridge and microwave on the property, he still brought them to me. And he had to have gone to the store for all that food and medicine.

I didn't want him to do that.

Didn't want him to feel obligated.

Don't want him to treat me differently from the other employees when it comes to employee business. And where I live and the stuff I own is employee business.

What we do off the clock is another thing altogether.

Which is why I need to talk to him.

But, like he said, might as well eat while it's hot.

I use the edge of my fork to cut off a chunk of meatloaf.

My taste buds rejoice at the juicy seasoned beef, and I wonder how a meal can be so bad in one instance and so good in another.

I take another bite as I remember the frozen meals I'd had with Mom growing up.

The RV we lived in was small. Cramped.

There was a platform bed at the back. The space underneath was supposed to be for storage, but she wedged a futon mattress under there and that was my bed.

It was fun when I was little. My own mini cave to hide in.

And some nights, if I was scared from a storm or if Mom was *in a funk*, she'd put her head at the foot of the bed so it was above mine and hold her hand down.

We'd twine our fingers together and she'd tell me stories.

Of a future she had planned.

Of a magical world with sparkling creatures.

Of nothing at all.

And it was perfect.

On those nights.

But other nights, while we took turns using the microwave before sharing the small booth-style table, she'd mutter about how expensive it was to feed two people. How crowded the RV was. How she had no privacy.

Like I had a choice in being hungry. Or being fucking born.

I remember comments she made just like that over a frozen meatloaf meal.

I was fourteen.

I got my first job the next day.

It was probably illegal. But I got paid in cash and was able to buy my own food.

And that's what I did.

For the next sixteen years.

No one has bought me food but myself since then. Not like that. Not groceries.

Not until Sterling.

CHAPTER 108

STERLING

COURTNEY KEEPS QUIET WHILE WE EAT, AND NO ONE bothers her about it.

Everyone assumes she's still tired from not feeling well, but I saw the expression in her eyes when she looked up at me.

It was conflicted.

Like a mix of gratitude and guilt.

And I know the thing she *wants to show me* isn't a thing at all.

Courtney wants to thank me while also telling me to take everything back.

I'd bet all my money on it.

Waiting to stand until Courtney cleans her plate, I press my palms to the table. "Court, you want to show me that clamp you need a replacement for?"

She blinks at me, those dark lashes fanning over her cheeks.

My question was very specific. One she can hardly deny.

And one that will allow us to walk over to the Storage Shed without question.

Though, of course, after we cross the driveway, I'll just lead her to her door and tell her to go lie down.

CHAPTER 109

COURTNEY

"UH, RIGHT. YES." I FINALLY REPLY TO STERLING.

It took me way too long to recognize that he was playing along with my *need to show him something*.

Two of the guys stay at the table and two get up with us.

Sterling stays quiet at my side as we walk down the path. And he keeps staying quiet after the other two peel off toward the Bunk House.

When we go a little farther, around a bend in the path that should put us out of view, he presses his hand into the small of my back.

Instead of tensing because we're touching *in public*, my body relaxes.

There's still so much I don't know about Sterling, but I don't need an explanation for why he makes me feel safe. He just does.

Our boots crunch across the driveway, and I finally glance up at the man next to me.

His trimmed, short beard snags my gaze, and by the time I look up to his eyes, they're already looking down at mine.

He lifts his brows in question.

I lift mine back.

"See something you like?" His voice is just as cocky as the question.

I roll my eyes. "Just noting the gray hairs."

He narrows his eyes. "Smart-ass."

A small laugh pops out of me. "Rude."

The hand on my back slides up my spine and over to my shoulder.

Then Sterling surprises me by pulling me into his side.

I exhale.

"Sterling..."

"Just wait." He says it kindly. So I wait. Assuming he wants to wait until we're in the Storage Shed to talk.

But then he turns down the narrow dirt trail leading to my cabin.

We stop at the bottom of the stairs. His arm drops from my shoulders, and we turn to face each other.

I part my lips, but Sterling's large palm lands over my mouth, trapping my words at the same time his other palm cups the back of my head. Holding me in place. "No."

"No?" I mumble under his hand.

He shakes his head. "No, I won't let you ask me to return the food. Or the table or the appliances." He holds my gaze, and I know he can see my surprise. "We have a long way to go, but I'm starting to understand you, Cookie. And I get it." He leans in so our eyes are inches apart. "But you didn't ask me for anything. You don't owe me anything. And I'm not going to argue over food or fucking heat. And you're going to sleep in tomorrow, but you'll be awake and dressed by eleven, when the electrician is coming over to replace the heater. Until then, you'll leave the space heater on." He slowly slips his hand away from my mouth. "Tell me you understand."

"Sterling, I can't—"

His palm covers my mouth again. "I told you what to say, Courtney. Don't argue with me."

He's not being mean; his voice is just... serious. And I feel it between my thighs.

I give a small nod.

He lowers his hand again. "Tell me."

"I understand," I sigh. "But I don't agree—"

He spins me around before plastering his hand back over my mouth.

I feel his breath against my cheek.

His nose ghosts over the shell of my ear. "You always going to fight me, Honey?" A tremble rolls over my skin as he takes a deep inhale against my temple. "I'm more than okay with that." He presses a soft kiss against my hair. "But not today."

Then he walks me up the steps and reaches past me with his free hand to open the door.

We're standing on the threshold, his hand still over my mouth, his hard body pressed against my back.

"Have a cookie, then go to sleep."

With a gentle push from my boss, I step into the cabin.

Sterling pulls the door shut, and while I stand stunned by the whole interaction, the deadbolt whirs closed behind me.

He's impossible.

A soft feeling wraps around my heart.

He's so impossible.

I don't know if I can accept all of this, but for tonight... I will.

And I'll search for those cookies.

Chapter 110

Sterling

If someone asked me if I was avoiding Courtney, I would say no.

And I would be lying.

After last night's meatloaf, she did as she was told and stayed in her cabin.

I know because I watched.

And today, I told her to clean the women's restroom while her new baseboard heater was being installed.

Which is a legitimate task, even if I did peek in earlier to confirm the place was already squeaky clean. I also spotted her little cactus in there, so I figured it must be a place Courtney likes.

Liking a bathroom sounds weird on the surface, but it's a whole building just for her. So it makes sense as a refuge of sorts.

And if I sat in her cabin the whole time the electrician was in there, so what? I wasn't about to leave him alone to rummage through her things.

And if after the electrician left, I went into her bedroom and swapped the pair of underwear I took days ago for a pair of new, slightly used panties...

Well, I never claimed to be a well-adjusted man.

My fingers twist in the soft fabric still stuffed into my pocket as I stand in my bedroom.

Courtney's lights are still on, but I'm sure she'll be going to bed soon.

I want to be in there with her.

Want to climb into her bed and twist my body around hers. Again.

But she needs to rest. And now that she has a properly heated cabin, I'm sure she'll sleep better without me pawing at her.

So I'm keeping my distance.

At night, so she can get back to one hundred percent. And during the day, so she can't argue with me about all the new items in her cabin.

It's the right call.

I'm sure of it.

But tomorrow, I'm heading out for a few nights with Fisher's group, and I don't think I can go that long without seeing her.

CHAPTER 111

COURTNEY

My phone rings, but it's a number I don't recognize.

I set the phone on the table and go back to securing the little black cape around Spike. The matching item to her classic witch's hat.

My phone vibrates with a text.

It's from the same number.

> Unknown: Answer the phone, Cookie.

My lips part.

Sterling?

"Duh." I roll my eyes at myself. Literally no one else calls me Cookie.

The unknown number calls.

I purse my lips.

I want to talk to him. Would like to hear his voice.

But Sterling left this morning after avoiding me, so I'm a touch annoyed with him right now.

I let it ring once more before I answer the call. "Hello, Sterling."

There's a low hum on the other end of the line that sounds a lot like appreciation. "Court."

My hum is less appreciative. If he's calling me Court, that means someone is close enough to listen.

"Is there something I can do for you, Sir?" If that comes out suggestive, that's his problem. I'm just asking.

He grunts. "Fisher forgot the cooking oil."

"I swear I packed it." I hear Fisher protest in the background. "I remember putting it in your truck."

Sterling grunts again. "We need it for tomorrow's dinner. I think it's on the counter in the Food Hall. Can you bring it here by four?"

"Sure. Um, where is *here*?"

"I'll send you directions. Make sure to download the offline maps since you'll lose service at some spots." His tone is no-nonsense, so I make a mental note to do as he says.

"Okay. Need me to bring anything else?" I don't know if he's planning to reimburse me for gas, but considering the fact I don't need to rush to buy groceries anytime soon, I can spare the expense.

"No. Just the oil. And your overnight bag."

"Okay—Wait. What overnight bag?"

"It's a two-hour drive. Once we're done eating the fish fry, it'll be dark." I can feel the command in his voice. "You're not driving home in the dark, Court."

I drag my teeth over my lower lip. "Is it, uh, *tent* sleeping?"

I'd really like to see Sterling, but I don't know about that whole sleeping on the ground thing.

"No. It's one shared cabin."

"It's a shack," Fisher calls out.

Sterling lets out a heavy sigh. "It's not a fucking shack. It has bunks and windows and a fireplace."

"And no electricity or water," Fisher adds on.

"It has water," Sterling argues back. "It just happens to be outside."

"Next to the outhouse."

I scrunch my nose at the outhouse comment.

Shared room and a no-electricity bathroom. Definitely *not* a sexy camping trip.

"Ignore him," Sterling says into the phone. "Just pack your things, Court. And come to me."

A flash of me on all fours with Sterling kneeling before me pulls a gasp from my lungs.

Sterling gives me a low hum, then the call disconnects.

"This says I'm here," I tell my Jeep as I continue to slowly drive down the narrow gravel lane.

I followed the directions Sterling gave me. And I'm right on time. But I don't see any signs of a cabin or a shack. Or Fisher's or Sterling's trucks.

I glance back down at the GPS on my phone.

Still says I'm here.

I glance back up and scream, slamming on my brakes.

Sterling shakes his head like I'm overreacting. Like I didn't just almost run him over.

He steps up to my door, and I hit the unlock button with one hand still pressed to my chest.

"I could've killed you," I gasp.

Sterling rolls his eyes. "You were going two miles an hour."

I drop my hands to my lap. "It would've been a slow death."

The side of his mouth pulls up in a playful grin. "Put the shifter into park."

I don't see the other vehicles, but I do as he says. "Where—"

Sterling grabs my knees and spins me so my feet are hanging out of the Jeep and I'm facing him.

With one hand, Sterling grips the back of my neck. "Hurry up and kiss me."

He pulls my mouth to his.

And I melt into him.

There is no other option.

I tilt my head.

His tongue swipes along my lips.

And I open for him.

He moves forward, clutching my side with his free hand and shoving my knees apart with his hips, getting as close as he can.

I moan.

He's so... hot.

His touch. His tongue. His body.

I press my hands against his chest.

His strong muscles flex under my fingers.

I open my mouth wider as I slide my hands up over his shoulders.

Sterling drags his palm down my neck until he's circling his arm around my back.

I arch into him. Aching to feel him press against my core.

I arch farther, then slide off the edge of the seat.

I yelp but feel Sterling's lips smile against mine.

I don't fall.

Of course I don't.

Sterling's hold on me tightens, and he hoists me up into his arms.

When he starts to walk, I break the kiss.

"W-what are you doing?" I'm gasping for air, struggling to get the question out, simply from making out with this man.

"I'm driving." Sterling, thankfully, sounds just as breathless as he circles the front of the Jeep.

Which I'll pretend is from the kissing and not the carrying.

"Okay," I pant while tightening my thighs around his hips.

I don't really care what his plan is. All I can focus on is the friction between us.

Each step has his cock pressing against the seam of my jeans, right where I want him.

Just not quite hard enough.

"Open the door, Courtney."

I look around and see we're at my passenger side door.

Letting go of Sterling with one hand, I grab the handle and pull the door open.

Sterling moves like he's going to deposit me into the seat. But he pauses, then presses my back against the side of the Jeep.

He hugs me tightly as he rocks his hips into the juncture of my thighs.

"Fucking hell." He groans and does it again. "I wanted to see you, but I think it might kill me to have you this close and not fuck you."

I drop my head back against the vehicle and match his groan.

Hearing Sterling admit that he wants to fuck me...

My fingers claw at his shoulders.

I want that so bad.

One of his hands moves to grip my ass. "This is my penance."

I drag my nails up the back of his neck into his hair. "Penance?"

He nods and presses his nose to my temple, inhaling. "I took that oil out of my truck."

It takes me a second to understand what he means.

And when I do, a laugh bursts out of me. "Fisher was so certain he packed it."

"You won't tell on me, will you?" His lips brush my skin with each word, and a shiver bounces down my spine.

I give my head a small shake. "It'd be kinda hard to explain."

Sterling huffs as he shifts us away from the side of the vehicle and lowers me to the seat.

I slowly release my hold of him, and our bodies disentangle.

When Sterling stands back up, looking down at me, the unspoken understanding hangs between us.

The agreement that we don't want anyone to know about us.

For the boss-employee aspect of it.

For the special-treatment-possibility aspect of it.

For the I-rely-on-him-for-everything aspect.

Not to mention the fact that we've only fooled around a couple of times. Even if Sterling mentioned wanting to *fuck me,* he hasn't.

True, the emotions I feel for Sterling when he's around, or when he's not around, seem bigger than just some physical fling. But the truth is we haven't slept together.

We hardly know each other.

And according to my contract, I'm only here until the end of December.

"Legs in." Sterling's voice is low, like he's having the same thoughts I am.

Instead of talking to him about it, because I'm a chicken, I obey and face forward.

He carefully shuts my door, then I watch him circle back around the front of the Jeep and think about why I'm here.

He wanted to see me.

He wanted to see me so much he sabotaged Fisher's packing.

A lightbulb bursts inside me.

He took that oil out of his truck before they even left. He knew ahead of time that he would want to see me. This sneaky little act was premeditated.

Sterling starts to climb into the driver's seat but has to wedge himself back out when he doesn't fit.

"How short are you?" He gripes as he uses the bar under the seat to slide it back before hoisting himself back in.

"Not that short." I bite down on my laugh as he still struggles to get comfortable. "I'm perfectly capable of driving, you know. You could've just directed me on where to go."

"True," Sterling admits, finally shifting into drive. "But then I wouldn't have gotten to carry you around like I did."

"True." I mimic him. "You also could've stayed on the side of the road, path, whatever this is." I wave out the windshield. "Rather than jumping out in front of me."

"You could've kept your eyes on the road. Then you would've seen me slowly step out of the woods."

"Yeah, well..."

"Good argument." Sterling keeps his gaze forward, but I can see another one of his secret smiles trying to appear.

So, I poke him in the side, high up on his ribs.

His arm snaps down so fast that it makes me jump back with a yelp.

He shoots me a narrow-eyed look. "What are you doing?"

I give him a wide-eyed look back. "Are you ticklish?"

"Absolutely not."

My mouth drops. "I can't believe it. *The* Mr. Black is ticklish."

"I just said I wasn't."

"I heard." I nod. "And you're a liar."

He slides another look my way. "You saying you're *not* ticklish?"

"I would never tell such an untruth."

Sterling shifts closer to his door, putting more space between us.

And I finally lose the battle against my laughter. "Relax. I'm not going to tickle attack you."

His elbow is still pressed firmly to his side. "Mm-hmm."

I settle back into my seat, then, without turning my head, I walk my fingers across the center console between us.

Sterling's hand snaps out, grasping mine.

We drive in silence, and I try to steady my heartbeat, but it's hard to focus on our surroundings when all I can think about is the way his rough fingers feel against my skin.

Holding hands shouldn't feel so... intense. But everything with Sterling is intense.

It's just how he is.

We bump along the narrow drive, and as we round another corner, the trees thin and I spot a couple of structures ahead of us.

Before us but off to the left is a square brick outhouse with a shingled roof and a metal door.

Still an outhouse, but it's like something you'd expect to see at a rest stop, not in the middle of the woods. Honestly, better than I was expecting.

No regrets about bringing my own toilet paper though.

The outhouse is set a few yards away from the strip of land designated for parking, giving the illusion of privacy.

Straight ahead in the parking area are two pickup trucks—Sterling's, Fisher's.

And to our right is a gazebo and the cabin.

The gazebo-looking thing covers one big, square picnic table.

The cabin looks to be one room, like Fisher said, and that's where everyone, including me, will be sleeping.

Sterling steers the Jeep next to the trucks and puts it in park.

I wait for him to turn off the engine and climb out before I follow.

Since I've been spending the last few days doing minimal work and sleeping late, I haven't spent much time with the four guests. But they've seemed nice.

They're all sitting around the square table, unbothered by the cold but wearing thick layers.

I lift my hand in a wave as I make my way to meet Sterling at the back of the Jeep.

They all cheer, saying something about fish, and I find myself smiling by the time Sterling has the back door open.

He slings my backpack—containing my clothes and a small selection of toiletries—over his shoulder and picks up the jug of oil in one hand and the paper bag of groceries I purchased on the way here in the other.

"Where's your coat?" he asks, looking over my non-coat-wearing body.

"Um." I shrug a shoulder.

Sterling heaves out a breath. "Do you not own a winter coat?"

"I've never needed one."

"Well, you need one now."

I nod. "And I'll buy one soon." His head gives a curious tilt, and I hold up my finger. "Don't you dare, Mr. Black."

"Don't I dare, what, Miss Kern?"

I resist the urge to glance around, knowing that will make us look guilty. But I still shuffle closer, lowering my voice. "Don't you dare go out and buy me one. You've already done too much. And if you do more, I'll end up spending my whole paycheck just paying you back."

Sterling takes a step forward, nearly closing the distance between us. "You will do no such thing, Cookie." He leans in close enough that I can feel his exhale on my lips. "And if I want to buy you things, I'll buy you things."

I curl my hands into fists at my sides.

I don't know how to deal with this possessiveness.

It's overwhelming in its intensity.

And confusing in its sincerity.

"You're so..." I can't think of the right description.

The side of his delicious mouth pulls up. "I'm so what, Honey?"

I sway toward him.

Honey.

Why do I love that so much?

"Got the oil?" Fisher asks from mere feet away, and I almost jump out of my boots.

"God dammit." I press both my hands to my chest. "What is with you people?"

Fisher's brows raise. "You people?"

My heart is still thundering in my chest, but I wave a hand at the two men. "You people who like to jump out of nowhere."

Sterling looks completely unbothered. Like he wasn't startled at all, and he doesn't care that Fisher walked up on us standing so close. *Inappropriately* close.

"I hardly jumped out of nowhere." Fisher snorts, eyes bouncing between me and Sterling.

My boss shakes his head. "If you'd been watching the road..."

"Yeah, yeah, whatever." I brush him off and reach for the grocery bag in his hand.

Sterling lifts it out of my reach.

"Seriously?" I drop my shoulders and give him a look.

"Seriously. Go take a look at the river before the sun sets. We'll get dinner ready." Sterling uses his chin to gesture toward the gazebo.

I look in that direction. "River?"

And then I spot it.

Beyond the gazebo, the land dips to reveal a wide strip of water.

It's beautiful.

"But." I turn back to Sterling. "I got a few things to share." I reach for the bag again, but he uses his long arms to pass it over to Fisher.

"We might be idiots who forget things," Sterling says with a straight face, "but I'm sure we can figure it out."

I throw my hands up. "Fine. I'll do nothing."

"You'll go grab my spare coat out of the back seat of my truck." Sterling gives me yet another command. "Then you'll go to the river."

"I'm okay, I swear." I can feel Fisher's intent gaze on us, and I work to soften my tone. "I have two sweaters and, a, um, flannel on. I promise I'm warm."

Sterling just stares at me.

And keeps staring at me.

My nostrils flare as I take a long inhale. "Fine. I will get your coat."

"Good..." Sterling says the word like it's supposed to be followed by another word but cuts himself off.

After a heartbeat, my cheeks start to heat.

He was going to say good girl.

Thankfully he caught himself because that would be a hard thing to pass off as casual in front of Fisher.

Assuming it's not locked, I hurry over to Sterling's truck, away from the men.

It's a four-door pickup, so I try the rear driver's side first and find a heavy khaki winter coat thrown across the back seat.

I really don't need it.

I'm not cold.

But with the truck blocking me from everyone's view, I bring the stiff material up to my nose.

It smells like him.

Biting my lip because I know I'm going to look like the biggest hypocrite, I pull the giant coat on over my layers and zip it up.

The material covers my ass and the sleeves are too long, but the warmth is immediate.

I may not need it. But I like it.

After shutting the door, I shove my hands into the pockets of the coat, and my fingers are met with something soft.

Still out of view, I pull a worn knitted hat out of one of the pockets, the logo for Black Mountain Lodge stitched onto the front.

"Fuck it."

I pull the hat on.

Dressed like I'm expecting a blizzard, I round the truck and walk over to say hi to the guests before making my way to the river.

And the river is... stunning.

It's a new type of peace. One I didn't know to crave.

This is different from the mountain view behind Sterling's house. It's smaller... more intimate than a view that goes on and on forever.

It's... grounding.

I lower myself onto a bench made of logs and watch the water flow past me, swelling and rolling around the rocks below.

Unconcerned by the obstacles ahead of it.

And as I watch, I decide I want to be like this river.

Take each day one moment at a time.

I'll be aware of the big picture.

Aware of my future.

But for now. For these next couple months. I'm going to live in the moment.

Obstacles be damned.

CHAPTER 112

STERLING

WATCHING COURTNEY EXPERIENCE SOMETHING NEW IS quickly becoming an obsession.

She sat down by the river, wearing my coat, watching the water flow by, until food was ready.

Then she joined the rest of us at the table for her first fish fry dinner.

It's nothing fancy. But it's fresh caught. Well seasoned. And hot from the pan.

I know it's delicious, but I couldn't even taste my portion because I was too busy staring at Courtney while she consumed hers.

Her eyes closed with every bite.

My balls ached every time she licked the grease and salt off her fingers...

It was torturous.

If it was socially acceptable, I'd have taken my dick out and stroked it while she ate.

But then I would've embarrassed myself, coming in seconds, because now I know what it feels like to have her lips wrapped around my cock.

"What was that?" Fisher asks from beside me.

I didn't say anything, but I must've made a noise thinking about my Courtney and her... skills.

"Nothing. Hand me that." I point to a plastic container.

Fisher doesn't press for more as we put away the rest of the dinner stuff.

Out here, everything needs to be secured and brought inside. Bears will mostly leave people alone, but it's best not to entice them with fishy oil or sugar.

Sugar.

I smile at the paper bag on the table.

When Courtney showed up with that extra bag of groceries, I didn't think much of it. Probably because I was still thinking about her legs wrapped around my waist and my tongue in her mouth.

But when I pulled the items out, I had to stop myself from stomping down to the shoreline and fucking her right then and there.

Because she brought cookies. Several different kinds, a container of each. Along with muffins and pastries. *For breakfast* she said, when I raised my brow at her.

The crunch of boots draws my attention.

"Need any help?" Courtney asks as she stops across the table from me.

I shake my head. "We're wrapped up."

"Oh, well, I can help bring it inside." Her hands are hidden inside the long sleeves of my coat, but I can see her fidgeting, and I wonder if she's doing that thing she does where she digs her damn thumbnail into the pad of her finger.

I should buy her gloves so she doesn't hurt herself doing that.

"Go get ready for bed." There are four posts holding the roof of the gazebo up, and each post has a lantern hanging from a hook, fighting off the darkness that has settled over the mountain. I nod toward one of the posts. "Take a lantern with you. There's a hook on the back of the outhouse door to hang it on."

Courtney bites her lip as she takes the closest lantern down.

Fisher is still standing here with us, so I can't demand she put her eyes on me. But I'm also not going to ignore the obvious signs of nervousness she's displaying.

"What's wrong, Court?"

Her eyes dart up to mine. "Nothing. I just..." She glances over at Fisher. "I brought my overnight bag like you said. But I didn't bring any blankets or anything." Her shoulders lift, then drop. "I wasn't thinking."

"I didn't tell you to bring any because I have extra in my truck," I tell her.

Her mouth forms a silent *O*.

"Go put your pajamas on. You can help me make up your bunk when you're done."

She bites her lip as she nods, then carries the lantern back to the cabin to get her backpack.

"Handy you have extra bedding packed." Fisher says it casually, but I hear the suspicion.

"It pays to be prepared." It's a douchey, condescending answer. But it's not a lie.

"Uh-huh." He picks up an armful of items. "Still don't know how the oil ended up in the Food Hall," he grumbles as he walks away.

I almost snort but clear my throat instead and pick up the rest of the food.

It's not like I yelled at him for *forgetting* the oil, so I don't know why he can't just let it go.

I cross paths with Courtney as she cuts back across the clearing toward the outhouse.

Her eyes are on mine the whole time, and I seriously wonder if it would be disgusting for our first time to be in an outhouse.

She passes me, and I carry on to the cabin.

It's for the best.

I would be happy to fuck her anywhere. On the ground. Against a tree. Over the hand sanitizer in the outhouse.

But Courtney deserves better.

I don't know what her past boyfriends have been like. But I'm going to be better than them.

Boyfriends.

That word doesn't feel right in relation to my Cookie.

For starters, I'm too fucking old to be someone's boyfriend.

Then there's the fact that we haven't slept together. Or talked much.

And... I'm her boss.

I step into the cabin, and Fisher moves out of the way so I can set my armful down next to the rest of the food on the small counter in the back corner of the cabin.

"Want me to go get the extra bunk stuff out of your truck?" Fisher asks, attention zeroed in on my features. "Or do you want to do it?"

This feels like a test.

And as much as it annoys me that my employee is the one doing it, I can respect it.

"Go ahead and grab it. There's a bed roll and blankets under the back seat. Bring it all."

He dips his chin. "Pillow?"

"No pillow." I knew I'd forget something. "She can use mine."

The side of his mouth twitches. "You sure you can go without, old man? I could always lend her mine."

"I'm sure, *Junior*. I've used rolled-up shirts for pillows more times than you've—"

A loud belch cuts me off, and we both turn to look at the man responsible.

Fisher laughs. "Damn, dude."

The man pats his belly. "Wanted to get that out before the lady came back."

I roll my eyes.

I'm going to owe Courtney after making her share a cabin with all these men.

But hopefully their snores and body noises will cover the sound of me climbing out of my bunk and into hers.

CHAPTER 113

COURTNEY

"NIGHT, EVERYONE," ONE OF THE GUESTS SAYS, THE bunk creaking as he climbs into it.

I thought I would feel more awkward staying in here with everyone, but the guests are all lifelong friends. Older guys who spent the whole night laughing as they told us stories of all the shit they've gotten into over the years.

It's been fun, having a beer while we were all spread around the cabin. But even though it's not that late, I'm tired and just as ready for bed.

The beds in here are bunk beds, like the guest cabins back at the Lodge, but these are handmade with the ends attached to the back wall. There are four sets total, with a couple feet of space between them.

Hanging down from the ceiling between each bunk is a curtain, making an effort at privacy. It doesn't go around the front, so it's just a thin barrier on either side of each bed, but I'm grateful no one will be able to see me sleeping. Unless they get up to pee, then they'd walk past the head of the bunks and could look at anyone.

And I know the head of the bunk is the end closest to the

middle of the room because Sterling told me to set up my blankets that way because the wall end is colder.

The more you know.

Sterling gets up from the folding chair he's been sitting on and starts to turn off the lamps.

There are no real ladders for getting to the top bunks, just the supports on the end for climbing.

The last lamp turns off, but the free-standing fireplace in the far corner of the room gives off enough glow to still see by.

Fisher bumps his shoulder into mine as he moves to the second set of bunk beds. "Night, Court. Glad you could come hang out with us."

I smile. "Thanks, I'm glad I could come out too."

"Everyone is glad. Now get in bed." Sterling steps between us.

"Extra sweet dreams to you, Sterling." Fisher teases our boss for his gruffness.

"Uh-huh. I'll be sure to wake you up at five so you can help me make breakfast," Sterling says to my coworker as he nudges me toward the bunk we'll be sharing, placing his palm over the spot where Fisher bumped into me.

Fisher groans and reaches for the boards to climb up to his top bunk. "I'll give you my pillow if you promise not to do that."

His comment makes me look at the bottom bunk next to where I'm standing.

"Where's your pillow?" I ask Sterling.

He heaves out a breath. "Don't worry about it. Get in bed."

I press my lips together, but I can still see Fisher watching us, so I keep my questions to myself and start to climb.

It takes some maneuvering, and I feel a little weirded out by the height, but I eventually get myself seated on the top bunk.

The thin camping mattress thing is actually pretty comfortable.

My pajama prep earlier consisted of changing into sweatpants and removing my bra. So after I shove my legs under the blankets, I drag off my layers of sweatshirts, leaving me in Sterling's flannel.

I toss the sweatshirts to the foot of the bunk, against the wall, trying to create more of a barrier between my feet and the cool wall.

If I have to get up to go to the bathroom, I'll put one back on since I don't want anyone but Sterling to see the outline of my nipples. But I really hope I can hold it until morning. Because lantern or not, I don't want to make that walk in the dark alone.

In fact...

I twist to see where Sterling is and jolt when I find him standing right beside me.

He lifts a brow. "Need something?"

"As a matter of fact, I was going to ask a favor." I keep my voice low. "If I have to go to the bathroom in the middle of the night, can I wake you up to walk with me?" It's an innocent question, but I still don't want to be overheard.

Sterling nods. "Yeah, Courtney, I'll walk with you."

Hidden behind the curtain that hangs between our bunk and the one Fisher is sleeping on, Sterling reaches up and runs his hand down one of my braids, sending a bolt of heat through my stomach.

"Go to sleep." He gives the end a little tug before dropping his hand.

I let my cheeks puff out on an exhale.

Obviously nothing is going to happen here, with a bunch of other people in the same room, but if we don't have sex soon... I might combust.

I start to lie down. But then Sterling starts unbuttoning his flannel.

When I pause, so does he.

I scoot down, then roll onto my side, tucking my hands under the pillow so I can watch.

Sterling shakes his head but gets back to undressing.

The flames from the fireplace shadow his movements, turning the simple act into a stage-worthy strip tease.

I want to cheer him on. But since we're not alone, I stay quiet.

Naked from the waist up, Sterling shoves his jeans down his legs, and my eyes lower to the front of his boxers.

His very tented boxers.

His jeans drop to the ground, and he steps out of them before folding the denim and setting them on the ground next to the bed.

How he can sleep in practically nothing when it's still rather chilly in here, I don't know.

But I sure do appreciate it.

Sterling grips his dick through his boxers, and even in the almost dark, I can see him squeeze his length.

A small sound leaves my throat, and I quickly turn my face into the pillow to muffle it.

And I keep my face in the pillow because it smells like him.

After filling my lungs with the foresty scent of Sterling, I slowly lift my head.

He's still standing there, watching me.

I sneak a hand out and motion him closer with one finger. He steps forward, leaning in until his face is inches from mine.

"Is this your pillow?" I whisper.

"It's yours tonight."

"But what will you use?" My eyes are on his lips.

"Don't worry about me, Honey." His words are quiet. Just for me.

I lift my eyes to his. "You can come up here and share it with me."

His mouth pulls into a full grin.

"What?" I can't help but smile when he does.

He lifts a hand, brushing his thumb across my cheek. "I was already planning on it."

My muscles relax. "Good."

The bed is basically the same as the one in the Laundry Cabin. Maybe a full? Certainly not a queen. And there's a foot gap between the edge of the bunk at my back and the wall—just enough to make me wonder why they didn't put it directly against the wall… Unless they left the gap for *cold wall reasons*. But if we cuddle real close, no one should fall off.

Sterling drags his thumb along my jaw. "Rest your eyes. I'll climb up when everyone's asleep."

Then he lowers out of view.

CHAPTER 114

STERLING

ON MY BACK, HANDS FOLDED ON MY CHEST, HEAD resting on a rolled-up T-shirt, I stare at the bottom of the bunk above me.

It's been forty minutes.

I can't hear any more whispered conversations.

No sounds of anyone still trying to get comfortable.

Just heavy snoring.

Slowly, I roll out of my bed.

I shouldn't be doing this.

Shouldn't chance it.

Not with Fisher on the other side of the curtain.

But even that isn't enough to stop me.

If Fisher is still awake, and if he's looking, he'd see me climbing up the front of the bunk, so I stay on the side, keeping the barrier between us.

Of course, if he gets up to piss and looks this way, he'll easily see two of us up here. And I'd give it fifty-fifty if he'd say something.

But he's a *mostly* respectful kid. So I don't think he'd creep like that.

Wouldn't creep the way I do.

Gripping the edge of the top bunk, I place a foot on my bunk to boost myself up.

The frame creaks.

The sound is loud, but not louder than that asshole snoring.

Courtney doesn't even stir.

Swinging my leg up, I maneuver until I'm on all fours and I can pull her pile of blankets back.

How she can sleep with so many clothes on, I'll never understand.

But then I look at her flannel-covered body, and I think it might be even sexier than her sleeping naked.

Naked is great, but wrapped in my clothes is even better.

I slip my legs under the blankets and lower myself.

These beds are hardly fucking big enough for me on my own, so the two of us together is going to be a tight fit.

But it's a sacrifice I'm willing to make over and over.

Courtney is facing me, hands once again entwined under her chin, but she scooted over before falling asleep, leaving just enough room for me to lie on my back.

Like the last time I crawled into her bed while she was sleeping, I slip my arm under her neck. But this time, I pull her into my side until she's half sprawled over my chest.

She makes a murmured sound of comfort, and I press my lips to her forehead, shushing her quietly.

Courtney nuzzles into my chest.

Her one hand is trapped between us, but the other closes in a fist on my stomach.

Thinking about the last time when she squeezed my hand and told me she liked it, I link our fingers together.

Then, in almost the same position I'd been in on the lower bunk, only a thousand times more comfortable, I close my eyes and let the soft sound of Courtney's breathing lull me to sleep.

CHAPTER 115

COURTNEY

A HINGE SQUEAKS, AND COOL AIR SWEEPS ACROSS MY face.

I burrow farther into Sterling's side.

Sterling's side.

I crack my eyes open.

My cheek is plastered to bare skin. Chest hair tickling my nose. My head rising and falling with each slow breath Sterling takes.

It's ungodly comfortable.

Like so comfortable it shouldn't be legal.

I breathe him in.

How is it possible to feel so... at ease with a man I barely know?

Because even though I've been in Colorado for a couple weeks, I still don't really *know* Sterling Black.

I look at our hands, fingers laced together on top of his body.

I gently flex my fingers.

His hand is so much larger than mine. His fingers are rough, filled with strength, yet capable of soft touch.

I flex my fingers again.

No matter where this goes, his kindness, his touch... it's healing something inside me.

Even with those first few miserable days, he's more than made up for it.

He explained. And he apologized.

I press my teeth into my lip.

I suppose I owe him an apology, too, for trying to blackmail him that first day.

That same squeak from earlier sounds and that same gust of outside air blows over us, followed by the thud of footsteps across the floor.

Someone must've gone to the outhouse.

My eyes widen.

Someone is up.

It's still dark out, but it's getting lighter.

They might've seen us.

I listen closely, straining my ears.

The creak of a bed frame signals the person going back to sleep, but I can't tell which bunk it is. It doesn't sound like the one closest to us, which would hopefully mean it's not Fisher who's up. But I can't be certain.

"Sterling," I whisper.

He doesn't respond.

I wiggle my fingers free of his grip and tap my fingertip against his chest. "Sterling."

The arm around my back tightens, and I hear a small rumble in his chest. But that's it.

I need him to wake up, but his sleepiness is so cute I find myself smiling.

"Sterling." I flatten my hand on his chest and give him a little shake.

The hand on my back slides up over my shoulder.

I think he's going to hug me to him, but then his hand is reaching around and clamping down over my mouth.

I grin under his palm.

This man is such a goober.

Then I remember what I learned yesterday.

I shift back, just enough to make room for the hand that's trapped between us. Then I dart it up, wiggling my fingers in his armpit.

Sterling's eyes snap open.

The palm over my mouth stifles my laugh.

The arm around my back squeezes me to him, but my fingers are already at their target. Still wiggling.

In a blink, Sterling twists toward me, rolling me onto my back until he's looming over me.

With his hand off my mouth, I work to keep my breathing quiet.

We're right on the edge of the bunk. And if I wasn't so turned on—looking up at his mostly naked body, feeling his hardness against my thigh—I'd be worried about falling off the bed.

"Morning," I whisper.

His eyes drop to my mouth. And stay there. "Morning, Honey."

Honey. Gah.

I shift, that hardness against my leg feeling harder with each moment.

Then I remember why I woke him up.

I use my head and brows to gesture toward the rest of the room. "Someone was up."

Sterling lifts his head and looks around.

"Shit," he whispers, then drops his full weight onto me.

All the air gets pushed from my lungs.

"Five more minutes." His lips graze my ear on each word.

I shove at his heavy body.

He rolls his hips.

I squeeze my thighs together.

He nuzzles his face into my neck.

"Can't. Breathe," I grunt.

He lifts off me, and I fill my lungs.

Smirking, he presses a kiss to the tip of my nose, and I swoon.

Then he shuffles over and swings down off the side of the bunk.

Gaping, I roll onto my side as he lowers himself to the ground. The biceps. The shoulders. The pecs.

Those dips above his hips where his stomach muscles flex.

I roll back onto my back.

I'm not prepared to look at *all of that* this early in the morning.

The soft rustle of clothing signals that Sterling is getting dressed. A bittersweet necessity.

There's a metallic zip, then I feel something depress the bedding beside me.

Rolling my head to the side, I find myself looking into Sterling's eyes as he leans against the bed.

And he looks ready to film a fucking movie.

A Western, probably. Not some corporate thing. Nevertheless, it's not fair.

I must be making some sort of expression because his cheek twitches. "What?"

"You're too handsome," I tell him, keeping my voice just as quiet.

He stares at me for a long second before shaking his head. But I catch the way his mouth tries to smile.

"You're tired" is his response as he reaches out to run a finger down my—probably frizzy—braid. "I'm going outside. When I come back, I'll walk you over to the outhouse if you have to go."

The suggestion is enough to have my bladder nodding.

I start to pull down the blanket. "I can go with you now so you don't have to make the trip twice."

He shakes his head as he smirks. "Not going to the outhouse. Just gotta pee."

"But..." I scrunch my nose when I realize what he means. "That's not fair."

"It's not. But it sure is handy." He holds up two fingers. "Two minutes." Then he walks away.

To go pee in the woods.

Or into the river.

Or literally wherever the hell he wants because he has a penis.

I've never been more jealous of someone's genitalia in my life. Because although the outhouse isn't as disgusting as I was expecting, it's still an outhouse. And that toilet seat is going to feel like ice against my butt cheeks.

Silently cursing Sterling for his urinating abilities, I spend the next two minutes struggling to climb down from my bunk.

My feet hit the floor just as the door opens again, and Sterling waits as I pull on one of my sweatshirts and boots.

I keep my eyes forward, not looking back at the other bunks, as we step out into the crisp morning together.

Even though the darkness is lifting, Sterling holds a flashlight beam ahead of us, and when we reach the outhouse, he hangs the light inside for me.

"I'll wait right here," he tells me.

When I open the door a few minutes later, he's exactly where he said he'd be.

The hand sanitizer is drying on my hands, but I still make him go over to the water spigot so I can wash them properly. They have a special type of camping soap that's okay to use for washing hands and dishes in the open, and I feel less gross after using it. But I can't stop my yawn as we approach the cabin.

Sterling places his hand on the small of my back. "Go back to sleep for an hour. You can head back to the Lodge after breakfast."

I tip my head back to look at him. "You're staying up?"

He nods. "I'll get the fire going. Prep for the day."

"Do you want help?" I try to keep the wince out of my voice.

Please say no.

"I got it." He strokes his hand up my spine. "Go back to sleep."

"If you insist."

He dips his chin, then drops his hand away from me.

Sighing at the loss of contact, I open the cabin door and step inside.

I toe my boots off and head back toward our bunk.

"Morning."

My head jerks over at the whispered greeting. I hadn't noticed the man standing a few feet away.

I lift a hand to Fisher. "Morning. Good night."

He grins. "Going back to bed?"

I nod.

"I'll do the same if the boss doesn't make me help him." Fisher uses his arm to cover his yawn.

I hold up crossed fingers. "Good luck."

I'm standing at the end of my bunk when the door closes, marking Fisher's departure.

The guests are still all asleep, but Fisher saw me up. He knows Sterling is outside. And I know Sterling isn't coming back in. So...

I grab the pillow off the top bunk, then crawl into the lower bed.

Climbing up top just sounds like too much work.

I burrow under the bedding until I'm nearly hidden, then I pull the blankets up to my nose.

And with memories of Sterling's warmth wrapped around me, I slip back into sleep.

CHAPTER 116

STERLING

IT'S LATER THAN I INTENDED. ALREADY AFTER DARK. But I'm here.

My heart thuds loudly inside my chest as I pull my truck up to the front of my house and turn the engine off.

Fisher and the guests are spending tonight on the river again, but I told them I had to go help out the other campsite.

And I did. I drove over to where Glen and Simpson have a group of hikers. I helped them with dinner. I used the showers at their campground. And then I told them goodbye.

Because I'm spending tonight at Black Mountain Lodge.

I slam the truck door and stride across the gravel.

Only I'm not going to sleep until I bury myself inside Courtney.

CHAPTER 117

COURTNEY

I SPIT OUT THE TOOTHPASTE AND TURN THE faucet off.

I thought I heard something—like a vehicle—but when I listen now, there's nothing but silence.

Stepping out of my little bathroom, I leave the light on and head to the bedroom, picking up my phone.

I've been debating all evening if I should text Sterling.

We haven't before, except for him telling me to answer his call.

But now... It feels like I should.

Sterling sabotaged Fisher's packing just so I could spend the night with him.

And that was, well, perhaps a bit much. But it's also kind of sweet. In a *serious Sterling* sort of way.

Squaring my shoulders, I type out a message and hit send.

Me: Have a good night, Mr. Black.

Only a few seconds go by before a reply comes in.

Boss: I plan to.

My brows lower.
I plan to.
What the fuck does that mean?
Then I hear the sound of the deadbolt unlocking.
And my heartbeat triples.

CHAPTER 118

STERLING

I SHOVE THE DOOR OPEN AND STEP INSIDE.

Courtney is standing at the opposite end of the cabin. Phone in hand. Wide eyes on me.

And my blood sizzles with anticipation.

CHAPTER 119

COURTNEY

STERLING KICKS THE DOOR SHUT, AND THE SOUND OF IT slamming feels like electric paddles on my heart.

He's here.

In my cabin.

And there's no one to stop us.

No reason for us to hold back.

I toss my phone onto the dresser.

Sterling flips the lock on the door.

I take one step forward.

Sterling takes four strides.

And we collide.

CHAPTER 120

STERLING

HER HANDS REACH FOR ME, AND THAT'S ALL THE permission I need.

Her arms circle around my neck.

My hands grip her ass.

And when I lift her off the ground, her legs tighten around my hips.

Chapter 121

Courtney

Heat floods my core, and I moan as I press my lips to his.

Sterling slides his hands lower as he boosts me higher. And I can feel his fingers press so closely to my core.

Sparks ignite inside me, and I wiggle in his grip.

His fingers flex, and I feel the heat of his palms through my thin pajama pants.

My lips part, and he deepens the kiss.

His tongue pushing into me.

I open wider.

And I feel his hardness pulse against me.

Groaning, I tilt my hips into him, and his matching sound vibrates against my chest.

"Sterling," I pant against his mouth.

"I know," he replies.

Then he starts walking.

CHAPTER 122

STERLING

WHEN THE FRONT OF MY THIGHS HIT THE EDGE OF THE bed, I loosen my grip on Courtney, letting her slide the few inches down until she's sitting on the bunk.

But I keep her on the edge.

Legs still spread around my hips, our bodies pressed together.

She's at the perfect height like this.

Perfect for me to slam into her.

I'm so close to having her.

And I'm so hard it hurts.

So eager that I'm afraid I might black out.

But demons couldn't drag me away from Courtney right now.

Not a force in the world could keep me from plunging into her heat.

She reaches out for my shirt.

But I beat her to it, gripping the fabric in the middle and yanking it apart. The little metal clasps all click open.

Courtney starts to smile, looking like she might make a comment about the snap buttons. But then her hands are on me, running over my stomach and up my chest, and her jaw goes lax.

While she's distracted, I grab the bottom of her T-shirt and pull it up.

Her hands slip from my body as she raises her arms.

Her bare tits appear from beneath the fabric, and I can't wait.

Leaving her shirt bunched around her neck, I bend down and take one of her nipples into my mouth.

Hands dig into my hair, holding me closer.

I suck on the soft flesh, letting my teeth drag over her taut nipple.

My fingers close around her other breast, massaging it, feeling it. Then, as I suck harder, I pinch her nipple between my fingers while I bite the one that's in my mouth.

"Oh god." Her grip in my hair tightens, and her heels press into my sides.

I switch, moving my mouth to the other breast, plucking at the nipple I just finished sucking.

"Please, Sterling." Courtney's needy cry sounds like fucking music.

I flatten my tongue and lick up her chest. "Please what, Honey?"

"Please..." She tugs on my hair, and I pull back enough to see the flush on her cheeks.

Standing up straight, I grip myself through the front of my pants. "You want my cock? Is that what you're begging for?"

Courtney nods, releasing my hair and sliding her hands back down to my chest. "Yes. That's what I want."

I'm torn between wanting to hear her say naughty things and nutting over her not being able to.

I grip her wrists and bring her hands down to my jeans. "Take my dick out, and I'll give you what you want."

A whine leaves Courtney's throat as her fingers scramble to undo my button and pull my zipper down.

"That's it." I stroke a thumb over her cheek. "Feel how hard you've gotten me."

She shoves my jeans and boxers down, and they drop around my feet.

I exhale, and she inhales as her hands wrap around my length.

"So hard." She says it with awe, like she hasn't had my cock in her mouth before.

"All for you." I drag my hands down her body and grip the hem of her pants.

Courtney releases her hold on me and helps to shimmy her pants off.

No underwear.

She tosses her pants aside as I kick off mine, my boots going with them.

"Fucking delicious," I grit out as I spread her legs, a hand on each knee.

I start to bend down, wanting to get my mouth on her pussy again, but she grips my shoulders, nails digging into my skin.

"You promised." She pulls me to her.

I groan and squeeze the base of my dick. "I'm going to fuck you, Honey. I promise." I seal my mouth to hers. "I just wanted to eat you first. Get you ready."

She's shaking her head before I finish.

"I'm ready." Her legs tighten around my sides, pulling me closer. "I'm ready."

I want to lick her.

Want to make her come before I shove my dick inside her.

Want to make sure she's really ready to take me.

But I'm not a fucking saint.

And I'm not going to deny my girl.

Not when I can see the glisten between her legs.

With a firm grip, I rub the tip of my dick over her slit.

Her slick pussy is hot against my cock.

Dragging my eyes up from where I'm positioned at her entrance, I reach up with my free hand and palm the back of Courtney's neck.

I tighten my grip. "Eyes up here."

She lifts her gaze, eyes locking on mine.

I shift my feet, and the head of my dick starts to push inside her heat.

Courtney's fingers press into my shoulders.

I slowly push my hips forward. Sinking in an inch.

Her mouth parts as she sucks in a deep breath.

"You okay, Honey?" I let go of the base of my cock and grip her ass.

I push in another inch.

She's tight.

So tight.

Like her pussy is trying to keep me in place and keep me out at the same time.

I lower my forehead to hers.

My hand on her neck feels like the only thing keeping her upright.

So slowly, gritting my teeth, I sink in another inch and shift my feet closer to the edge of the bunk.

"Tell me you're okay." It's getting hard to talk. But she's not responding, and I can't make myself stop, so I need her to reply. "Courtney."

"I'm okay." She drags her nails up the back of my neck, fingers into my hair. She slides her other hand down until it's pressed to the center of my chest.

"Good." I push in another inch.

And another.

She gasps. Her head drops back.

I seal my mouth to her neck.

And I push in another inch.

I dig my fingers into the soft flesh of her ass as I hold her in place. And keep pushing.

Until I can't get any deeper.

Until we can't be any more connected.

CHAPTER 123

COURTNEY

PLEASURE AND THE PERFECT AMOUNT OF PAIN overtake my body.

It's so much.

His cock is filling me so full.

He's almost too big.

But it's exactly enough.

Because it's Sterling.

All of Sterling.

I hold him to me, hands moving to his shoulders, as my body works to accept him.

I can feel *everything*.

Tears prick at the corners of my eyes, even as I squeeze them shut.

The feeling of *him* is just so intense, it's overwhelming me.

My pussy pulses around him.

The sharp pinch of his intrusion is starting to fade.

And I'm ready for more.

Chapter 124

Sterling

My balls squeeze, and I press my open mouth against Courtney's bare shoulder as I breathe.

Two breaths. Three.

One more.

Then I lift my head. And pull my hips back.

I look down between us.

She's still perched on the edge of the bunk, legs spread, pussy swallowing the tip of my dick.

I flex my fingers against the back of Courtney's neck as I feel her tip her head forward, wanting to look too.

I ram my hips forward.

Courtney claws at my shoulders as she cries out.

I do it again.

She curses.

I pause.

We watch each other.

Chests heaving.

Fingers digging.

"Don't stop." Courtney's whispered request sends a shudder down my spine.

I pull almost all the way out of her hot slit. "Don't worry, Honey. I'm not stopping until you come on my cock."

I lower my head, and she arches her neck as I thrust forward.

Our bodies connect like a lewd puzzle as our mouths wrestle to taste as much of each other as possible.

And something swells in my chest as I hug Courtney's body to mine.

CHAPTER 125

COURTNEY

HIS COCK IS SO BIG. SO THICK AND FILLING THAT I can't catch my breath.

I can't catch my heartbeat.

Teeth graze over my tongue, and my pussy clenches in reply.

I thought I'd had sex before.

I thought I knew what sex was.

But Sterling Black is like nothing I've ever experienced.

His muscular body looms over mine.

His strength surrounds me. Holds me up.

His heaving breaths... His sweat-slicked skin...

His cock.

Goddamn, his cock is glorious.

And he keeps going.

Keeps pumping into me.

I've never been so stretched.

Never felt so free.

CHAPTER 126

STERLING

HER TIGHTNESS DRAGGING UP AND DOWN MY LENGTH IS too good.

Too much.

And her clinging to me.

Moaning around my tongue.

Tits rubbing against my bare chest.

It's sending me toward the edge.

And I need to keep my word.

I need to make my girl come before I do.

Courtney breaks the kiss, and our heaving breaths fill the room.

She says something, but I can't hear it over the ringing in my ears.

I pull my hips back, then shove them forward.

"What'd you say?" I'm leaning back in. Wanting her mouth on mine again.

Then she repeats herself.

"I'm on the pill." Her lashes flutter as she tells me. "In case you..."

Christ.

I groan and shut my eyes.

In case I want to come inside her.

Yes.

Yes, I'd like that very much.

I snap my eyes open and move my hand from the back of her neck to the base of her throat.

Then, I push.

CHAPTER 127

COURTNEY

I LAND ON MY BACK, THE MATTRESS ABSORBING THE contact.

The glow from the bathroom light in the hall illuminates the bedroom enough that I'm on full display.

Laid out. Arms wide. Legs spread. Nude.

A deep rumbling sound rolls out of Sterling's chest.

My back arches.

"Fucking death of me," Sterling says as he grips my hips and yanks me a few inches toward him, holding me with my ass halfway off the bed.

Then he starts thrusting again.

Slamming his hips forward.

Stuffing my pussy full of dick with each stroke.

He gets so deep there's a twinge of pain.

But... I like it.

I think I really like it.

The ache Sterling's cock causes is... exhilarating.

And I already want to do this again.

I want to do this every night.

My body slides up the bed with each slam of his hips, and I search for purchase. But my fingers only close around blankets.

"Arms up." He slides his hands up my body until he's palming both my tits, his rough fingers hot against my soft flesh.

"Arms?" I blink at him.

"Over your head, Cookie. Put your hands on the wall." Sterling pinches my nipples. "Brace yourself."

I reach my arms straight up.

Lying like this, sideways across the small bed, my hands reach the wall.

And I brace myself.

Sterling gives my nipples a tug, then he moves his grip to the top of my thighs, right where they crease at my hips.

Holding me firmly, he goes back to working his cock in and out of me.

I can feel my tits bounce with each collision.

Can feel everything bounce.

Can feel the head of his dick dragging against that spot inside me.

And he has me so close.

So fucking close.

CHAPTER 128

STERLING

COURTNEY'S NECK IS ARCHED. HER VISION IS unfocused.

I release my hold of her with my right hand.

And I watch her expression as I press my thumb down on her clit.

Her mouth drops open. Her hips lift. And she lets out a deep moan.

My body reacts with hers.

Watching her like this... it's so fucking hot.

It's making me so fucking hard.

She squirms.

And I know she's close.

I circle my thumb.

Her pussy clenches.

I thrust deeper.

Her moans get louder.

I press my thumb down a little firmer.

She cries my name.

I feel my balls pulse.

And I need her to go over.

Slamming deep, I let go with my other hand, reach up, and tug on her nipple just as I rub her little clit faster.

Her hands leave the wall, dropping to grip my forearms.

Her nails dig into my skin.

And I know she's ready.

"Eyes up here," I grit out.

She opens her eyes.

"Now come."

Nails scrape across my arm. And she combusts.

Her body arches off the bed.

Her pussy contracts around my cock.

And I explode.

I rock my hips against her.

Staying as far inside her pussy as I can while I flood her with my release.

CHAPTER 129

COURTNEY

MY MUSCLES QUIT WORKING ALL AT ONCE, AND I MELT into the bed.

Sterling's body is still shuddering, hunched over mine, hands braced on either side of me.

He's still inside me.

Still stretching me.

And I don't know if I'm dead or in an unfamiliar state of euphoria, but either way, I'm happy.

I'm happy with whatever version of life or death this is. Because I've never felt more satisfied or more sexy.

And if this is real life, I'm going to need more of it.

CHAPTER 130

STERLING

WHEN I FEEL LIKE I CAN FINALLY SEE STRAIGHT, I LIFT my head and meet Courtney's glassy gaze.

She looks well and truly fucked.

And my inner beast preens.

We did that.

Her lips pull up into a soft smile.

She looks so pleased. So at ease.

With me.

My stomach gives a twist. Part disbelief. Part wonder. Part something new.

Don't get ahead of yourself.

It's just one fuck.

Not a forever.

But...

I swallow.

"Can I stay?" My voice comes out scratchy.

Her smile grows. Her relaxation a balm to my racing thoughts.

"Like overnight, or..." She glances down to where we're still joined.

I groan. "Overnight, Cookie."

344

"Then yes." Her answer sounds suddenly shy. And that makes me all the more certain that I want to stay.

Standing upright, still inside her, I reach down and grip Courtney's ankles. Then I lift her legs straight up until they're pressed together in front of me.

The position tightens her core around me, and I can't stop myself from pulling partway out, then pushing back in.

It's all too much on my sensitive dick, but her moan makes it worth it.

"Stay," I tell her, flexing my grip on her ankles before letting go.

I grunt when I slip free of her heat.

And she lets out a little squeak when I drag my fingers down her slit, needing to feel the sticky warmth.

I smirk.

Naked, I stride away from my messy pinup girl and head into the bathroom.

I blink against the brightness.

Then I freeze.

The sight of red streaking across my dick is making my brain glitch.

It's not a lot.

I don't think it's from a period. I've had period sex. Doesn't bother me in the least. But it doesn't usually look like this.

Without cleaning myself off, I turn back around.

CHAPTER 131

COURTNEY

HANDS AGAINST MY STOMACH, ANKLES CROSSED, LEGS straight up in the air, I feel exposed but surprisingly not self-conscious.

A man doesn't fuck you like Sterling just fucked me if he doesn't like your body.

Heavy steps announce Sterling's return.

I start to lower my legs, but he grips my ankles in one hand, holding them in place.

I look to his other hand, but it's still empty.

"I'm going to ask you a question, and I want an honest answer." His serious tone sends a tendril of unease through me.

"Okay..." I slide my hands up to cover my tits, suddenly feeling that self-consciousness I thought I'd lost.

He uses his free hand to pull one of my hands away. "Don't cover yourself from me."

I huff out a breath and drop my other hand back to my stomach. "Don't freak me out with lead-ups. Ask your question."

His eyes stay on mine. "Are you a virgin?"

I feel my mouth literally drop open.

The hell?

"No, Sterling. I am not a virgin." My tone is bland.

He rolls his eyes. "*Were* you a virgin?"

Is this man for real?

"At one point in my life? Yes. An hour ago? No." I widen my eyes at him. "Do you want me to tell you about my first time?"

The hand on my ankle lets go and smacks my ass.

I yelp. And then I can feel the mess of bare sex leaking out of me.

"Can you get me some tissues or get out of the way?" I ask, bending my knees.

"I'll clean you up when you tell me why there's blood on my dick." He reaches back between my legs, running his fingers down my slit again.

"Sterling," I gasp.

He pushes a finger inside me.

I groan.

"Tell me." He sounds distracted. But the fact he's casually playing with my pussy tells me he isn't disgusted by the blood. Which is good because that would be ridiculous.

"I wasn't a virgin," I tell him calmly. "But you're... big. And... enthusiastic."

The finger inside me stills. "I hurt you?"

His question is so quiet I almost miss it as he slowly pulls his finger free.

"No—"

"Fuck." He holds his hands up. Like he's afraid of hurting me more.

What a moron.

"Sterling," I snap. He meets my gaze. "Quit acting weird. I like it rough. Now go get me some tissue."

I watch his jaw work before he spins and strides back to the bathroom, toned butt cheeks on full display.

He's back a moment later and stays quiet after handing me a clump of tissues.

He keeps waiting until I sit up and start to slide off the bed.

"Dammit, Courtney." He darts forward and grips my waist to help me down.

"I'm fine," I tell him, but he doesn't let me go. Our still naked bodies pressed together.

He reaches one hand up to lightly grip my chin. "Are you telling me the truth? Do you really like it rough?"

His tone is even, but his eyes are heated.

"I do. Though I'll admit, it's a new revelation."

"How new?"

I drag my teeth over my bottom lip. "Very new."

Sterling makes a sound low in his throat. "You better be telling the truth."

"Why's that?" I can't help but ask.

He slides his hand around from my chin to the back of my neck. "Because if some other man ever got rough with you…"

"That's never happened," I tell him honestly. "Never in the bedroom and never in any other way."

He flexes his jaw as he nods. "Go get dressed."

CHAPTER 132

COURTNEY

When I step out of my little bathroom, I find Sterling sitting on the bed, leaned back against the wall, with a bag of sandwich cookies in his lap.

All the lights are off in the cabin, but one of the camping lamps has appeared at Sterling's side, set to low, filling the room with a nice glow.

Silently, I climb onto the bunk.

I'm in the same pair of pajamas as earlier, and he's in boxers. Just boxers.

I sit facing him. "Cookies?"

He nods, then holds the open package out to me.

This is one of the food items that he left in the cupboard.

I select one, the chocolate filling too much to resist, and take a bite.

He does the same.

"What's your favorite dessert?" I ask before taking another bite.

"Apple pie." His eyes stay on mine. "What's your favorite cookie?"

"All of them." I smile. "But a classic chocolate chip is hard to beat. Do you cook?"

He tips his head side to side. "Some. But my skills are limited to specific dishes."

"Like what?"

"Chili. Steaks. Spaghetti." He shrugs and takes out another cookie. "Or whatever leftovers I can get off Cook." He holds the cookie out to me, and I take it, even though I'm still working on my first. "You cook or stick to mini pies?"

I pop another bite of cookie into my mouth. "I don't mind cooking, but I think I'd like it more if I had a big kitchen. My last place had the biggest kitchen I've ever had. But it was still cramped." I use my empty hand to gesture toward the other end of my Laundry Cabin. "The microwave is a major improvement here, thank you. The just-add-water stuff can get old."

He sets the bag between us. "What was your last place like?"

"Just your typical outdated and overpriced apartment building."

"Is that why you left?" Sterling sounds like he's trying to be cautious. "Because it was overpriced?"

Do I want to explain to Sterling just how broke I am? No, no, I don't.

But I will.

Because there's something between us.

And because every time he finds out there's something wrong with my living conditions here, he's fixed it.

The mattress.

The appliances.

The food.

The heat.

Maybe I don't *owe him*, because my life is my own and I don't owe anyone anything.

But maybe I need to try to trust someone.

It's been a long time since I've had someone to trust.

I push away the tightness growing in my throat. "I moved into that building when I got the job working as the on-site maintenance person. It didn't pay much, but my apartment was included. And I needed that."

He tilts his head to the side. "Why did you need that? Where were you living before?"

I shove more cookie into my mouth, wondering how far back I should go.

I swallow my mouthful, then sigh.

Fuck it.

"I grew up in an RV with my mom," I tell him. "And by the time high school graduation came around, I knew I had to find somewhere else to live. It was too crowded for the both of us." Sterling nods like he understands. And even though I'd moved to the bed above the front seats by the time I was a teen, it was still too small. Even if it had been a big fancy RV, I still would have needed the space. "Financial aid meant I could go to college. And getting a job as an RA, a resident adviser, meant I had free room and board. So as soon as I was able, I moved onto campus. And I managed to keep that arrangement the full four years."

"What was your major?"

I blow out a breath. "I couldn't decide on anything I really wanted to do, so I ended up with business administration. Honestly, I hated it. I never got bad grades, but school wasn't easy for me. And I always wanted to be out doing things. But even jobs that don't seem like they need degrees still wanted one. So, I stuck to it."

Sterling lets out a hum of understanding. "I get that."

"Did you go to college?" I'm curious now that we're talking about it.

He shakes his head. "No. School wasn't my thing either. And living out here, there were always guide positions open."

"Guides like the guys here?"

Sterling nods and reaches for another cookie. "Pretty much. I'd already been working for some of the tour companies during the summer. Hunting, fishing, camping, whatever they wanted.

And when I was done with high school, I was able to start full time. It's what appealed to me most."

"I was wondering... why don't you offer hunting trips?" I've wanted to ask since I started.

"Liability. Too many idiots who think they're a good shot. And too many hotheads who get pissed if they don't shoot something. If people want to catch their own food, they can do a fishing trip."

"Makes sense," I agree, grateful the Lodge isn't overrun with rifles on a regular basis.

"Did you move back in with your mom after school?" Sterling shifts back to the previous topic.

"No." I snort, trying to picture it. "Even if she hadn't taken off, I'd never move back into that sardine can."

CHAPTER 133

STERLING

My teeth are touching the cookie, but I don't bite down.

Taken off?

Her mom took off?

"I found a studio apartment that rented month to month and moved there after graduation. I was still working the jobs I had in college, but when I found the listing for my last job, I jumped on it. I wasn't exactly qualified, but I'd had to fix a lot of shit in that RV, so I knew enough." She keeps talking, but I'm still stuck on her mom *taking off*. "I think I was there for like eight years? But then the building got purchased, and I lost my job."

I blink at her. "You were there for nearly a decade, and the new owners just fired you?"

What the fuck?

"Yeah. Said they would *use their own people*. Which meant I lost my job *and* that I had to start paying rent. Which, I'll add, was much more expensive than it was when I first moved in." Courtney lifts a shoulder, like that didn't devastate her life.

"That's shit."

"Kinda was. But then I found this gig." She smiles at me. Fucking smiles.

And I see it all so clearly now.

Courtney losing her job through circumstances out of her hands.

Her housing situation flipping on her. Costing her more than she could afford.

Her finding the job at the Lodge, packing up her life, and driving across the country to start over.

Courtney finding me.

Me telling her I wouldn't hire her.

The way she must've felt...

Fuck.

The way she must've felt when I told her no. When she had nothing to return to.

I put the cookie back in the bag.

"I'm sorry." My voice is hoarse.

Her smile wavers, but she keeps it from falling. "It all worked out. So, when did you buy the Lodge?" She changes the topic.

I feel like a piece of shit. And I want to apologize for my behavior, but if she doesn't want to talk about it, I won't force it. "I bought the land when I was thirty, then spent a few years building my house and the cabins while I continued to work elsewhere. But now, Black Mountain Lodge has been open for twelve years. And in that time, I've bought up more property, especially from my old bosses when they retired."

"That's pretty clever." Her expression is impressed, and I like it more than I should.

"Thank you. Most people don't know it, but all the cabins and camping sites we take guests to... I own them."

Her brows lift. "Really? Even the guys don't know?"

"Pretty sure they all think I rent them from someone else. And since it keeps them on schedule clearing out and cleaning up..." I shrug. "Why mess with a good thing?"

Courtney snickers. "Clever boy."

"I have my moments." I reach back into the cookie bag and take out the one I put back.

"So..." She closes one eye, and I pause with the cookie halfway to my mouth. "How old are you?"

Not expecting the question, I take a moment, trying to remember how old I am, before I answer. "Forty-six."

She smiles. "Forget for a minute?"

I grunt and bite the cookie.

"When's your birthday?" She asks me what should've been the obvious next question.

But I'm still caught off guard.

And I don't want to tell her.

But I can't really refuse.

CHAPTER 134

COURTNEY

"OCTOBER FIFTH," STERLING TELLS ME.

"Oh, that's..." My smile fades.

That was this month. A few days after I started.

Was that the day we got the new mattresses?

Time has been a blur since I got here, but I would've remembered if anyone said anything. I was definitely eating in the Food Hall by then.

And no one said anything.

Did anyone even know?

"It's not a big deal, Cookie." Sterling's voice is soft.

He can probably read the emotions as they cross my features.

"Does anyone know?" I keep my voice just as soft.

"Don't think so. No reason to." He sounds like he means it. Unbothered.

But I... I don't really have anyone who celebrates with me either—with the exception of my mom calling me each year. The one day I'm guaranteed a call, along with Christmas. So, I get it. I would give the same answer. And I'd mostly mean it.

But I was also mostly alone. Working by myself. Living alone.

Sterling, though, was surrounded on his birthday, by all of us, and no one said a thing.

Why does that feel so much worse?

"When's your birthday?" Sterling asks me, breaking the silence.

"March twenty-third," I answer.

"What's your favorite color?"

The heaviness that was settling over me lifts. It's such a silly question for one adult to ask another. But I kind of love it.

"Forest green." It's always been green, but I think my time living amid the pine trees has altered my answer. "What's yours?"

"Light blue. Do you have any siblings?"

A small laugh bubbles out of me at the way he's all over the place with these questions. "No. Just me and my mom. Never met my dad." When his mouth twists, I realize it's not really something people say casually. But it's the truth. I know the man's name. But he wanted nothing to do with my mom when she got pregnant, so I want nothing to do with him. Easy as that. "You have siblings?"

"Two pain-in-my-ass brothers. We don't see each other too often. One's in Denver, near where my mom lives now, and the other is out in California. And a dad I wish I didn't know." I feel anger coat my features, but Sterling waves me off, once again reading my thoughts. "He wasn't abusive or any shit like that. Just worthless. In and out of our lives for the first handful of years until he up and moved out of state. Then we'd go years without hearing from him. Finally, one day, my mom stopped taking his calls, and that was that."

"Sucks." I pick up another cookie, then hold it out. "To shit dads."

Sterling huffs out a laugh and taps his partially eaten cookie to mine. "To being better off without them."

We take bites at the same time, savoring the sweets and the truth.

"So." I lick the crumbs off my fingertips. "You said you built your house. Does that mean you helped design it?"

Sterling nods and tells me about the process. How he hired a builder and then an architect. Tells me about the layout he wanted, and what he would do differently now that he's older, has more money, and has lived in the house for a while.

While we talk, we get under the covers.

I snuggle into Sterling's side and place my head on that perfect spot between his chest and shoulder. And we keep talking.

He asks why I always wear my hair in braids as he gently drags his hand down one.

I tell him it's for function, to keep my hair out of my face, and that it's just become a habit.

He tells me he likes it.

I tell him I like his beard.

He asks me about Spike.

I explain how she's my pet, and I love her.

He asks me if I know how much I talk out loud while I'm working.

I ask if he knows how much he scowls while he's working.

We talk about all the other properties he owns, and I ask how the outhouses get cleaned.

He asks me how I feel about living in the mountains.

I tell him that I can communicate with bears now.

He gives me advice on what to do if I see one again.

I ask if he's ever had pets.

He's quiet for a moment before he tells me about the dog he had growing up.

His fingers trace circles on my arm as he talks about the lab mix his family adopted from the shelter.

His fingers still when he tells me how hard it was to put him down when he got old and frail.

I rub circles on his chest as I tell him how much I'd love a dog. How, if I had one, I'd want it to be one that sticks to my side all day.

He asks what breed of dog I'd want.

"I wouldn't care." I close my eyes, imagining it. "I just think it would feel good to save one from a cramped kennel. Give them a home where they could run around a bit."

As I say it, I see the parallel. The way I want to help someone avoid the enclosed existence I've felt trapped in for far too long.

Sterling kisses the top of my head.

Then he does it again, with his arms tightening around me.

I press my lips together.

Then I blow out my breath and ask him what his favorite season is.

He tells me fall.

And when he asks me mine, I tell him spring.

Sterling explains what the winter is going to be like up here.

I promise him I'll buy boots when I buy my jacket.

And I resist the urge to ask him if I'll still be working here in January.

It's a fair question. One I will eventually need an answer to, but asking about it right now feels wrong.

So I don't bring it up.

Instead, we talk about how we both hate the holidays. How he avoids his family drama and chaos by working through them—either on real work outings or going out on trips with his bachelor friends.

I explain how I still talk to my mom, but it's not often. And that I've rarely been able to afford to travel to see her. And how she claims it's always too far to drive back *just for one day*.

I admit how much it hurt over the years. And how I've come to terms with it.

And then we keep talking.

Sterling tells me about the time he went rafting with his friends and nearly drowned as a teenager. How he got grounded for a month, and his mom made him eat brussels sprouts with every meal as added punishment.

"That's actually pretty brilliant." I smile against his chest

"Joke's on her. By the end of the second week, I'd started liking them."

"Seriously?"

I can feel him nod. "If she'd just given me plain steamed ones, I probably would've hated them the whole time. But she was eating them, too, and clearly got sick of having them plain. So she started roasting them with maple syrup or sautéing them in butter." He rubs his hand over his stomach. "I need to ask Cook to make some soon."

We talk more about food and getting in trouble.

Where I kept my head down in class, Sterling apparently got sent to the principal's office on the regular.

We keep telling stories.

Keep tracing patterns on each other with our fingertips.

We keep sharing.

We make up for all the times we didn't talk.

And when Sterling curses, pointing out that the sunrise is starting to glow around the curtains, I feel like I know him.

I feel like we've known each other for years.

I feel like I can call Sterling Black my friend.

CHAPTER 135

STERLING

I REACH DOWN TO THE HAND COURTNEY HAS ON MY chest and lace our fingers together. "Go to sleep, Honey."

"But it's almost time to get up." She yawns, and I close my eyes at the feeling of her open mouth against my bare skin.

"There's nothing for us to do until the groups come back, and that won't be until eleven at the earliest."

Courtney lets out a sleepy hum. "You'll stay?"

"Yeah." I give her fingers a light squeeze. "I'll stay."

And as she slips into dreamland, I think about everything we talked about.

Think about the things I told her that I haven't told anyone.

Think about the series of events that brought her to me.

I hate that part. Hate all she's been through. Hate how she's had to do it all on her own.

I understand what it's like. But I hate it for her.

And as I follow her into unconsciousness, I do something I haven't done in a long time.

I think about the future.

CHAPTER 136

COURTNEY

I FEEL LIKE I'VE HAD A PERMANENT BLUSH ALL DAY, SO I thank Helios for removing the sun from the sky and making it dark enough that no one can see the color in my cheeks anymore.

"Court, you want another beer?" Simpson asks as he stands from his spot next to me.

I automatically glance at Sterling, even as I tell Simpson yes.

Sterling is on his third as well. And I have to admit, the idea of drunken sex with that man is *very* appealing.

"Thank you." I accept the opened bottle from Simpson.

When I woke up this morning—at eleven, when the alarm Sterling set on my phone went off—I was alone. But his side of my small bed was still warm.

I did my best to seem cool and collected over lunch, then busied myself stripping the beds in one of the cabins and starting the laundry.

The group I didn't have the fish fry with is still here. They live farther away and paid for an extra night so they could leave tomorrow at dawn rather than today after lunch. Which is why three men I don't know are sitting around the fire with the Lodge employees.

They seem nice enough, but they also have a *dude bro* vibe that I don't have the energy for. So I'm sticking to my conversation with Simpson and Fisher while catching as many glances of Sterling as I can.

CHAPTER 137

STERLING

I watch Courtney drain the last of her third beer while nodding at something Simpson says.

When they both stand, I press my own bottle to my lips and tip it back.

The fire is dwindling, and one of the guests has already gone to bed. But I've been waiting for Courtney. Because I'll be damned if I don't sleep in her bed again tonight.

I should find a way to get her into my house.

Into my much larger bed.

I lower the empty bottle.

Though there is merit to the small bed.

Less space. More contact.

"Good night, everyone." Courtney lifts her hand in a little wave.

The embers are giving off the faintest light, but even in the dark, Courtney is beyond tempting.

Her bed.

Definitely her bed tonight.

Fisher also gets up, and there's a round of good-nights as he and Simpson walk off with Courtney between them.

I'm debating how quickly I can get up and follow when one of the two remaining guests gets to his feet.

He's the quiet one.

Been polite.

Didn't drink much.

But he's been watching Courtney.

She's an attractive woman. The only woman here. So I get it.

But when he gives the group a nod and walks off into the dark, I get to my feet.

Chapter 138

Courtney

"Night," I say as I let Fisher take my empty bottle.

He and Simpson break off toward the Bunk House, and I continue on the path toward my cabin.

The air is crisp, and I have Sterling's flannel on under my thickest sweater.

The extra layer is warm, but that's just a bonus. I could wear any of my other shirts, but the flannel makes me feel close to him.

Makes me feel like he's with me.

My boots crunch over the gravel, and I tip my head back as I walk, looking up at the stars.

The moon is a sliver tonight. Beautiful and picturesque. But leaving the world dark.

I look back down at the path in front of me.

I forgot my flashlight in the cabin. And I know I should probably worry about running into Lady Bear, or some other forest-dwelling creature, but I'm more focused on being proud of myself.

My first day here, I couldn't fathom walking all this way in the dark.

Now it feels like... home.

Home.

What an idea.

I know I've used the word before, thinking about this place, my cabin. But it feels... bigger now.

Home feels like more than just where I'm sleeping.

If I wasn't buzzed, the thought might choke me up. But—I smile in the night—I am buzzed.

And I'm certain Sterling is going to come to me tonight.

And I don't care how sore I am *down there*. I'll welcome him with open legs.

CHAPTER 139

STERLING

RED DOTS MY VISION.

Courtney is crossing the driveway.

And the man is following her.

My hands open and close at my sides.

He. Is. Following. Her.

I keep my footsteps silent as I trail a few paces away.

This is my land. My property. I know how to move through it without making a noise.

And the fact this guy is doing the same... I doubt this is his first time following a woman.

I want to call out to Courtney.

Want to warn her.

But I also don't want to frighten her.

And I want to make sure my rage is correctly placed.

I'll give this man the distance between here and the Laundry Cabin to change his mind.

But if he goes all the way to her front steps, he won't be walking away.

CHAPTER 140

COURTNEY

EXCITEMENT FILLS ME AS I PLAY THROUGH IMAGES OF what will happen tonight.

As I cross the driveway, I start to hum the tune to "Side to Side."

And I grin to myself as I continue on the narrower path, the final stretch to my cabin.

A second night in a row with Sterling Black will surely have me walking sideways.

CHAPTER 141

STERLING

I GRIT MY TEETH.

My woman is fucking humming.

She's being stalked by the worst kind of predator, and she's fucking humming.

But if she's going to unwittingly give me cover, I'm going to take it.

I lengthen my stride, closing more of the distance between me and the man.

Courtney sways as she starts up the steps to her cabin.

The lights are off inside.

The light is off over her front door.

Nothing but darkness surrounds her.

She keeps humming as she makes it to the top step.

Unaware of the man standing at the base of her stairs.

He pauses.

Waiting for her to unlock the door.

He's silent.

He's not here to hit on her.

He's here to harm her.

I'm five strides away.

And when I hear the deadbolt unlock, I sprint the final steps.

CHAPTER 142

THE FUCKING CREEP

My blood simmers when I hear the lock turn.

Go on, bitch. Open the fucking door.

I lift my right foot and place it on the bottom step without making a sound.

Handy that they gave the woman her own cabin. A place she can fuck everyone on staff in private.

The door to the little cabin opens, and the whore steps over the threshold.

I saw the way she was looking at all the men.

I saw the way she looked at me.

She was practically asking for it.

I climb another step.

The door starts to close behind her.

I lunge forward, reaching for the edge of the door, all of my weight on my right foot.

My mouth opens in a smile.

But then my foot is forcefully yanked out from beneath me.

My hands grapple but find nothing.

I'm too slow.

Too confused.

My face connects with the top step.
Pain explodes through my brain as I feel my nose crunch.
But I'm still moving.
I didn't fall.
Someone is dragging me off the stairs.

CHAPTER 143

COURTNEY

I FLIP THE INSIDE LIGHT ON JUST AS THE DOOR CLICKS shut behind me.

I stop humming, thinking I heard something. But it's nothing.

Turning the deadbolt—to please Sterling—I go back to humming.

Time to get ready for bed and wait for my boss to find me.

Chapter 144

Sterling

I give the man's ankle a violent jerk, and I feel something pop in the joint as I drag him off the steps.

Courtney's door clicks shut.

I know he's going to scream any second now.

I twist his already injured ankle. Hard.

He turns with the movement—the body's natural reaction to try to stop the pain.

But that just puts him flat on his back. Which is exactly where I want the Fucking Creep.

I drop on top of him.

Straddling his torso.

His eyes are wide. His face covered in blood from his broken nose.

And I'm too furious to be controlled.

Controlled is the last thing I feel.

His mouth opens.

But I can't let him speak.

If I hear a single word. If he tries to lie to me. If he tries to justify himself. I'll kill him.

And I need him silent.

I will not let him terrorize my girl.

Releasing my rage, I slam my fist into his chest.

I hear the air get stuck in his lungs.

His diaphragm is seizing.

It's not a death blow.

But it'll keep him quiet.

The thud of Courtney locking her deadbolt settles over me.

She's safe.

And I'm going to keep her that way.

I throw another punch.

My knuckles collide with his cheekbone.

My other fist connects with the other side of his face.

I think about what would have happened if I wasn't following him.

I punch his already broken nose.

He tries to push me away.

I think about the fear Courtney would have felt if he'd shoved through her door behind her.

I grip one of his hands in both of mine.

And I squeeze.

I squeeze as hard as I fucking can.

He writhes.

He claws at me with his other hand.

But I'm picturing Courtney's eyes full of fear.

I'm remembering her telling me how no one has ever been rough with her.

And I'm thinking about how I want that to be her truth forever.

I feel the crunch.

Feel the fragile hand bones failing.

And I squeeze fucking harder.

His diaphragm finally releases, and he drags in precious oxygen.

I drop his hand and punch him in the face again.

He grunts.

Knees pound against my back as he rocks side to side below me.

I reach back and thrust my fist down.

My form isn't good, but it's good enough.

I do it again.

And again.

His tiny dick taking each hit.

A sharp cry finally leaves him.

I lean forward and slug him in the chest again.

If this motherfucker dies from lack of oxygen, that's on him.

He swings at me with his unbroken hand.

And I fucking grin when I catch it. "If you insist."

My hands are already sore.

My knuckles are split.

But nothing will stop me from fucking up his second hand.

I interlock my fingers, his hand trapped between mine, and I squeeze.

I think about Courtney asleep against my chest.

I think about her fingers entwined with mine.

I think about her telling me that her mom would hold her hand like that to comfort her when she was young.

And I think about this fucking piece of shit man beneath me.

I think about the damage his hands could do.

And still gripping his crushed fingers, I wrench my hands down.

His wrist snaps.

"Uh, Boss?" Fisher's voice breaks through the haze surrounding me.

I glance up, annoyed I didn't hear him coming. "Yeah?"

Fisher makes a choking sound as he looks between me and the man I'm sitting on. "What's, uh, going on?"

I hear the next set of footsteps a moment before Simpson steps up beside Fisher.

The fucking creep beneath me starts to breathe again. "H-help me." His voice is garbled. "H-he's killing—"

I release his broken wrist and slam my fist into his chest again.

I think I feel a rib crack.

Good.

When I look back up, both of my employees move their gazes to Courtney's cabin.

"Was he—" Simpson's voice cuts off.

He thinks of Courtney as one of his daughters, and even in the dark, I can see his features shift. Rage and fear. The same mix that's poisoning my blood.

I keep my voice low. "He was going to." I turn back to the man and punch him in the face again. I look back up to my guys. "She doesn't know."

Simpson holds his hand out to me.

I'm not done with the Creep, but I still take Simpson's hand and let him haul me up.

He grips my shoulder with his other hand, steadying me.

Adrenaline is still coursing through my body, and I take the moment to calm my breathing.

A thud sounds behind me.

Turning, I watch Fisher kick the man on the ground.

In the ribs. The leg.

When the man rolls onto his side, Fisher kicks him in the ass.

And I decide the kid is alright.

Chapter 145

Courtney

Face washed, teeth brushed, and lotion applied, I turn off the lights and head into my bedroom.

I know Sterling is going to come to me tonight.

The looks we shared over the fire weren't casual.

They were as heated as the flames.

And I'm ready for him.

Wearing his flannel, a pair of black panties, and nothing else, I climb into bed.

I consider texting him, asking how long he'll be, but I set my phone down on the edge of the bunk instead.

I can be patient.

And I can wait while I rest my eyes.

CHAPTER 146

STERLING

The lights go out in the Laundry Cabin.

Simpson steps past me and delivers his own kick to the back of the man's thighs. "Bastard," he hisses.

With my girl climbing into bed a few yards away, the need to get this man away from her becomes unbearable.

I bend down and grip his ankles, aware one is probably broken, and I start to drag him.

He lets out a cry.

I drop his ankles, spin to face him, and drop to one knee.

He holds his mangled hands up.

I bat them away with my left hand, then crash my right fist into his chest. Again.

As he once again struggles to breathe, I put all my weight onto his chest as I brace against it to push myself back up.

Fisher nods at me with impressed approval written across his features. "Want me to drag him?" he asks quietly.

I shake my head and scoop up the man's ankles again, then start dragging him. "Leon wasn't drinking tonight. Go wake him up and have him pull his truck up to the house."

"On it." Fisher barely has the words out before he's running away into the dark.

"What else you need?" Simpson asks, his voice full of emotion.

I'll get there.

But not yet.

I'm not ready to be anything but furious yet.

"I need you to stay here and keep an eye on his buddies. Don't interact if they come looking for him. Play dumb." I look over at Simpson, and he nods. "I'll figure out something to tell them in the morning."

We reach the front of my house, and I drop the man's feet.

He groans.

Simpson kicks him.

"I'm not sure how many more hits your ribs can take," I tell the man. "So maybe shut the fuck up on your own, yeah?"

Simpson stands by my side as we stand over the Creep.

"You did good," Simpson tells me after a minute of silence.

I stare down at the man at our feet. "I want to kill him."

The man whimpers.

Simpson lays a hand on my shoulder. "You did good."

Headlights cut through the woods, then Leon's pickup comes into view.

It's a big red thing with a topper. Ideal so no one can see our cargo, and so our cargo can't fall out.

"Keep kicking him if he tries to move," I say to Simpson before jogging into the dark.

I'm back from the Storage Shed in less than a minute with a length of rope in my grip.

Fisher, good with knots, helps me tie the man's hands behind his back. Then we use the excess rope to tie his feet together before we not-so-carefully lift him into the back of the truck.

"You're in the back seat," I tell Fisher. "You can keep an eye on him through the rear window." I roll out my shoulders. "My old ass can't sit twisted like that."

Fisher huffs a laugh as he climbs up into the back seat. "Maybe not, but your old ass can throw a punch."

I grunt and grip the *oh shit* handle to pull myself up into the passenger seat.

Leon is still behind the wheel, having stayed seated, quietly listening to classic rock while we hog-tied a man.

He turns his head to look at me. "Where to?"

That's it. No other questions.

"The Inn."

Leon nods, then shifts into drive and does a U-turn, heading down the driveway.

As we reach the end of the drive, we pass the gate that's permanently open.

It's not electric. Just a hunk of metal with a chain and rusted open padlock.

It wouldn't help security-wise for guests who are already here, but maybe I need to start closing it at night. Or install a security system on the Laundry Cabin. Something with a panic button.

As Leon turns out onto the road, he stomps on the gas, and the rear of the truck fishtails onto the pavement.

There's a thud, then a cry from the bed.

Leon looks at me. "Oops."

Fisher snickers, then heaves out a deep breath. "I'm so fucking glad you were there." I glance back, catching his eye. "After we got to the Bunk House, Simpson and I were both feeling weird about that guy. Didn't like how he left the same time as us." He shakes his head. "We decided to check on Court, make sure she got to her cabin alright. Then we heard the scream... My heart fucking stopped for a second. We thought it was her."

I work to swallow.

I was right there.

Right fucking there when that slimy fuck tried to get his hands on Courtney's door.

Even if he'd gotten his fingers on the door, I never would've let him touch her.

I have to keep reminding myself.

He never would have fucking touched her.

I was right there.

I flex my fists.

But he still got too close.

I pull my phone out of my pocket and dial Rocky.

"Sterling."

"I need a favor."

He hums on the other end of the line. "Consider me interested."

"You know those security cameras you have behind your office building?"

"What cameras?"

The start of a smirk pulls at my lips. "I have some trash for your dumpster."

"A happy camper?" I can hear the humor in Rocky's voice.

Leon hits the brakes harder than necessary as we approach a stop sign.

There's another thud. Another cry.

"He's not that happy," I answer.

"Noted. I'll make sure none of my staff head that way for the cigarettes they think I don't know about." He pauses a moment. "You need anything else?"

"That's plenty. I'll owe you."

"I'll remember," Rocky states before hanging up.

Leon chuckles. "Curious what sort of favor that man will ask for."

"Me too."

We stay silent for the rest of the drive until we near the Inn, then I direct Leon where to go.

Rocky Ridge Inn is a long two-story motel built into the side of a mountain, with the bar front and center. But about a quarter mile down the two-lane highway, around the bend in the road, is a small building. This is Rocky's office. But from the one time I set foot in it, I saw it's mostly just used for storage.

"Behind there." I point out the windshield.

Leon pulls the truck around the far side of the building, revealing the dumpster.

There are dumpsters closer to the Inn, but I don't want to leave this human garbage right next to someone's motel room.

Leon puts the truck in park, then relaxes in his seat, clearly planning to stay put.

Fisher and I open our doors at the same time and meet at the back of the truck.

I drop the tailgate and open the back window of Leon's topper.

Blood is smeared across the truck bed.

Guess I'll owe Leon a favor too.

"How do you wanna do this?" Fisher asks, eyeing the man.

I reach out, gripping the rope binding the man's feet, and drag him to the edge of the bed.

He groans.

"Got your knife?" I ask my employee even though I know he does. He always has his fishing knife on him.

The man in the truck bed starts thrashing. "You can't do this," he cries.

"I can do whatever the fuck I want," I growl and punch him in the kidney. "And if you say another fucking word, this knife is slicing your throat. Under-fucking-stand?"

The sound of steel clearing leather has the man stilling.

I look over and Fisher holds his knife out to me, handle first. Looking totally okay with me threatening this man's life.

With my free hand, I grab the man's ankles again and yank him so his legs are hanging off the back of the truck.

I slice through the rope binding his feet together, then fist the front of his shirt and drag him the rest of the way out of the truck.

"Stand up," I command when his feet hit the ground.

He stumbles.

Fisher slaps him. "He said stand the fuck up."

I bite down on the inappropriate urge to smile.

The Creep manages to stand, his weight all on one foot, and I hand Fisher's knife back to him.

I pat the man's pockets until I find his phone, then I pull it free.

"Password." When he doesn't reply, I look up and meet the man's swollen eyes. "Your face is too fucked up for facial recognition. So you can either tell me your password and I can call an ambulance for you, or I can smash your phone right here, right now, and you can walk your ass to town." You can't see the Inn from here, and chances are he doesn't know there's a thriving business around the corner.

I drop his phone onto the pavement.

I lift my boot.

"One, one, six, four," he rushes out, his words garbled. Probably from his broken face.

"There. That wasn't so fucking hard." I slap him on the back.

He stumbles forward and falls.

But with his arms still tied behind his back, his landing is... rough.

"Ouch." Fisher makes a face.

I type in the code, and the phone unlocks.

It takes me a moment, but I get all of his contacts deleted. All his texts deleted. Call log wiped. Messaging apps deleted.

It won't stop him from getting a hold of someone, but it's going to make it a hell of a lot harder. Especially if he's not one of the few people who still memorize phone numbers.

I drop the phone back on the ground, then look up at Fisher. "Help me lift him?"

"Can do."

We step up on either side of the man who is face-first on the ground and each grip him under the arm.

He's crying now.

And to be fair, he's in tough shape.

Broken fingers.

Broken wrist.

Sprained or broken ankle.

Broken ribs.

Broken nose.

Jaw fucked up.

And those kicks had to hurt.

But he needs to save his energy because it's getting colder.

Not cold enough to kill him overnight. *Probably*. But cold enough that he's going to want to climb out of this dumpster and get to his phone sooner rather than later.

His best bet will be calling for an ambulance.

But ambulances come with questions. And cops.

Sure, he can give them my name and the name of the Lodge and explain exactly what happened.

But he'd have to explain *exactly* what happened. *Why* I attacked him.

If it would actually land the Creep in jail, I'd call the cops myself. But I stopped him before he broke the law. So calling them wouldn't do shit.

But beating the man half to death has been very satisfying.

And hopefully his surgeon sucks, and his hands cause him pain for the rest of his miserable life.

"Cut his hands," I say to Fisher as I nod down to the man's tied hands.

Fisher drags the blade over one of the man's palms.

The man cries out.

I raise my brows.

Fisher's mouth forms an *O*. "You meant the rope."

"I meant the rope."

Fisher slices through the rope, and once they're free, the man jerks his arms in front of him, holding them to his chest.

"Up on one," I say to Fisher.

"Am-Ambulance," the man chokes out.

"They'll come when you call them. One." I grunt as we lift the man by his hips and armpits, then drop him headfirst into the partially filled dumpster.

There's more moaning and crying as the contents of the dumpster rustle around before everything goes quiet.

I don't know if he passed out. Or if he's just playing dead. Either way, he got less than he deserved.

As we walk back to the truck, I drop my hand on Fisher's shoulder. "Appreciate what you did tonight."

He dips his chin. "We're the Black Mountain family. We look out for each other."

"That we do." I nod. Then I nod again before I crack a smile. "You meant the rope," I say with a lightly mocking tone.

Fisher grins.

SHOWERED AND DRESSED IN NEW CLOTHES, I CLIMB THE steps to Courtney's front door.

I type my master code, and the deadbolt unlocks.

But I don't enter.

Not yet.

Watching that man lunge up these steps... That was the scariest thing I've ever witnessed.

And I'm so glad... so fucking glad Courtney didn't see it.

I take a deep inhale of the night air.

I don't know if it's the right call, but I'm not going to tell her.

Knowing what almost happened won't help her.

And I want to tell her to listen better. To be aware of footsteps behind her.

But I don't want her to be afraid.

I don't want her to look at every guest with suspicion.

I don't want her to not feel safe.

I take another breath.

The visual of him following her is going to haunt me.

But the way he fell face-first when I dragged him off the stairs...

That was satisfying as fuck.

My knuckles throb as I flex my fingers.

I've had enough pain and violence for the night. It's time for comfort.

I open Courtney's door.

CHAPTER 147

COURTNEY

Cool air flows around me, and I groan, reaching for my moving blankets.

"Shh." The sound is low.

"Sterling?" My voice feels scratchy.

"Go back to sleep, Honey," my boss whispers as his body settles against mine.

His front to my back.

"I tried to wait." I let him jostle me as he slips one arm under my pillow and one around my waist.

"I know." His hand finds mine, and our fingers slip together. "I'm sorry I'm late."

Warmth fills me.

From his body. From his touch.

I sigh, my eyes never opening. "I'm glad you still came."

Something presses against my hair.

Peace fills the space around me.

I'll always come for you.

I'm not sure if I hear the words or think them. But as I slip into sleep, Sterling holds me just a bit tighter.

A DEEP GROAN RUMBLES AGAINST MY BACK.

I wiggle against the movement.

A mouth presses against my neck.

A rough hand drags up the side of my thigh before palming my ass.

"Fucking hell, Cookie." Sterling's fingers flex against my flesh. "You sleeping in nothing but my flannel and a pair of panties?"

I hum in reply, wanting more of his touches but also wanting to stay asleep.

But then I feel the tongue against my skin at the same time his hand slides around the front of my hip. He cups my sex, the thin layer of cotton the only thing between me and his thick fingers.

He starts to rub.

His middle finger pushing the fabric firmly against my entrance.

Then dragging up.

I groan as the pressure hits my clit.

He makes a matching sound.

I arch my back as my breathing becomes heavier.

Sterling's hot breath heaves against my neck. "You're so fucking warm." His hand leaves my pussy to grip my thigh. "Open for me."

I lift my leg and let him guide it up and back until my foot is hooked around his calf.

He moves his hand back to my center.

With my legs spread, his whole hand fits over my core, gripping me.

He grinds his palm into my clit, and as I press my ass back into his hard length, I'm reminded of the first time he got me off. When he pinned me to him in the dark woods.

When he ground against my ass.

I want to feel that again.

That energy.

And I want it now.

I bring my leg back down from over his, but before he can protest, I reach down and start to shove my panties off.

He moans. "You gonna let me into your sweet pussy, Courtney?"

I nod, shoving the fabric down more.

Sterling pulls away from me, then tears my panties off the rest of the way.

As soon as they're off, he climbs over me.

I'm still on my side, and his hard cock is pressing into my hip.

Him in only boxers. Me in only his flannel.

"How do you want it?" He grinds his dick against me.

"Like..." I gasp for breath when he palms my breast, balancing his weight on one hand. "Like that first time. In the woods."

"You want me to finger you, Honey? Is that what you want?"

I shake my head. "I won't say no, but..." He huffs a breath that's too sultry to be a laugh. "I meant..." I'm getting so turned on I reach down between my legs and start rubbing my clit.

Sterling grips my wrist and pulls my hand away from my core.

With his hold, he uses his position above me to roll me onto my front.

He yanks the pillow out of the way, and then Sterling traps both of my wrists over my head in one of his hands.

"You can touch yourself when you're alone. But if I'm here, I'm the one with my fingers in your slit." Sterling lowers himself so he's lying on my back.

His thighs are spread to either side of my hips, and his boxer-clad cock is wedged against my ass.

"Now tell me what you meant about doing it like we did in the woods," he demands with his lips next to my ear.

I flex my core, causing my glutes to squeeze around his length.

He rocks his hips. Just like I wanted him to.

"Like that," I pant, head turned to the side, sucking in air.

He rolls his hips again. "Like this? Does my Little Worker want it from behind?"

Little Worker?

Sweet Mother Hera.

"Yes, Sir."

Sterling lets out a curse.

He releases my wrists, and I feel him shift his weight.

Then the heat of his bare cock slaps down on my ass.

"You wet for me?" Fingers press between my legs from behind.

I shift, trying to widen my thighs.

I'm pinned.

His thighs trapping my thighs.

His weight above me.

"Fuck." His fingers find my slickness. "I don't want to hurt you again." The tip of his finger presses inside me. "But you feel ready."

His hand pulls away. Then I hear him spit.

Followed by another groan.

The tip of his dick is bumping against my entrance, and I just know he's stroking himself.

I turn my face into the mattress and moan.

I don't even try to look back to see him because the mental visual of him spitting into his hand is enough to have my body reacting.

If his fingers were still between my legs, he'd feel me getting wetter.

"I'm going to fuck you now, Miss Kern." The blunt tip pushes into me. "If it's too much, tell me."

I tilt my hips, taking him deeper.

We both groan.

He pulls his hand away from his cock and rolls his hips as he flattens his body over mine.

He sinks in slowly.

But he doesn't stop.

Just keeps pushing.

Sinking deeper.

My fingers curl, gripping the sheets.

Then my hands are caught again, Sterling's strong grip pulling my arms straight.

With his other palm, he grips just above my hip. Grips and pushes me down into the mattress.

He lets out a sound that almost seems painful as he presses his hips all the way against me.

He's as deep as he can get.

And I'm trapped.

Hands held hostage.

Body pinned with his.

It's hard to breathe.

I can't move.

And I feel like I'm stuffed so full I might burst.

Something pulls on one of my braids.

His teeth.

My already sizzling body lights up when I realize it.

Sterling is biting down on my hair.

I tip my head to the side, increasing the pull.

There's a growl.

Then my boss starts fucking me.

CHAPTER 148

STERLING

I CAN'T STOP.

Can't slow down.

Can't do anything but fuck my girl into the mattress.

She's squirming beneath me.

Whimpering and moaning.

Trying to get away while also arching her back and trying to take me deeper.

And I simply can't stop.

Our bodies slap together.

The sound of her wetness fills the room.

Her pussy is trying to fucking swallow me with each thrust I take.

I press my fingers harder into her soft side. Trying to hold her still as I slam my cock home.

I try to keep some of my weight off her.

Try not to crush her.

But I need her.

Lifting my head, I look at where I'm holding her hands in one of mine.

It's still dark, barely dawn, but I can see the dark marks where my knuckles have split.

I can see the faint bruising on my forearm from where the man tried to claw me through my shirt.

And I can see my girl safe beneath me.

I shove my hips forward.

I can feel my girl's warmth around me.

I pull out and slam back in.

Courtney moans, and I revel in my girl alive beneath me.

And hearing her, seeing her, feeling her, has me on the brink.

I let go of her hip and shove my hand between her body and the mattress.

Courtney lifts her hips as much as she can.

It's only an inch.

But it's enough.

My fingers reach her slippery clit.

I don't ease into it. I just start rubbing.

My movements are jerky.

My tether is fraying.

Courtney starts getting louder.

Starts squirming more.

Starts to squeeze her thighs together.

I keep going.

Keep thrusting.

Keep touching.

"That's it, Honey." I circle her clit. "You're choking the life out of me." I kiss the back of her neck. "Let go."

I shove in as far as I can.

And she breaks.

Her cries are loud.

Her hands fight my hold.

And her pussy clamps down around me.

She comes and comes, and the wetness coats my dick.

I rock into her.

And I clench my jaw.

But when she calls out my name, I can't hold back anymore.

Releasing her, I lean back onto my heels, and I start to come as my cocks slips free, sending the first pulse of my release across her ass.

Then I grip my length and stroke the soul out of my dick.

Painting Courtney's flannel-clad back in my seed.

It's filthy.

It's animalistic.

And it's my new favorite sight.

My girl wrapped in my clothes and covered in my cum.

Still hard, I push back into her. Just to make her squeal.

Chapter 149

Courtney

Opening my front door, I roll my shoulders back and stretch my neck side to side.

The ache that had been starting to fade between my legs is deliciously back.

I inhale the morning air, letting my eyes fall closed.

I didn't get my drunken sex last night, but morning sex with Sterling did *not* disappoint.

The sound of the dryer running behind me has me biting down on a smile.

I couldn't see Sterling when he came on my back, all over his flannel. But I could hear him.

And those grunts will live in my memory forever.

I squeeze my thighs together.

This is not the time to relive that particular moment. I have work to do.

And I especially can't think about Sterling planting a kiss on my ass cheek after he cleaned me up and stripped the flannel from my body.

He's such a mix of gruff and swoon that my body just melts around him.

So when he pulled the blankets back up to cover me and told me to go back to sleep, I did.

I blink up at the bright blue sky, then drop my gaze to where I'm going.

I pause with my foot in the air, my face scrunching up.

There's blood on my top step.

Ew.

I step over it.

I've seen a few patches of feathers around the property, where birds met with violent ends. And even though I don't see any feathers, I'm sure some creature met its end here.

My shoulders shimmy in a shiver.

As I cross the driveway, I hear voices and turn my head toward Sterling's house.

He's standing on his patio, hands in his pockets, talking to two of the guests who are still here.

Simpson is with them too, and when he spots me, he lifts his hand.

Waving back, I smile but keep walking.

Sterling's eyes move to mine, and I hold his gaze for two thudding heartbeats, then I look away, casual as ever.

There's something kind of exciting about having an illicit affair with my boss.

And I understand the reasons for keeping us secret, even if we haven't actually discussed it.

But it's getting harder to deny my growing feelings for Sterling.

And I know we'll have to talk about it at some point. But today... Today I want to do something special for him.

The Food Hall is empty when I reach it, but someone has already been in to turn on the lights.

As I go through the routine with Big Joe, I wonder if Cook is going to make breakfast for the guests before they leave.

If he is, I'll have to wait until later in the morning to execute my plan. But if there isn't a group breakfast, then Sterling shouldn't come in here.

Just as I wonder about breakfast, Cook comes through the door.

"Morning." I smile. "I was hoping you'd be here."

Cook puffs up his chest. "Well, don't you know how to make an old man feel appreciated."

I laugh. "We all appreciate you. We'd starve without you feeding us."

Some more literally than others.

"Yeah, yeah." He walks over and grabs two mugs out of the cupboard.

"Are the guests staying for breakfast?"

Cook shakes his head. "Nope, they're on their own."

"Gotcha. I just saw them talking to Sterling, so I wasn't sure." I shrug. "I thought they'd be gone already if they have a long drive."

"They should be outta here soon. Heard something about one of their guys leaving early." Cook holds out the mugs. "Now tell me what you need."

I pour our coffee as I tell him.

Cook closes one eye as he looks at me. "What for?"

"Just have a craving."

CHAPTER 150

STERLING

I can smell lunch before I even open the door to the Food Hall, and my stomach lets out a grumble.

Stepping inside, I can see that everyone is already here. But my eyes still find Courtney first.

She's standing over by Cook on the other side of the counter. And on the counter is the pizza I could smell from outside.

Cook doesn't make homemade pizza too often. Claims the crust is a pain in the ass. And judging by the amount he needs to fill two large trays, I don't doubt it.

But it's one of my favorite meals.

I flex my fingers. Usually Cook only makes pizza for special occasions, and I have to wonder if he did it today because of the way we handled that man last night.

He wasn't with us, but the guys are all close, so I wouldn't be surprised if the whole story has been shared among them already. Probably last night when we got back, considering they all sleep in the same damn room.

But so long as no one says anything to Courtney, it doesn't bother me.

I get into the back of the line and arrange it so I'm getting slices off the tray in front of Courtney.

She seems extra small today, standing all the way over there, on the other side of the counter.

Or maybe the small feeling is more equated to fragility. And my fear of something bad happening to her.

I give myself a mental punch in the face.

She's right here.

Right in front of me.

And this morning, mere hours ago, she was underneath me.

Alive as ever with my seed streaked across her back.

Courtney presses her lips together, trying to stop a smile. And failing.

"Court." I dip my chin.

"Hi." It comes out a little breathy. She clears her throat. "Um, how much would you like?"

It's my turn to press my lips together.

She rolls her eyes. "How many slices of pizza?"

I hold my plate out. "As much as you can fit."

Shaking her head, she piles five squares on my plate.

Since it's just the employees in here, everyone is spread out over two tables rather than crammed onto one. Giving us more elbow room.

I pick the only empty bench, sitting across from Fisher, ensuring that Courtney can sit next to me if she'd like. And it only takes a minute before she sets her plate down to the left of mine.

But instead of sitting, she goes back behind the counter.

Curious, I watch as she pulls out a rectangular metal pan from a hidden shelf under the counter.

My brows pull together as she carries it over and sets it on the end of our table.

"What's that?" Leon calls from the far end of the other table.

I don't look over at him.

Because all of my attention is focused on the large pan next to me that's filled with... cake.

I slowly lift my gaze up to Courtney.

She's looking across at Leon. "It's a cake."

"What kind?" Simpson asks.

"Funfetti with cream cheese frosting." Courtney picks up a knife and starts to cut the cake into slices.

"Fun what?" Leon asks.

"Funfetti." Fisher repeats Courtney's answer.

Cook brings over a stack of small side plates and sets them down next to Courtney.

"It means there's sprinkles inside the cake," Simpson explains. "It's my youngest's favorite."

I stare at the slice of white cake full of multicolored spots as Courtney sets one on a plate.

She hands it to Fisher and tells him to pass it down.

Courtney repeats the process until everyone at both tables has a piece.

Cook finally grabs his own food and drops down next to Fisher, then starts up a conversation with the kid.

While Courtney is setting down her own piece of cake next to her plate, I look at the table.

At the pizza.

At the cake.

At the bottles of root beer Cook shared with everyone out of his personal stash.

It looks like we're having a damn party.

Courtney places her hands on the table as she climbs onto the bench.

As she twists, her hand moves so it's between my plate and the edge of the table over my lap.

It's casual.

Nothing.

But when she sits down and moves her hand, there's a small slip of paper left behind.

I grab my napkin and bump the paper off the table and into my open palm.

It's a scrap of lined paper, probably torn off a page from the clipboard.

Picking up a slice of pizza with one hand, I carefully unfold the note in my lap with the other.

And the two words slither off the page and under my skin.

Happy Birthday.

I flatten my palm over the paper.

I blink.

I swallow.

I blink again.

Then I set the pizza slice down, push my plate to the side, and replace it with the cake plate.

My fork falls through the fluffy slice.

If Courtney had asked my favorite cake flavor that night when we stayed awake talking until dawn, I would have said chocolate.

And I would have been wrong.

Because when I take a bite of my birthday cake, I swear it's the best thing I've ever tasted.

CHAPTER 151

COURTNEY

"Cake first?" Cook's question draws my attention up from my plate.

Sterling makes a noise of approval. "No offense."

I didn't want to look at him while he was opening his birthday note.

I'm not a spy. I don't know how to be clandestine.

But looking at him now, as he shovels another bite of cake into his mouth... It feeds something inside me.

He likes it.

I did something for him, and he likes it.

"None taken." Cook chuckles.

I look between the men, trying to understand the joke.

Sterling puts the last bite of cake into his mouth, then immediately reaches for the spatula sticking out of the pan and serves himself a second slice.

I start to grin but end up gasping. "Oh my god, your hand."

Before I can think about what I'm doing, I reach for him, gripping his left sleeve.

The hand nearest me is resting on the table, and I stare down at the damaged skin.

"Court—" He cuts himself off from saying my full name.

And it reminds me that we are boss and employee right now. "It's nothing."

I release his sleeve but keep looking at the cuts across the top of his knuckles.

Then he sets his second slice of cake down, and I get a look at his right hand.

And it's so much worse.

"Sterling." It comes out as more of a scolding than I intended, and the room goes silent, all attention on us.

My boss turns his head to face me, eyebrow lifted. "Yes?"

I glance around and confirm that, yes, everyone is looking at us.

I bite down on my lip.

"What'd I miss?" Leon calls out, leaning over the table to look this way.

"Court was yelling at Sterling." Cook grins as he calls it out.

"I was not yelling," I say reasonably.

"Huh?" Leon asks.

I mirror his position, leaning over the table, and say it louder. "I was not yelling."

"Kind of sounds like yelling," Simpson chimes in.

I blow out a breath and pick up a slice of pizza, shoving it into my mouth.

It doesn't take long for conversation to start back up around the tables.

Taking another bite, I try to look at Sterling's hands out of the corner of my eye.

His left hand is down on his thigh, inches away from my own, with a corner of paper showing from beneath his palm.

The few dark lines of broken skin look painful, but it's nothing compared to his right hand.

Every knuckle on that hand is split. Wide cuts that look like they need bandages span his middle two knuckles, and the top of his hand is covered with discoloring that will surely darken into bruises.

Sterling was in a fight.

He had to have been in a fight.

But when?

He didn't have those marks last night. And this morning...

I was too sleepy, and then ravaged, to even notice his hands.

But it's not like he could've been in a fight since leaving my bed a few hours ago.

I lift my eyes and take in his profile.

There are no signs of bruises on his face. No signs of injury anywhere other than his hands.

As I'm staring at his unharmed jawline, Sterling turns to look at me.

He holds my gaze for a beat, then tips his head to my plate. "Eat your lunch."

CHAPTER 152

STERLING

I FEEL LIKE AN ASSHOLE AS I STAND FROM THE TABLE, not saying anything to Courtney.

But what can I say?

Thank you for making me the best birthday cake ever?

Thank you for being so fucking sweet while also not making a big deal of it?

Thank you for being alive and unharmed and the best thing that's possibly ever happened to me?

I carry my plates over to the dishwasher and wonder how I can take some of that cake back home with me.

I stare at my knuckles as I set my plates in the rack.

How could I have forgotten about my hands?

I left Courtney's cabin while it was still dark, so even though I started my day with my hands all over her delectable body, she didn't get a chance to see the damage.

Though it's hardly as bad as it looks. Just a handful of cuts.

I don't get in fights. It's probably been fifteen years since I've taken a swing at anyone. But I've never walked away from one with so little to show for it.

I've also never beaten a man quite so badly.

As I stand from the dishwasher, I put a hand on the counter, then twist, just a bit, side to side, to stretch out my back.

Okay, so maybe I have more aches and pains than just my hands. But that's from exerting myself in ways I usually don't.

The image of Courtney pinned below me flashes in my mind.

I've been exerting myself in all sorts of ways recently.

When I look back to the tables, I see Courtney scooping out more slices of cake for guys who want seconds.

Considerate of her.

I wait until she sets down the spatula, then I stride over to the table.

Courtney didn't take a second piece for herself, so I scoop one up for her, then set it and the serving utensil on her plate.

"I have a call this afternoon," I say loudly enough to catch everyone's attention. "I'm talking to that tech company about booking a trip for their whole team this spring. So I'll be unavailable for a bit."

"This that software company you were talking about last month?" Simpson asks.

"Uh-huh." I nod. "I'm quoting them an extra fifteen percent since we'd be filling literally every bed with nerds, so we'll see."

There's a round of groans as the guys remember some of the past guests we've had who were simply not suited for the outdoors. But we don't discriminate.

We just charge more.

I lift the cake pan. "Everyone who wanted a second piece got one?" I ask the crowd.

There's a rumble of affirmative noises.

"Good." I nod.

Then with a third of the pan still full, I carry it out the door.

CHAPTER 153

COURTNEY

WALKING BACK TO MY CABIN, I LOOK UP THE DRIVEWAY at Sterling's house.

I haven't seen him since he left lunch, carrying the whole cake pan.

Some of the guys called after him as he did it, laughing over his apparent sweet tooth.

I buried my smile under the second piece he'd given me, sure he was hoarding it because it was his birthday cake.

I consider texting him, wanting to know if he'll be around tonight, if he'll come over. But that feels awkward.

I literally live in the cabin next to his. If he wants to see me, or be seen, he knows how to make that happen.

Sighing to myself, I carry on past the driveway.

The proximity makes hookups easy, but it also makes it hard to set expectations. If this was a normal situation with a guy I was... *seeing*, I wouldn't expect to bump into him every thirty minutes.

I need to chill.

Of course, just as I tell myself that, as I near my cabin, I start to slow.

Then I stop.

Because attached to my cabin, lining the steps that lead up to my front door, are railings.

Hand railings that match all the other cabins.

"When did he...?"

I move toward them, hands outstretched.

My stairs aren't wide. And the top step is hardly bigger than the other steps. But more than once, I've been nervous about falling off them.

And now...

I grip a railing in either hand.

I try to shake them.

They don't move.

This man.

I turn, intending to go to Sterling's front door to thank him in person.

But then I remember him mentioning that call.

I don't know what time that was supposed to be or if he'd still be on it, but I don't want to interrupt his work.

Honestly, sometimes I forget that being here *is* work.

But Black Mountain Lodge is Sterling's business. His livelihood. His way of paying his employees.

I bite my lip.

I won't knock on his door, but I will send a text. Even though the idea seemed so absurd a moment ago.

Because I can, I climb to the second step, then lean against the railing before I take my phone out of my pocket.

Me: Thank you for the railings.

Not in a hurry, I continue to lean, tipping my head back and breathing in the evening air.

My phone vibrates a minute later.

Boss: You're welcome.

Boss: I'll be out late tonight. Behave yourself.

I purse my lips.

I always behave myself.

And what does he mean he'll be *out late*?

It can't be with another woman, right?

And does late mean he'll be late climbing into my bed while I'm asleep again? Or is it late like he'll be tired and go straight to his own bed?

I shake my head and slide my phone back in my pocket.

No need to jump to conclusions.

If I don't see him tonight, I'll see him tomorrow.

I DON'T SEE HIM TOMORROW.

CHAPTER 154

STERLING

I FEEL LIKE SUCH A PRICK.

I really am busy. Trips into town, avoiding Courtney... It's hard work.

But I need some time for my damn hands to heal up. I don't want her asking me more questions.

I TYPE IN MY CODE AND UNLOCK COURTNEY'S DOOR.

I managed another day without talking to her. Always had someone else near me when she was around so we were never one-on-one.

But I can't hold out any longer.

I'm leaving tomorrow with another one of the crews. And I thought I could leave without touching my girl. But I was wrong.

So fucking wrong.

I make sure to close the door quietly behind me and leave my boots in front of the dryer.

Then I strip on my way to Courtney's bunk.

Her lights turned off two hours ago.
I'm sure she's fast asleep.
I just want to hold her.
Breathe her in.
Feel her warmth.

CHAPTER 155

COURTNEY

THE WOODS I'M WALKING THROUGH MORPH INTO A city park.

It's summer, and the pavement is radiating heat.

I'm so warm.

And... I'm in a dream.

My dream self takes a slow breath.

I love it when I know I'm in a dream.

And not because it means I'll have a nice dream, but when I know it's a dream, I don't have to feel scared if something creepy happens.

I keep walking, tipping my face up to the sunshine.

There's something familiar about this place.

And when I look around, I realize it's not a park but a campground.

And the pavement has turned to gravel.

I breathe in the thick, humid air.

This is the last place I lived with my mom inside that RV.

The same RV shimmering to existence before me.

The brown and tan coloring is the same.

The off-white curtains hanging on the inside of the windows are the same.

The silver sun reflector propped on the dashboard, spread across the length of the windshield, just how I remember it.

I watch as high school me opens the side door.

She jumps down the step... and suddenly, she and I are the same.

I'm standing with my back to the RV.

And I'm just... so fucking over it.

So over living like this.

I want a house.

I want a house with space and rooms and privacy and furniture that I don't even use because my home is bigger than what's necessary, but it's still what I need.

I clench my fists, grit my teeth, and scream silently in my head.

And the desperate feeling that I felt then.

That I still feel now...

It's so fucking real.

It's so fucking real.

The need for freedom and escape but also for someone to take care of me.

The need for someone to just take care of me.

For someone to give to me freely. With abandon.

For someone to share without strings or guilt.

For a place to call home.

To *really* call home.

I want to tell my younger self that it's okay.

That we get out and make our way.

I want to tell her that we find what we need.

I want to lie to her.

I want to tell her that we've built that house.

I want to tell her that I have a big walk-in shower.

That our life gets easier.

That we have someone to take care of us.

My vision blurs, and I peel off from high school me.

Becoming two people again.

And I know I can't lie to her.

Because I can't lie to myself.

I watch, feeling useless as younger me wipes at her eyes and starts walking.

She's going to work.

But then the world shimmers again, and everything around us transforms back into woods.

Younger me keeps walking.

And I follow her.

I follow her to the Laundry Cabin.

But she doesn't stop. She doesn't even look at it.

She walks all the way to Sterling's house.

Younger me stops at the base of the stairs, the dream stairs looking so much longer than the real-life stairs.

I stop beside her, looking up.

I can feel the desire to climb the steps and go inside.

I can feel her hope.

"That's not for us," I tell her.

Even though I know the emotions I'm feeling are my own.

Younger me turns to current me. "Maybe it could be."

The door at the top of the stairs opens.

It's dark beyond the threshold.

It's so far away.

But... *maybe it could be.*

"What if it's not?" I whisper.

"What if it is?" she whispers back.

I can feel the warmth of Sterling surrounding me.

And that hope... that damn hope I've clung to for so long...

I take a breath.

I lift my foot to the first step.

And I fall.

Jolting myself into wakefulness.

CHAPTER 156

STERLING

COURTNEY'S BODY JERKS IN MY ARMS WITH A GASP, startling me awake.

Then she shudders.

I'm the big spoon to her little spoon, and when she shudders again, I tighten my grip on her. "Easy, Honey."

Her head moves on the pillow. "Sterling?"

I press my nose against her hair.

I'm about to say something along the lines of *better not be any other men climbing into your bed*, but before I can get it out, I hear her sniffle.

"Courtney?" I lift my head, trying to see her face, even though it's dark.

"I'm okay." She sniffs again. "It was just a dream."

Fucking hell. She's crying.

"Well, I'm not okay. You shaved a year off my life, scaring me awake like that." I loosen my grip on her. "Now come here and console me."

She wiggles. "I am here."

There's another sniff.

"Not here enough. I need your front." I grip her shoulders and start to shift her.

She grumbles but turns until she's facing me.

I wrap my arms back around her, pulling her close.

Courtney inhales, like she might say something, but I press my palm to the back of her head, pulling her face into my chest. "Shh, go back to sleep. I got you."

CHAPTER 157

COURTNEY

I SQUEEZE MY EYES SHUT.

It was just a dream.

A mashup of subconscious thoughts.

Nonsense.

It shouldn't make me cry.

But waking up to *him. Here.*

Telling me he has me...

Sterling strokes his hand down my back.

And it only makes my heart ache more.

It was just a stupid dream.

"Sleep, Honey." Sterling's voice rumbles through me.

I should ask him about his hands.

Ask if that's why he's been avoiding me.

Ask why it looks like he got in a fight.

But I'm too tired.

And he's too comfortable.

When I wake again, the sun is rising and Sterling is gone.

Chapter 158

Courtney

Three days.

Sterling has been gone for three days with one of the groups, without a goodbye.

Without so much as telling me he was going.

I wouldn't have even known they were coming back today if it wasn't for Cook.

Yeah, I could have texted Sterling myself. I have his number.

But he has my number too.

And he's the one who left.

The windows on the front of the Storage Shed let in some of the daylight from outside. Enough for me to see the array of wrenches in the tool chest before me. But seeing them isn't the problem. I can't even remember what I came into the Storage Shed for.

I slam the drawer closed.

Tipping my head back, I close my eyes.

This is why I shouldn't have gotten involved with my boss. It's affecting everything.

There's no escape from thoughts of him when I'm living on his property.

The door to the shed opens.

I can't see around the shelving that takes up the center of the room in front of me, but Cook is the only one still at the Lodge.

"Need me for something?" I call out, knowing it's too early for lunch.

The door closes, and footsteps sound from the other side of the shelves.

I stay where I am, needing a moment to calm myself before I take my frustration out on Cook.

The footsteps round the corner beside me.

"I do need you for something." Sterling's voice curls around my throat.

I freeze for a heartbeat.

Then I whirl on him.

"You." I point my finger at him.

He's already right there.

So close.

"Me." He steps forward. Forcing the tip of my finger into his chest.

"You..." I can't think straight with him this close. "You left."

He nods. And steps closer. "I'm back."

My stupid heart squeezes.

He's back.

But for how long?

Sterling grips my wrist and lifts it, taking the pressure off my fingertip.

He presses a kiss to the back of my hand, then sets my hand on his shoulder.

I lift my other hand and press it to his chest.

I don't really want to stop him.

I don't really want to stop him from touching me.

But I feel like I need to put up some sort of protest.

His heart thuds under my palm, then he grips that wrist too.

Repeating his action, he kisses my fingers, then places my hand on his other shoulder.

My eyes start to burn, and I focus my gaze on his throat.

Why does he have to be so confusing?

Sterling closes what's left of the distance between us. And even though his movements are controlled, I can feel his hardness pressing into me.

He's not unaffected.

And then he proves it by reaching up and gripping my braids.

"Eyes up here." His voice is rough.

I obey.

Because I can't stop myself.

But I refuse to completely give in.

I've had too long to sit with my thoughts.

"What happened to your hands? Who did you fight?" I dig my fingers into his shoulders.

To hold him away... To keep him close... I don't know anymore.

CHAPTER 159

STERLING

I GENTLY TUG HER BRAIDS, TILTING HER HEAD BACK just a little more, needing to see her neck. Needing it exposed to me as I tell her this.

Needing her to trust me.

Like I should have trusted her.

I still won't tell her the full truth. But with distance... I realized distance is the last thing I wanted.

"I'm not a violent man," I tell her.

My hands around Creep's fingers, crushing them.

"I need you to know you're safe with me," I ask of her.

Creep landing face-first on her steps as I drag him into the dirt.

"I need you to not be afraid of me," I beg of her.

The pop of bone as I break Creep's joints.

Her shoulders relax even as she clings to me. "I'm not afraid of you, Sterling."

I let her braids slide through my fingers as I drag my hands down their length.

"Tell me what happened." Her hands move to the sides of my neck, holding me.

I fill my lungs.

CHAPTER 160

COURTNEY

I FEEL HIS NECK FLEX ON A SWALLOW. "THERE WAS A man who was going to hurt a woman. He needed to be taught a lesson."

Oh.

I keep my eyes on his.

He was protecting someone.

A woman.

My tongue peeks out to wet my lips.

I have to ask.

I don't want to ask.

But I have to.

"Are you... seeing someone else?" It comes out as a whisper.

The side of his mouth pulls up. "Cookie, you think I'd keep your dirty panties in my nightstand if I was seeing another woman?"

My lips part.

Then close.

My dirty panties?

"You... what?" I can't believe I heard him right.

Large hands grip my hips as he lowers his mouth until his lips are just an inch away from mine. "You unravel me, Courtney

424

Kern. I've never felt more unhinged. More undone." His hands start to roam. One slides around and grips my ass. The other moves up my side until it's just underneath my breast. "I'm on my second pair. And I'm going to need to swap them out soon."

My breathing is coming out in pants. "Swap them out?"

He rocks his hips against me. "Yeah, Honey. Swap them out. Because they smell more like me now, and I need them to smell like you."

Oh gods.

He's talking about smelling my panties.

Why is that hot?

Why am I getting so wet?

"What—What do you do with them?" I can't stop myself from asking.

The hand on my ass slides around until it's wedged between us, cupping my sex.

"I'll show you sometime." He rubs me through my jeans. "Would you like that?"

I nod.

I frantically nod.

He groans and finally, *finally*, presses his mouth to mine.

The second I feel his tongue lick across my lips, I open for him.

Sterling takes the opening, deepening the kiss.

And maybe I should resist.

Maybe I should make him tell me more.

But when he starts to undo my pants, I don't care about what I should do.

I only care about getting his hands on me.

About getting his dick in me.

My zipper gets pulled down. And I reach for his.

Chapter 161

Sterling

Courtney's little hands reach into my jeans and grip my length through my boxers at the same time I slip my fingers into her panties.

She's soaked.

I moan.

My girl is a fucking freak.

And I'm obsessed.

"That get you hot, Honey? Thinking about me wrapping your panties around my cock as I jerk off." I wiggle my middle finger into her slit, getting it slick.

She tugs my boxers out of the way and pulls my aching dick out.

"Is that what you do?" she pants, gripping the base of my cock in one hand and stroking the length with the other.

Our lips brush with each word.

Our breaths mingle.

Our pulses race.

I drag my finger up to circle her clit. "That's what I do." I slide my finger back inside her. "Then, when I'm ready to come..." I add a second finger. "I hold them against my face." Courtney lets

426

out a whine as her pussy clenches around my fingers. "I breathe in the scent of your pussy while I come all over myself."

"I..." Her fingers tighten around my cock. "I want to see that."

My balls pulse.

I'm too fucking close to the edge.

"Soon," I promise her. "But right now, I'm coming in this hot little slit."

I shove my fingers deeper, then pull them out of her heat, dragging them up over her clit before I free my hand and grip her hips.

Using my hold on her, I twist her around. "Brace yourself, Honey."

Courtney slaps her hands down on the top of the tool chest.

I grip the top of her pants and shove them and her panties down her hips.

Her bare ass is too much of a temptation.

I bring my hand down, spanking her perfect cheek.

She leans forward, arching her back. Presenting herself to me even more.

"God damn." I stroke my length once. "I'm not gonna last. So I need you to come fast," I tell her as I line up with her entrance. "And I'm gonna need you to be quiet."

I press in just an inch.

Her channel pulses around me.

I hold still.

And in the silence, I know she can hear it too.

The voices.

"Sterling," she gasps.

I lean over her back, one hand still on the base of my cock, squeezing, the other braced next to hers on the tool chest.

"Not a sound," I whisper against her ear.

Then I let go of my dick and shove my hips forward.

CHAPTER 162

COURTNEY

I'M SO WET.

So ready.

But he's still so big.

And I love it.

The sting of stretching around him adds to the pleasure that bursts through me.

Turning my head, I bite down on the fabric of his sleeve to keep from crying out.

Sterling lets out a sound, but it's low. Just for me.

The voices outside are getting louder.

Sterling drags his cock out, then pushes back in.

Again and again.

He fucks me.

And my vision goes a little blurry. Stars dancing in front of my eyes.

Then his hand is between me and the tool chest. Reaching down between my thighs.

I try to widen my stance, but the pants bunched around my thighs keep me captive.

Sterling tilts his hips and shoves in deeper than he was before.

My lungs start to let out a mewl of enjoyment, but the sound of the shed door opening freezes the noise in my chest.

Sterling doesn't move.

Doesn't pull out.

We're hidden by the shelving.

No one can see us.

Not yet.

I bite down harder on the flannel between my teeth, and Sterling presses his open mouth to the side of my neck.

Fisher's voice is clear as he talks to someone about lures.

Next to the door is a large bench where the guys store some of their gear.

I hear a thud as something heavy is set down.

There's no need for them to come farther into the shed.

Please don't come farther into the shed.

There is no way we'd pull apart quick enough to not get caught.

No way...

Sterling's fingers start to rub my clit again.

I squeeze my eyes shut.

Fisher is still talking.

The door is still open.

Sterling rubs faster.

And holy fuck. I'm going to come.

The pressure increases on my bundle of nerves, and I feel myself edging closer to the drop-off.

But I can't do anything to stop it.

I can't move to grab his hand.

I can't whisper to him.

I can't do anything to stop Sterling from making me come.

His hips start to pulse.

Small movements.

Tiny jerks.

But enough.

S.J. Tilly

I hold my breath.
Sterling licks a path up my neck.
My pussy clamps down around his cock.
The door shuts.
And I come.

Chapter 163

Sterling

The click of the door closing acts like a dam opening.

Courtney shatters.

Her body vibrates.

Her pussy flutters around my length.

And I unload myself deep inside her.

CHAPTER 164

COURTNEY

STERLING CHUCKLES AGAINST MY BACK, AND I FINALLY unclamp my teeth from his shirt.

Gulping in air, I shake my head. "I can't believe that just happened."

"I can't believe you came so hard." He lifts his head enough to scrape his teeth against my neck. "You dirty girl."

The sensation sends a shiver down my spine, causing my muscles to spasm around his length.

Sterling hisses, and I can feel him shifting as he stands straighter. "Sorry, Honey, but there's nothing in here sanitary enough to clean you up."

"Huh?" My brain is still fuzzy because he's fucking right. That orgasm was... intense.

Instead of clarifying, Sterling pulls out, then pulls my underwear up into place.

Oh. Right. Clean up.

I grimace and clench my core muscles.

But then the back of my underwear is pulled away from my body, and Sterling's wet dick is sliding down between my cheeks, just once, before he pulls away again.

Did he just try to clean his cock off?

There's a growl, then a palm smacks down against my ass.

I jolt, and I can feel the mess he made start to seep out of me.

"Sterling," I snap while still trying to be quiet.

He just chuckles again and pulls my pants up.

When he tries to do the button for me, I slap his hands away.

"Secure your own pants before someone shows up," I tell him as I do my own before turning around to face him.

His eyes are hooded, and even though I can still sense his humor, he looks as thoroughly fucked as I feel.

"You go first." He dips his head and presses a quick kiss to my lips. "I'll wait a few and then leave."

I nod, agreeing because I need to get to my bathroom ASAP to clean up.

I take one step before Sterling stops me. "But Cookie, leave those panties on the floor for me."

"Want some help?" Fisher calls out to me from down the path.

I pause, arms full of bedding as I leave one of the guest cabins. "I'm good, but thanks."

"If you're sure." He lifts a hand. "See you at the fire."

"I'll be there." I nod, then turn away from him toward my cabin.

Thankfully, the sun is setting, so Fisher wouldn't have been able to see the blush on my cheeks.

I still can't believe I had sex in the fucking Storage Shed.

And I can't believe Sterling was getting me off while Fisher was on the other side of the shelves.

I shake my head.

That should not have been so hot.

My back is starting to ache from lugging laundry around, and I'm excited to be nearly done.

But voices I don't recognize have my steps slowing.

All the guests left earlier, after lunch.

A lunch where I spent the entire time looking at my plate, not making eye contact with anyone. Certain if I did, they'd know what had happened between Sterling and me in the shed.

It was uncomfortable, and I'd rather not think about it, but the point is, there shouldn't be any unknown voices here.

When I reach the driveway, I see them.

Parked in front of Sterling's house is a pair of pickups. And next to the trucks are three men I don't recognize, plus Sterling.

They're talking. Casual stances.

One of the guys is holding a Crock-Pot, another has a case of beer in each hand.

Friends.

They look like a group of friends.

And I can't help but wonder why Sterling didn't tell me he was having people over.

I mean, we were a little busy when we were together earlier.

But he didn't mention it at lunch either. Or at least not that I heard.

And if his friends brought food, I doubt Sterling is coming to the bonfire tonight.

A tiny voice in the back of my head wonders if he'll invite me to join him and his friends inside.

Still walking, my movement must catch Sterling's attention because his eyes lift to meet mine.

The shift in his gaze does not go unnoticed. And all heads turn to face me.

Me. With my arms full of dirty sheets and my hairline frizzy with sweat.

Looking my best.

The only guy not holding something lifts his hands. "Hi, there."

I smile at him, hoping it doesn't look as strained as it feels. "Hello."

This is not how I wanted to be introduced to Sterling's friends.

The other two nod in my direction, one of them grinning. "And who might you be?"

"Oh, um." I glance at Sterling.

"This is Court." *Sterling uses my work name. To his friends.* "She's the new maintenance person."

The new maintenance person.

I roll my lips together.

Something hot wraps around my heart.

"Oh, right." One of the guys smiles. "The new Marty."

I swallow down the tightness.

The new Marty.

No one special.

"That's me." I feel like I choke on the words. "Nice to meet you guys."

They all repeat the sentiment back to me.

My arms are straining, but I lift my bundle of laundry an inch. "Better get back at it."

"That's enough for tonight, Court," my boss tells me.

I glance at him and nod.

The tiny voice in my head that was hoping for an invitation cowers away into the back corner of my mind.

I'm not getting an invite.

I'm getting a dismissal.

It shouldn't hurt.

And I shouldn't have expected anything different.

Sterling doesn't invite me into his home when it's just the two of us.

Why would he start now?

"Have a nice night." I force my voice to sound bright.

I'm a handful of yards away, cutting across the driveway, so hopefully no one notices the heat in my cheeks.

Or the shine in my eyes.

I tighten my grip on the laundry and quicken my pace.

Getting away from Sterling and his friends as fast as I can.

Chapter 165

Sterling

The guys asked a few questions about Court, but I answered them blandly. Feeling like a bigger and bigger asshole with each word out of my mouth.

I want to tell them she's mine.

That I'm becoming unhealthily attached.

But... she works for me.

She is my maintenance person.

And I don't want to admit that I, the boss, am sleeping with one of my employees.

It's a bad look.

It's an unfair balance of power.

It's unethical.

If I could tell them she was my girlfriend... Maybe that would be better.

But right now, telling them I'm just sleeping with her feels wrong.

Then again, treating her like she was just another employee felt fucking horrible.

I scrub a hand down my face.

Maybe if I had remembered what today was, I could've talked

to her. Maybe set some expectations or something. But I'd completely forgotten.

It wasn't until I got a text letting me know they were on their way that I realized it was my night to host.

So I had thirty minutes to clean up my living room and dig through my freezer to make sure I had enough frozen pizzas on hand to throw in the oven.

We watch most of the football games at the Inn, but we each take turns hosting once throughout the season.

Since my schedule is so chaotic, I don't get to watch most of the games, but tonight is my night. And it was too last minute to cancel.

"Anyone need anything?" I ask as I push up from my chair.

Everyone shakes their heads, plates still half full.

In the kitchen, I look out the window in the direction of the firepit.

I can't see it from here, but I hope Courtney is there.

I hope she's enjoying herself.

And I hope the look I saw on her face wasn't real.

I hope I didn't hurt her.

CHAPTER 166

COURTNEY

ALONE IN MY BED, I LET MYSELF FEEL EVERYTHING I DID my best to block out this evening.

I let myself feel the disappointment.

In myself.

In Sterling.

I pull the blankets up to my chin and roll onto my side.

It's always my bed.

Always my cabin.

Always on his terms.

Clasping my hands together, I close my eyes.

I thought I could let it play out. But I'm not even done with my first month here.

If I'm this messed up now, how will I make it two more?

I take a deep breath and let it out slowly. Knowing what I have to do tomorrow.

CHAPTER 167

STERLING

WHEN I GET TO THE FOOD HALL FOR LUNCH, COURTNEY is already seated.

She's at the end of her bench, with Simpson next to her and Leon across from her.

Nowhere for me to cut in.

I try to catch her eye, but she doesn't look up from her conversation.

It's not like she usually makes a show of greeting me, but this feels... like I should be worried.

Gathering up my plate of food, I try to see if Cook's expression will tell me anything, but he's his usual self.

I consider sitting at a whole different table, but I can't make myself do it.

I need to be near her.

Leon gives me a nod as I set my plate down next to his. And Courtney finally lifts her gaze to mine when I sit.

Her smile looks... off. "Hi, Boss."

Her greeting hits me like a slap.

Boss.

The guys call me Boss.

It's not a big deal.

But Courtney doesn't call me that. Not since she first started. Not since she hated me.

I knock. Feeling like an idiot. But it's still early evening, and it doesn't feel right to just walk in.

Except she doesn't answer.

I press my ear to the door, but I don't hear any signs of Courtney inside.

It's possible she's ignoring me.

Like she did when she slipped out of the Food Hall after lunch, but it's more possible she's taking a shower.

For a moment, I consider going to the women's restroom. She wouldn't be able to avoid me if I walked into the shower with her.

The idea of showering together is one I'd like to explore.

But something's off between us right now.

And I know it's my fault.

And I need to find a way to fix it before I throw myself at her again.

Sighing, I turn around and lower myself to her top step.

If someone sees me, I'll...

I scrub a hand over my face.

If someone sees me, I'll tell them to fuck off.

Thirty minutes later, my girl appears.

Her hair is wet and twisted in loose braids.

She's wearing a sweatshirt and soft pajama pants, ready to stay in for the night.

And I feel a pang in my chest because there's no sign of my flannel anywhere.

The others might not have noticed when she wore it. But I did.

And she's not wearing it anymore.

I stand as she approaches, taking the few steps down so we're on even ground.

Courtney is holding a bundle in her arms. Her towel wrapped around her clothes from earlier.

And she looks just like she did last night.

Cautious.

A little nervous.

Alone.

I flex my hands at my sides.

I want to reach for her.

But I don't know if that's what she wants.

I don't know if *I'm* what she wants.

CHAPTER 168

COURTNEY

I SLOW AS I APPROACH MY CABIN.

And Sterling.

Instantly, my hands feel clammy, and my stomach starts to twist.

I've spent all day going over what I want to say to him.

I've literally run through a dozen variations of how to start this conversation.

But now that he's here, standing in front of me, all my words are getting jumbled up in my throat.

Because I don't want to do this.

I don't want to end this.

But I don't want to feel *like this* even more.

I stop when I'm a few feet away.

"Sterling," I say. Just as he says, "Courtney."

He reaches out and takes my towel-wrapped clothes from me, setting them on the steps behind him.

When he faces me again, I don't know what to do with my hands.

I didn't want to do this holding laundry, but now that I don't have something to hide behind, I feel even more raw.

We watch each other for a moment. And the expression on Sterling's face... It's vulnerable.

And it sends a crack through my rapidly beating heart.

"Sterling." I have to swallow to keep going. "I... I'm not good at this."

He shifts like he might come closer, but he doesn't. "Not good at what, Honey?"

Honey.

Why does he have to call me Honey?

I press my lips together and gesture between us. "Whatever *this* is. I'm just not good at it."

"This?" He shifts closer this time. Just an inch.

I nod.

Fuck, I hate this.

"I think..." I take a breath. "I think we need to stop. Go back to what we should've been."

"And what is that?" His voice is too quiet for me to read his emotions.

I lower my gaze to his chest.

I can't look into his eyes anymore.

I feel like I won't be able to look into his eyes again. Not after this.

Not once we're done.

"Boss and employee." It comes out as a whisper. "We should just be boss and employee. Until I leave at the end of December."

CHAPTER 169

STERLING

MY LUNGS ACHE.

Until I leave.

I stop myself from pressing a hand over my heart.

I don't want her to leave.

"Why would you leave?" I ask.

Do you really want to hear her say she doesn't want to be near you?

Do you really want to hear you aren't enough?

Do you really want to relive that? With her?

I need to hear it.

I need to hear it in order to move on.

"Why?" She lifts her hands and drops them. "Because that's when my contract is up. Because you never really meant to hire me. Because..." Her chest is rising and falling in time with my own. "Because I've never had a fuck buddy, and I'm not good at it, Sterling." She shakes her head. "I'm just not good at it."

She...

I shift an inch closer, ignoring the comment about her contract.

"We're not fuck buddies, Courtney."

"Okay." She still won't meet my gaze as she lifts her shoulders. "Like I said, I've never had one."

I reach out and gently grip her chin. "Eyes up here."

Finally, she lifts her gaze. "I'm sorry."

"What are you sorry for?"

"That I couldn't do casual." At her side, I see her pressing her fingertips together.

My heart drums inside my rib cage.

It's right there.

The thing I think she's trying to say is right fucking there.

"Why can't you do casual with me, Courtney?"

She drops her gaze to my mouth before lifting it again. "I've never done it before."

I slowly shake my head. "Tell me the real reason."

CHAPTER 170

COURTNEY

I SWALLOW.

Why is he making this so hard?

Why can't he just accept it and move on?

This right here is why I can't keep it casual with Sterling.

Because the thought of him *moving on...* The idea of seeing him walking into his house with another woman... It makes me sick.

I force myself to keep my eyes focused on his, even as I take a step back, breaking his hold on me. "I can't do casual because I don't feel casual about you, Sterling. Alright? I can't keep doing this and feeling like... like a secret. I thought I could. But I can't."

Sterling keeps staring me straight in the eyes. "Is that all?"

I just told him I have feelings for him, and that's his reply?

I take another step back.

"That's all," I whisper.

He dips his chin. "Good."

Anger sneaks through the hurt swirling inside me. "Good?"

"Yeah, Cookie." He takes a step toward me. "That's really fucking good."

"What—"

Before I can ask him what the fuck he means, he takes another step, bends, wraps his strong arms around my hips, and scoops me up and over his shoulder.

"Sterling," I hiss.

He doesn't say anything, just starts walking.

"Sterling, what are you doing?" I try to look around. "Someone might see us."

"Good."

Good is becoming my new most hated word.

I press my hands against his lower back to steady myself as I bounce against his shoulder.

I hear the change as he steps onto the gravel of the driveway.

"I will tickle you." I threaten him with the only thing I can think of.

Because what in the actual hell is he doing?

"You wouldn't dare." His tone is completely calm now.

I reach for his sides.

He slaps my ass.

"Mr. Black," I snap.

"You only call me that in bed." He soothes his hand over the spot he spanked. "And not today. Today it's Sterling."

CHAPTER 171

STERLING

WITH MY WOMAN OVER MY SHOULDER, I FEEL LIGHTER than I have in a long time.

She likes me.

Courtney *likes* me.

And she's not leaving.

Not now. And if I can play my cards right, not in two months.

"If you want to talk more, we can go inside." Courtney is trying to use a *reasonable* voice. And it makes me grin.

I shift my grip on her, sliding my hand from where it was looped around outside of her thighs to between her legs.

She squeezes her legs together.

Which only serves to trap my hand.

"We are going inside," I tell her.

"But my cabin..."

"Not your cabin." I shake my head. "My house."

Her hands press into my back again, and I feel her trying to lift herself. "But we never—"

Someone clears their throat.

I stop walking, and Courtney stops talking.

Turning my head, I find Fisher and Simpson standing on the other edge of the driveway.

448

Courtney lets out a sound that can only be described as a squeak.

I school my features. "Something you guys need?"

Fisher's eyes are bouncing back and forth between my face and Courtney's.

Simpson snickers. "Nothing that can't wait."

I focus on Fisher, giving him an opportunity to say something if he needs to. He's the closest in age to Courtney. She's incredibly attractive. He's single. And I've seen how easy they are together.

It would make sense if he had a thing for her.

He can't have her, but it would make sense.

Fisher runs his tongue along his teeth, then his mouth spreads into a grin. "Like Simpson said. Tomorrow at lunch should be a good time to... catch up."

I let the side of my mouth pull up, then I start walking again.

Striding to my front steps.

CHAPTER 172

COURTNEY

I KEEP MY FACE AVERTED FROM MY COWORKERS AS Sterling walks toward his house.

I don't exactly understand what is going on with Sterling, but I'm certain I don't want to have the rest of this conversation in front of anyone.

We walk for a few moments before I feel something press against my hip.

"Did you just kiss me?" I keep my voice low even though I can't see anyone anymore.

The hand between my legs shifts, and I'm well aware of how his touch is affecting me.

"Yeah, Cookie, I kissed you. And I'm going to do more than that in about two minutes." As soon as he finishes speaking, we start climbing the stairs to his front porch.

I tense.

Sterling is strong, obviously, but I don't want to move and make him drop me down the steps.

"I got you." He answers my silent worry.

I got you.

The same words he told me just the other morning. When I woke up with tears in my eyes.

And when we reach the top of the stairs, Sterling slowly lowers me to my feet.

My head swims for a moment, and Sterling lays his hands on my shoulders. "I don't want to be casual with you either, Courtney. And I should have done things differently since the first time." His thumbs stroke along my throat. "I should have taken you to my bed the first time."

"You don't—"

"I do." He slides one hand to the back of my neck. "I'm sorry I didn't do this better. If I think on it, I probably thought that you'd feel more comfortable in your own space. But considering how things started for you in that cabin..."

I press a hand to the center of his chest. "It's a good cabin."

He shakes his head. "Whether it is or not, I want you in here, with me. Now. Tonight. Tomorrow. Any time you feel like it, I want you to stay with me."

"Sterling..."

It sounds... too good.

Too easy.

Sterling pulls away from me.

He opens the front door, the unlit room dark beyond the threshold. "Let's start with tonight."

He holds his hand out to me.

And it's just like my dream.

"That's not for us."

I take a deep breath.

"Maybe it could be."

I place my palm in his.

And everything changes.

CHAPTER 173

STERLING

HER HAND IS WARM IN MINE.

And when I walk Courtney into my home, it all feels different.

CHAPTER 174

COURTNEY

WE PASS A KITCHEN WITH A SMALL PIECE OF PAPER stuck to the front of the refrigerator. The *Happy Birthday* message is the only thing on the surface.

And I feel a piece of my armor unlatch.

We walk through the living room. A place with comfortable furniture but no decoration.

And I see more of Sterling.

I feel more of him.

Of his life here.

And I squeeze his fingers.

We climb the stairs. Side by side.

And I take in his beautiful home.

But I recognize the loneliness.

His loneliness.

And more of my defenses fall away.

We enter his bedroom, and he turns me to him.

I match his embrace.

I reach for his shirt as he reaches for mine.

We watch each other.

We undress each other.

And we fall onto the bed with each other.

CHAPTER 175

STERLING

HER BODY IS WARM BENEATH MINE.

Her breathing is shallow.

Her eyes are open. And she's showing me so much.

She's showing me so fucking much.

And I'm taking it all.

Her legs spread.

Her back arches.

Her gasp is delicious.

She's taking all of me.

And I'm sinking deeper.

Into her body.

Into her mind.

Into her timeline.

She's accepting me.

She's clinging to me.

She's crying my name.

Her heat is surrounding me.

And I've never felt like this before.

I'm aware of every inch of her.

I'm aware of each inhale she takes.

I'm aware of the way she trembles.
My hands search between us.
And I find what I need.

CHAPTER 176

COURTNEY

I LET GO.
   In Sterling's arms.
   In Sterling's bed.
   I let go.
   Because *what if it is?*

CHAPTER 177

STERLING

WITH MY FACE AGAINST HER HAIR AND HER ARMS around my neck, we break.

Her cries are muffled when she presses her mouth to my shoulder.

My groans are dampened by her holding me tightly.

And together, we fall.

CHAPTER 178

COURTNEY

"SHOULD WE REALLY DO THIS?" I ASK FOR THE FIFTH time, flexing my fingers against his hold.

Sterling looks down at me with such patience and adoration that I sigh.

He's not changing his mind.

Not that there's really a point trying to hide what we are now. I have no reason to believe that Fisher or Simpson wouldn't have told the other guys what they saw, which was Sterling carrying me like a caveman to his house with his hand between my legs.

I've already brought up all my concerns this morning.

What if they treat me differently?

What if they get mad for some reason?

What if they ask when it started?

And Sterling reasonably answered all my fears.

He won't let them treat me differently.

No one has any reason to get mad.

They won't ask questions like that. And if they did, he'd admit he had a thing for me since day one.

I force the hand not in Sterling's grip to relax.

This morning has been... great.

I woke up naked in Sterling's amazingly comfortable king-size bed.

I asked him why he ever let us cram onto my mattress while I tugged on his hair as he went down on me.

I used his shower, which was way nicer than walking forever to use the public ones.

And he made me coffee, with his coffee maker, before I was even dressed.

Truly, it was the best morning I've had in a long time.

And we have a few days before the next round of guests, so Sterling had already declared this as a day off for everyone. But Cook still planned to make lunch. So... we're going to lunch.

Right now.

Reaching out with his free hand, Sterling opens the door to the Food Hall without breaking our connection.

I step through first, my arm extending behind me until Sterling steps up to my side.

Everyone turns to look at us.

Everyone.

Because we're the last ones to get here.

I drop my gaze and try to let go of Sterling's hand, but he doesn't let me.

And then I instantly feel like a jerk because this isn't just about me. This is about both of us. These are his employees. Men he's known a whole lot longer than he's known me.

Sterling doesn't stop though.

He doesn't make a speech.

He just keeps walking.

My arm extends out in front of me until I break out of my frozen state and catch up.

The room is silent as we pass by the tables and approach the counter.

This is it.

No going back.

And I need to do my part. Because Sterling and I... We're in this together.

Stopping across from Cook, Sterling lets go of my hand, then places his palm on my lower back. "You first."

I relax my shoulders.

I stop biting my lip.

I lift my head.

And I smile.

Because Cook is smiling.

Beaming.

And it's the exact reaction I needed.

I don't know what expression everyone else is making, but knowing Cook is happy is enough for me.

He holds out a plate for me, piled high with pasta smothered in a pink sauce.

I take it, not saying anything because I can't think of the right thing to say.

And because I'm not sure I can speak just yet.

Sterling slides his palm up my spine, stopping when his hand is at the base of my neck.

It's a soothing move. But also a claiming move.

And even though I'm too chicken to turn around, I'm certain all eyes are still on us. And these touches... They won't go unnoticed.

"Just no making out in my kitchen, alright?" Cook holds a plate out to Sterling.

The man beside me takes the offered plate with his free hand. "No promises."

I nudge my elbow into Sterling's ribs. "We promise."

Cook winks at me. "Already his better half."

My cheeks, which were already warm, flare even hotter.

We haven't even had the discussion about labels yet, even though I'm pretty sure it's safe to say Sterling is my boyfriend now. *Pretty sure*. But calling him my better half seems a bit intense.

Sterling just grunts, then uses his hold on me to turn both of us so we're facing the tables.

And like I suspected, everyone is watching us.

Some of them look serious. Some have smiles on their faces. But we all stare at each other until Sterling speaks.

"Any questions?"

That's it.

Any questions?

I almost roll my eyes.

Leon raises his hand.

Sterling sighs, presumably over the hand raising. "Yes, Leon?"

He lowers his hand. "Does this mean she's switched loyalties, or can we still talk shit about you in front of her?"

Sterling slowly turns his head to look down at me, brows raised.

I look at Leon. "We can still talk shit."

He grins.

And then, one by one, everyone relaxes, their smiles growing, the chattering building.

I was so focused on how they might feel toward me that I didn't consider anything else. Like the fact they might worry about their own workplace atmosphere.

I take a deep breath and shove away my remaining doubts.

These are good guys.

And even if I started as an outsider, they won't turn on me now. Not when we've become friends.

My heart gives a little squeeze.

Because it's true. These guys are my friends.

I have friends.

And a man.

And potentially... a future.

CHAPTER 179

STERLING

COURTNEY EXCLAIMS SOMETHING FROM UPSTAIRS.

I can't make out the words, but I'm guessing she found her pet cactus on the bedroom windowsill.

Or her clothes in the closet.

Or her pillow on the bed.

She's slept here, showered here, eaten here, for three nights in a row. I'm just making it easier.

CHAPTER 180

COURTNEY

Lips press against my temple. "I gotta run into town."

"Mmkay." My reply is as sleepy as I feel.

"Go back to sleep. You have thirty before your alarm. I'll see you at lunch." He kisses me again, then stands. "Don't make it weird."

That has my eyes cracking open.

Don't make it weird?

"What are you talking about?" I ask. But Sterling is already striding out of the room.

Then it dawns on me.

It's the last day of the month.

And that means I'll get my first paycheck from Black Mountain Lodge.

I blink at the ceiling.

Sterling's bedroom ceiling.

This is the payday I've been counting on since before I even started.

Since the day I was told I got the job.

At the time, I'd been in... such a bad place.

Financially.

Mentally.

I needed this so badly.

And when I got here... it took a few days, but I got settled.

I got a cabin to call my own.

I got a homemade lunch every day.

I got coworkers who became my friends.

And I got Sterling.

I got stability.

And I kept my position by being good at my job.

A job I've come to enjoy.

I take a deep breath.

The relationship I'm building with Sterling has nothing to do with my paycheck.

I won't make it weird.

CHAPTER 181

STERLING

THE MOMENT I OPEN THE DOOR, I SMELL THEM. THE mini apple pies Courtney told me she was making.

I've been gone on another outing, and the nights away were just as frustrating as I knew they'd be.

But I still took the time to detour on the way home.

Courtney has bought a few things for herself since getting paid last week, but she hasn't splurged on snow boots or a proper winter jacket.

So I did.

And I just know the faux fur-lined hood is going to be adorable as fuck on her.

I grin as I head up the stairs, toward the sound of the shower.

If I time this right, maybe I can see her dressed in nothing but the jacket.

CHAPTER 182

COURTNEY

COFFEE MUG IN HAND, I WALK TO THE BACK DOOR, looking for the source of the sound that woke me up.

It's rhythmic.

It's...

I hold the mug away from myself as I choke on my coffee.

It's Sterling.

Chopping wood.

With a literal axe.

As snowflakes slowly dance around him.

And his shirt is open.

Of course it's open, because he's working up a sweat.

Composure gathered, I lean against the doorframe and take another sip of my coffee.

We got our first real snowfall a couple weeks ago, and that was the first time I saw Sterling light a fire in the living room fireplace.

I knew it was real wood crackling away as we snuggled together on the couch watching a movie. But I guess I hadn't considered where that firewood came from.

The continued thuds from outside are proof that the wood comes from Sterling.

Not feeling guilty in the least, I settle in and watch him.

Knowing damn well I'm going to insist he goes into the hot tub tonight to soothe his muscles.

And knowing just as well that I'll join him.

I smile as I greet our next round of guests.

Three cabins' worth.

All women.

It's the most excited I've been for group lunches, wanting to talk to all of them.

But it's the most grateful I've been for basically moving into Sterling's house. Because I only have to share the shower with him.

The second paycheck is just as awkward to accept.

But I keep my promise of not making it weird.

CHAPTER 183

STERLING

I LOOK OVER AT MY PASSENGER SEAT. "THIS IS A GOOD idea, right?"

Golden eyes blink back at me.

I nod. "It's a good idea."

Driving slowly, I pull into the garage and shut the door behind me after I turn off the engine.

My mind keeps oscillating between doubt and excitement. But it's too late to turn back now.

Opening my door, I let Ben out of the truck.

He follows me to the door that leads into the house.

"Okay, you stay here," I tell him.

Ben stares back at me.

I nod. Then head inside.

Courtney is standing near the stove, oven mitts on her hands. "Hey."

"Hello." Something in my tone clearly gives me away.

She turns to face me, head tilting to the side, eyes narrowing. "What's going on?"

Her suspicion is adorable. "Nothing bad. I promise."

"But something."

I rock back on my heels. Wondering again if I did the right

468

thing. But knowing if she'd been with me, the outcome would've been the same.

"I got... something." I can't quite get myself to say it.

"And that something is...?" She lifts a brow as she puts her mitt-covered hands on her hips.

I think about how to start but decide it's easier to show her.

I grip the handle for the door leading to the garage, and I open it.

Chapter 184

Courtney

I watch Sterling, wondering what he could possibly be surprising me with this time.

He already bought me all the winter clothes I could possibly need.

All of my things are already inside his house.

Everything I could...

My breath catches.

And my muscles freeze.

Because...

Because...

Tears flood my eyes.

I feel stupid for crying, but I don't care.

Because the most beautiful dog in the world just walked into the house.

It's black and fuzzy and comes up to Sterling's knees and... It's the most perfect dog I've ever seen.

"Oh my god." I heave the words out as tears roll down my cheeks. "Who is this?"

Before Sterling can answer, I drop to my knees, tossing the oven mitts behind me.

It's a dog.

A real dog. Here.

I hold my hands out, and the furry black animal trots toward me.

No hesitation.

No growls or whimpers.

"Ben, this is Courtney," Sterling says in a quiet voice. "Courtney, this is Ben."

"Hi, Ben." I let out a watery laugh. "I love your name."

People names for pets have always been my favorite.

Ben slows when he reaches me but doesn't pull back when I press my fingers into his fur.

"You have such pretty eyes," I tell him.

He chuffs.

"Sorry." I stroke a hand down his side. "I meant they're very handsome."

"I see I'm no longer needed here." Sterling chuckles as he lowers himself to the ground next to me.

My smile is so big it's hurting my cheeks. "Where did you get him?"

Ben leans forward and licks the side of my face.

"Ew," I laugh as Ben tries to climb farther into my lap.

I shift onto my butt, and he plops himself right on top of my legs. Feeling heavier than he looks.

Sterling lays one arm over my shoulder while he reaches out with the other and scratches the top of Ben's head.

"I got him from the shelter in town. They said he's a lab-collie mix, but who knows." He shifts to scratch behind Ben's ears. "Ever since that night we talked about dogs... I've wanted to take you there to look for one." I raise my eyes up to meet Sterling's. "I should have waited for you. But I was driving past, and I wanted to see..." He lifts a shoulder. "I know we said we weren't doing gifts..."

I nod. Because that's true. We agreed that we wouldn't exchange gifts for Christmas, which is only a few days away.

"But as soon as I saw him, I knew he was meant to be yours."

Gratitude fills my chest. "He's mine?"

Sterling nods. "He's yours."

CHAPTER 185

STERLING

I WANT TO TELL HER THAT BEN IS *OURS*. THAT HE belongs to both of us like she belongs to me.

But the tears rolling down her cheeks are filling my lungs. And I can't find the words.

I'll tell her later.

Explain later.

Tonight, we'll just be a family.

CHAPTER 186

COURTNEY

I LOOK DOWN AT MY RINGING PHONE.

It rings a second time.

A third.

And on the fourth, I blow out a breath before answering it. "Hi, Mom."

"Merry Christmas, Courtney." Her voice is cheery. Happy and bright and not a trace of discomfort, despite the fact that we haven't spoken on the phone in months. "How's the holiday weather in Colorado?"

So she remembers the text I sent her months ago about moving. I wasn't sure since the only response she gave was just a thumbs-up.

"It's actually really nice," I tell her truthfully as Ben runs up onto the back deck and drops his stick at my feet.

I pick it up, lean back, then toss it as far as I can.

It's above freezing today, but there's still a fair amount of snow on the ground.

Sterling and the guys shoveled all the pathways between buildings. And then Sterling shoveled paths through the backyard for Ben to run through. So even though I'm still getting used to this winter weather, it hasn't been hard to get around.

And it doesn't bother Ben in the least. Which he proves by leaping off the edge of the low deck, straight into a pile of snow.

"Courtney?"

I catch myself grinning at the goofy dog. "Sorry, I was distracted by, um, my boss's dog."

If I told her it was *my* dog, she'd ask too many questions.

So, I'll pretend Ben belongs to Sterling.

Even though he feels like he belongs to both of us.

I'll also pretend I'm still living in the Laundry Cabin.

Telling Mom I moved in with my boss would most definitely spark a lecture.

And fair points or not, I don't want to hear it.

I don't want to hear how it's a bad idea to move in with a man, who is your boss, who lives on your jobsite, without having a real discussion about it.

I don't want to hear how it's a bad idea to spend two months living comfortably together, sleeping together, cooking dinner together, without discussing what happens in one week, when January starts.

And I don't want to explain that I'm wildly in love with him.

That I fall more in love with him every time he walks through the front door.

Every time he inhales me like he needs the scent of me filling his lungs.

Every time he groans against my neck.

Every time I fall asleep with his hand clasping mine.

I can't even explain how a part of him feels like a part of me.

How I breathe easier with him in the same room.

How I sleep deeper with him at my side.

How I smile more with him in my life.

I press my free hand to my chest.

Sterling has been off on a retreat for the last two nights, and I miss him so fucking much.

He told me he would cancel. That he planned this trip before we met. That he'd rather stay home.

But I wouldn't let him.

Didn't want to ruin his plans with his friends.

And I'm regretting it so much.

Fuck his friends. I want my Sterling.

Ben drops the stick at my feet again, and I toss it.

My mom is still talking. Telling me about her drive to Florida, her plans for the holidays, her next destination. Unaware of my inattention.

I keep making the right sounds. And she keeps going until I hear someone knocking on her door. The rattling sound ingrained in my memory makes me wonder how long that damn RV will keep running.

"That's the neighbor." She calls anyone in the same campground as her a neighbor. "We're doing a potluck. Gotta go."

"Have fun."

"Always." I can hear her smile. "Love you."

Then the line cuts.

"Love you too." I sigh.

Ben bounds up the steps, but instead of dropping the stick, he plops his body onto the deck.

I crouch so I can run my hand down his back. "You're such a good boy." He lifts his head, his tongue lolling out. "Should we have some snacks before our holiday dinner?" Ben licks his chops. "Come on."

Half the guys are gone, but half of them are still here, and Cook is making us dinner.

I have a variety of full-sized pies cooling in the kitchen as my contribution.

Sometimes the Lodge is booked with outings over the holiday, but this year it isn't. So we have a few days before the next group arrives on New Year's Eve.

Opening the door, I step back as Ben trots into the house.

He's so happy here.

I vow not to let the call with my mom, or my spiraling thoughts, depress me.

I have a dog. A real, actual dog.

And I have a boyfriend whom I love. Who I'm almost certain loves me too.

I will not be depressed today.

As I walk into the kitchen, I spot Sterling's laptop on the counter.

I know we need to have our talk soon. About me working here.

I like working here. But...

I open the laptop, then open the web browser.

If this is going to work long term for us, possibly forever, I need to start looking for a different job.

My hands hover over the keyboard.

I've always searched for new jobs out of desperation. If I'm not on a deadline to find something new, I could look for something I *want* to do, not just the first thing available.

And if we stay together... If I officially move in here with Sterling, then I don't need to look for a job that has room and board included.

A tendril of excitement weaves through my ribs.

The options are endless.

I stare at the blank search bar.

And I keep staring.

And the longer I stare, the more that excitement turns into anxiety.

My throat tightens.

I have no idea what I want to do.

Literally not a fucking clue as to what I should type.

I dig my teeth into my lip.

I... I don't know what my passion is.

I've never had one.

My gaze lowers to the keyboard.

The letters stare back up at me.

I try to think about things I like.

Sterling. Ben. Spike. Baking pies.

Pies are the only thing on that list that I could do anything with. But I'm not trained. I don't have any experience. And I like making them, occasionally, for fun. But they aren't my passion.

I lower my hands to my side, leaving the search bar blank.

CHAPTER 187

STERLING

I WALK A FEW MORE PACES DEEPER INTO THE WOODS before I take my phone out of my pocket.

The reception out here is trash, but I have two more nights before I head home, and I know the call from her mom yesterday took its toll on Courtney.

She didn't admit it straight out, and we've only been texting since I left, but I could tell.

I curse at the two bars of service but know it's the best I'm going to get. And even if the signal cuts out on us, I want to hear her voice.

It only rings twice before she answers.

"Sterling." Courtney practically gasps my name, sounding out of breath.

"Cookie. You're not supposed to be working." I picture her lugging loads of laundry around, working up a sweat because she puts her whole damn heart into her job.

She laughs. "Not working, just playing tag with Ben."

Ben lets out a playful bark, as though he's confirming.

A smile that feels almost wistful pulls across my lips. "Well, that's fucking adorable." She snickers. "You gonna have dinner with the guys?"

Courtney makes a sound of agreement. "Yeah. Simpson got back today, so I think everyone will be here."

Ben barks again, and the sound that comes out of Courtney can only be described as a giggle.

Fuck, I miss them.

I clear my throat. "Ben doing okay?"

"He's so great. No accidents. He cleans his bowl every meal. *Don't you, you good dog, you?*" She changes her voice as she talks directly to the dog. "We're still working on sleeping in, but I think he just likes going outside too much."

"He probably likes the treats he gets every time he comes back in." I say it like I didn't do the same thing those few days I was home after getting him.

"It's a strong possibility." Courtney hums. "Can I ask you something?"

"Always," I reply.

Not wanting to move and mess with the cell signal, I lean against the trunk of the aspen I'm standing next to and wait for her to ask whatever's on her mind.

"How did you find your passion?"

My brows furrow. "What do you mean?"

"I... I was just thinking the other day about passions. People always talk about them, like it's just something they always knew about. But... I don't have one." There's a tone of defeat in her voice, and I hate it.

"Honey, I've seen you passionate," I tell her, meaning it.

She huffs. "I know I have the capability, but I mean like specifically. I don't have a passion. I don't even have a hobby."

"Dressing up your little cactus doesn't count?" I realize that sounds kind of dickish, so I try to clarify. "Sorry, that was a serious question, but it sounded rude. Honestly, I don't know anything about hobbies. I literally live where I work."

"That's what I mean though." It sounds like she's pacing. "The Lodge *is* your passion. I know you told me that you'd been doing guide work since high school, but which came first?"

"Like the chicken or the egg?"

"Yeah. Did you become passionate because you worked for those other companies, or did you seek out those jobs because you knew you wanted to do them? And... Did you ever have doubts? Or were you always all-in?"

I blow out a breath. "I don't remember ever making a conscious decision about it, but growing up out here, I spent a lot of time exploring the woods. My hometown is about an hour from the Lodge, but the terrain was the same. Mountains and woods and wildlife. It just became my... happy place, I guess you could say. Plus it was a way to avoid my parents, homework... Typical kid shit. So when I found out I could get paid for fucking around outside, it was a no-brainer. Some jobs I liked more than others, but that was mostly about the people I had to work with."

"Sounds nice," Courtney says softly. "So, you never considered anything else?"

I roll my lips together. Not wanting to answer.

"That's a yes." She snorts after my extended silence.

"It's a yes." I sigh.

Courtney makes a sound in her throat. "Your hesitation makes me think it was about a woman."

A laugh jumps out of my chest.

She snickers. "I'm right, aren't I? You don't have to tell me if you don't want to."

"No, it's okay." I push off the tree and start my own pacing. "I want to preface this by saying I have *zero* feelings for this person. I don't hold any sort of candle for her. I don't think about her with longing."

"Yeah, yeah. You're over her. I get it," Courtney teases me.

I roll my eyes at myself. Of course, this woman of mine would be understanding.

"So..." she prompts.

"So... she was my high school girlfriend. And like every couple that age, we planned our whole lives out. She would go to college, get her teaching degree. I would keep working full time, overtime, until I could afford my own guide business. We would live in the town we grew up in, working our careers... But she went to college out of state, and after the first year, she came home and told me it was over. She said she liked living *in civilization* and that she'd never be happy living with me *in the woods*."

I shake my head remembering it.

I let her dismissal twist me up for so long. And for what? I can't even picture her face anymore. I'd pass her on the street and not recognize her. And even if I did, I wouldn't care. I have my Courtney now.

"What a twat," Courtney spits.

Goddamn, this woman is it for me.

I smile at her anger on my behalf.

"It took me a while to get there, but yeah, you're right. Unfortunately, at the time, I was still young, dumb, and full of pride. And her rejection made me doubt myself. And my passion." I circle back to the original question. "I never quit, but I cut my hours and got a temp job in an office."

"In an office?" Courtney repeats incredulously.

"It was very temporary."

My girl laughs. "I'm trying to picture you at nineteen, playing nice with people in button-downs... that aren't flannel."

"Yeah, well, I couldn't picture it either. I was there less than a month before I decided I'd rather live alone than live that sort of lifestyle. It just wasn't for me. *Isn't* for me," I correct. "And it proved to me that we didn't love each other the way I thought we did. It wasn't like..." I swallow the rest of my words.

It wasn't like us.

I didn't love her at all.

Because it didn't feel like this.

CHAPTER 188

COURTNEY

I LEAN AGAINST THE COUNTER.

He was going to say *us*.

He was going to say *it wasn't like us*.

As in he loves me.

That has to be what he was about to say.

I blink, forcing away the dampness building in my eyes.

"Sterling—" a noise drags my attention to the kitchen window.

"Courtney, I—"

"Sorry, hold on, someone is here." I watch as a somewhat beat-up blue SUV pulls up to a stop in front of the house.

"What do you mean? Who is it?" Sterling's tone has completely changed. Going on alert.

"I don't know." I keep watching as a man, about my age, exits the vehicle. "It's a guy. He parked in front of the house. Are you expecting anyone today?"

"No. Do you recognize him?"

I focus on the man's face. "No, I don't think so."

"Keep me on the phone. I'm going to text Simpson to come to the house so you aren't alone with him." The audio changes, and I picture Sterling switching me to speaker.

"Okay." His reaction seems a bit overkill, but I do like the protectiveness. "I'm going to hold you at my side."

The man outside is looking around, but I know it's only a matter of moments before he climbs the steps to the front door. And I'd rather meet him outside the house than on the threshold, so I hurry across the kitchen and swing the door open.

Sterling says something, but I can't make it out.

"Hello." I greet the stranger.

Ben slips out the door with me but stays by my side.

The man lifts a hand. "Hey, there. I'm looking for a Sterling Black."

He's being friendly, but I stick to a partial truth. "Right place, bad time." I smile to soften it. "He's busy at the moment, can I help you?"

The man approaches the base of the stairs, hand out, so I hurry down the steps to meet him.

"I'm Dale Norton." I place my hand in his as he speaks. "I'm a few days early, but I'm the new maintenance guy."

I stare at the man, Dale, not comprehending.

"Sorry, what?" I croak.

The new maintenance guy.

A few days early.

Panic starts to claw at my throat.

He's here for my job.

My contract that ends December thirty-first.

My...

My heart fucking aches.

A muffled sound comes from my phone.

But my ears are ringing. And I can't make it out.

"Marty said it shouldn't be a problem to come a couple days early. Said a bunk should be open." Dale sounds a lot less upbeat than a moment ago, and I'm sure the devastation I feel is showing on my face.

I shake my head and force my mouth into a smile. "No, that's fine."

Movement past Dale catches my attention.

Simpson is striding toward us, concern written all over his face.

"Court, you good?" he calls out.

Dale lets go of my hand and turns toward the newcomer.

"I'm good." My tone is fake, but I keep my smile in place as I gesture to the man in front of me. "This is Dale."

Dale holds his hand out.

Simpson shakes it but keeps looking at me.

I wet my lips. "He's the new maintenance person."

Simpson rears his head back.

I shake mine, needing him to accept this.

I don't want to make a scene.

"Could you show him where to park?" My question is a plea.

I need Dale away from my—*Sterling's* house.

I need him away from me.

Simpson nods, and I don't wait around for more.

Spinning, I hurry back up the steps, Ben on my heels, as I rush back inside.

My replacement is here.

I close the door, then lean against it as I suck in air.

Sterling wouldn't do this.

He wouldn't just replace me and kick me out.

I lift the phone to my ear. "Sterling?" I whisper.

"Court—"

The connection is choppy.

It sounds like he's moving.

I don't have much time before I'll lose him. So I ask the only question that matters right now. "Did you know?"

His harsh breaths come over the line. "I—" His answer breaks up. But the next part comes through clear. "I forgot."

Then the call drops completely.

I forgot.

Not *I didn't know.*

CHAPTER 189

STERLING

HEARING THE MAN ASK FOR ME BY NAME SENDS A JOLT of unease through me.

No one should be showing up at the house.

And I hate that it's happening with Courtney there alone.

Her words are muffled, but then she must shift her grip on the phone because the audio suddenly comes through clearer.

"He's busy at the moment, can I help you?" Courtney sounds polite, but I can hear her hesitancy.

There's a pause before I hear the stranger speak.

"I'm Dale Norton." My brows scrunch at the name. Why does that sound... "I'm a few days early, but I'm the new maintenance guy."

No.

Fuck.

No. No. No.

My pulse jolts to a sprint.

And I start to run.

"Sorry, what?" Courtney's voice cracks, and I don't know if it's from the connection or if...

"Courtney!" I shout into the phone.

I need her to hear me.

Need her to lift the fucking phone to her ear.

Snow crunches under my boots and branches slap at my body, but I keep running.

This can't be happening.

This cannot be fucking happening.

I'm missing words.

The connection between us is breaking up as I race toward my truck.

"He's the new maintenance person," I hear Courtney say, and I assume Simpson is there.

There's more that I miss.

My truck is in sight.

"Sterling?" Courtney whispers into the phone.

"Courtney, please listen." I can hear the line cutting out.

"Did you know?" Her question is hard to understand. But I hear it.

And it breaks my fucking heart.

"I didn't know he was coming." I'm breathing heavily, and I know it's from panic more than from running. "I forgot Marty emailed me. It was before—"

The call fucking drops.

"Fuck," I shout as I reach my driver's door.

I have a four-hour drive home through mountain passes with little to no service.

And no time to spare.

CHAPTER 190

COURTNEY

"I KNOW," I TELL BEN.

He gives me the side-eye.

"I know." I say it more forcefully this time. "I'm aware I'm being petty. But it's all I have right now."

My perfect dog huffs, then lowers himself to lie on the women's room floor.

I have absolutely no reason to come shower out here, other than pettiness. And the fact that I don't want to be naked in Sterling's house.

He sent a text saying that he was coming home and not to leave.

That was it.

I'm coming home. Don't leave.

But it was enough to have me crying on the floor with Ben curled in my lap, bony butt hanging off my knees because he's too big to fit.

I wasn't going to just leave.

True, I'd already grabbed an armful of my clothes out of his closet and carried them over to the Laundry Cabin. But it was just some of my belongings. And Ben's dishes.

Because if tonight ends in a fight—or a breakup—I needed to

have enough of my belongings in my old cabin to get me through a few days.

My reflection blurs as I drag my brush through my wet hair.

I blink the stubborn tears away.

It didn't sound good, Sterling admitting he forgot about my replacement. But I've had hours to dwell on it, and I know I need to hear him out.

Because I know Sterling.

I know him better than I think most anyone does.

And if he wanted to break up with me...

I purse my lips and blow out a breath.

I'm trying so hard to be mature about this, but even thinking the term *break up* sends my pulse into a tailspin.

If Sterling was planning on ending it, he wouldn't have gotten me a dog.

I look over at Ben, who is watching me from the floor.

Then again, Sterling could maybe see giving me a companion before kicking me out into the cold as a decent thing.

Except for the cost.

Eyes locked with the golden ones watching me, I feel another traitorous tear slip down my cheek.

"No matter what," I promise Ben in a shaky voice. "No matter what, I'll take care of you. Okay?"

Ben blinks up at me.

And I make a mental note to google if dogs can eat ramen.

On cue, my stomach growls.

As a surprise to no one, I did not attend dinner tonight.

Simpson didn't come back to the house after showing Dale around. There was no need. And when he appeared in the Food Hall with my replacement, I'm sure the rest of the guys pieced it together.

Thankfully Sterling left all the food in the Laundry Cabin when he moved the rest of my things into his house two months ago.

Two months.

Such a short time.

A lifetime.

Long enough to fall for someone.

Short enough to doubt their intentions.

That damn tightness twists around my throat again.

I don't want to doubt Sterling.

I don't want to move out.

I don't want to search for my passion without him.

My shoulders slump.

I want to trust him.

I want to stay.

I want to have a home here.

My lungs burn, and I open my mouth, sucking in a deep breath.

"One day at a time."

Blankly staring at my reflection, I twist my hair into braids, then wrap my clothes into my towel.

Just like old times.

"Okay, Ben, let's go."

I pull open the bathroom door, and Ben steps out ahead of me.

I won't leave, but I won't wait for Sterling in his house either.

It doesn't feel right.

The sky is clear tonight. The half-moon isn't especially bright, but the light glows off the snow lining the path, making it bright enough to see by. And since I forgot my flashlight, I appreciate it.

It's been nice these last few days, but nightfall always brings the cooler air.

I fill my lungs and work to calm my nerves.

I don't know if Sterling sent that text the moment he left or sometime later, so I don't know when he'll be getting home. But it could be soon.

And I know I won't be able to sleep until he gets here and we talk.

My eyes are focused down on where I'm walking when Ben starts whining.

"What's—"

A man-shaped form steps onto the path in front of us.

CHAPTER 191

STERLING

MY HEADLIGHTS FLASH ON SOMETHING, AND I SLAM ON my brakes.

For a long second, too long, I stare at the gate pulled across the end of my driveway.

"What the fuck?"

I shift the truck into park.

The gate that is always open is closed.

I unbuckle my seat belt.

It's not just closed. Someone shoveled it free, swung it closed, and—I squint my eyes, not believing what I'm seeing.

They put a new padlock on it. Locking it shut.

Ice so cold it burns fills my veins.

I reach into my back seat and grab the item I always keep there.

With my other hand, I dial three numbers as I climb out of my truck.

Then, for the second time today, I start to run.

Chapter 192

Courtney

"Hello?" My tentative voice barely carries over the sound of Ben's whimpers.

The man walks forward.

"Dale?" I take a step back.

I can't see the man well. But I know it's not one of my guys.

Then he steps into a beam of moonlight, and I can see it's not my replacement either.

But I recognize him.

He was a guest here. A while ago.

My fear morphs into terror.

He shouldn't be here.

And I shouldn't be out here alone.

No one knows I'm out here alone.

"What do you want?" I don't want to hear the answer, but I can't stop the question from coming out.

He takes a step forward. Toward me. "I want to ruin your life the way you ruined mine."

What?

He doesn't make any sense.

I barely even talked to him when he was here.

But sense doesn't matter. Not with men like him.

Not with men who would approach you in the dark.

He takes another step, leaving only a couple yards between us.

I throw my clothes bundle at him.

"Run!" I yell the command at Ben as I spin and take off back toward the bathroom.

My blood is sizzling with adrenaline.

My body feels like it isn't mine.

If I can just get through the door.

There's a lock—

A hand grips the back of my sweatshirt.

I stumble.

But the man's hold on my shirt keeps me from falling.

I start to struggle.

I won't go easy.

I won't—

Cold metal presses against my throat.

I flinch.

And a sharp sting slices my skin.

A cry flies from my mouth, and my hands reach up on reflex.

He shakes me, and the knife cuts me again.

"Shut the fuck up," he hisses.

I try not to shiver with disgust at having him this close to me. At feeling his hot, disgusting breath on my neck.

Ben is barking now.

Standing a few feet ahead of us, hair on end.

Tears I didn't realize I was crying flow from my eyes.

It's okay, I want to tell Ben.

I'll be okay, I want to promise him.

Please don't come closer, I beg of him.

I'm shaking so hard I feel another sting of metal across my skin.

"Walk forward." His command is followed by a shove to my back.

My eyes dart to the shower building.

I was trying to get there so I could lock myself inside. But I plant my feet.

I won't go in there.

Not with him.

"Bitch, move." Rage laces his words.

"I don't understand. Why—"

The knife shifts so it's pressed tight against the underside of my jaw.

"Your fucking boyfriend fucked up my hands so bad, I lost my fucking job," he spits out. "They're still so bad I might just slice your throat on accident. So *walk*." He shoves me harder.

The blade breaks skin.

Ben lunges forward, and the creepy man tries to kick past me at Ben.

"Stop," I cry.

He shoves my back again.

I squeeze my eyes shut.

My neck hurts so bad.

I can feel the warm stickiness of my blood trailing down my skin.

Lifting my shaking hands, I hold them palms out and shush Ben.

I need to think.

I can't go into the bathroom with this man.

I won't.

My body—my hands and elbows and knees—is the only weapon I have.

I don't know if I'll get away before he cuts too deep, but I'll try.

I'll fucking try.

I pull in a trembling breath, preparing myself.

Then we both freeze as the undeniable sound of a shotgun being cocked fills the darkness around us.

CHAPTER 193

STERLING

FEAR AND RAGE WRESTLE INSIDE MY RIBS.

I knew whoever shut that gate was here for something bad.

But I wasn't prepared.

Nothing could have ever prepared me.

I keep the shotgun pointed at the ground, my finger next to the trigger, as I take in the scene.

The Fucking Creep has a hold on Courtney, probably gripping her shirt. And he has a knife to her throat.

He has a knife. To my girl's throat.

"Stay there!" the man shouts.

Courtney finally opens her eyes.

Tears are rolling down her cheeks.

And her neck... I can't look at her neck.

Not yet.

I take one step forward.

"Don't come any closer." He seethes. "I'll fucking kill her."

I hold Courtney's gaze. "I got you."

The words are barely audible, and it's dark, but I know she can see my mouth as I say it. I know she can read my lips.

Footsteps approach from the side, and I glance over to see Fisher and Cook crossing the driveway.

The Creep shifts his attention back and forth between me and the other guys.

Panic builds in his jerky movements.

"Surrender and I won't shoot you," I say in a loud, clear voice.

"I'll never—" His head whips to the side.

Toward the woods.

And then I hear it.

The deep, huffing breaths and heavy footsteps... of a bear.

Chapter 194

Courtney

"Lady Bear," I whisper.

She's so large.

So ethereal and intimidating as she appears from the woods.

And as she lifts her head to sniff the air, I remember I'm bleeding.

Lady Bear takes another step closer, and the knife leaves my throat.

I try to take a step back, wanting to give her the distance she deserves, but then two hands slam against my back, shoving me toward the bear.

CHAPTER 195

STERLING

COURTNEY STUMBLES AWAY FROM THE CREEP.

And that's all I need.

I take two fast strides forward, halving the distance between us.

Then I squeeze the trigger.

The shot explodes from the end of my weapon and blasts through the man's knee.

He crumples to the ground.

CHAPTER 196

COURTNEY

THE LOUD GUNSHOT PULLS A SQUEAK OUT OF MY CHEST as I fall to the ground.

Feet away, Lady Bear rears up to her hind legs, and I freeze.

My heart is beating so fast I think I might be having a heart attack. But I stay still, lying uncomfortably on my side, trying not to move a muscle.

Even with this massive bear looming above me, I feel safer than I did a moment ago, because I'm not alone anymore.

Sterling is here.

He got here just in time.

Seconds pass, and I finally make out the pained sounds coming from the creepy man.

I was busy falling, so I couldn't see exactly what happened, but I hope that gunshot was Sterling shooting him.

Ben lets out a sound of distress, and I search with just my eyes until I find him. Fisher is holding his collar, keeping him out of harm's way. And another layer of relief settles across my shoulders.

Then the ground vibrates as Lady Bear drops back down to all fours.

I hold my breath as she looks down at me.

Her nose twitches, then she turns to look at the man who attacked me.

The man is clutching his leg, letting out moans of pain, but his head is lifted, looking at Lady Bear with terror in his eyes.

Part of me wants her to rake her claws across his throat. To make him bleed like he made me bleed.

I want her to rip his fucking head off.

I want payback for the way he made me feel.

But then I remember the gun in Sterling's hands. And even if the awful man might deserve death, Lady Bear doesn't.

In the calmest voice I can manage, I speak to Sterling. "Please don't shoot her."

Sterling is holding still, keeping his eyes on the big girl inching closer to the man, who is bleeding a hell of a lot more than I am.

"I won't." His calmness is more convincing than mine. "Unless she tries to hurt you."

"She won't hurt me." I will the words to be true. "Right, Lady Bear? You're a good bear." She turns her head back to me. "You're so pretty." The tears I thought were done continue to fall from my eyes.

The bear is so close.

She turns back around, sniffing in my direction.

"Thank you for showing up when you did." I mean it. I mean it so much. "I love you," I whisper, meaning that too.

Her eyes sparkle in the moonlight.

And then she's gone.

Lumbering back into the woods.

I exhale.

My neck and side muscles ache from holding myself up.

The quiet is broken when the creepy man screams loudly.

I turn my head to find Simpson pressing his foot into the man's destroyed knee.

"You fucked up coming back here." My mild-mannered

coworker leans his weight onto his foot, and the man on the ground screams louder.

And just like that, my brain can't handle anymore.

I flop onto my back.

CHAPTER 197

STERLING

"FISHER," I CALL OUT, AND AS SOON AS HE LOOKS MY way, I toss my shotgun to him.

He releases Ben's collar and catches the gun.

I don't wait for him to point it at the man on the ground.

I race Ben to our girl.

I slide the last foot on my knees. "Courtney." I reach for her, my hands tentative but needing to touch her. "Cookie, talk to me."

She's flat on her back, eyes closed. And if I hadn't heard her talking to that fucking bear a moment ago, I might think she was passed out.

I lean over her, one hand braced on the ground, the other gently cupping her cheek. "Eyes up here, Honey."

Her eyes blink open.

Relief swamps me.

And I collapse on top of her.

My forehead drops to the snow next to her head, and my lungs seize.

She's alive. She's alive. She's alive.

Hands press against my sides, fingers curling in my shirt.

"I'm okay." Courtney's words are quiet. Just for me.

And my body trembles.

Her fingers flex, then her hands run up and down my sides.

"I'm okay, Sterling." Her hands slide around my back until she's hugging me. "I'm okay."

"I'm not," I say back just as quietly. "I'm so fucking sorry. I—"

A fur-covered head clunks against mine.

Courtney lets out a half laugh, half sob as one of her hands leaves my back. "My boys."

Forehead going numb from the snow, I lift myself up.

The hand still on my back slides around to my side, then up to press against my chest. Over my heart.

Ben whines and nudges his nose against Courtney's temple.

"I'm okay," she says again, this time to the dog.

There's a thud behind us, then another loud cry from Creep.

Ben darts over to the man on the ground and barks in his face.

Courtney lets out a chuckle. "He's starting to feel courageous."

The man yells something at Ben, and I watch as Fisher kicks him. Again.

Everyone here loves that damn dog.

"Come here," I say to Courtney as I shift around until I'm sitting with my legs crossed.

She holds her hands out and lets me pull her up and into my lap, her side against my chest.

I hug her close with an arm around her back. I use my other hand to ghost my fingers over her chin. "Let me see."

Her lips press together as she lifts her chin, just an inch. But then a sound leaves her throat.

"Shh." I press my palm to her cheek. "If it hurts, don't move. I'm sorry I asked."

Tears start falling from her eyes again. "It's not..." She pulls in a shaky breath. "I was so scared."

I cup the side of her head and pull her into me.

My heart shreds as she cries against my chest. And I have to keep reminding myself that I got here in time.

And when that sends panic coursing through my system—because what if I hadn't gotten here when I did?—I remember that damn bear.

Courtney's bear.

I press a kiss to the top of her head.

Even if I hadn't gotten here right when I did, that bear would have saved her.

We're gonna have to find a way to feed that bear for the rest of her life. I just know it.

New footsteps sound on the gravel, and I kiss Courtney's hair one more time before looking up to find Cook and a man I don't recognize, who must be Dale.

The man's eyebrows are raised, but he doesn't say anything about the scene before him.

It's a point in his favor.

If I came across a man with a shot-up knee, being kicked by one of my coworkers, stepped on by another, shotgun aimed at his chest, and a crying woman with a bloody neck sitting in the lap of my boss... I might have a reaction.

Guess we'll keep Dale on the payroll.

"Cook." My friend looks at me, eyes moving to Courtney as she reaches up to wipe away her tears. "An ambulance is on the way. I need you to get the bolt cutter out of the shed and open the gate. That fucker there put his own padlock on it." I look at the new guy. "Dale, go with him."

New guy nods at me just as Simpson lifts his foot and stomps down on Creep's knee again.

Creep's wail is shrill before he goes blissfully quiet. Passed out.

"'Bout fucking time," Simpson grumbles. Then he looks at me. "You already called it in?"

I nod, still holding Courtney as tight as I can. "As soon as I saw the gate was closed, I knew something was wrong." I run my hand down Courtney's braid. "I just told the dispatcher to send an ambulance and hung up."

Simpson nods at Courtney. "She okay?" His voice is quiet, but Courtney hears him because she lifts her head.

"I'm fine." She brushes at her cheeks again. "Just rattled."

With her head raised, I use the opportunity to look at her neck.

It's too dark for me to see it well, but it looks like her whole neck is smeared with blood.

"Courtney." The distress is back in my voice, and she jerks her attention back to me.

She reaches toward her neck but doesn't touch it. "It's not that bad."

Destructive rage floods my system.

I look up at Fisher. "Shoot him again."

Fisher chambers a new round.

Courtney laughs, honestly laughs, as she places a hand over my mouth. "Don't shoot him."

Simpson kicks Creep in the side.

Ben barks.

Courtney snorts.

And her humor is enough to have my rage subsiding. Just a bit.

Cook and Dale jog into view, with the new guy carrying the heavy bolt cutter. They both look this way but don't stop, disappearing down the driveway toward the gate.

"That's the guy you beat up, isn't it?" Courtney asks, eyes back on Creep.

"It is." I shake my head. "I should've told you. But I didn't want you to be afraid."

"What did he do?" she asks.

Simpson can hear her question because he kicks him again.

"He was following you... Was trying to get into your cabin." I don't tell her how close he was. And I don't need to because now, wherever she goes, Ben will be at her side, paying attention when she isn't. "I got to him before he could do anything. Tried to teach him a lesson." I heave out a breath. "I underestimated him." I make sure Courtney is looking at me. "I'm sorry. This is my fault. I never thought he'd come back."

She shakes her head. "Stop that right now. You couldn't have known. And I'm glad it was me and not some other woman." She brings her fingers near her neck again. "Now that he's done this, he'll go to jail, right?"

I nod. "He should. You have..." I swallow. "Injuries. And we have witnesses."

"Got you one better." Fisher hands the shotgun to Simpson, then takes his phone out. "Started recording when we got here. Got him holding Court at knifepoint and shoving her toward that bear." He does something on his screen. "Got one short version and a longer one with you blowing his fucking knee out. Which one do you want me to share with the cops?"

I shake my head. This kid. "It's not exactly a secret that someone shot him."

Fisher lifts a shoulder. "Maybe not, but in the confusion—with the bear and all that—maybe we can't remember who did it."

"Appreciate the offer, but I'll own it. It's not like I killed him. And when the rumors get around, people will know not to mess with my girl." The faint sound of sirens breaks through the night. "Simpson, put the gun on the ground behind me."

He steps away from Creep, who is starting to moan himself awake, and empties the shells from the gun—putting them in his pockets—before setting the firearm down a few yards behind me.

Red and blue lights bounce off the trees as Cook and Dale step up to join the group.

"I can get up," Courtney tells me.

I press a kiss to her forehead. "You can stay right here."

Chapter 198

Courtney

STERLING PAUSES. "MAYBE WE SHOULD WAIT."

I smile at the man. "You said you wanted to show me something."

His eyes drop to my neck and the bandages the EMTs put on my cuts last night.

"Sterling. They're just scratches. I can walk a bit."

Honestly, I want to stay inside and cuddle up with him and Ben on the couch all day. But Sterling told me he wanted to show me something. So I'm going to let him show me something.

He puffs out his cheeks, then nods. "Okay. But if it's too much, tell me."

"I promise I will."

Sterling takes my hand, and we start down the path that leads from his back deck to the little lake behind his house.

Ben bounds ahead of us, turning back when he gets too far away, then darting back down the path.

I take a long inhale.

It's beautiful out today, the sun making it feel warmer than it is. But I'm still wearing my new winter jacket and boots.

Sterling insisted.

Just like he insisted on tying my boot laces.

And making me breakfast.

And holding me in his arms all night.

I don't need him to baby me like he is, but I think he needs it.

Even when I told him I'd taken some of my things to the Laundry Cabin, he just kissed me and told me he understood.

Then he told me he'd be moving everything back into his house today.

I really am obsessed with this man.

I squeeze his fingers.

He squeezes my fingers back, and we walk in silence.

Past the lake.

Up a hill.

Through more woods.

Until we end up in a clearing.

It's beautiful.

The big blue sky.

The gentle slope of land...

"I don't have a ring yet." Sterling's words have my feet stopping.

I look up at him, heart pounding. "What?"

He turns to face me, taking both my hands in his. "I don't have a ring yet, Courtney Kern. But I'll get one. Because I want you to stay with me. Now. Forever. Into the mystery that happens after this life." He rubs his thumbs across the sensitive skin of my wrists. "I should have talked to you about all of this sooner. When I knew..." I watch his throat work. "When I knew I loved you, I should have told you."

Brightness erupts behind my ribs. "You..."

The side of his mouth pulls up. "I love you."

A part of me knew it. So much of me felt it.

But to hear him say it.

"I love you too." It comes out quietly, too choked with emotion to be loud.

"Good." He lifts one of my hands and presses it to his chest.

I flatten my palm over his heart as he lets go to brush his thumb over my cheek.

Then, carefully, to avoid my bandages, he moves his hand to the back of my neck.

"I want to build a home here with you." His eyes move to the side, looking at the land around us. "I've thought about it over the years. Figured I might someday. But I want that day to be now. And I want it to be with you." He looks back down, gaze on mine. "You can work at my side. You can find something else to do. You can change your mind a thousand times. Whatever it is, we can find your passion together."

A sob bursts out of me.

Because I believe him.

And because I can picture it too.

Sterling leans down and presses a kiss to my forehead. "Can I tell you another thing?"

I blink through the tears and nod.

His smile is so warm and full of love that I know it's an image I'll keep in my mind forever.

"Ben was never just for you." The dog hears his name and presses his body between our legs. "He's ours. Our baby. And if you want more furry babies, or human babies, I'll have as many or as few as you desire. I'll do anything to keep you. You just tell me what you want."

I look around at the towering trees. At the snowy mountain peaks in the distance.

I picture the ground covered in wildflowers.

I imagine a herd of dogs.

And maybe one child.

And I feel something that must be joy blossom inside me.

Never in my wildest daydreams would I have thought this life was possible.

Never had I imagined a man like Sterling would be the one to change my life.

I slip my hand free of his grip and place it on his chest next to my other one.

"I just want you," I tell him truthfully. "I'll take the rest of it, but I don't need it. I only need you."

We exhale together.

The doubt. The worry... It vanishes from between us.

Then Sterling Black's mouth is on mine.

And I close my eyes.

Because this is it.

The start of my forever.

Epilogue 1

Courtney

STERLING IS SITTING ON THE COUCH, WAITING FOR ME to join him for movie night.

Ben is sleeping on his bed under the dining table.

And I'm ready to enact my plan.

It's been three weeks since the attack.

I'm healed.

That horrible man is going to end up in prison.

The new guy is fitting in great.

And Sterling is still treating me like I'm made of glass.

But that ends tonight.

He eyed me when I came down from upstairs, dressed in a skirt. But he didn't say anything.

He's probably assuming I want us to get handsy during the movie.

He'd be mostly right.

Smiling to myself, I reach up under my skirt and pull my underwear down my legs.

STERLING

"HONEY, DO YOU WANT—"

Courtney walks into the room, and my brain glitches.

The sight of her in that fucking skirt was enough to have my dick reacting. But now...

Now it's the panties dangling from her fingers that have all my attention.

"You had a question for me, Mr. Black?" Her voice is sultry. Suggestive.

"What are you doing, Miss Kern?" I start to stand.

"Stay." She snaps the order.

And I drop back onto the couch, my eyes lifting to hers.

Courtney steps in front of me, but instead of climbing onto my lap, she sits on the coffee table.

And I only now notice that it's shoved a few extra feet away from the couch.

Naughty girl.

"Open your pants," she commands.

I don't know what this new power-play kink is, but I am fucking here for it.

I flip my button open and drag my zipper down.

Her gaze is hooded. And from the look of her, I bet she's just as hot for it as I am.

Courtney slowly spreads her knees. "Take it out."

Christ.

The material of her skirt drapes down, blocking my view.

I lift my hips and shove my jeans and boxers down.

My cock bobs free, and I grip it.

Her cheeks flush as she watches my dick harden.

"Now show me." She tosses her panties at me, and I catch the scrap of fabric. "Show me what you do with them."

They're warm.

I groan and bring them up to my face.

As I inhale, Courtney grips the hem of her skirt and lifts the fabric. Exposing her bare pussy.

Proving the cotton over my nose and mouth was just removed from her body.

I take another inhale, and precum drips from my dick.

My girl makes a sound, and I open my eyes.

I hadn't meant to close them.

I curse when I see her fingers slide through her slit.

There's no mistaking the glisten between her thighs.

I lower her panties and wrap them around my cock.

One hand grips the base of my dick tightly. The other grips the pussy-scented fabric.

And then I stroke.

I drag my fist up and down.

I watch her fingers push inside her entrance.

I watch her rub her little clit.

I watch her reach up and play with her tits through her shirt.

I watch her watch me.

I watch her get close.

And when I know we're both *right there*, I slide off the couch and walk on my knees toward her.

"You ready to come, my Little Worker?" I growl.

Courtney nods. "Hurry."

As soon as I can reach her, I bend and lick up the length of her slit.

She cries out.

I do it a second time, but that's all I can handle.

She reaches for me as I crawl forward on my knees and shove my cock inside her.

Her panties bunch at the base of my dick.

The fabric rubs against Courtney's clit, and she throws her arms around me, pulling me close, as she comes around my length.

And I leave them there, panties wrapped around my cock, getting soaked by my girl, as I release deep inside her pussy.

Epilogue 2

"Do we have to go?" Sterling grumbles against my neck, his body pressed against my back as I dry my hands over the kitchen sink.

I shake my head as I examine the new sparkly band tucked against my other sparkly band, only that one has a large square-cut emerald in the middle. "Sterling, it's our wedding reception."

"Yeah, but we saw them all this afternoon."

I twist in his hold until I'm facing him. "Mr. Black. Your employees are trying to do something nice."

"Mrs. Black." He smirks. "*Our* employees are trying to suck up to you."

I roll my eyes even as I smile.

He's been calling me that every chance he gets.

"They only do that because they know I'm the nice one." I cup his face and pull him down for a kiss.

Sterling is great to his employees, but with the building of our new house over the past year, he's been a little extra stressed. And maybe a little extra grumpy to anyone who isn't me.

But our house is complete, furnished, bigger than we need, and absolutely perfect.

And we moved into it two weeks ago.

Really, our employees are probably just excited about their new lodgings and are hosting this little reception as a thank-you.

Because along with building this house, we did a little remodeling to the old house—converting the garage into three more bedrooms and adding a bathroom. So now Sterling's old house is the new Bunk House and Black Mountain Lodge has an extra guest cabin.

A big one with a washer and dryer that we can charge more to use.

It's not in use at the moment. Because at the moment, we're closed for celebration.

But one of the guest cabins is occupied... by Marty.

We didn't have a bridal party. We just got married at the courthouse. But we flew Marty out to be one of our witnesses, because if it wasn't for him...

If it wasn't for Marty's lack of attention and that damn name cutoff on the application, none of this would have happened.

I smile against Sterling's lips.

Some of the best things in life happen by accident.

Sterling's mouth smiles against mine. "What is it, Wife?"

"Just thinking about you, Husband."

He hums. "Good. Now let's go, before I drag this dress off you."

I pull away from him, my bright green sundress shifting around my legs.

Sterling whistles as we walk past our sunroom—filled to the brim with plants and cacti—to the front door.

Paws claw against the wood floor as our four dogs sprint through the house, then barrel through the door Sterling holds open.

It's a crazy pack of misfit rescues. And I swear I've seen Ben, more than once, bouncing through the woods with a big furry beast much larger than any of our dogs.

I step outside, and Sterling follows, lacing his fingers through mine as he shuts the door behind us.

And I decide that tonight, when we get home, I'll tell him about the human baby we'll be adding to our herd.

HELP PROTECT LADY BEAR AND HER REAL-LIFE COUNTERPARTS

Climate change is one of the biggest threats to wildlife.
   If you can't donate, then spread the word.
   The bears can only save us if we help save them.
   https://www.nature.org/en-us/

Acknowledgments

I would first and foremost like to thank Mother Nature. Specifically the Rocky Mountains and all the bears who live within.

Moving to Colorado was the inspiration for this series, and it's so damn beautiful here, I will never get tired of it.

Special shout-out to my mom for keeping up with my somewhat absurd deadlines. I appreciate how many times you read these books for me!

Thank you, Kerissa, for not being completely dead inside. Sorry I spoil the plot for you while I'm writing, but I appreciate your feedback always. You're the best friend and PA a girl could ask for. Never Leave Me.

Thank you, Nikki. Your reactions while you read for me are everything. They truly give me life and keep my spirits up when I need that extra positivity.

To my cousin Ali, I adore you. I don't know how you speed-read so fast, but I live for your voice memos and feedback. Especially your tears. Give me all the tears.

Gabby and Sam, your encouragement is everything, and I love you guys.

Liz, you see me at my worst... literally, those Zoom angles and my unshowered self... but you don't judge, you just encourage. I don't know if I could've hit this deadline without you. So here's to another year of writing. May we one day do it leisurely.

To my editors, Jeanine and Beth. You both make me look so smart, and I love you for it. Because of you, no one knows that I'm complete shit at spelling.

Lori, my talented cover designer, I don't know what I'd do without you. You always knock it out of the park.

To Wander and his team, never stop what you do. I appreciate you so much.

To my ARC readers... you make me smile.

Mr. Tilly, you grew up a city boy, but you're a mountain man now. No ragrets.

And to everyone out there who reads to this very last line, I'm glad you're here.

About the Author

S. J. Tilly was born and raised in the glorious state of Minnesota but now resides in the mountains of Colorado. To avoid the snowy winters, S. J. enjoys burying her head in books, whether to read them or write them or listen to them.

When she's not busy writing her contemporary smut, she can be found lounging with Mr. Tilly and their circus of rescue boxers.

To stay up to date on all things Tilly, make sure to follow her on her socials, join her newsletter, and interact whenever you feel like it! Links to everything on her website www.sjtilly.com

Also By S. J. Tilly

DEAR ROSIE,

The Bite Series

(Holiday Novellas - Baking Competition)

SECOND BITE

SNOWED IN BITE

NEW YEAR'S BITE

The Mountain Men Series

MOUNTAIN BOSS

MOUNTAIN DADDY

BOOK 3 - END OF 2025

Made in United States
Orlando, FL
04 April 2025

60139540R00295